Her Cowboy King

Her Cowboy Prince

The King's Cowboy

For my sisters, Clio and Grace
I would move across the world for you

BEFORE

Markus Jaroka would never regret that his last night as a free cowboy was spent camping with his brothers. They went up into the craggy mountains of Montana, breathing in the scent of pines and lounging around the flickering flame. A night of bedrolls and beers and in-jokes that had all three men smearing tears off their faces. His brothers were his lifeblood, the land his home. Farewells didn't get much sweeter.

He knew Tommy wouldn't regret it either. In town, his brother used his downward-tipped hat as a social shield, adding shadow to his reputation as an enigmatic lone rancher. But Kris—who'd landed the lion's share of cowboy swagger and a coyote's ferocity to boot—would likely have preferred to devote his last night of freedom to a woman, making the most of his feral-edged charm.

None of them knew they were about to be bucked from ranching life forever.

They rose before sunrise. Doused the embers, shouldered their belongings, and hiked through wilderness to their ranch in Sage Haven. Routine was to dump their packs at the homestead and hit the stables, but the tread of the three brothers faltered as they emerged onto the back meadow of their property.

Their father, Erik, sat on a wooden stump by the far gate.

Tommy adjusted the strap of his bedroll. "What's he doing here?"

"No other way to reach us." Guilt fringed Kris's voice. Phone reception didn't follow them into the mountains, and it had been his idea to go camping.

"I'm sure everything's fine," Mark said, despite his unease.

"He's in yesterday's shirt. Still buttoned wrong." Tommy spoke under his breath, observant as ever. "He hasn't slept."

Kris swore and lengthened his stride.

"He probably just fell asleep in the armchair again." But Mark clenched his fists as they crossed the field.

Their dad stood as they neared, raising a hand. It tremored, outlined against the dawn sky.

"Morning, Dad." Kris offered from Mark's right.

Erik nodded once. "Boys."

Boys, sure, or twenty-five-year-old men with a profitable quarter horse ranch between them. They stopped a few paces away, planting their feet and swinging their packs to the ground.

Erik's smile was tight. "Good night out there?"

"Cold," Mark said. "What'd we miss?"

"Is Mom okay?" Tommy moved in beside Mark, and a moment later, Kris appeared at his other shoulder.

With his brow creased, their father looked at each of them in turn, his features softened by regret. "She's . . . fine. She's worried." He let out a turbulent breath. "We had news overnight."

Mark's gut warped as he braced for the worst. Had their father received more test results? Was it bad? No matter what, Mark would hold it together for his parents, for his brothers. Steadily, he asked, "What's happened, Dad?"

"My brothers and nephew were in an accident yesterday. I'm afraid they didn't survive."

Faint with selfish relief, Mark lowered his head. His parents were okay. The deaths of his uncles and cousin were tragic, but he couldn't pretend to mourn men he'd never met. Men who'd never shown a spark of interest in Mark or his family.

"How?" Tommy's question was quiet.

"Balcony collapse," Erik said. "They were banqueting under the night sky."

"All three of them?" Kris sounded sick.

Mark jerked his head up as his brother's tone kicked him in the gut. His own nausea rose fast. In one swift tragedy, their father had become the sole surviving Jaroka of his generation. Which meant—God above, it meant . . .

Mark spoke as if a firm word could stop fate. "No."

"But that—" Tommy choked on his own voice.

Kris turned his back, cursing roughly.

The field tipped, a disorienting slant, and Mark struggled to hold his balance. This wasn't possible. The mortality of his uncles had always seemed like that of legends—their deaths were unthinkable.

They were royalty, after all.

"This is—" *No.* "Not happening."

His dad spoke gently. "It *has* happened, Markus."

Kris hadn't turned around. His body was rigid. "There must be someone else."

Tommy was stark white and swaying. He held his hat loosely by his side, his other hand deep in his dark hair. "There is no one else."

"But Dad." Panic controlled Mark's pulse, pushing it hard. "Your health. You can't take this on." The stress would surely accelerate his Parkinson's disease. "You need peace and quiet in the country—not a country to rule."

His father nodded slowly, heavily. "I hate that you're right."

"It's true." Kris spun around, his lip curling in outrage. "This can't be expected of you."

Tommy had stopped moving. His hat lay in the grass by his feet.

"Tell us what we can do to stop this." Mark could take time off the ranch. They all could. Shock knotted the thoughts in his head, but once it eased, he'd hunt down the world's best lawyers, doctors, activists. Anyone who would fight for his father against the burden of hereditary monarchy. "We'll work this out."

Tommy clamped a hand over his shoulder. "Mark," he said, his voice strangled.

Mark covered his brother's hand with his own. "I'll sort it out. Don't worry."

"I know you will." Their father sagged back down onto the tree stump, features breaking. "Your mother and I discussed this all night. Like you, she forbade me to accept my responsibility. I'd be stupid to ignore my condition." Remorse filled his sigh as he looked at them all. "I'm so sorry, boys. I've decided to abdicate."

He looked at the firstborn of his triplet sons.

"Mark, the crown will fall to you."

NOW

1

Kiraly had a new royal family.

Princess Ava Veisi stared out the luxury car window as the royal convoy of Kelehar navigated the twisted city streets. An entire nuclear family of royalty that had been out of public mind and memory for a quarter century. How had that been possible? She eyed the car in front, catching sight of her parents in the back seat. Her iron-handed, duty-defined parents.

Looking away, she suppressed the scream that lived at the back of her throat. It would convey too much. Envy that the Jaroka family had lived undisturbed for so long. Resentment that their return prevented her annual trip to Monaco. And frustration that it had consequently barred her own escape from the public eye.

She'd planned it. A cover story. A traveling companion. A route of safe houses all the way across the Luxembourg border and beyond. New lines fanned out from her eyes from the sleepless nights she'd spent obsessing over it—the years she'd spent glaring intently at that end goal.

And it had been torn from her just days before she could pull it off.

Her next inhale was shaky. She could handle this.

"Pretty city," Cyrus murmured beside her.

With ugly memories. She eyed her older brother. He was a national treasure back home, valued for his scrupulous reputation and kind heart as much as his olive skin and coal-black hair. He was a sweet man with genuine sympathy and gentle good looks, and as heir to the Kelehar crown, his future as king couldn't come soon enough.

"You see beauty in everything," she answered.

He raised a lush black brow. "You should follow my lead."

"Not in a place like this."

His tongue clicked. "You know it's beautiful."

She offered a compromise. "It's a nice city if you like the provincial."

His lips quirked. "Snob."

"As I was raised." She swung her gaze back out the window.

The tiny country of Kiraly folded neatly in between its neighbors, with its one and only city built on the slopes of an expansive mountain range. The whole capital felt jumbled, like the cobbled roads, houses, and buildings all shoved each other aside in a perpetual race to the palace at the top.

It was a magnificent palace. The white limestone exterior was luminescent against the lush green of the rising mountains beyond, and the towers and turrets and balconies gave the Romanesque design a striking asymmetry. She'd once lost her breath standing in the tallest of those towers, staring out at the surrounding peaks and valleys speckled with vivid glacial lakes.

She'd once almost lost a whole lot more inside those walls.

Swallowing bitterness, she looked away.

The streets spun this way and that, a steep maze that led ever upward connected by laneways and shortcuts constructed of more steps than she wanted to imagine climbing. Cobblestone steps fit narrowly between restaurants and cafés, concrete steps ran parallel to roads in place of sidewalks, and wooden steps passed under the latched gates of private homes. Steps, everywhere.

It all looked like too much work. These people needed hiking boots just to buy fruit and flowers.

Market stalls claimed any corner or curb wide enough to balance a table. Cafés were slotted in poky storefronts, customers spilling onto the pavement beneath colorful shade cloths, while upmarket establishments offered large umbrellas to protect outdoor settings from the spring sunlight. She caught sight of appetizer platters and wine, and her stomach shifted as she momentarily forgot her nerves.

It was a culture of shared food and bright clothing. She'd never admit how much she adored the way these people dressed —fitted coats of butterfly blue, skirts of violet, and turmeric yellow scarves. In color, at least, she might fit in.

"Who knows?" Cyrus spoke again, his voice low. "This new American king might be nice too."

Markus Jaroka might also be a snake. "I don't do wishful thinking."

"I heard there are five brothers, all born together."

"Five?" She'd heard two.

"And that they knew nothing about their lineage until last week."

She eyed him. "That seems unlikely."

Cyrus smiled. "I also heard the princes grew up spoiled on Hawaiian beaches."

Why didn't that surprise her? "So, they're beach-party brats."

He elbowed her. "The other story is they grew up in New York. Lawyers, all of them."

"That bodes well," she said, her voice dry. "Train men to think without feeling, then put them in charge of a country."

"Cynicism doesn't become you, Ava."

Yet she had become cynical. She held down a heave of regret. She'd tried to ignore the rumors—they put a rotten churn in her system. She looked back out the window, apprehension tight around her middle. The one consistent fact in a fog of speculation was that their father intended to abdicate due to ill health, passing the crown to his firstborn son, Prince Markus Jaroka. She knew nothing about Markus, but his name circled her like a torture master.

He posed a very real threat to her future.

"I don't care who Markus is or where he was raised," she said. "I want nothing to do with him."

Cyrus didn't answer.

"I'm just here to reconnect with Zara," she finished, quieter, and battled nerves the size of monsters at the thought alone. There would be no *just* about that visit. "You'll still help us?"

Her brother didn't hesitate, but his whisper was sad. "Of course."

Longing scraped down her ribs. She missed Cyrus—missed being able to talk openly with him. Conversations such as this were painfully rare. Years back, he'd distanced himself, making an outward show of his disapproval, his disappointment in her. Their parents could never suspect he was on her side. Nor did they, for just months ago, they'd granted him additional responsibilities as Crown Prince and thus the power to help her.

"Thank you," she whispered, looking at her lap.

Again, he said, "Of course."

Hands clenched, she returned her attention outside. The city was officially in mourning—though the black banners lining the main streets appeared to be a formality only. In contrast to the dark fabric, the atmosphere was buoyant, excited, as the people prepared for the arrival of their new royal family.

She couldn't blame them.

She'd been to Kiraly once before, three years ago, accompanied by her parents, who'd sought a marriage between her and the heir apparent at the time, Prince Aron. The prince had been briefed on her visit. It would be an advantageous match for both kingdoms and pressure came from all angles to form a union. At just twenty years old, she had already been devastated by the expectations of the crown. Crushed and without the reserves to fight, she'd seen no way out of her duty.

Then she'd met the prince. Had he been courteous or cool-mannered or even half-mad, she'd have stayed coddled in her numb stupor and done as she was told. But at their first meeting —a moment of alone time staged so blatantly by their families that she'd felt sick—he'd stroked her cheek in greeting and allowed his fingers to graze her breasts on the way down.

Yes, plural. His hand had zigzagged for maximum coverage.

"Marry me," she'd said, because duty came before dignity.

Then she'd spat on his cheek.

It'd had the desired effect.

Humiliated and furious over Prince Aron's rejection, her parents had aborted their pursuit of a strategic alliance—until several days ago, when all known Kiralian royalty had died in an architectural crumble, and out of the wreckage strode fresh game for her parents' matchmaking hunt.

Officially, she was here to attend the funeral. But she had been left under no illusions. She was a pawn once again.

Cyrus nudged her.

She kept her shoulders back and stomach tucked in, her eyes locked on the city outside. "What?"

"Hold out your hand."

She did, confused when his fist moved in and cool metal thudded onto her palm. His fingers slid over hers and forced them closed.

"A ring?" The band was thick and unadorned.

"It was our grandfather's wedding ring." His shoulder pressed against hers as he pretended to look out the window beside her. An act in case their parents should somehow see them. "Dad said I should have it."

She opened her palm. "And you should."

"Our parents are fixated on your marriage, not mine. Why should you deal with that pressure without a family heirloom for your troubles?"

She inhaled around hope and fear. "I'm planning on getting something much more rewarding."

He tilted his head. "I still want you to have the ring."

"And do what with it?"

"Propose to someone you want to marry," he said.

Affronted, she glared at him. "Are you mocking me?"

Curse those long, dark lashes that embodied his innocence.

"You know what I intend to do here, Cy." Sabotage her parents' plan to offer her hand to the new king of Kiraly. She'd done it once without thinking. With her mind on the task, Markus would be running from her before spring had finished settling. Then she would shed royal life, once and for all. "Wearing a ring is not on the list."

Her brother's gaze was gentle, but he tucked his hands firmly in his pockets when she tried to give the heirloom back. "That's why you need to be on the giving end, sister."

She was sure her nostrils flared. "Instigating something I don't want isn't empowerment."

"I didn't say to offer it to the new king." Sympathy coated his reprimand. "Offer it to anyone you choose—whenever you choose." Hand out of his pocket again, he encased her fist. "By this token, the crown of Kelehar supports your choice."

Oh. That wasn't fair. Her breath caught, and she swallowed hard at her brother's big heart. The ring dug into her palm with the thorns of bad memories. "Even if he's an accountant? Or a gardener? Or a carpenter?"

She didn't say violin tutor. But it hung in her silence.

"Especially then."

"Oh, Cyrus." She almost pressed her forehead into his shoulder. "I wish you were king already."

That impossibility was a waste of a wish, for their father was fighting fit. Unless a tragedy befell the king of Kelehar, Cyrus wouldn't ascend for decades. The ring changed nothing—if she married, it would have to be blue blood. Her parents would tolerate nothing less. Her only freedom lay in never marrying at all, and she clung to that with everything she had.

Cyrus still held her hand and she remembered, back when her heart had bled fresh, he'd once said to her, *"It kills me, Ava, that I can't figure out a way to make you happy that doesn't involve faking your death and smuggling you away across the seas."*

"Could we try that?" she'd responded. *"I'm all for death by leopard attack, if you're short on ideas."*

His hollow laugh had echoed with sadness.

Now, he whispered, "What are you thinking?"

She lifted her head as they approached the palace gates. Something inside her reared up at the sight, a captive yanking violently against her chains, wild-eyed and powerless. It was the entrance to a world she'd finally been on the verge of escaping.

"I'm thinking," she said, turning back to him with a composure that only went skin deep, "perhaps Kiraly has leopards."

The people of Kiraly were in for a shock.

After a life spent surrounded by ranchers and small-town

folk in Sage Haven, Mark hadn't considered how strongly he and his brothers emanated *cowboy*. Sitting in the private jet that shot them away from home toward an unfamiliar city in the middle of Europe, it struck him that they'd suit royal life like muddy boot prints on a silk carpet.

The flight attendants seemed startled by their rough-edged presence, honed from long days and brutal work. Their hardened bodies made a mockery of the lushly padded reclining chairs, for they could just as easily find comfort in a bedroll on a flat patch of earth. Country-tanned skin jarred against the sophisticated white cabin, their dark hair was untamed, and then there was their sheer strength of will that meant they refused to be anything other than who they were—royal expectation be damned.

Thank God his brothers were coming with him.

Earlier that morning, their mother had suggested they wear suits. Kris had outright refused. Their shirts already had buttons and collars, and they were cowboys, damn it. If that meant arriving in denim and leather and hats, so be it.

"They want their princes back," he'd said, "this is what they get."

Mark had almost pointed out that their arrival was a matter of duty, not public pressure, but duty demanded they show up, not dress up, so his brother's point stood.

Tommy took a couple of tablets a few hours in, the medication downgrading his quick-breathed anxiety into a fidgety unease.

Kris leaned forward, elbows on his thighs, frowning into space. Eventually, he asked an attendant for food. "Surprise me," he said, passing back the menu. "I'm not fussy."

Mark sat, jaw tight, holding the envelope containing his father's official letter of abdication.

When the plane landed at a royal private airport, they were

told the angle of the palace grounds forbade an airstrip, so they were respectfully relocated into a helicopter. Before long, the chopper closed in on Kira City—the beating heart of a kingdom otherwise occupied by farmland, mines, and mountains.

He'd thought it wouldn't be so bad. They could still live among mountains.

But the Alps were nothing like the Rockies.

His mountains were rugged—dry, with a high-desert kind of sparseness. Hiking at home was rough. Nature gave no handouts, sometimes throwing in a bear to keep up the challenge. But the mountains outside the chopper were lush, bright green, and bursting with spring. The angles were sharper, more vertical in their ascent from deep valleys, and they rose around him like prison bars.

None of it looked like home.

The city was scattered down the bottom end of a particularly vast mountain, constructed like someone had dropped a collection of streets and buildings and left them where they'd landed. A turquoise lake glinted at the base of the slope, while above the city, a thick forest ascended into snow.

This was the nation that, according to the news he'd read online, eagerly awaited the arrival of the Lost Princes.

His skin chilled. Right in the center, above the city and below the forest, was the palace.

"It's a beast," he observed over the sound of the chopper.

"Sprawling," Kris shouted back.

"Not sprawling." Tommy looked out the window as if it might shatter all over him. His large fists were curled on his thighs. "Dogs sprawl in the sun. Drunks sprawl on benches. That place . . . it dominates."

Tall with a great throne hall and rising turrets, the building's architecture was a statement of wealth and power. Ostentatious, built to both spellbind and intimidate. The white exterior blazed in the sun, stinging his eyes, contrasting the dramatic shadows cast from surrounding towers. He couldn't judge the size from overhead, but his father had told him that it once concealed an army of men and horses, and observers had been none the wiser. The royal property fanned outward with extensive gardens, garages, fountains, stables—

He looked away, repulsed. His horses had been his riches, plain and simple. This was too much.

And too soon, the helicopter descended behind the palace.

"There are people lined up." Agitation pinched Tommy's words. He'd pulled back from the open hatch. "Hundreds of them."

Kris clasped Mark on the shoulder. "Your lead, man."

Mark borrowed strength from his brother's grip. He wasn't ready for this. But he nodded, sliding the crumpled envelope into his bag as he stood. He'd free-fallen through the past forty-eight hours since his father had delivered the life-altering news. Now he felt on the verge of the impossible.

Head spinning, he slung the bag over his shoulder and disembarked.

The air smelled different. Clean, empty, with no familiar waft of warm earth or musky bite of leather. With his heart burning, he settled his old black hat on his head and focused on the man awaiting them clear of the chopper.

Tall and elegantly thin, the man wore a traditional suit of deep blue, edged with a thick gold braid. He stood with his hands behind his back, his head lowered respectfully.

"Your Royal Highness," he greeted, bowing, and then repeated the greeting to Kris and Tommy as they settled in beside Mark. "I'm Philip Varga. I was the late king's royal advisor and have been acting as regent during the interregnum."

"Philip." Mark extended his hand, his mouth dry. "I'm sorry for your loss."

Pain flashed across the man's face. "Thank you." He shook Mark's hand. "I knew your father. I've missed him a great deal. You are—all of you—his spitting image."

They nodded, silent, not so much out of their depth as in the wrong ocean.

Mark cleared his throat, but the reluctance lodged there didn't budge. "This is from our father," he said, reaching into his bag and drawing out the envelope containing the letter penned by Prince Erik of Kiraly, irrevocably renouncing the throne to immediate effect. It had been dated, signed, and witnessed by his three sons and a lawyer from Kiraly who had flown over for that very purpose. That single piece of paper with a few simple paragraphs would shift the weight of power forever.

"Ah." Philip eyed the envelope, the fold between his brows suggesting he knew exactly what it was. "Perhaps this isn't the appropriate time. Such a weighty matter might warrant a touch more ceremony than at the foot of a helicopter."

"Right." Ranch living demanded things get done the moment they needed doing, but he put the envelope away.

"I will arrange for an assembly of witnesses this afternoon." Philip spoke quietly, yet the words howled in Mark's ears. The moment that letter was opened, the instant his father's abdication was officially received, Mark would be named as king.

King Markus of Kiraly.

He rejected the title on instinct. He wasn't a king. He'd tried. Since the news had first stunned him, he'd tried to believe it, stretching the concept in his mind, but it had come no closer to fitting him. Disbelief formed a crater low in his gut, a hollow sensation he couldn't get around. His life of ranching couldn't be over. Yet a part of him suspected it had been secured by the same quick-release knot he used on the horses—one easy tug and it all unraveled.

"The funeral is the day after next." Philip moved the conversation on. "The late king, heir, and prince are currently lying in state." When the brothers didn't respond, he lowered his voice with a wince. "I'm dreadfully sorry, but I'm struggling to tell you apart."

"Markus," Mark said, his voice numb. His name didn't sound like his own.

Kris gave a one-sided smile. "Kristof."

Tommy seemed to take advantage of Philip's power of deduction and said nothing.

"I see." Philip gave the same smile of apology that the brothers had received all their lives. It betrayed he had no confidence he'd be able to tell them apart if they so much as swapped places. "You look stunned. How do you feel?"

Mark gave a tight smile. "Fine."

"Popular," Kris said, surveying the rows of people.

Again, Tommy didn't answer. He eyed the steep forest at the edge of the palace grounds, his hat tilted down to shadow his face.

"Obvious question." Kris tucked a hand into his front pocket, lowering a shoulder. "Are the deaths of our family being treated as suspicious?"

"Not at all!" Philip looked horror-stricken. "The police extensively assessed the site for signs of tampering. The only evidence they found was of poor workmanship. Please, don't even think on that. Now." He clasped his hands together. "Is there anything we can organize to make you feel more at home? This must be quite disorienting."

"Some time alone," Mark requested on Tommy's behalf, "to ground ourselves."

"And maybe a sandwich." Kris returned his attention to the lines of people. "Thanks."

"Consider it done. Now please meet your household."

Philip angled himself and gestured to the welcoming party. Two immaculate lines formed a walkway from helicopter to palace, both rows two-deep, presumably with the lower-ranked positions concealed at the back. "From the chief of staff and house manager, to advisors, guards"—he pointed farther down the line—"and on to the chefs, grooms, and valets."

All stood erect, gazes fixed on the stone paving at their feet. Every single person held a bouquet of indigo flowers.

"Bluebells." Philip met Mark's eyes steadily. "Our national flower."

Unlike the streamside bluebells back home, these were more delicate, scattered along the stem instead of bunched. Even the things that should be the same were different.

"Gifts to honor their future king," Philip finished.

Mark nodded and slipped further into the crater of disbelief. Then he forced a smile at his brothers. "Let's say hello, shall we?"

"They've arrived, Princess."

Ava glanced up from her laptop as her personal guard, Gul, poked his head around the door to her private guest chambers. Physically, he intimidated. Wide-shouldered and bulky with muscle, he stood above most people and made no effort to reduce his impact by softening his stance or ducking his head. The glow of his personality was concealed behind a severe face and impassable gaze, a matter of discomfort for many, and the very reason he fit the role of her protector and companion.

Now, Gul's black eyes shone, and his lips pressed together, kicking up in the corners. She knew that look.

He wanted to talk.

Sighing, she snuggled deeper into the armchair. The

fireplace was lit beside her, unnecessary for the warming spring weather, but she was on edge and nervousness made her cold.

"They're not what we expected." He had a subdued voice, at odds with his large physique.

"Then you'd better restrain me." She returned her attention to her screen and typed a few words. "I'm about to run right into Markus's arms and embarrass us all."

"You master everything you do, Princess," he said, "off-the-cuff sarcasm included."

She threw him a half-smile and let him get away with that.

After a pause, he said, "There are three of them."

"Really? I'd heard—"

"Three," he repeated firmly. "You want to know more, but I won't share unless you look up."

"I'm trying to forget why I'm here." And she'd been succeeding by writing an email to Zara to schedule a meeting for the following day. She met Gul's frustrated gaze and her temper softened. None of this was his doing. He was one of the few friends she had, even if she couldn't decide whether or not she could trust him. "I'll meet these three brothers soon enough, Gul, and then I won't be able to unlearn what I know. Please don't talk about them prematurely. You know my position."

Inclining his head, he fell silent and clasped his hands behind his back. He glanced around her suite, features curious as he popped his lips quietly. Then—"They're not what we expected *at all*—"

"Please, don't." She shook her head. "Not yet."

Whether he remembered his place or heard the sadness in her voice, he yielded. "Of course. My apologies. Please don't hesitate to ask if you require anything further."

As he backed out the door, she said, "Gul?"

"Yes, Princess?"

Her shoulders dropped a little. "I'm glad you're here with me."

His smile was gentle. "So am I, Princess." With a nod, he closed the door.

She looked into the flames beside her. Three brothers: two princes, one king.

She *had* to get out of here.

♘

"You greeted everyone." Philip's narrow face was red as he rushed into the parlor. The doors closed behind him and one look at his openly dumbfounded features told Mark the man intended to be formal in public only. "Literally, every single person!"

Mark shared a look with Kris, brows raised. Half an hour earlier, they'd been escorted to this immense parlor and granted solitude and sandwiches. The route had stunned him— expansive halls and endless corridors, marble floors, picture- perfect courtyards—and he'd reeled at the reality that this palace was his new home.

He and his brothers had to *live* here.

Mark rested a hand on the back of an emerald velvet armchair and addressed Philip. "They were there to welcome us, weren't they?"

"Ceremonially speaking." The man put a hand to the side of his face. "A few nods here and there would have been adequate acknowledgment. Oh, the city's going to go mad with this."

Kris set his coffee on the table beside him, stiff with insult. "Were we out of line?"

"As royalty, you set the line," the man said, attention moving from brother to brother. His gaze lingered on Tommy, who kept

23

his back turned as he studied the collection of books displayed in a grand case. "But this is certainly unprecedented."

Mark straightened. "We've always made time for our employees. That's not going to stop now."

Philip covered his mouth, muffling a sound of disbelief.

"We're hardly about to ignore those who serve the crown." Kris leaned his hip against the table edge and crossed his arms.

"Hardly," Philip echoed. "The palace is in uproar about the identical dark-haired, blue-eyed princes who look servants in the eye while asking their names." Mark frowned as the man's voice hitched with a hint of . . . was that excitement? "And not just one, but three. That's three times the likelihood of seeing any one of you in the palace on a daily basis. The corridors will be teeming with staff trying to catch sight of you. It's already a frenzy out there. And they'll never know which brother they've seen, because I can't even tell you apart."

Dutifully, Mark and Kris recited their names.

Thanking them, Philip assessed each of their faces—the usual hunt for clues that might help him tell them apart next time. Not that Mark had ever understood the difficulty. Their differences seemed obvious. Tommy's introverted tension and the chip in his front tooth when he actually opened his mouth. The perpetual tousle Kris gave his hair and disheveled posture to match—he sauntered on the move and lounged when at ease. And Mark, well, he'd been told he was their grounding force.

"Add to that," Philip continued, "the saviors look like they've stepped out of a Wild West film." He threw his hands in the air and muttered, "No one within our borders is going to get any sleep tonight."

There was a room-wide pause.

"Wild West?" Tommy looked over his shoulder, brows high.

"The hats, you think?" Mark asked.

"Boots?" Kris kicked out a heel.

24

"The shirts, the jeans, the sun-browned skin." Philip's gestures darted between them. "The accents, the strut, the complete lack of superiority toward people who would never in a million reigns expect you to speak to them. The gracious acceptance of I-lost-count-how-many bouquets of bluebells . . ."

Mark eyed the table and the huge pile of woodland posies.

Tommy turned fully, lifting his chin. His eyes glinted with an edge that proved soft-spoken did not mean mild-mannered. "You think we should have stayed in Montana."

"No, Tomas." At that, Philip's shoulders sagged and his face split into a relieved smile. "I think you boys are exactly what Kiraly needs."

2

Mark paced his suite, not even trying to sleep. What was the point? He hadn't slept properly since his future had been reset. That first night at home, his thoughts had fixated on his brothers. They'd rarely been apart, only during their college years, and never across oceans. But just because he had to step up to the throne didn't mean they all had to sacrifice their lives in Sage Haven. The next morning, he'd told them to keep the ranch running and live their lives. He'd be fine on his own.

He'd ended up in a horse trough for being a martyr.

Discussion over.

Now, agitation spun through him. They were here. They had each other. But what were they supposed to do? What was *he* supposed to do? He'd handed his father's letter to a group of parliamentary witnesses that evening, and tomorrow would dawn on his new reality.

He'd already been given the monarch's chambers. He hadn't touched anything—he'd hardly sat down. The four-poster bed had crimson hangings that matched the curtains and silken rugs. The chandelier and crystal lampshades cast a garish sparkle onto the gold walls, and was that three-seater couch all velvet? It seemed as if his uncle Vinci had needed constant reassurance of his own wealth, which fit with the unflattering picture Mark's dad had painted of the late king.

Flicking off the lights, Mark moved to the grand windows overlooking the city. His forearm pressed horizontal along the glass, his brow resting on top. Breathing in, breathing out, and longing for basic comfort.

He didn't belong here.

Thank God his dad had been the youngest of three brothers, unlikely to ever take the throne—and thank God he'd got out before Mark and his brothers were born. What if they'd grown up surrounded by all this needless extravagance? What if their values had aligned with those of the late monarch, indulgent and vain and carelessly spending the nation's money? Their upbringing would've been a hell of a lot different to calling a Montana farmhouse home and horse-strewn meadows their playground.

They'd taken pride in the ranch. The quarter horses, the staff—the very land that had been in their care. They'd all intended to live out their lives in that town, content with their stock and the earth beneath their feet.

Again, he breathed in, breathed out, and tried to keep his mind together. Opening his eyes, he gazed down at Kira City where lights glittered and people slept.

His people.

Unsettling or not, he couldn't ignore that truth. He shifted his arm to grasp the window frame beside him. This upheaval had thrown him a mile—but if he wallowed in self-pity for the life he'd lost, it would be as detrimental to Kiraly as his uncle's self-indulgence.

This was his duty. Time to pick it up and shoulder it as best he could.

If he could run a ranch with his brothers by his side, then he could let this city be his property, the people be in his care, and have his brothers continue to lend their strength beside him.

He'd protect them in return. Tommy's anxiety would make royal life a battle and although Kris would never admit it, having his world torn out at the roots was hitting him hard. With his tendency to act out under stress, Mark would shield him until he found his feet. This was difficult enough without public scrutiny.

He straightened. He couldn't let his own title intimidate him from the work that had to be done. In Kiraly, there would be no stress, no scandals, no overspending—just the uncomplicated ruling of a straight-shooting king.

That, he might be able to manage.

Sudden light woke him. Startled, he sat up on the bedcovers and saw someone tying back his curtains, washed out by the blinding morning sun. Had they knocked? Shouldn't he have given permission for them to enter? Throwing his legs over the edge of the bed, he blinked and focused on the immaculately uniformed man with white-blond hair across the room.

"Hey," he said, confused. "I can do that."

The man turned, heels meeting, and bowed deeply. Older than Mark, though not by more than a decade. "Your Majesty," he said in a voice hushed with reverence. "My king."

Mark closed his eyes briefly. It was official.

"Morning," he said.

"Good morning." The man gestured to a tray on Mark's nightstand. It held a cup of steaming coffee and a newspaper. He returned to attention, making faultless posture look like rest.

"And would you like me to lay out your clothes today, Your Majesty?"

What? Mark pulled a face. "No. I'll manage."

"Very good, Your Majesty." And with that, the unidentified man turned and headed to the door.

"Hold on there." Mark rubbed his face. "I met you yesterday, didn't I?"

The man halted, turning back. "You did, Your Majesty."

"And—who are you, again?"

"I am your manservant, Your Majesty."

"Right." Something inside him recoiled. *Servant.* "I don't suppose we could call you my first man instead?"

The man gazed at the wall behind the bed. He hadn't yet made eye contact. "Of course, Your Majesty."

Great. Except—why did the man look dismayed? "Oh, I'm not demoting you," Mark said quickly. "Same position, new title. What's your name?"

"Adam Boller, Your Majesty," he answered, his voice low, eyes still on the wall.

"Were you my uncle's"—he almost couldn't say it —"manservant, too?"

The man shook his head. "No, Your Majesty."

Newly promoted, then. Mark smiled on a casual nod. "Congratulations."

He gave a small smile. "Thank you, Your Majesty."

"Adam." Mark rolled his shoulders and reached for the coffee. "You can't keep calling me that."

The man blinked, startled.

"I've spent my life on a ranch in Montana," Mark said. "Everyone I've known has looked me in the eye, shaken my hand, and called me Mark. No one's opened my curtains or brought me coffee and a paper." It put him on edge, as if he was lazy and superior, and he'd never been either. "The only way I can cope with all this is to be the man I've been for the past twenty-five years. To do that, I need you to treat me like anyone else."

Adam stood silently for several seconds. Then he spoke, his voice cautious. "That goes against my training, Your Majesty."

"I get that. It's your choice."

After a beat, the man's gaze dropped to his. "I'll try, Your —Mark."

Mark smiled, relieved. "Thanks," he said, and tried the coffee. It was sweeter than the grounds he'd always brewed before dawn. Someone had prepared it for him. Someone he probably met yesterday but might never meet again. He'd always done everything for himself—he didn't like to imagine that one day, he might drink coffee or eat meals without thinking of how it had ended up in front of him.

"To be honest," Adam said, "few of us knew you and your brothers existed. Rumor suspected one of you, but not three." His smile was tight. "It's thrown everything into quite a state."

Wait. "People really didn't know we existed?"

"You spent your lives hidden in American mountains." Adam cleared his throat lightly. "The royal family certainly never spoke of Erik. I've heard there was . . . tension between them," he finished carefully.

Tension was putting it mildly. Mark's father had effectively banished himself from Kiraly when he had left the kingdom in a statement against the hedonistic values of the monarch. Apparently, King Vinci had banned any mention of Mark's parents in the media after that, lest Erik's judgement call gain support and spread into public opinion.

Still, Mark hadn't realized the ban had been so effective that the nation hadn't known he and his brothers existed until now.

"We never planned to end up here." Mark looked out the windows. "Our existence wasn't supposed to matter."

"Heirs always matter." Adam paused and asked quietly, "You . . . don't want to be king?"

Mark let out a breath. "Let's just say it makes me uncomfortable."

"Right, yes." The man winced. "Considering your current discomfort, I'm sorry to inform you that you'll be monitored by security at all times beyond these chambers."

Dismay hit Mark like a backhand. "Oh."

"The cameras inside the palace are discreetly positioned, if that helps. And those who will personally monitor you both indoors and out are like shadows. You'll hardly notice them."

Not notice people trained to watch his every movement? Mark ran a hand up and over the bridge of his nose, trying to subdue his swell of alarm. "And my brothers? Will they be monitored?"

Adam inclined his head.

"Do I have the power to dismiss security?"

The man paused. "You have ultimate power."

That statement simply refocused Mark's alarm.

"May I assist with anything else?"

Yes. He needed a distraction. "Tell me something about Kiraly every morning. Big, small, heartbreaking, funny. Doesn't matter. I don't know enough."

"Gladly." Despite dropping the formal address, Adam's pause seemed just long enough for a silent *"Your Majesty."* "The palace has eighty-two private bedrooms and one-hundred-and-forty-eight bedrooms for staff. It also has reception rooms, two grand ballrooms, libraries, restaurants and bars, a cinema, swimming pool, art museum, concert hall . . . There is a full list somewhere. I'll find it for you. If you ever require the use of any such facilities, I shall ensure preparations are made for your visit."

Preparations made for Mark to visit a room in his own

palace? His next breath was thin, difficult. "Thanks, Adam," he said. "Do you have a room here?"

"No. I live in the city." Then he added, "And the entire west wing is closed."

"Closed?"

"The late King of Kiraly was renovating—then Prince Aron made use of a balcony under construction for a family banquet. He believed the contrast of culinary extravagance against a background of paint tins and plasterboard would hold visual appeal for . . ." He paused, looking pained, "Instagram."

Mark grimaced. It was tragically obvious how the banquet had ended.

"Prince Tomas and Prince Kristof are eating breakfast in the parlor." Adam gestured toward the door, his arm at a perfect ninety-degree angle. "To your right, down the stairs at the end of the corridor, left, and then the fourth door on the right."

"Can't I just make myself a piece of toast?" He knew the answer, but some masochistic part of him needed to confirm just how tightly his freedom was bound.

"Oh no, Your—uh . . . sir." At that, Adam almost smiled. "If I'm to treat you like anyone else, then I should tell you that will never happen."

Mark's stomach sank as he offered a friendly nod.

"Will that be all for today?"

No. There would be waiters at breakfast, security shadowing the corridors, and footmen at the doors—the services were seamless and inescapable. One manservant would never be all.

Mark would never fend for himself again.

"Yes, thank you." Resigned, he added, "Perhaps don't open the curtains so wide tomorrow morning. And a stronger coffee would be great. No sugar."

"Very good, Your Majesty." Adam bowed again. "Very good."

When Mark strode into the enormous parlor, boot heels echoing off the polished floor and a pair of guards in his wake, he found Kris lounging at the head of a gargantuan table set for three and Tommy standing by the window, looking out at the palace gardens. The cream walls and blue furnishings matched the outside view—the nearby garden beds bloomed blue and white and violet.

Two guards were positioned on either side of the doorway inside. His own guards peeled apart to join them. Several waiters stood silently a discreet distance from the table.

Their breakfast had never had so many spectators.

"Morning," Mark said to all.

"These breakfast sandwiches are monsters." Kris swiveled around, gesturing at the platters. "Almost as good as the ones at Rose's Diner."

"Big call." Mark sat and almost leapt out of his skin when a waiter silently appeared at his side. "Ah—I'll dish up, thanks," he said, horrified that the man intended to help him select from the platter right in front of him. The waiter bowed with a murmured, "Of course, Your Majesty," and returned to his position. For crying out loud, this was weird. He tried to ground himself with breakfast table talk. "Get any sleep?"

Tommy glanced around and shook his head.

"I think I hallucinated from fatigue at one point." Kris poured a mug of coffee and pushed it at Mark. "Did you get a manservant, too?"

Mark grimaced. "Yes."

"Mine might quit." Kris stretched back in his chair and

grinned. "I was missing when he came in to wake me, and only once he'd shouted my disappearance down the halls, gathering a search party, did I wander back up with my own breakfast." His brows rose as his grin widened. "Not done, apparently."

Jealousy pinched Mark. "You found the kitchen?"

"Is that surprising?" This from Tommy.

"I found many things," Kris said, reaching for his plate. "Did you know there's an aquarium on the ground floor?"

"Tell me when you find a library," Tommy said.

"Oh, and there's a microbrewery somewhere."

Tommy's mouth quirked. "Close second."

Mark raised a hand, eyeing his brothers. "You know we'll be watched by security from now on?"

"Yes." Tommy turned back to the window.

"That lot already trailed me to the kitchen and back," Kris said, jerking his chin toward the guards. "Not very chatty, are we, Peter? Hanna?"

Two of the guards shifted slightly. The young woman murmured, "No, Your Highness."

Mark shot his brother a smile. "Try not to get on their nerves. They've already been lumped with the unlucky task of following you everywhere."

"Why, though?" Kris returned the smile even as his eyes narrowed. "They wouldn't explain. Have you been given a security briefing?"

"Not yet." His attention moved to the guards. "Should we be concerned?" he asked.

One cleared his throat. "Standard protection for a member of the royal family, Your Majesty."

"Right." Mark tried not to think about what else would become a standard part of their new lives. Instead, he focused on his brothers' well-being. "Keep busy today. Sunlight and movement. Try to convince our bodies we're back home. Sleep might come easier tonight."

"I'm going to hike up there." Tommy nodded at the alpine woods behind the palace.

"I'll head into the city." Kris tapped the tabletop. "Avoid culture shock by diving right in."

"Philip wants to meet with me," Mark said. "Then I'll make myself useful outside." Exertion cleared his head, and shared work often relaxed tongues. He wanted to get a feel for the Kiralian people from the ground up.

Then he noticed his brothers exchanging a glance.

"What?" he asked.

Tommy raised a brow. "Is the plan to continue avoiding the fact you've woken up as king of Kiraly?"

Mark's gut roiled. "Yes."

"Easy," Kris concluded, and returned to his meal.

Easy for Kris, sure, but Mark spent the next twenty minutes stuck in a battle between hunger and the inability to stomach food. Then Philip joined them, the ceiling-high wooden doors sweeping closed in his wake.

"Your Majesty, King Markus," he greeted grandly, his gaze darting from one brother to the next. His gaze settled expectantly on Kris seated at the head of the table. He bowed low.

When he looked up, Kris was chewing and jerking a thumb in Mark's direction.

The man shifted his attention, his cheeks growing pink. He repeated the bow. "Your Majesty. It is an honor to welcome you to your duty."

Forcing a smile, Mark answered, "I'd be more comfortable with my duty if you used my name."

Philip's hum in response made no promises, though his

shoulders relaxed fractionally as he examined the plate of breakfast sandwiches. "I trust you slept well."

Mark skirted around answering. "Want to join us?"

The man pulled back. "No. Thank you."

"There's muffins," Kris said.

Philip's nose scrunched lightly. "I avoid sugar. Now, Markus, our briefing will be conducted in your study in under an hour. Kristof and Tomas, please take the day to settle in. Training will begin tomorrow."

"Training?" Kris raised a brow. "I thought you said we were just what Kiraly needed."

"I stand by it." Philip regarded him levelly. "Your decency and modest upbringing will lead to honorable ruling. But that does not mean I will allow this royal family to dissolve into swaggering informality that will encourage judgement and disrespect. I believe you are good men, but you are not royal men. You must be both. It's my duty to protect the reputation of this monarchy and I'll not have your boots dirtying my table, so to speak."

"Point made," Kris said, but his slow smile betrayed the monarchy's reputation wasn't safe yet.

"You might encounter guests who have traveled here for the funeral," Philip continued. Standing with his feet together, arms down, he resembled a very tall gate post. "Some a considerable distance. They're exceptionally interested in you all, so be prepared for questions."

"Definitely going hiking," Tommy murmured, moving to sit opposite Mark.

"Dinner tonight will be a private affair, as the house is still in mourning, but there will be a meal with guests at some point after the funeral."

Apprehension dug a hole in Mark's chest, but he nodded. "Thanks, Philip."

The older man inclined his head and turned to leave. "Oh, and Your Majesty?" He glanced back over his shoulder, breezy, offhand.

"Yes?"

Philip didn't quite look him in the eye. "I should tell you."

When he didn't continue, Mark squared his shoulders toward him. "Yes?"

"One such party of guests, the king and queen of Kelehar, have brought their daughter with them. The very delightful Princess Ava."

"Right." He nodded once, blankly.

Philip scratched his nose and said swiftly, "It's no secret they seek a strategic marriage."

Mark almost dropped his coffee as Kris choked on his second muffin.

"A strategic marriage," Mark echoed, setting his mug down.

"Correct."

He stared. "With me?"

"Also correct."

No. Not also correct. That didn't make any sense. "That's still a thing?"

Philip cleared his throat, not quite meeting Mark's eye. "Yes, Your Majesty."

The pressure of Mark's heartbeat pounded high in his neck.

"Uh-oh," Tommy murmured.

Mark's face was cold. "You mean it only still occurs in places like Kelehar, don't you, Philip? Not here."

Shifting uncomfortably, the older man promptly busied himself with the formerly repulsive task of choosing a muffin.

"Philip?" he pressed, hands bunching.

"Hmm?" Philip straightened, holding two cherry muffins aloft. "You're king, Markus. Your choice of life partner is entirely up to you."

Foreboding gathered in his skull. His brothers seemed to be holding their breaths beside him. "But?"

The man sighed. "It would be a very beneficial union for Kiraly, Your Majesty. I suggest you consider it seriously."

Ava couldn't get out of the palace fast enough. She'd woken to the light shuffles of her maid, bolted down breakfast, pulled on jeans and a fine caramel jumper, and then flew down the stairs to corner her father in the east guest parlor.

"Father." She strode up to his table set for one. Fragrantly fresh bread was surrounded by small bowls of cheese, walnuts, dates, and garden herbs. Chai awaited him in a small glass, blushing brown, with several sugar cubes beside it. He had always preferred a simple breakfast, despite his position. "I'm taking a car into town."

He lowered his phone to frown at her. "Are you?"

She tapped her fingers against her thigh. "Yes. Can I have my pick?"

The king of Kelehar watched her, dark gaze steady. "What business do you have in town?"

"A meeting about the shelter."

He raised a brow. "You're not going to run off again, are you?"

In response, she pressed her molars together so hard they slid and squeaked.

Sighing, her father reached for his tea. "Of course you can take a car, Ava, love. Any except the Cerulean." Then his gaze shifted to Gul behind her and his expression hardened. "Take a second vehicle and four other men."

Dismissed, she left for the royal garage without another word.

She chose the Vermilion.

Energetic and prickly, it was her favorite model. Noise suppression muted the roar of the engine, but it vibrated through the pedals as she accelerated out of the palace gates. Luxury cars were Kelehar's largest export, each and every one the height of prestige and comfort. Vermilions pushed the sporty end of the spectrum, but the seat was plush and the interior timber-lined, and three people would fit uncomfortably in the backseat if circumstances really demanded it.

A collection of their best cars always traveled with the Veisi family. Flown over in advance to meet them, for Keleharian royalty would ride in nothing less.

Kira City citizens ignored her as she edged the car down the steep streets, engine revving at the crawling pace. It was a typical disregard for a place that attracted the cream of the wealthy as tourists. Ostentatious vehicles were nothing new.

Halfway down the mountain, she approached the intersection where Zara had suggested they meet. The nearest corner housed an old pub. A blackboard was mounted on the unkempt exterior and elbows stuck out of the open windows. On the sidewalk, a busker played guitar, attracting a small throng of tourists, and Ava scanned the bustle for Zara Nguyen.

I'll wear yellow, Zara had written in her emailed response last night. *You won't miss me.*

The only reason Ava didn't miss her was because she was standing on the lip of the curb, leaning out over the lane, peering intently through Ava's windscreen. Not noticing her would have meant hitting her with the side mirror.

Zara's hand shielded her eyes and her straight black hair fell to her waist. There was nothing yellow about the gray loose-knit coat that fell to mid-thigh, or the textured green scarf, or the fitted black jeans. Then a woman pushed a pram away from the sidewalk and revealed that Zara's chunky boots were as bright as canaries.

Ava waved, nervous now, and pulled up beside her.

The door flew open and Zara shoved her head inside, background sounds rushing in around her: singing, shouting, and the hum of traffic.

Ava leaned over. "I hate to embarrass you, but I think you've overdone the yellow."

"Oh shit." The woman stared with delighted dark eyes. "It is you! I should've expected you to rock up in the automotive equivalent to a sneer, Miss Princess."

"I prefer to think of it as a cocky grin." She glanced in the rearview mirror. Gul was at the wheel of the security car behind her, blocking the road as he waited.

Zara hesitated. "I don't have the class to ride in this."

"And I don't have the time to elevate you right now."

The woman pulled a face. "Dilemma."

Ava rolled her eyes with a smile. "I meant, get in."

Smiling back, Zara collapsed onto the passenger seat. As she reached for the door, a man called out from the pub doorway. "Hey, Zara, babe, where's my kiss goodbye?"

"Up your ass," she called back and slammed the door.

With her smile growing, Ava accelerated away from the curb, remembering this woman's tongue from three years ago. She had a big heart but came without padding, so heaven help her conversational partners if they were precious.

The car all but juddered along the busy street. People were everywhere, crossing in front of her, cycling, calling out to others as they stepped off the curb. This city was far too relaxed. Ava tapped the wheel. "How do you feel about the open road?"

"I so love it," Zara said. "I'll direct you."

They took backstreets down the slope and cut away from civilization. They ended up on a road with the mountains looming on one side and grassy meadows dotted with cows on the other. Ava sped up, feeling the increasing distance between her and the palace like fresh space in her lungs.

Beside her, smelling like coffee and tacky deodorant, Zara was struggling to take off her jacket in the confined space.

"Will I get locked up if I elbow a princess in the face?" One arm burst free, jerking toward Ava.

She eyed it. "Only for a little while."

"Manageable." Zara threw her jacket on the backseat and flopped against the headrest. She was older than Ava, in her early thirties. Weariness lined her face. "God, I'm tired."

Ava flipped down the sun visor. "How is the shelter?"

"Productive, ceaseless, and depressing."

"Would you like to talk about it?"

"Nah, not really." She regarded Ava, her head still against the rest and her hair smearing into the beginnings of a tangle. Voice growing somber, she asked, "How're you holding up?"

"With goals." Ava adjusted her grip on the wheel. "They keep me focused."

If she looked down and saw the bleak shadow of her existence, she might dissolve into it.

Zara kept watching her. "I didn't think you'd be allowed to drive yourself around."

"It's the one thing I am allowed to do on my own." Ava glanced in the rearview mirror. Gul and his team followed close behind, proving even this freedom was limited.

Her friend hummed, unimpressed.

"Our cars are our national pride." Ava reached the speed limit and crept over. "As a member of the royal family, not only did I have to learn to drive, but in a way that showcases our vehicles."

"Weird."

41

"Growing up with diamond chimes singing above a gold-embedded crib warps one's yardstick for weird."

Zara stared, appearing unsure whether she should laugh or muffle her horror.

"Add servants waiting hand and foot on a toddler," Ava said, "and the yardstick snapped entirely."

"I like you." The woman grinned. "I'm not nearly as weird as I thought."

She gave a small smile in return. "Yes, you are."

Zara laughed. "You're mouthier than when I last saw you."

Ava's smile faded. "I was preoccupied." If one could be preoccupied by debilitating grief.

And Zara had given her focus. This woman without padding had tossed a guiding light into Ava's dark skies and ordered her to walk toward it every day. "Set up your own women's shelter," she'd said. "You might not be able to control your own life, but you can give other women the chance to take control of theirs. Shift your restless energy into positivity. I'll help you." And every day since they'd met, Ava had lived by that light, seeking Zara's advice and friendship in emails along the way.

"Now don't get me wrong, sweetcakes, I'm happy as hell to see you." Zara reached out and patted Ava's thigh several times. Few could touch a princess without permission—yet the startling sensation soothed Ava like oil on parched skin. "But you were supposed to be in Monaco right now, doing all the, you know, fun things." Her pointed glance seemed to say, *like escaping across the continent*. "I've been hanging out for the go-ahead to take over management of your shelter. Tell me you're only here for the funeral."

Ava stared through the windscreen and didn't answer.

"Oh, balls," the woman muttered.

"King Markus." Ava's insides curled like leaves near a flame.

"I'm supposed to make a good impression so he'll agree to marry me."

Zara ran a hand over her face, cursing. "But we had a plan! I can't believe those Jaroka bastards up and died like this."

"It was most selfish of them."

Zara snorted. "Is this Markus even in the country yet?"

"He arrived last night."

"I heard he's got six brothers and they're all geniuses from Harvard."

"Tell me none are interested in marriage and I might pretend to care."

Zara side-eyed her with a grimace. "Do you have a revised plan?"

"Nothing decent." Nerves clung inside her throat. She focused on the road, the reliability of the pine trees one after another. "Just to be so horrendously disparaging of the concept of a lifetime together that he'll agree it's a bad idea."

"Sounds piss-weak, if you ask me."

Stinging at the bold criticism, Ava reminded herself not to be precious. "Yes," she agreed.

"Considered the honest approach of telling him you'd rather eat concrete at the bottom of the ocean than be married off to a king like an auction item?"

"And hand him a power trip at my expense?" Ava had met too many powerful people to ignore that sharing what she wanted exposed her vulnerability. Forcing her into something she didn't want gave them greater power—her parents had taught her that lesson time and again. This life wasn't about honesty and negotiation. It was about dominance. She shook her head. "He'll realize I have no choice and use it against me."

Zara raised a finger. "This is where I should point out the low probability of him actually being soulless enough to exploit the true wishes of a woman. But I deal with the consequences of assholes every day, so I'm not going to bother."

The road bent hard, taking them into sweeping green farmland.

Zara spoke again. "This isn't an arranged marriage, though?"

"No. Strategic."

"Gross."

"Marriages of state are traditional for royalty. And I'm the lucky winner who gets to try to keep tradition alive for this slice of history."

"Not if I can help it." Zara blew out a hard breath. "So, if you're being pressured into this, and he's only just flown in fresh from the student library, what's to say he's not being pressured on his end, too?"

"He could be." Ava had thought of that. "But if Prince Aron could decide against marrying me, then Markus certainly can. Future kings and sovereigns can make their own decisions here, regardless of expectation."

"Okay. God, this better end well," Zara muttered. "I'm going to throw a curveball here—what if you like him?"

Ava almost laughed. "Then I'd have the added torture of liking someone I couldn't be open with." No one else could know what drove her. It wasn't safe. "I still wouldn't want to marry him as badly as I want to get out of this life. It'd be better if we hated each other on sight."

And Cyrus wondered why she embodied cynicism.

Zara tapped her fingers on the dashboard. "Okay, so you need to buy time while Cyrus and I work out a new escape plan. Somehow, we've got to make you disappear before the eyes of your guards back there, with the added complication of vanishing inside a security-monitored palace."

And all before she returned to Kelehar in a few short weeks. Panic flooded her. A princess couldn't disappear in her own country, not without being recognized by everyone she encountered. This had to happen abroad. The strategic match between her and the king was an unrelated yet chilling obstacle. "The word impossible keeps springing to mind."

"Nah." The woman's hand returned to Ava's thigh for another few pats. "Leave it with us. You focus on shaking off the king's interest, because a formal royal engagement would definitely complicate your disappearance. We'll take care of the rest."

Ava's inhale wavered. *Impossible, impossible, impossible.*

Zara looked at her. "We could discuss king-ditching techniques, if you want?"

She nodded stiffly.

"Let's strengthen your method. Give it a little twist, because I'm not sure being openly disparaging will do the trick. But we *do* want him to decide that it's a bad idea, definitely."

Ava tilted her head, listening.

"You could act as if you're committed to the marriage— like you'd do anything for your duty. But be the kind of woman he can't stand. You'll have to figure out what that is on the fly."

"Provide examples, please."

"If he's pretentious, mock him. If he's a cocky little shit, tear his ego to shreds. If he's a decent guy, be cruel. When it reaches a point of maximum intolerability, chances are he'll decide against the marriage."

Ava turned the plan over in her mind. "It could work."

Zara gave a grim smile. "It's all I've got."

Then Ava would have to judge fast, aim low, and hope for the best. She tucked the idea away like a one-step plan to her better future. "What about you? Any dilemmas that'll make me feel better?"

"Oh. Yes." Zara turned her face away and pressed her

forehead against the window. "I have a crush on my housemate, but he knows and is going to move out."

Surprised to receive instant gossip, Ava asked, "Are you sure?"

"Painfully," Zara confirmed, her forehead remaining on the passenger window. "He moved in a few months ago. I needed help covering my mortgage. He's always been distant, but I find that kind of mysterious. I've given signals recently. Prolonged eye contact. Smiles. Little touches. And he's become even more distant."

Ava frowned, taking a left-hand turn up the mountain. "Explain the part where you think he's moving out."

"He's hardly been home for days. And when he is, he doesn't talk to me. He hardly answers when I ask about his day."

"Could he be busy at work?" Ava attempted reassurance, hiding her confusion. The man sounded far from appealing.

"He works in the palace. Serving somehow—he wasn't specific. I suppose it's been hectic there this week, considering . . . but I was passing his room the other night when he came out. I saw inside—he had bags packed." Zara's sigh was dejected. "He knows I like him and he's balls-deep in freak-out mode."

Ava hung her fingers from the base of the steering wheel, unsure how to help. Friend duties were unchartered territory. "You could ask him out for a drink?" Surely resolution aided moving on. "Find out for certain."

"I'm not the kamikaze type."

Out of ideas, Ava said, "I'll be staying in the palace for a few weeks. If you need to talk, you're welcome to visit me."

"Thanks."

After a few minutes of watching the scenery slip by, Ava said, "We haven't spoken about work yet."

"Let's not today. I could do with a break."

And so they spoke of inconsequential things until Ava returned to the cluttered streets of Kira City and parked opposite the bland building of the women's shelter that Zara managed.

Zara's hand brushed Ava's shoulder, the touch soft as a feather. "It's selfish, but I really am happy to see you."

Throat tight, she said, "Me too."

"Don't worry, sweets. It'll all work out." Zara's words of comfort were surprisingly gentle, and Ava remembered the same tenderness in her friend on the bleak night they'd met. Ava's tears had fallen for hours, and Zara had sat with Ava's head in her lap, stroking her hair and murmuring like a mother to a baby. This woman came with padding, after all, cushions upon cushions crammed into every corner of her heart.

Then Zara exhaled roughly and added, "And if it ends badly, we can go drink 'til we're shit-faced and tell the world to get fucked."

3

Philip kept Mark until midafternoon. The study was a grand tower room, wreathed in windows with views that made Mark's head spin. The walls were curved, and glass doors opened onto a balcony, welcoming new spring air into the room. Neither man used the head of the desk, but instead sat facing each other on plush armchairs. The conversation was grueling, if simply for the fact that three days ago, Mark had been overseeing soil testing of pastures, and now, he was being given a map of his future on which he didn't recognize a single landmark.

"Your coronation will be in six months," Philip told him. "Under usual circumstances, it would be held within a couple of months of your ascension, but given the . . ." He looked momentarily lost. ". . . profound tragedy, it was decided that a longer period of national mourning would be most appropriate. A Coronation Committee has been formed and the preparations have already begun."

Mark swallowed. Six months were required to prepare for one day? "Right."

"In the coming months, you'll be trained in the ways of a

king, from your specific political role within the state to forms of address; from the customs of other cultures to how to negotiate a trade deal."

Mark nodded once, still unable to shake the sensation of free-falling. This world was blurry around him, an unfocused streak as he plunged into its center. He had to find his feet before he was crowned. He bunched up the sleeves of his plaid shirt and ignored the pummel of his pulse.

"I should tell you upfront." Philip glanced down at the papers on his lap, rifling through them. "Kiraly is in considerable debt."

Mark stilled. "Debt?"

"Yes." The man sighed and held out a piece of paper. Taking it, Mark felt the impact of the negative figure like a blow. "It's external debt. Primarily to one exorbitantly wealthy country in the Middle—"

"How?" he interrupted, his dismay masked by the demand. Most countries were in some kind of national debt, but Kiraly was only small, and that figure was so *big*. It crushed him. He didn't know what the hell he was doing as it was, but to inherit such indebtedness . . . it splintered his confidence. "How did this happen?"

"Ah, well." Philip shifted, scratching behind his ear. "It's, you know."

Mark stared.

The other man practically squirmed. "I can't bear to speak ill of our late King Vinci . . . he wasn't himself since the queen died. But . . . you could say that his spending habits got a bit out of hand."

Cursing under his breath, Mark said, "Philip, in what matters did you advise my uncle?"

The man blinked. "Pardon?"

"We both know he was more interested in himself than in Kiraly. Did your advice support that?"

Philip paled. "Your Majesty. Your uncle wasn't a bad man. He just . . ." The advisor toyed with his cufflink. "He made bad choices, which I endlessly tried to talk him out of. Please believe me that Kiraly would be much worse off if it weren't for my continued efforts."

Mark held the man's earnest gaze—and believed he spoke the truth.

"You are, of course, welcome to select new advisors," Philip said next, in the soft tone of humiliation. "Those you can trust."

"No." Mark sighed. He'd needed to be sure. "You're not going anywhere."

Philip pretended to adjust his tie as he sank back into the cushions in relief. "Thank you, Your Majesty." He paused to breathe, hand on his chest. "I was head of personal security for sixteen years while acting as the king's advisor. I like to think I'm a valuable asset. If you have any questions, any at all, please come to me."

Mark didn't hesitate. "Why are you so sure we're what Kiraly needs? Why is *everyone* so sure? I've been reading the news. Public opinion of us is surprisingly positive. I don't understand." For all Kiraly knew, he and his brothers might be just like their uncles and cousin—settling in to rack up more debt.

Philip smiled. "I ran security. You think I didn't keep an eye on the outcast arm of the royal family? I've come to know you three. You're good men."

Mark balked. *Outcast?* His parents had turned their backs on the Jaroka royal family, not the other way around.

"I held a fleeting press conference before you arrived," Philip continued, "with the purpose of sharing that the Lost

Princes were decent and trustworthy and would be a great asset to Kiraly."

"You started the Lost Princes thing?" Then the man's previous words registered. "How did you keep an eye on us, exactly?"

Philip pressed his lips together. He glanced away. Then he said, "I'm no longer head of personal security and therefore no longer permitted to divulge that information."

So his advisor wouldn't spill every secret just because his king asked. Mark respected his discretion, even as it bugged him. "I'll ask the current head of security, then. Can I meet them?"

"I'll set up a meeting," the man replied, still looking away. "Plenty of other priorities first, I'm afraid."

"Sure." Fine by Mark. He'd had enough of business for the day. The pressure of it was gathering behind his eyes. "Tell me about yourself. Do you have a family?"

The question seemed to smack the color from the man's face. "I—no, Your Majesty." His head lowered. "Not anymore."

"I'm sorry." Uncomfortable, Mark swiftly reversed. "And you live in the palace?"

"Yes." Philip looked up, features composed, but sadness hung from his shoulders. "I'm available anytime you need me, day and night."

"Good to know." Mark nodded too many times.

Philip's gaze dropped to his knees. He picked at his trousers.

God, okay. Keep moving the conversation on. To what? *Anything. Ask him anything.* "What are the rules regarding the royal family having relations with palace staff?"

The man's head snapped up, eyes wide. "Pardon?"

"I'm not asking for me," Mark said hurriedly. "I meant Kris. He has a habit of looking for distractions." And he might not look very far.

"Ah." Philip paused. Then he nodded. "Yes, I did read that. A ladies' man." He cleared his throat, seeming to shake off whatever loss had overcome him. "It's not prohibited, but it's certainly not encouraged. The status inequality, you understand."

"Yes." Since Kris had none of Philip's discretion, Mark would have to talk to him.

"May I ask what's wrong with Prince Tomas?" Philip asked. "The reports were never clear."

Mark bristled and leaned forward, elbows on his thighs and hands clasped between. Voice low, he answered, "Nothing's wrong with Tommy."

"I apologize for my lack of tact." Philip spread his palms. "What troubles him?"

"He gets anxious." And he would get furious if Mark said anything more than that.

"I see." The man's brows rose. "Now, you'll all have new clothes tailored tomorrow—"

Mark's chin angled up. "We won't need them."

Philip looked stricken, his eyes darting to Mark's favorite old jeans. "It's just that—"

"You take us like this, or not at all."

Mark would surrender to duty—but Tommy and Kris had moved here for him, and he'd be damned if it stripped them of their very identities.

"Ah." Philip gave a quick smile and folded his hands on his lap. "I opt for taking you, Your Majesty, and my apologies." He paused. "You three brothers are the last of the line, after all. We'd have to scrounge back to a split in the bloodline to find someone to replace you. Awful business. Let's not think on it."

Dread belted Mark, hard and fast. It was alarmingly clear what *last of the line* meant for him.

Producing heirs.

Pressure sank deep into his shoulders.

"I'll try to do this right," he managed to say. "But that'll mean staying sane." The stranglehold royal expectation now had on his life—future family included—could drive him mad. "My brothers and I will need time for ourselves. Tommy needs space, if Kris can't travel freely he'll go crazy, and it'll be better for everyone if I can vent my stress on a morning ride. We are who we are. Is that going to be a problem?"

"Not at all." Philip straightened his lapels. "Your Majesty, I heard that you offered to make your own toast this morning. You ask for nothing compared to your predecessor. Of course, you should all have time to yourselves. In fact, I'd say we're finished here for today."

Mark rose to his feet. They hadn't spoken about the issue of strategic marriage, but there would be time to put an end to that after the funeral. He let it go. "Then I'll be outside."

"I can arrange a tour—"

"No, thanks. I'm sure I'll find somewhere to get my hands dirty."

If Philip had been standing, Mark suspected he'd have staggered from shock. "Dirty?" His advisor swallowed. "Our staff are exceedingly capable. I'm not confident you'll find anything to do."

Mark plucked his hat off the desk. "There's always work to be done."

Ava wished she'd worn softer shoes. Her own fault for dressing as inappropriately as possible for the palace and grounds tour, but her choice of a fuchsia pink gown, tight around her figure and finely beaded, had been prompted by her mother barging into her room and demanding she put on walking clothes.

"Do you want me to attract a king or a gym instructor?" Ava had asked archly from the desk.

"We're hardly about to see the king outdoors, Ava. Be practical. You won't attract him with a broken ankle."

"True." Speculatively, she'd chosen her highest heels.

A petty victory, and the fury on mother's face when she'd appeared downstairs might have been worth it, if it weren't for the painful reality of her mother trying to sell her off. She'd packed such formal gowns on Ava's behalf, all for the purpose of looking her finest for King Markus at shared meals, evenings of entertainment, and whatever other social occasions her mother no doubt envisioned for Ava's stay following the funeral. Well. If her mother wanted her to dress up for the king so badly, she would, every chance she got—no matter how ridiculous.

Ava made it through the indoor circuit without much discomfort, but as the tour progressed into the centuries' old garden, along winding paths and quaint bridges, each stretch of nature displaying the flora of a different geographical origin, blisters formed fast.

"A princess never hobbles," Gul murmured from behind her.

"Nor does she tolerate smart-mouthed guards."

He paused. "Well, that's entirely untrue."

She held back a laugh. "I'm hoping to break my ankle."

"Shall I shove you?"

"Only if I haven't managed it by the time we circle back."

Cyrus shot her a despairing glance over his shoulder, but didn't comment.

The path soon beckoned them out of the cultivated gardens and into a woodland of brooks and ferns, stepping stones and follies. Pines towered in the near-distance—they were approaching the forest at the edge of the royal grounds. As the journey began to get particularly treacherous, Gul murmured from behind her, "Princess, your hair pins are slipping."

Thankful for the rest, she stopped to face him. He directed her to the loose pins, and she pressed them deeper into her heavy pile of hair. It was so thick, some days she longed to cut it short as a pixie. Waiting, she watched Gul's careful expression as he instructed her hands—and then watched shock flatten his features as his gaze caught on something behind her. Under his breath, he murmured, "Turn around, turn around, turn around."

She did as he begged and then stilled, stunned.

There was a small team at work at the edge of the woods. Fallen trees were being drawn out from the forest, sliced into sections with chainsaws, and then moved to several chopping blocks on which they were axed into pieces. Mundane, common work, and ordinarily, she wouldn't even glance in that direction.

But the man.

Oh, the man at the nearest chopping block was like nothing she'd ever seen. Shirt hanging open, his sun-browned skin swelled over wide shoulders and jutted down a stomach flat as a floodplain. His jeans were faded, threadbare over the knee on one leg, torn at the thigh on the other, and met brown leather boots. His belt had a brass oval buckle and his dark hat curled up at the sides.

Men didn't dress like that in Kelehar.

As she stared, the man positioned a stump, picked up his axe, and swung down hard. Muscles shifted, wood splintered, and her thoughts scattered.

"Ah." The guide had stopped the tour a short way along the path, evidently waiting for the princess to finish her hair. Now, the woman extended her arm in the woodchopper's direction with a flush riding up her face. "On our right, you'll see our beloved new sovereign, King Markus Jaroka."

The heat of horror burned Ava's skin.

King Markus?

Everyone in the group reacted differently. Her father stared, while her mother gasped and shot a look straight at her. Cyrus tilted his head, frowning, and Gul leaned in close, murmuring, "I told you they were unexpected."

Dismay held a knife to her throat. She didn't dare move. She *couldn't* move.

"Cowboys?" Cyrus sounded curious. "I didn't hear that one."

Then her heart thudded, for at a quick, quiet word from her mother, the guide hurried the group along. Cyrus sent her a glance stricken with apology even as Ava followed, desperate for this not to happen—not here, not now—but her mother spun around, and every strict line in her face decreed that Ava was to stay exactly where she was or the wrath of the crown would fall upon her.

"Oh, Gul, help me," she whispered, halting. Although she'd only spoken with Zara about him this morning, she hadn't anticipated encountering King Markus so soon. She wasn't ready for her fate to be set in motion. Not yet.

"I'm afraid I got the same look, Princess." Regret filled his words. "My hands are tied."

She nodded stiffly. Despite their friendship, she couldn't expect him to disobey the queen's orders and let Ava slip away. And so, she stood in her ridiculous finery, not a dozen paces from the lumberjacks, and waited for the king of Kiraly to notice her.

Her breath came uncomfortably fast. Her skin prickled, still too hot, but she forced the sting back from her eyes and turned away, her shoulders straight, her chin up. Her whole life, she had been groomed to best appeal to a king. She'd lost her childhood to a battering of lessons: etiquette, deportment, conversation, and later, politics and economics. Adolescence provided temporary relief, boarding at the world's most prestigious private school in Switzerland, but like a sweet dream, it had dissolved the moment she'd returned home. Even now at twenty-three, her life was a cycle of daily fitness training, public events, and enforced chastity. She had no freedom. She made very few of her own choices. And why? Her parents had dictated her life—stolen what she'd loved most—so that she could please a *cowboy*?

The absurdity of it choked her. The pain and humiliation. Heat flooded her eyes.

"He's looking, Princess." Gul's voice was soft.

"Make me angry," she begged, breaking apart at the world's sick joke.

"Not just looking," he said, "but taking you all in. And he likes what he sees."

She hauled herself onto that statement as if it were a lifeboat. Desperate to save herself, she worked herself up into a temper. So King Markus was just like his cousin. Leery-eyed and repulsive. How dare he presume to look at a palace-born-and-bred princess, when he knew nothing beyond dirt and dung?

Slowly, faking carelessness, she turned around.

The king was wiping his forehead with the back of his wrist. He'd lowered his axe, all the better to stare, though his chest still rose and fell from exertion. His brow creased at her attention; his jaw flexed.

"If you make him come over here, I can't promise not to touch him," Gul muttered.

Inhaling, she took the bait and began the uneven walk toward the chopping blocks.

King Markus cast a questioning glance at the man beside him, jerking his head in her direction. After receiving a nod and hurried hand gestures, he approached, his stride long and easy.

His features grew sharper as he neared. A straight nose, dark brows, and a strong jaw like bent iron. Eyes sapphire-bright and weighted with curiosity.

He stopped farther away than she'd expected.

"Princess Ava." With an accent that curled tightly around buttery vowels, King Markus seemed to scoop her name right out of her stomach. He plucked the hat off his dark brown hair, nodded once, and set it back on again. His other hand rested on the waistband of his jeans.

No, not rested. It *gripped*.

Not as relaxed as he let on.

Quickly, she judged that a man of the land wouldn't react well to disdain and superiority. She set Zara's plan into action, praying her friend was right.

Ava sniffed, keeping her features tight as her gaze swept him up and down. Her insides knotted at more than a glimpse of his bare chest and sparked as her attention tangled at the torn denim at his thigh. She shifted, thrown off-balance by her body's attraction to a man who could trap her entire future.

Indifferently, she looked back up. "And you're the king?"

"I am now." His answer was low, measured.

She didn't reply. All the better for him to hear the scorn in her silence.

His brow flickered. "I hope I haven't offended you by meeting under these circumstances." He gestured to himself, open-shirted and sweating.

"Not at all." He'd offended her with a great deal more than that. This union was like offering a Vermilion to a backyard mechanic. "When people wear their insides on the outside, they are so much easier to navigate."

His frown lowered.

Glancing down, she made a fuss over lifting the skirt of her dress off the ground. Pine needles clung to the fabric like a hem of spiked lace, and she shook it gently with a sigh. Making a play for his opinion on their marriage, she said, "Apparently we're to be wed," and casually looked up again.

His jaw clamped shut, and tension hardened the muscles in his neck. Interesting. Prince Aron had been quick to presume his right to her, but this king—he still hung back, leaving plenty of sunlight between their shadows.

Recovering, he slid a hand into his pocket. "I don't believe that's set in stone yet."

"How long have you been here, Your Majesty?"

He didn't pause. "Twenty-one hours."

"I'm not sure what life was like for you at home, but face value is a convoluted concept in politics." She raised her brows. "I suggest you don't believe anything for a long while yet."

He regarded her cautiously.

"Including me," she added, and instantly regretted deriding him with such a personal truth.

He ran a hand over his mouth. His brows were low as his attention moved over her shoulder, seeming to notice Gul. Her pulse tripped as he looked back to her, an unmistakable shadow of desperation in his eyes. She knew that expression: life moving too quickly in a direction he hadn't intended. He was struggling to grab hold of anything familiar or of his own choosing. Well, that *was* interesting.

The cowboy was drowning in the deep end.

"I was told it would be my decision," he said, his words firm.

"Your decision." She repeated it quietly, dropping the hem of her dress back onto the pine bed.

"And yours." He spoke like it was obvious. "What kind of marriage would it make otherwise?"

"One of strategy and political benefit."

Wariness gathered in lines on his brow. "And your choice will support that?"

She struggled to hold onto her dignity. She prayed he wouldn't discover she had no choice at all. "Of course, no matter how it will pain me to do so."

He raised his brows.

"Look at me." She extended her arms a little to the sides, as if to display her ancestry and upbringing. "And look at you."

As his frown returned, something about him changed. A subtle mood shift that edged his shoulders back and settled his stance more firmly between both booted feet. Then the cowboy king said in a voice of gravel, "My insides don't align with your outsides, Princess Ava?"

She stared back at him, expressionless.

Chin level and eyes hard, he said, "It's been nice meeting you." And with that, he lifted his hat and returned to the sweaty task of chopping wood.

It was a start. Cautiously optimistic, she made her way back to where Gul stood, side-on, neither watching her nor allowing her out of his sight.

"Well?" he murmured, falling into step behind her.

"He wasn't thrilled by me."

Her guard didn't respond until the path threaded beside an artificial stream, where the splashing of an immense fountain could conceal the impropriety of him asking, "And what was he like?"

"Green," she said, though her stomach curled at his innocence. Markus was so new to his position that he hadn't seemed like royalty at all. She might have been talking to an actual lumberjack. Not that it mattered. That lumberjack had a world of power over her and that made him dangerous. "They'll mold him around his duty. I just have to get in first."

"You could have spat on him."

"I try not to recycle strategies." Heaven forbid she became

predictable. "I want to go directly back to my rooms. I shall not be rejoining the tour."

"Yes, Princess."

The blisters set a slow pace back to the palace.

A bird trilled nearby as Gul said, "My offer to shove you still stands, if that would brighten your day."

A smile rose above her unease. "What did I do to deserve you?"

His answering smile came a beat too slow, and with a lurch of her heart, she remembered exactly what she'd done. She remembered the act, the aftermath, and the agony. She remembered, with sorrow hard in her throat, that even this friend was here to prevent her from escaping her duty.

They walked on in silence.

"You met her?"

Kris spoke from where he lazed on Mark's bed, his bare feet dangling over the edge of the mattress. Tommy sat on the silken rug, his legs extended with his back against the wall and a book splayed face-down beside him. A giant gold-framed mirror hung above his head.

Mark paced. "I couldn't avoid it. She was touring the grounds."

"Evaluating her future estate," Kris said.

"Kristof." Tommy smiled faintly. "Not helping."

"She likes the grounds more than she likes me. I'm beneath her." Their encounter irritated Mark like a bug bite that became more swollen the more his mind scratched at it. "Looked at me like I was a mangy dog."

"Not the kind to feed strays, huh? That's good, right?" Tommy eyed him from beneath tired lids. Mark had hoped the day's hike would put color back in his brother's cheeks, but he looked pale and worn out. How Tommy would cope with tomorrow's funeral was anyone's guess. "The strategic marriage is a non-issue."

"She wasn't convinced of that."

"Philip said it was your decision," Kris reminded him, getting comfortable on the bed and shifting around to tug the covers over himself. Then he half-sat up, peering at the mattress beneath. "Hey, where are your sheets?"

"Pulled them off. They were silk."

"Silk sheets." Kris rested on his elbows, pulling a face. "What's with this place?"

Tommy snorted.

"Philip said it was my decision," Mark repeated, uneasy. "She said I was stupid to believe that."

"What does she look like?" Kris asked.

Mark's midsection tightened. "What does that matter?"

"There are only hundreds of people around here. I want to pick her out."

Uncomfortable, Mark kicked off his boots under a winged armchair. "Olive skin. Big dark eyes. Dark hair all pinned up. She managed to look down on me even though she only comes to about here, heels included." He held a hand against his chin. "She spoke in this considered way, like she'd had training in pronunciation or something, and her voice was sort of low and rich, and her mouth was . . ."

Enthralling.

An amused, "Uh-oh," came from the bed.

Mark ignored him. "And she was wearing a full-length gown thing, like it was a state dinner instead of a stroll in the gardens. If she dresses like that all the time, you won't miss her."

"Wait, you said heels. Out there?" Kris shook his head with

a laugh. "Classic. Was she trying to break an ankle or something?"

Mark raised a shoulder.

"Describe the dress," Tommy said.

Damned Tommy.

"I don't know—pink?" He wished that was all he'd noticed. The fabric had been wrapped around the soft squeeze of her waist and the curve of her hips, falling loose in a floor-length skirt. He'd seen no bra straps over her smooth shoulders—not that he'd been looking—and the neckline had swept down, not too low, just low enough that her skin had begun to swell before it disappeared beneath the fabric at her breasts. And the back of the dress, when she'd walked away from him and he'd foolishly looked back, had scooped—

He saw Tommy glance at Kris, brows raised.

"Right." Kris grinned. "That memory just swallowed you whole."

Mark eyed him, his gut sinking. "So?"

His grin widened. "So I'm guessing she looked good."

"Yes, she looked good." Curse his brothers. They didn't get it. They hadn't been there—hadn't felt the brutal jolt of reality that the princess was real. The strategic marriage proposition was *real*. Not some offhand suggestion for him to consider in the isolation of his study, but a possible future closing in. "Your point?"

Tommy shifted, bringing a knee toward his chest, his foot flat on the rug. "Maybe the princess wasn't as bad as she seemed, but you don't know how to be interested in women anymore."

His skin heated. "What?"

Tommy spoke carefully. "You and Sally were together a long time."

His pride twisted. He should've known their camping trip would come back to bite him. He'd shared too much.

"Don't worry about it." Kris rolled onto his side, propped up on an elbow. "We'd both figured you hadn't been with anyone since Sal."

Mark clenched his teeth. "A seven-year relationship proves I know how to be interested in someone."

"A seven-year relationship that spanned most of high school," Tommy pointed out quietly. "How long since you broke up? Four years? I hate to say it, but your one-time experience at asking out a fourteen-year-old girl doesn't really transfer to knowing how to pursue a woman at twenty-five."

Not true. He just hadn't met anyone he'd wanted to pursue.

"I know this is rich coming from me." Tommy scratched at the rug beneath him. "But don't let your fear of the unknown stop you from being interested in her, if you would be otherwise."

Kris stretched with a yawn, his shirt riding up over the top of his jeans. "And at some stage, you're going to have to get back in the—"

"Enough." Irritated, Mark eyeballed them both. "Thanks for your concern, but she was rude and condescending, and sure, beautiful too, but I'm not interested. And before you get any heated ideas, Kris, I strongly suggest you don't go there either. End of story."

His brothers exchanged a glance.

"Okay." Kris shrugged, lying back down.

"Sure." Tommy picked up the book beside him and resumed reading.

With a scowl, Mark resumed pacing.

"Princess," Gul spoke softly from the doorway. "I'll be going down for dinner shortly."

Ava glanced up from the report she was reading in her sitting room. She had already dined, bathed, and changed into her favorite nightclothes, and was now curled in a cushy armchair with the intention of making headway on the paperwork spread across the table beside her. Her women's shelter usually provided a decent, if temporary, distraction. "Enjoy your meal."

"Erwin will take over. He won't intrude unless you call."

"Thank you." Then she called out louder, "Thank you, Erwin!"

A muffled, "Of course, Your Highness," came from beyond the door.

"Well," Gul said, standing as bold and daunting as ever, "I'll see you in the morning. I'll be off now."

She smiled in farewell and returned her attention to her work. It didn't take her long to realize that Gul remained across the room, making no move to follow through on his grand announcement. With a sigh, she flipped open a spiral-bound book from the pile beside her, hunting for notes. "I don't want to talk about him," she said, eyes on her work.

There was the *click* of the door closing—with Gul on the inside. "But he's a cowboy, Princess." His words were imploring.

She flicked up a glance. "Have I previously made discussing cowboys a habit for that to be a relevant argument?"

Unfazed by her sharp tone, he said, "You could start."

Sighing again, she put down her pen. "Fine." She faced him properly, tucking her legs beneath her. "Sit down. You have three questions."

Gul made himself comfortable on her divan, splaying an arm along the sloped back and feet crossing at the ankle. He grinned. "Isn't he something?"

She clicked her tongue. "Really? You want to waste a question on that?"

"It's not a waste." His usually impassive face was at ease and his gaze was fixed on her with interest. "I want to know whether you think he's something."

"If you like that kind of thing," she said, raising a shoulder dismissively.

"*Do* you like that kind of thing?"

Deep down, she wasn't sure. "Not when he's the king and I'm expected to please him."

"What did he smell like?"

She scoffed, taken aback. "I didn't inhale him, Gul."

"Perhaps you should have. Was his accent as hypnotic as his body?"

"Why would you ask that?" She drew her legs more securely beneath her. "This isn't about whether I think he's sexy or want to write his initials in my diary. This is serious. I could be trapped with him for the rest of my life."

He sobered. "I understand that, Princess."

"But you still want to know if I think his accent is attractive?"

His eyebrows pulsed above a straight face.

She raised her hands in frustration. "In another time and place, yes, I'd probably think so."

"He worked alongside those laborers like they were equals," he said.

"Because he doesn't know his place," she said. "That's dangerous for a king."

"But it's kind of captivating. He's strong and capable, not limp-handed and useless. Don't you find that appealing?"

"Gul." She crossed her arms, hiding from his voracious questioning. He'd long surpassed three questions. "You can count."

He didn't flinch from the blade in her tone. "Do you think he could be kind?"

The angle of that question struck her fears. "Did my mother ask you to do this?" she asked, dismayed by the sudden thought.

He blinked. "What?"

"Order you to cast that man in a positive light so I'd be more agreeable?"

"Of course not." The glint in his eyes fell to the darkness of offense. He sat straighter, relaxation gone. "I worry about you, Princess, and I'm concerned that you believe you'll be able to deter him. If your plans don't succeed, I want you to be able to find hope in your situation. I've heard what the palace staff are saying about him. Good things. And he didn't look evil from where I was standing and that's more than I can say about the last Jaroka you met. King Markus might not be that bad."

Gul's words sliced something open inside her, and her sudden fear that he was right—that she might not succeed—made her lash out. "You marry him, then," she said, distressed. "If you find him so hypnotic."

And as quickly as it had blinded her, her fear was replaced by the bright sear of regret.

Gul rose to his feet woodenly, his features tight. Hurt shuddered in his next breath.

"I'm sorry." She stood, papers falling. "That was—" A cruel reminder that such unions were impossible back in Kelehar. "Forgive me."

"There's nothing to forgive."

They both knew he lied.

"I didn't mean—" She cut herself off. It didn't matter what she'd intended. Helpless, she offered him the freedom to escape her. "Perhaps you'd like to eat now."

"Yes, thank you."

She remained standing as he departed, her teeth tight. Why

was she like this? Useless at being a friend, too quick to take swipes at others to protect herself. He'd offered her succor for a future eventuality and she'd stabbed him for his trouble. It was a dark irony that she desperately fought to avoid marriage while he longed for marriage to be permitted to him and whomever he came to love.

Huffing out a disgusted breath, she sat and shoved her books aside. She would achieve nothing tonight. Not even the shelter could distract her from the sting of her own selfishness.

4

Mark awoke to dawn and dread that today was the funeral. A mournful event made worse by the expected widespread attendance and his first official public appearance as king. The world would be watching him on this stepping stone toward his coronation—watching Kris and Tommy, too, Kiraly's mysterious rancher-to-royal princes.

Tommy . . .

Concern pressed at his solar plexus. Tommy said he'd cope, but the ceremony would be immense. Packed with guests. Hundreds of curious, prying eyes. Handshakes and condolences. And then the burial—smaller but still full of strangers. Mark let out a breath.

They'd get through it.

Hauling himself out of bed, he stuffed his hands into his hair. His day had been planned. Consult with his full team of advisors after breakfast; bury three of Kiraly's most powerful men at two; nip back to the palace to meet his prime minister at five; and dine privately with his brothers at six.

At the base of the bed stood a clothes rack displaying a black suit, tie, and sharp white shirt. Glossy black shoes waited neatly on the floor. The kind of clothes Mark had only worn a few times in his life and always at circumstantial knifepoint. He sighed, feeling the prick of the blade yet again as he turned to Adam.

His first man was setting down a tray with coffee and newspaper on Mark's bedside table, his gaze absently surveying the bed. Then he stilled, eyes wide and appalled.

"Your Majesty," he said, and then seemed to catch himself. "Mark. You have no sheets."

"Oh." Mark glanced over his shoulder. "They were silk."

Adam straightened. "I will arrange for the finest cotton sheets."

"That'd be great." He paused. "Actually, is there anyone around here who could tone down this whole suite? And for my brothers too?"

The man looked at him in disbelief. "You want it less . . . royal?"

"Got it in one."

"I'll make arrangements at once, Your Maj—Mark."

Mark smiled as he reached for the coffee mug.

"Sorry." Adam shifted, eyeing his own feet. "I'm trying."

"I know. And I appreciate it." Mark stretched his neck. "Do you drink coffee, Adam?"

"Tea, actually."

"Then could you arrange for tea to be added to the morning tray?" This daily ritual needed softening. A shared drink would help.

Adam blinked. "Of course."

Mark smiled again and took his coffee to the window. The sun was coming over the horizon, the early light hitting a band of houses high on the mountainside, and they shone in the honey-stoned landscape. Far below, the dark shapes of boats were buoyed on the blue-green lake.

"It's an attractive city," he said, seeking a distraction from the day ahead.

"Yes."

"What do you like the most about it?"

Adam thought for a while. "Its duality," he said. "In one glance, it's a luxury destination for the wealthy. World-class resorts by the lakeside offer exquisite restaurants and boutique shopping strips, all with stunning natural views. But then you turn your head and see that while entertaining the highest class of global society, the city is also a home. People live on those steep streets, working to please the tourists, or laboring on the farms and in the mines. After a day's hard work, they come together to laugh and sing in shabby courtyards and crowded bars. It's not an easy life, but those people have the strongest legs in all the world and the liveliest of hearts."

Mark gazed down at the city of two faces. "Well said, Adam."

"Thank you."

"And what can you tell me about Princess Ava?" She was knotted in his tension tangle, another thread to complicate the mess in his head. It sickened him that maybe, to be a good king, he needed to realistically consider the notion of strategic marriage.

"Of Kelehar?" The man sounded surprised. "She is very lovely."

Mark waited, and after a period of silence, turned to see the man looking conflicted from where he stood by the bed. Evidently, *lovely* wasn't the whole truth.

"Your words will stay in this room," Mark assured him.

"It's just that . . ." Adam's already soft voice dropped. ". . . she spat on the late Prince Aron."

Confounded, Mark said, "S*pat* on him?"

"She requested he marry her and then spat in his face."

71

"How do you know that?"

Adam flushed, shifting his weight. "Word travels downstairs, Your Majesty."

"When did it happen?"

"A few years ago. He declined her proposal, as you can imagine."

Mark frowned. Ava had already been here to marry into the Kiralian royal family? She'd clearly disdained his cousin but had still returned for a second attempt, despite feeling no warmer toward Mark. That bad omen unsettled him. Philip had claimed the union would be beneficial to Kiraly, but it must be even more advantageous to Kelehar. Surely only the greatest of outcomes would have Ava pursuing marriage with men she clearly scorned. Unless she didn't scorn them specifically.

She might be utterly awful to everyone.

"How does her temperament seem this visit?" he asked.

"I couldn't say," Adam answered, hands clasped behind his back. "She arrived with her own attendants, so we avoid her wherever possible. If she spits on princes, we dread to discover how she treats those who serve her."

With a nod, Mark let the subject drop.

He didn't want to know either.

"It looks like the king is an early riser, too, Princess," Gul said.

Ava sat on a cushioned chair by her sitting room window while her maid, Esther, arranged her hair. Gul stood in front of the next window along, hands behind his back and feet apart, faultlessly dressed and groomed. His neck craned curiously as he spied on the gardens three floors below.

"He must start his day with a ride," he said.

"Tell me more of these facts about the king." She rubbed her fingers over her eyes. "Then I can forget them en masse."

"He's coming out of the stables. There, see? Leading that piebald beauty."

Her gaze shifted across the quaint labyrinth of shrub-lined paths to the stables. Despite the early morning shadows, she could make out King Markus tugging at the straps of a saddle, his other hand on the horse's neck. A cluster of dogs surrounded him, tails wagging. On her last visit, Ava had learned that the late king of Kiraly had bred Bernese Mountain Dogs and let them roam freely around the palace and grounds. The kennels were situated beside the stables.

King Markus gave a final yank of the saddle strap before kneeling down and disappearing from view behind the horse. The dogs converged, their tails picking up speed.

"He's popular with animals," Gul said.

"With humans too," Esther mused quietly.

Ava chose not to ask what she meant. Wincing at the tight tugs on her scalp, she watched the king lift himself onto the horse's back and take off toward the mountains. Perhaps he sought an early morning ride for privacy, or exercise, or to clear his head.

Half a dozen guards on horseback rode out after him.

Ava looked to Gul. There was one thing she and the king had in common.

Privacy was relative.

Ava didn't observe much of the funeral. It was vast, somber, and silent. Monarchs, politicians, and other dignitaries sat close to the front of the great palace chamber. Residents of the city had turned out to fill the road and great steps leading to the palace in an admirable display of respect for a family that had indulged at their expense.

She sat with Cyrus and her parents, unable to see the Jaroka brothers, and tried desperately not to remember Prince Aron's haunting smirk or his touch on her breasts—not while his loss was being publicly lamented.

When the procession moved to the private royal cemetery, a sanctuary of draping vines and sunlight, bold sculptures and breathless quiet, her position put the cowboy triplets in full view.

She couldn't look away.

Shoulder to shoulder, facing the people, these brothers looked like true royalty. With their hands clasped behind their backs, they formed a line of three, all strong and captivating in black suits, their hair the color of overturned earth and eyes like the same midday sky. Even still and silent, their bond was almost palpable, an aura of fraternity that could admit no one else. She suspected authority wouldn't be divided among these brothers but multiplied by the power of three.

She couldn't distinguish Prince Kristof from Prince Tomas, as she knew nothing of them bar their names. One kept his face downcast, hands in fists and body taut, while the other stood with his chin angled upward, his confidence bordering on cocky, his hair a roguish mess.

But she knew Markus, positioned in the middle, wearing a sash the color of bluebells secured with a large pin of the Kiraly royal insignia. Even without the sash, she'd recognize that frown and the caution in his eyes. She'd seen his stance, the braced line of his spine. Her gaze lowered briefly—she'd also seen the workman's body concealed beneath the façade of his formal suit.

Swiftly, she turned her attention back to his brothers.

As the prayers finished and the caskets were lowered, grief

got the better of one of them—the taut brother. His lowered face was pale. His chest moved rapidly. His hands were balled so tightly by his sides, his knuckles were the color of bone. Near instantly, the other two moved in, turning their backs to shield their brother from view.

The congregation's silence deepened, and she knew she wasn't the only one straining to hear the prince's ragged breathing and his brothers' gravelly murmurs.

Then the anguished prince was backing away, turning, striding stiffly across the cemetery. Several guards trailed him, and in moments, they'd all passed through a vine-coated archway and were gone. King Markus and his roguish brother returned their attention to the burial, lowering their heads as if nothing had happened.

Strange. The new royal family was rumored to have never met their late relatives. So why the grief-stricken breakdown?

She eyed King Markus. His stare was set on the filling holes in the ground. Regret lay heavy on his brow, but his jaw was strong and his features composed. Not a man grieving loved ones, but more prepared, focused, like he was laying mental groundwork in anticipation of the challenges to come.

Watching him, her heart kicked beneath her breastbone. She wasn't here to be distracted by family intrigue. She had her own groundwork to lay.

She'd seen the desperation of a drowning man when they'd met. That desperation surely lingered beneath this new resolve. While he was dealing with the new weight of the crown, she planned to make herself an extra burden, too much too soon. She must force his instinct for survival to push her aside.

If she didn't succeed, the Kiralian crown would drown her instead.

"No one even noticed," Kris said. "Don't worry about it."

"No one noticed?" Tommy's head snapped up from where he sat on Mark's simple gray couch. The private suite had been refurbished with unexpected speed. From the furniture and bed linens to the floor rugs and wallpaper, it was minimal, neutral, and infinitely more comfortable. "I fucking lost it," Tommy said, raising an angry hand. "Everyone noticed."

"It was a funeral." Mark sat on the couch opposite. Unease clenched his gut—Tommy hadn't held it together. How the hell were they going to handle this going forward? "Your family died. Distress makes sense."

"Yeah, and it wasn't even that bad." Kris kicked back on a chair at a wooden table. Keeping his distance, Mark noticed, because he had a habit of getting too close when Tommy was worked up. Kris's gaze was sharp and steady. "It was worse in your head."

"Not once I got out of there." Tommy ran a hand over his mouth. "It was a full-blown attack. I hardly knew where I was. It's any wonder my guards didn't call for help. Goddamn it. I'm sorry."

Kris shifted in his chair. "What the hell for?"

"Our first public appearance and I bolted."

"At the end," Kris snapped. "You stood with us the whole time. Don't turn this into something it wasn't."

"I panicked." Tommy leaned forward, elbows on his spread thighs. "I couldn't handle it."

"There were a lot of people," Mark said.

"A lot of pressure," Kris added. "None of this shit's familiar—"

"Don't," Tommy said quietly, furiously. "Don't say it like it makes sense."

Mark swung a concerned glance at Kris. The problem was

that it *did* make sense. Tommy's debilitating anxiety was a direct result of his near-death experience three years ago.

"Don't tell anyone it was a panic attack." Shame was thick on Tommy's features. "Not even Philip. I don't want word to get out that I'm a nutcase."

Mark frowned. "Anxiety doesn't make you a—"

"Promise," Tommy interrupted, his eyes narrowing.

"Okay," he answered, holding back a sigh. He doubted Philip would comment. The man had been lost in grief from funeral to burial, his eyes red-rimmed, tears flowing.

"Sure." Kris raised a shoulder. "Who am I going to tell? Let's play cards already."

Night had descended by the time a knock came from the sitting room door. Mark called permission to enter, distracted by his cards. As usual, Kris had won almost every hand.

"Excuse me, Your Majesty."

Mark turned at the sound of Adam's voice.

"Hey, Adam," he said, being mindful to face his cards away from Kris as he looped an arm over the back of the chair. "Come on in."

Adam took one step inside, his gaze down. "I apologize for the interruption, but I was just in the kitchen—requesting that cup of tea for your morning tray—and who should I encounter, but Princess Ava."

Kris made a noise across the table. "Odd place for a princess."

"It seemed that she was looking for me specifically." Mark's first man looked uncomfortable. "She asked me to deliver a message to you."

This couldn't be good. "Go ahead."

"She, uh." Adam shifted his weight. His fingers tapped against his side. "She asked me to tell you that she sleeps on the left."

Mark almost dropped his cards. "Sorry?"

The man flushed. "She sleeps on the left side of the bed, Your Majesty."

A slick, uncomfortable heat grew in his chest. What game was she playing? The message was inappropriate, and she must know it.

"Okay," he said finally. "We can all guess why she wants me to know that."

Adam's gaze remained downcast. "She said, *so he can get used to sleeping on the right if necessary.*"

God have mercy. Had Princess Ava swept into the kitchen, nose turned up at the smell of half-washed dishes, dressed in bold funeral black, and announced her sleeping preferences for all to hear? The surrounding staff must have been intimidated, baffled, and by the end, plump with gossip.

"I see," he said faintly. "Thanks, Adam."

"Very good, Your Majesty." He closed the door behind him.

Slowly, Mark turned to face his brothers. Kris had a frozen grimace and Tommy was biting his lips together very tightly. Neither of them made eye contact.

They sat in silence until Kris finally asked, "Well?"

"Well, what?"

His brother released the grin Mark just knew he'd been suppressing. "Which side do *you* sleep on?"

5

Ava hated what she was about to do. The morning air was cool and the stone bench was cooler still under her skirt. She sat beneath a lightening sky, pretending to enjoy the open air while pinning her awareness on the stables. She wasn't suspiciously close, but within shouting distance. Her hand on her lap formed a tight fist.

In bed late last night, she'd called Zara. "My problem," she had said beneath layers of autumn-colored quilts, "is that he seems to be a nice man. Everyone says so."

"That's not a problem." Zara's voice had been groggy. "You remember the strategy?"

If he's a decent guy, be cruel.

Ava had sighed. "Yes."

"What do you want then?" The question had been blunt and gentle at the same time. "To be nice to a nice guy and end up married to him? Or let your goals keep you focused?"

Ava shifted on the bench. Not twenty minutes ago, she'd observed King Markus go for another dawn ride from her window. Determined to get out of this country, out of the binds that held her, she'd immediately looped on her jacket and boots and come downstairs.

Gul had followed as she'd passed the stables and then circled back to sit on this bench. He now stood a short distance from her, frowning. "I always thought you were a cat person."

"I am." She ran her fingers through the long, soft coat of the palace dog that had settled beside her.

"So . . . ?"

"So this one followed me and I'm patting it."

"Okay." He sounded skeptical.

The dog sat with beautiful obedience, gazing at her with guileless brown eyes. Aversion pushed her attention away and her fingers buried a little deeper into its hair. Manipulating innocent creatures—and she'd thought her selfishness could sink no lower. But these were desperate times.

"And you're happy sitting here in the cold patting a dog?"

"Yes," she said.

He paused. "Okay."

Eventually, the pound of hooves announced the king's return and she turned, feigning curiosity, to watch the clutter of guards on his tail. King Markus had his plaid sleeves rolled above his elbows and even from this distance, she could see his breathing was labored. The horse's coat shone with sweat. He rode hard.

He dismounted, conversed with several grooms in what looked to be a polite refusal of assistance, and then led his horse around the back. Ava almost rolled her eyes. Of course his majesty was tending to his own mount.

She waited, tension stiffening her posture, and inadvertently met Gul's gaze. His glimmering eyes clearly suspected her of deliberately placing herself in the king's path, like a schoolgirl lingering after class for a chance to encounter her crush.

"You're hopeless," she murmured, looking away.

The dog was watching her sideways. He was too well trained to beg outright, but aware that her fist concealed a cube of salty cheese that she'd pocketed from her morning platter.

"Good boy," she said, resting her closed hand by her side.

The dog shifted on its haunches, expectant.

She flipped her palm when King Markus emerged from the stables. He strode with a distracted air, unrolling his sleeves and ruffling a hand through his hair. The dog made its move, interpreting the cheese reveal as an invitation, launching to its feet and seeking out the treat by her side. Her thumb brushed its damp nose.

Then she shrieked and leapt back. The atmosphere of the garden shifted abruptly; staff straightened, heads turned, alertness spread.

"It tried to bite me!" The dog shrank back as her foot brushed its rear. She jerked her knee to imply impact. "Get back!"

Gul glided between her and the dog. "Stand clear, Your Highness."

She sensed that the king had halted across the yard, staring at her. Her heart pounded. Would this work?

"Punish him," she ordered Gul loudly and watched her guard's eyes widen in horror.

He looked over his shoulder to where the confused dog sat. "I don't think it meant—"

"I order it. Punish him!"

"Princess," he murmured urgently under his breath. "I don't know what you expect of—"

"Fine, I'll do it." And she surged forward, outwardly furious, internally begging for someone to intervene. Everyone was motionless around her. Why wasn't the stable master rushing forward? Had she miscalculated? Surely a groomer must interfere at least?

No one moved. She was in a vacuum, the air pulling out of her ears and lungs.

"You wretched animal!" She slammed her own self-respect as her palm rushed toward the creature's side. She halted the movement a fraction before hitting the rump, but performance or not, she knew the dog was frightened. Her heart lunged in her ribcage, pounding for help as she pointed at the dog and shouted another reprimand. When still no one came, she raised her hand again, pride sinking to her toes. "You should be chained—"

"Excuse me, Your Highness," came the cold voice of the king very close behind her. "I'll have to ask you to stop."

She snapped a glare over her shoulder as relief dizzied her. He was a single stride away, his shoulders back, top lip curled in disgust. His blue eyes were hard. Gul stood rigid beside him, his face lowered.

"It was going to bite me," she said, her hand still poised.

King Markus stood tall, motionless. Dressed as a common cowboy yet exuding command. "You said before that it *tried* to bite you."

She glanced away, pretending to regret that slip.

"You appeared to be feeding it," he said.

Surprise tripped her. He'd noticed her, even before she'd caused a scene? "My fingers aren't food, Your Majesty," she said derisively, facing him. "That is precisely the problem here."

His lips twisted. His gaze remained flat.

"It's untrained and should be chained up, not wandering the grounds hurting innocent people. This is why I loathe dogs. I would never keep them. When I'm queen, this one will go first."

"I'm sorry for your distress." His gaze had moved to the cowering dog.

"You don't sound sorry."

"Believe me, I deeply regret this incident." Then he clicked his fingers by his side and said, "Come here, boy," and the dog darted to his heel with its tail between its legs. When he looked back at her, the king's gaze was dark with criticism, steady with blame, and despite herself, her skin heated with shame. She wanted to lower herself in his esteem, and yet her pride shied from this man's judgement.

She looked away, her chin high.

"Would you like me to escort you safely inside, Your Highness?"

"Not with that animal by your side," she said, with as much loathing as she could manage.

And so, without another word, the king led the dog away.

She sat on the stone bench. She tucked a few strands of hair behind her ear and then eyed his retreating back, struggling to keep her posture dignified. It was difficult to be on the receiving end of repulsion and feel victory, especially when paired with her own regret.

It had worked. That was what mattered.

"You made him come so close to us," Gul muttered, his words accusing.

She exhaled shakily before answering. "I'd expected the stable master." She'd intended the king to witness the scene and judge her for it, not to come himself.

"He smelled like a rough woolen blanket."

Momentarily thrown, she frowned at her guard.

Gul didn't explain. Instead, he asked, "Did you truly expect me to hurt it?"

"No. I thought someone would come sooner. Everyone in this place knows those dogs are incapable of harm."

"You're playing a strange game, Princess."

Her whole life felt like a strange game. She stood suddenly.

"I need to change before breakfast. I've got dog hair all over me."
She set off toward the palace, her regret expanding at her
guard's silence. "I'm sorry I put you in that position, Gul," she
said quietly, slipping off the emerald silk scarf from around her
neck and passing it to him. "A less ugly task . . . dispose of this
for me. The dog slobbered on it."

That was a lie, but she noted the way he folded the fabric
ever-so-precisely and tucked it inside his pocket. He was a man
of such kindness and deliberation—and he was stuck minding a
self-serving princess.

She halted on the path. He stopped an instant later,
glancing at her in question.

"I really am sorry," she said.

He scanned her face. "It's just . . . you know I like dogs."

She did. "And so I knew you wouldn't actually harm it."

"But what if I had? For you?" His gaze was earnest. "You
should work harder on your backup plans."

Backup plans scared her. They meant believing the true
plan could fail. She ducked her head, not a nod, exactly, but an
acknowledgement of his words.

They continued walking. As they passed through the wide
palace doors, he said, "You know I'll have to report this to the
queen."

Her gut scrunched, but she said, "Yes."

It wasn't until they reached the door to her guest chambers
that she said softly, "Gul, do you think I hurt it?"

"You hardly touched it, Princess. But you'll have lost its
trust."

She kept her face lowered, unmoving when he opened the
door and stepped back.

He cleared his throat from above her. "I could see what you
were trying to do. And I'd say you made a very poor impression

indeed." His soft voice was low. "Shall we find the dog later? I can visit the kitchen for a bribe."

Gratitude raised her eyes. "Yes, please."

"Better get changed then." Gul smiled gently. "You'll be late."

U

In his rooms, Mark showered off the hard ride. Agitation over the princess had him pushing his shirt buttons through the wrong holes twice as he dressed. Philip wanted him to marry a woman who spat on princes and kicked dogs? The strain of expectation pulled low in his chest. He really didn't need this right now.

He'd spoken to the stable master who'd kept a close eye on the dog—Dolce—while it had been with the princess. Apparently the dog had been enticed to her side by treats.

"She was feeding him little pieces, Your Majesty," the older woman had said grimly. "Such a gentle dog, but he must have startled her by asking for more. I'm sorry to say that, in my opinion, she overreacted."

No kidding.

He exhaled all the way down the stairs, almost colliding into Kris as he strode along the corridor toward the breakfast parlor.

"Hey, Your Majesty," Kris said with a grin as Mark fell into step beside him.

"You're supposed to bow," he murmured, and regretted the comeback when his brother halted and dropped low at the hips. A couple of staff bustled out of a nearby room, caught sight of the prince bowing to his king, and instantly fell into various poses of respect.

Mark bit back a groan when the guards trailing him and

Kris, evidently not to be left out despite their discreet distance, also bent at the waist.

Smiling for show, he stepped hard on his brother's foot. "That's enough," he said through his teeth.

The pair of cleaners glanced up as the brothers passed. Kris flashed them a quick grin and murmured, "How're you going there?" Both blushed scarlet and swiftly lowered their faces again.

"What did we talk about?" Mark asked under his breath.

"What? I can't say hello?"

"Not in that tone, you can't."

Philip was waiting at the closed doors to the parlor, beaming as he stood at attention. "What a heartening display of loyalty," he said, his head tilting.

Kris grinned at Mark. "You say bow, I say how low."

"Knock it off."

Philip's smile didn't falter as he gestured to the doors. "Now, I mentioned there would be a shared meal with funeral guests, so this morning, you're hosting a semi-formal social breakfast. Most guests depart before lunch."

Kris nodded and raked his hand through his hair from nape to forehead.

Mark glanced down at his black-and-blue-checked shirt and jeans. "Now?"

"You wanted to be yourselves, didn't you? This is an opportunity to make acquaintances and form connections." Philip's hand was poised to give the signal to the doorman. The large wooden doors reached the high ceiling, inherently dramatic like everything else in the palace. Discomfort thudded in Mark's pulse. They were literally about to make an entrance. "Oh, and after breakfast, Markus, please proceed to your study to begin training."

At a light scuffing sound, Mark glanced over his shoulder

and saw Tommy rounding the far end of the corridor, running a hand wearily over his eyes. Like them, his brother was expecting the usual quiet breakfast for three.

Mark gave a short, low whistle.

His brother halted, looking up, and Mark and Kris both whipped their hands in front of their throats to signal abort mission. Tommy stiffened, and with a nod, turned and disappeared.

"But, but—" Philip raised an alarmed hand after him.

"Just us this morning." Kris clasped the man's shoulder and turned him to face the parlor. "Shall we?"

Displeased but trumped, Philip waved his hand and the doors parted.

A woman inside began announcing, "His Royal Majesty . . ." then paused, her eyes darting between the brothers in alarm. Two, not three, and introducing the wrong brothers could be a protocol disaster. As Philip whispered in her ear, Mark smiled patiently and for the first time in his life, considered the practicality of wearing nametags. The woman started again. "His Royal Majesty, King Markus of Kiraly and His Royal Highness, Prince Kristof."

Their usual breakfast table had been removed, making space for the several dozen dignitaries that filled the room. Mark continued smiling as he nodded once to the left, once to the right, and breathed easier knowing Tommy had retreated. Beside him, Kris raised a hand in a small wave and said, "Hey there."

After a series of smiles and raised brows traveled through the room, conversation resumed.

Philip leaned toward Kris and muttered, "Remind me to start your lessons in formality as a matter of urgency."

Kris looked unfazed. "Sure thing."

Uniformed footmen appeared, their silver trays bearing

fancy canapés. The funeral guests were smartly dressed, prepared for a final meal before the return trip home. All but one, Mark noted as unease twisted like barbed wire beneath his ribs.

"I'm guessing that's our delightful princess," Kris murmured, gazing across the room.

She had changed since their outdoor encounter. Her dress was new-growth green. Floor-length, it wrapped around her from left to right like the curl of a fern frond, gathering in a coil over one shoulder and falling in a stream down her back. Her raven hair was spiraled loosely on the crown of her head and wreathed in a circlet of silver leaves.

"Oh." Philip's eyes were bright. "You've already had the pleasure of meeting Princess Ava?"

Mark paused. "We've spoken."

"Please do speak again," he said, far too enthusiastic. "Now, shall I make introductions?"

For what felt like the better part of an hour, Philip introduced guests to both Mark and Kris, and they held separate conversations side by side. Mark exchanged simple pleasantries about the palace, accepted well-meaning advice on royal life, and dodged heavier discussions on policies and agreements. By the time the introductions were over, his stomach was clawing for food. He'd have to let the waiters know they were welcome to interrupt when breakfast was concerned.

"Sustenance." Kris appeared bearing a tray of mini round things on sticks.

"What are they?" Mark asked, hesitating.

His brother paused. "They are delicious."

"You took the entire tray?" People had noticed, particularly the red-faced Philip.

"I asked first," Kris said. As he offered it to Mark, he asked more seriously, "Holding up?"

"Somehow." Mark chose one. It contained rice and herbs and tang and magic.

His brother's gaze seemed to extend beyond the parlor. "I miss the constant smell of horses," he said.

"I miss the sound of them." A gentle nicker as he took their reins; a louder whinny that traveled from the stables at sunset. His dawn rides were too short, too busy with security guards, to fill the ache.

"I miss Sage Haven," Kris said.

"So do I."

"And Buck and Bull."

Mark smiled grimly. More than missing their dogs, "I worry about Mom and Dad."

Kris nodded and swallowed down another rice ball. "I'm worrying less than if Dad were here though."

True enough. Mark viewed the room, his mind on his parents, just in time to catch Ava casually extend her plate in front of the bodyguard standing beside her. The man didn't look at her, nor did his hard expression change as he picked up a pastry and popped it in his mouth. Ava's lips came startlingly close to a smile, and she gave the plate a little shake. The bodyguard quirked a thick brow down at her and put another two in his mouth. He resumed staring intimidatingly into the middle distance, chewing slowly.

Ava's features stiffened when she saw Mark watching. Discarding the plate, she left her bodyguard's side and moved toward him and Kris. Everything inside him tensed. If he ever found himself transported back home to live amongst the horses and hills, the last thing he'd miss about Kiraly was this princess.

"Here comes trouble," Kris drawled.

Mark hummed. *Trouble* was much too light a word.

"King Markus." Ava greeted him with a smile that hit his bullshit filter and fell flat on the marble floor.

"Princess Ava." Mark gestured to Kris. "This is Kristof."

She leaned around him to look at Kris, her smile still sweet. "Hey there," she said, a little too loudly.

Kris paused, his eyes narrowing. Then he held out his hand and said, "Call me Kris."

"Kris." Ava eyed his hand, eyed Mark, and then slowly accepted the shake. The closeness of her arm moving in front of him twisted strangely in Mark's stomach, and he shifted his weight, pulling back.

"And your other brother?" She retrieved her hand, her fingers curling into the green fabric at her chest. "Still overcome by grief?"

"Showing grief isn't a weakness," Kris said, his voice growing cold.

Her answering look was so puzzled, Mark almost believed she was serious when she said, "Isn't it?"

"And your brother?" Kris nodded at the young man of obvious genetic resemblance. "Is he the heir?"

Her gaze softened as she followed the gesture. "Cyrus is heir and a good man. Intelligent, kindhearted, beloved by our parents and country. He has everything and is everything."

Across the room, Cyrus held himself tall, composed—a stance that hinted at future greatness. When the man turned and caught Mark's eye, he smiled with such unmistakable goodwill that Mark could only believe Ava's assessment.

"Unlike me," she finished, bringing him back.

A gentleman would refute her self-deprecation. "You seem to have everything," Mark said, after a pause.

Her smile returned, pinned into place. "Cyrus and I will be staying in Kiraly for several weeks. We're having a holiday."

Foreboding ran through him. "Weeks?"

"Yes." Her dark eyes held his. "It will be a precious time to get to know each other before we're wed. Don't you agree?"

His gut hitched. He didn't respond; didn't dare get tangled up in this conversation again.

Kris extended the tray. "Rice ball, Your Highness?"

She looked genuinely startled. "Cowboys, kings, *and* waiters. My, is there anything you boys can't do?"

"Tolerate arrogance," Kris answered, exchanging the food tray for a glass of juice from a passing waiter. "I hear you think my brother here is beneath you." His chest widened in insult as he shifted closer to her, subtly cutting in front of Mark. "Let's talk more about that."

Mark placed a hand on his shoulder with a quiet, "Kris." His brother was tense beneath his palm.

Kris didn't relax. "Why would you want to marry a man you consider your inferior?"

Her expression flickered. "I am not incapable of sinking to his level, Kristof. I will endeavor to reduce myself so that I can please my king."

Kris didn't even try to hide the *what-the-fuck* face he pulled at Mark.

Mark, determined not to reduce himself to the cruelty of Ava's level, continued to hold his tongue.

"I feel it's my duty to ascertain your tastes in women, Your Majesty," Ava went on. "I'll do my best to imitate such traits. I'll become your type, and we'll be a perfect match."

Rankled and heading quickly toward pissed off, Mark murmured, "What makes you so sure you aren't exactly my type, Princess Ava?" because he doubted she'd have a quick-mouthed answer to that.

He swore fear widened her eyes before she turned away. Her chest moved with her breaths, and for several moments, she failed to acknowledge him at all. Then she glanced back and smiled too sweetly. "My mother's watching."

The queen of Kelehar was eyeing them from across the

room. She was younger than he'd expected, her hair dark and luscious like her children's and her features so alike her daughter's that Mark's instinct was not to trust her. She had a small glass of tea in her hand and suspicion on her face.

Mark smiled politely and Ava wiggled her fingers in a delicate wave.

"My mother is adjusting to the notion of having a cowboy in the family," she said, her eyes still on the queen. "I think she's half-expecting you to carry me over the threshold, bend me over, and throw a saddle on my back."

Kris spluttered, coughing juice out of his nose. He was immediately descended upon by Philip, who bore napkins and ushered him away from the princess, muttering about, "Unsightly party tricks."

Too appalled to respond, Mark struggled to keep his features neutral. He couldn't handle much more of this.

"How nice." Her eyes followed Kris across the room. "I've always wanted a fool for a brother."

Fury flooded him. Fists balled tight, he ordered himself to walk away. But a part of him refused to give her that power. "Leave me."

Eyes wide, she exclaimed, "Oh, a command. You're coming into yourself, King Markus."

"I can say it louder, if you'd like."

Her lips twisted as she glanced swiftly at her mother. Then she cast him an assessing glance, curtsied, and departed.

It took all of his self-control not to scowl at her retreating back. Instead, Mark met his brother's pissed gaze across the room as Kris wiped a napkin down his shirtfront. Kris's frown betrayed that neither of them cared much for royal life.

Mark wanted his horses back.

6

The bridle path was overgrown with grass and wildflowers. Blue sky gleamed between the towering pine trees on either side of the mountain track, and as their course veered, Mark slid a glance back at Tommy. Features clear, grip easy on the reins, his brother was casually surveying the sheer wall of forest on their left. He looked relaxed.

About time.

On impulse, Mark and Kris had fetched him after breakfast and suggested a ride. Philip would be at his wits end, desperate to continue his training, but this took priority. Tommy needed to shake off the previous day's panic attack, and after Mark's encounter with the princess, he'd take any kind of cleansing he could get.

They'd warmed up the horses before breaking into a canter, not speaking, just riding fast to the soothing three-beat pound of hooves. Only once the path had developed more juts and blind curves had they slowed to a walk.

"She's not the girl next door," Kris called over his shoulder from his position out front. "I'll give you that."

So they *would* be discussing her. Mark's back teeth met as

he angled his hat to block the harsh sunlight. "Rude and condescending, like I said."

"The juice still stings," Kris answered, rubbing his nose.

Tommy spoke from the rear. "She sounds like a real catch."

Kris glanced back before easing his mount to one side of the track. Mark and Tommy guided their horses to fill the space beside him. They continued three-abreast—doing their best to ignore security trailing them on quad bikes. It fractured the peace, but if the royal family wanted to canter, the guards would bring engines to keep up.

"But something wasn't right," Kris said, frowning. "Something about her feels off."

"Off?" Mark asked.

"Yeah, but . . . I don't know. I can't pinpoint it."

They rounded a bend and drew their horses in as the landscape unfolded before them. A natural clearing exposed a sweeping view of the alps, epic and white-tipped. The mountain range blocked the horizon with its dramatic formation, and Mark suddenly ached for the Rockies back home. Similar, yet so different.

The quad bikes idled behind them. Another difference.

Eventually, Kris shook his head. "How's this though?"

"I've seen better." Tommy gave a ghost of a smile.

Mark gave a laugh. "It might grow on me." Then he jerked his head in question and they continued at an easy pace, the bikes following. "How was the city, Kris?"

"Steep." Kris grinned. "Like who-the-hell-decided-to-build-a-city-here kind of steep. No one knew who I was—it was before our photos were taken at the funeral." He reached out, yanking a handful of leaves off a tree as he passed. "I pretended to be a tourist, intrigued by the monarchy in this quirky little country. Most people have high hopes for the new King Markus." He shot Mark a wry glance. "Apparently, Vinci didn't engage with his people. I mean, he was progressive—Kiraly has one of the best public health-care systems around. He passed fair-work regulations, marriage equality, and free university. So life's pretty damn good. *But* our uncle's involvement didn't extend beyond approving policies. No public appearances in years. No donations or sponsored events, not even invite-only banquets at the palace. He didn't acknowledge his people at all. He was a recluse and did nothing to stop Aron living like an entitled ass."

Mark frowned. "Philip hasn't mentioned that."

"Yet," Tommy said.

"Explains his reaction when we shook everyone's hand that day." Kris eyed them dryly. "But the Kiralians want to like us. They have a strong sense of national pride and we seem to have a good reputation already."

Mark gave a small roll of his eyes. That would be Philip's press conference at work.

Tommy nodded. "I've done a bit of digging too. They love their city and lands and community. A disengaged head of state couldn't take that away from them, but they've felt undervalued and disrespected. They want a royal family that will put this country and its people first."

Dread sucked beneath Mark's sternum. He could value his people. He could engage with them and treat them with respect. But the concept of putting the country first left him cold, because it implied *over him*. Over his desires and preferences and possibly even his values.

Like marrying for love.

Could he really do that?

Tommy continued, "Recent budgets include a hefty sum allocated to 'palace upkeep' and 'royal appearances,' which seems to mean unnecessary renovations and Aron's international travel."

There was also the money Mark had ordered for

normalizing their private suites. Guilt pinched him, and he felt the sway of self-doubt. Even trying to do right, he'd done wrong.

"We'll cut those categories," he said. "And others. Philip mentioned we're in debt."

"Only shitloads." Tommy sounded cynical. "Happy inheritance. And almost all of it owed to the family of your blushing bride-to-be."

That almost knocked Mark off his horse. "*What?*"

"What?" Kris sounded just as confused. "Why does Kelehar want an alliance if we're in debt to them?"

But Tommy's features had gone distant on the path ahead. His brow was low. "Christ. She's pretending."

"Sorry?" Mark battled to focus. His debt was to Kelehar?

"The princess. She's putting it on."

That hauled him back. "Putting what on? You're losing me."

"Everything," Tommy answered, his tone convinced. "It's an act."

"An act?" Her words came too smoothly. No one could pretend to have a whip for a tongue—she'd been born with that particular feature. "I don't think so."

"You haven't met her, Tom," Kris pointed out, leaning forward to eye his brother around Mark. "Pure rattlesnake."

"You've both talked about her. She was wearing another over-the-top outfit today, right?"

"Yeah." Mark slanted him a dubious glance.

Tommy looked between them, frowning like it was obvious. "And no one else was dressed like that? I'm thinking pant suits and rich person office-wear, but not gowns and heels. And you said she was wearing something similar the other day. She's in character."

Kris made a dismissive sound as he straightened. "Nah."

"A princess would know the appropriate dress code for a social breakfast."

Unease seeped through Mark at Tommy's suspicions. It was true—not even Ava's mother had been overdressed.

"Then there was the dog incident and you said that she claimed to want to imitate your tastes in women, but if that were the case, she'd have come in jeans and a sweater. She's doing the opposite."

Mark frowned. "Why?"

"Why else?" Tommy almost looked apologetic. "She doesn't want you to marry her."

"Then why would she talk about it like—" Alarm clenched at his throat. "Tommy. Why didn't you say because *she* doesn't want to marry *me?*"

His brother grimaced. The silence was tight.

Because maybe she didn't have a choice.

"No." Appalled by the idea, Mark reined in his horse. "No way."

"I don't know." Kris didn't look convinced. "I guess she sweetened up her expression when her mom was watching, but that could mean anything."

Mark exhaled roughly and shot a look over his shoulder. Tommy was guessing blind. He couldn't be right. And yet—he *had* seen fear in her eyes when he'd said she might be exactly his type. Genuine fear.

Sickened, Mark said, "I have to go meet Philip."

"We've got time to figure it out." Tommy's words were quiet.

"Yeah." Kris started tugging his horse around, following Mark's lead. "But Tom's probably wrong anyway."

"You guys keep going." Mark motioned to security. Several of the quad bikes slowed to a halt, preparing to follow him back. He swallowed bitterness. "See you tonight."

As he rode alone, he tried to ignore the sensation in the back of his mind that felt a lot like realization. His first meeting with

Princess Ava played in his head: how she had told him that face value was a convoluted concept.

Don't believe anything for a long while yet—including me.

He scowled at the endless pines and pushed his horse faster. No. She couldn't be under pressure to marry him. A strategic marriage was one thing, but not giving the bride or groom a choice? That kind of thing was medieval. Besides, she was intelligent and educated with the mental and social resources to refuse. It wasn't possible.

She spat on the late Prince Aron, Adam had said.

And Aron had turned her proposal down. No one would spit on someone they were willing to wed. As hair-raising as the notion was, Mark couldn't deny that it almost made sense.

Had she evaded one strategic suitor only to find herself face-to-face with another?

An hour later, Mark was sweating under his shirt. His sense of free-falling had accelerated so rapidly that if he met solid ground now, he'd shatter. Philip had greeted him in the study—red-faced at the delay—and immediately requested that they make their way to a private meeting room. Assuming it was related to his training, Mark had agreed.

Now, he sat opposite the king and queen of Kelehar. A cozy little group, just the four of them, knitted together by tension and secret words.

"This union would benefit Kelehar and Kiraly both," the older king began, his hands steepled in front of him.

Mark unclenched his teeth. Outrage scalded him from the inside out. How dare they gather as if all decision-makers were in the room? "Where's Princess Ava?"

"She'll be along," the queen said, dismissive.

Disgust burned him. "What possible benefit is there to Kelehar?"

"Your Majesty," Philip murmured beside him. "Your tone."

"His skepticism is admirable." The king held Mark's gaze in a death grip. "Your question refers to what benefit we can possibly find in a country as indebted as yours? The answer is in your mines, Markus. Palladium mines owned by the Kiralian crown."

Mark knew next to nothing about the mines. The gleam in the king's eye betrayed he suspected as much.

"Palladium is a rare and beautiful metal," the king continued. "Lustrous, silvery white. But perhaps you know that much?" He smiled. "Its primary use is in catalytic converters. It reduces noxious emissions and Kelehar has a booming luxury car industry. It's one of our main exports. Several years ago, our economy bordered on the brink of recession when our palladium supplies were withheld from a different source. Politics . . ." He shook his head. "If it happened again, the consequences for Kelehar could be disastrous. Economy is everything, don't you agree?"

Mark stared back. "Then let's make a trade deal."

"Trade deals can be broken, as we discovered the hard way," the queen spoke up. "But family always honors family."

The air felt thin. How could marriage be discussed like this? And where was their daughter? His hands formed fists under the table. "What will Kiraly receive in return?"

The king of Kelehar held his gaze. "We'll waive your debt."

Staggered, Mark excused himself to speak to Philip in the hall. His advisor hurriedly followed him out.

"What the hell is going on?" He rounded on the older man, furious that Philip had led him into that room unprepared. "Why didn't you tell me we owe that entire debt to Kelehar?"

"If you'll keep your voice down," Philip spoke quietly,

urging Mark farther away from the doors. "King Vinci mostly borrowed from Kelehar. They were always so willing to lend."

And now they held that debt against Mark's throat.

"Why is this conversation happening now?" He fought to buy time. "We buried my uncles and cousin *yesterday*."

"Politics doesn't grieve, Your Majesty."

"This is disrespectful."

"They're gone." Philip's callous statement was softened by the waver in his voice. "It's important that we focus on building a better future."

"You're talking like this is a political campaign." He turned away, struggling for calm. He couldn't catch his breath, couldn't find his feet. Kiraly had whisked away the life he'd loved, and now it attempted to determine his wife.

And it was only day four.

He faced his advisor. "I don't understand this."

"They get our palladium to secure the growth of their car industry, which supports the better part of their economy. And they'll wipe the outstanding balance of funds borrowed." Philip's words became breathless. "The *entire* balance, Your Majesty. This is unprecedented. We could put money where it's really needed again. Kiraly could thrive."

Mark breathed low into his lungs and still felt the clutch of suffocation.

"Besides, the crown of Kelehar is exceptionally wealthy," Philip added. "And it's always sensible to marry into money."

Mark shook his head. "Why would they offer to wipe the entire debt?"

"As a gesture of—"

"Bribery," Mark finished, cold at the truth. They were bribing him to marry Princess Ava.

Philip made a startled choking sound. "Your Majesty! Lower your voice. What outlandish reason could there possibly be that would necessitate *bribery* for you to marry their daughter?"

Only every second of exposure he'd had to her. She was unendurable—at least toward the men she didn't want to marry.

And her parents must know it.

"There must be other ways to pay off this debt," Mark said, even as dread settled deep in his chest. "Kiraly must be worth more than its mines."

"The traders make lovely juniper jam." Philip sighed at Mark's glower. "Tourism can't be relied upon exclusively. Nor can taxes. The debt will accumulate. I wouldn't encourage this if I didn't see it as the only way out."

"But—" Mark's heart was starting to hammer. "We don't know each other."

His advisor turned up his palms. "This kind of arrangement has worked out well in the past."

Aversion flinched through Mark and he asked, "You think it's fair to ask me to do this?"

"I want you to succeed, Your Majesty. Your cousin refused this very union to widespread disappointment. Much of the world adores Princess Ava for her charm and charity. I want you to make your people proud. You're the change we've needed for a long time, and this will start your reign on very strong footing. If you ascend to the throne with a new wife, Kiraly would celebrate. If you ascend with Kelehar as an economic ally, they would rejoice. But ascend without national debt? You could never do wrong."

Mark stared at him. He'd believed Philip was on his side. But he'd made a gross miscalculation.

Philip was on Kiraly's side.

Panic took hold. "Surely this can wait until I've settled in."

"Kelehar's economy was hit hard when their palladium supply was withheld. They want this secured now, before the king and queen return home later today. To hesitate would be an insult and would damage future relations." When Mark didn't answer, Philip went on, his thin hands moving as if molding the words midair. "Economic insecurity gives kings nightmares. You could grant him a sound sleep as early as tonight."

"What about my sleep?"

The man gestured vaguely, as if to say, *what about it?*

Mark stilled as another motive for the king and queen's haste dawned on him. Catch the heir before he adjusted to his position. Catch him unawares and pressure him into a quick decision, convincing him that this was what any self-respecting king would do.

He inhaled deeply, forcing his panic to the far edges of his mind.

Silently, he indicated that they return inside.

"Markus." The queen reached a hand out and placed it halfway across the table. "Would you please find Ava and escort her back here? I believe she intended to visit the rose garden."

So, she wasn't on her way here at all. He looked between the king and queen, suspecting they'd overstepped a line to see whether he knew it existed. No one ordered a king in his own palace. But a fair-mannered cowboy would do as a monarch instructed, whether he liked it or not. Were they testing him to see who they were dealing with, all the better to manipulate him into securing the engagement today?

Bitterness gathered beneath his solar plexus. They couldn't manipulate him into anything. But in this moment, he'd let them believe they could, because God above, he needed time to think.

Speechless, he nodded curtly and left the room.

He found Princess Ava seated on a bench near the tea roses. It was a pretty, secluded space on the grounds, and the air moved softly under a clear blue sky. Her bodyguard stood behind her, a muscled giant of a man with his hands clasped behind him. He faced away from the trail where Mark approached, gazing down at the dog lying at the princess's feet.

It turned out Dolce's affection could be won back with an exceptionally large bone.

It also turned out Ava didn't loathe dogs at all. Her back was to Mark, and she leaned forward, scratching Dolce behind the ears.

In conversation, the pair gave no sign they'd heard his approach.

"One day, I'd like to have my own garden," Ava was saying, and he hesitated at the unguardedness in her voice. She was dreaming of flowers while he bore summons from her parents. Interrupting this moment would be like saddling a prancing foal. With his chest heavy, he drew back. His guards, a respectful distance away, also stopped.

Her bodyguard spoke. "You have your own garden."

Ava continued to pat the dog. During breakfast, Mark hadn't noticed the way her green dress dripped down her back in a low vee, exposing a sweep of skin. If that level of magnificence was really a costume, as Tommy thought, she wore it with ease and authority. Sophistication was familiar to her, even if it was designed to alienate him.

Briefly, desperately, he wondered whether they could grow together. Close the chasm between their world views and find contentment in each other.

But he could never be more than he was, and even if she tugged on denim and a pair of boots, she'd still emanate superiority. Their upbringings were poles apart.

They would never be happy together.

"A garden exists with my name." Her voice was wry. "Others tend it."

"You would grow a beautiful garden, Princess."

There was a pause, then a laugh. "You're so good to me, Gul. We both know I don't know how to plant a flower, let alone sustain it." She gestured wide, silver bangles tinkling at her wrist. "I don't know what anyone does around here or at home. My meals appear out of nowhere, as do my clothes. My bed is always perfectly clean and comfortable for the season. I have everything done for me, and it's highly possible I don't even know what most of those things are. Only last year did it occur to me that someone's job must involve changing my toilet paper, because in all my life, I've never reached the end of a roll."

"Princess!" Gul sounded startled. "And stop claiming to be useless. You manage the shelter."

"I know," she said. "But all I mean is that I could never survive on my own."

Mark frowned at that comment. She struck him as the last person who would need to fend for herself.

"You're resilient," her man said. "I'm sure you'd be very self-sufficient."

"I'm not so sure." She turned to glance up at Gul, and Mark swiftly drew back into the rose hedge. A thorn latched onto his forearm—he deserved it for eavesdropping. Great impression he must be making on his guards. "I still can't work out what the king and those men were doing chopping wood the other day." His ears burned. "It's spring. Why chop wood right before summer?"

Gul chuckled indulgently but didn't answer. Evidently, he didn't know either. Then he said, "What's that?"

"Cyrus gave it to me."

Mark didn't risk looking to see what they were talking about.

Her bodyguard spoke after a few long moments. "It's beautiful."

"It's so I can marry whomever I want."

The air fled Mark's lungs.

The guard didn't comment.

Mark barely heard her murmur, "What if he wants the union, Gul? I'll have no choice."

"He won't want it." The bodyguard's voice hinted at doubt as he added, "You'll make sure he doesn't. You have time."

"I've tried to be awful."

"You have been," he answered softly, and sighed. "I thought that's what you were up to. He looked like he never wanted to see you again after this morning."

Mark shifted, uncomfortable at the accurate observation.

"His eyes are such an innocent shade of blue." She broke their conversation to murmur a few gooey words at Dolce. "I almost feel bad. But my parents intend to meet with him when they return at the end of my stay." She spoke with a bitter tone. "He has to hate me by then."

And with that comment, Mark was pierced by realization.

She thought he could be swayed by emotion—thought he was a leader who would put his own happiness before the benefit of his people. But a true king valued financial security and economic prosperity. A true king made sound decisions for the nation's greater good—not his own.

He'd questioned whether he could do that, but realized it wasn't about what he *could* do.

It was about what he *must* do.

He had to put Kiraly before his heart—and Ava's.

Gut heaving, he scuffed his boot on the path and moved forward. Gul turned, his eyes alert, and Ava spun around, her hand lifting from the thick hair of the dog. Dolce looked up, thumped his tail against the ground a few times, and resumed gnawing on the bone.

Mark ignored their alarmed silence and halted nearby. "Your Highness." He looked toward the bodyguard and nodded in greeting.

"King Markus." Ava slowly rose to her feet, her face impassive. "Please, don't let us hold you up. The wood will not chop itself."

Gul shifted, his eyes downcast.

Instead of bristling with insult, Mark allowed the blow to add color to his rapidly bruising self-respect. He should have noticed that she had no choice—should have realized she behaved with the venom of a cornered snake. Instead, he'd snap-judged her as a selfish princess, while condemning *her* for snap-judging *him* because he was a cowboy. He defined hypocrite.

Ava stiffened as he glanced at the dog. He didn't comment.

"I'm here for you," he said instead.

A beat of silence had her brow flickering down, confused.

"Your parents request your presence," he added.

She blanched but held her features still. "Excuse me?"

"They asked me to find you."

"King Markus," she said, with a rigid smile. "You mustn't allow them to treat you like a butler just because you're beneath them. Use your title like an untrained soldier might use a shield in war."

He frowned.

"At least try to preserve yourself," she said.

Sudden dread chilled him at her mention of preservation—at the reality of their union. *You three brothers are the last of the line.*

He'd have to ask this woman to open her body to him.

She'd recoil from that kind of intimacy, but expectation would demand it. She'd allow his touch out of duty, but it would feel wrong—*be* wrong—to enter her without her heart's permission.

He wouldn't do it. If they wed to politically benefit their nations, there would be no heirs.

He extended a hand toward the palace. "I'll show you the way."

He saw her panic set in then. In her shuddering breath; in the way she refused to look him in the eye. Without so much as a glance at Gul, she strode off along the path.

Mark walked a pace behind, his steps weighted. He couldn't actually do this, could he?

He had no choice.

He was king.

Inside the east atrium, daylight spilled from the stained glass bordering the ceiling. Ava slowed so he could take the lead, her face turned away, and he headed toward a large staircase with gleaming banisters supported by ornately engraved plasterwork.

As they climbed, she spoke from behind. "How much did you overhear?"

He didn't turn. "We chop wood in spring, let it season over summer, stack it in autumn, burn it in winter."

She was silent for a dozen steps. "Oh."

They continued on, a line of three, through vast spaces and around corners, until they reached the door to the meeting room. It was off a dim corridor, architecturally landlocked from windows and natural light. He paused with his palm on the handle, his pulse pounding, and looked over his shoulder. The silver wreath on her hair looked dull and her shoulders seemed to sag from where he stood above her. Her brown gaze met his and he caught a flicker of dread.

The same emotion heaved low in his abdomen. Taking an unwilling bride was not how he had envisioned starting his reign.

"That will be all." Her chin lifted, though the fright in her eyes remained. "I doubt this concerns you."

"It concerns me a great deal," he murmured, and stepped inside.

Ava froze in the doorway. Fear seized her bones even as her muscles bunched to bolt.

Her parents sat opposite the head advisor to the king of Kiraly. Her heart spluttered. She knew that look on her mother's face. The unbearable combination of authority, appraisal, and victory that instantly slapped aside Ava's naïve delusion of control.

This was happening.

No. Ava's pulse raced, and blood pressed hot and cloying to the inside of her throat. Please no. This conversation was meant for later—her mother had told her just that morning. *You'll win Markus over during your holiday. Then we'll come back and make him an offer fit for a king. He won't be able to refuse.*

Weeks away.

With time to plan another escape and disappear before any of this happened.

Not here, now.

No, please, Mama. No.

"Ava," her mother said, her hands folded neatly on the wooden tabletop, careless that she spoke over the shards of Ava's final hope. "Come and join us."

No one moved except King Markus as he quietly took his seat at the opposite end of the table. Ava knew that no amount of silver or fine embroidery could disguise her horror, but she kept her chin high and her shoulders rolled back. She struggled to pull her teeth apart.

"May I ask what's going on?" Her question was breathy.

"We are discussing strategy." Her father's attention was on a document, but he gestured to the chair on his left, closest to the door. "Sit down."

Adrenaline urged her to flee or fight. She could faint, as her body was also threatening, but this situation demanded presence of mind, because she might, *might,* be able to get out of it.

She sat down. The scrape of her chair legs tore at the silence like fingernails fighting against the hard floor.

"There, now we're all here." Philip spoke lightly to King Markus. "We see no reason to waste time, as you understand, Your Majesty."

The young king met the man's gaze, his features blank. Her insides convulsed. He was going to do it. She could see duty unsettling the innocence of his eyes, stirred up like sediment. He was going to agree.

Oh, God, no.

"We have legal documents drafted to officially bind this exciting agreement," Philip said. "We thought it best to be prepared."

A contract to enforce an engagement.

At her mother's sharp glance, Ava realized she'd whimpered.

"As we have discussed, both Kiraly and Kelehar will prosper from such a fitting union. And you will look so dazzling together." The advisor had the audacity to smile at her. Vision blurry with devastation, she swayed in response. "While you were out, we were discussing how best to celebrate. So many thrilling possibilities."

Celebrate.

She would start by passing out, and chase that with a lifetime of mute misery. She couldn't escape now. If she ran away after this, the political chain reaction could be catastrophic, with accusations of foul play, reneged deals, and possible out-and-out conflict.

She looked down as her goals dissipated. She saw the bleak shadow of her existence.

Her future was sealed.

She would never be happy.

"Now . . ." Philip angled his shoulders toward King Markus and paused as if to say, *go on.*

She clutched the edges of her chair. Blood throbbed beneath her temples. Every breath ripped; every second excruciated. It would be unbearable. Standing beside him, smiling when she must, tolerating his instructions, living an act for the rest of her life for the world couldn't know it was a farce. She would lose herself to bitterness and expectation—forget who she was without him. They could eat in separate parlors, go about their own business, but each day would end behind a closed bedroom door. He would have to touch her eventually—heirs wouldn't produce themselves. She waited with her eyes pressed shut, her face angled down at her lap.

No one moved. No one spoke.

She jumped, looking up, when the slide of paper scratched at her ears. Opposite her, King Markus sat rigid, his checkered shirt taut over tense shoulders.

He stared down at the contract. He inhaled, exhaled.

Then he lifted his head and looked her straight in the eye. "I do not agree to the proposed union between Princess Ava Veisi and myself."

Disbelief prevented her from registering his words. She stared.

"We will not be married. And that's my final decision."

7

"How *dare* you?" Ava's mother chased her into the private chambers and slammed the door so hard the windowpanes shook. Ava's lungs burned. She'd raced through the palace, but her mother had kept up in her anger, her heeled strides ricocheting off the cavernous ceilings, driving Ava's adrenaline higher. "What did you say to him? What did you do this time?"

"What did I do?" Ava flung herself around, her heart stumbling over her mother's cruelty. "What did *you* do? You were both going home today. This was meant to happen when you came back. Why didn't you warn me this morning?"

"Your father and I *are* going home today, Ava, and there was no warning to give." Her mother's breathing was loud, her skin flushed. Fury was thin on her lips. "You know it's why we're all here, yet you've schemed and ruined it already." Her arms shot up as she made a sound of incoherent outrage. "I hope you're happy!"

"Happy?" Ava turned away, pushing back a sudden onslaught of tears. The gall of her mother to even say such a thing. Facing her again, she said, "You've never wanted me to be happy."

Her mother ignored her. "Your father trusted me with this. This one thing that could guarantee economic stability." Her finger rose and her eyes blazed. "And you've tried to make me fail since the very start!"

"You? You're talking about the rest of my life." Ava's chest felt leaden. "This has never been about you."

"Because everything is about you, isn't it, Ava?" The words were scathing, delivered as her mother stalked toward her. "Your world has to be exactly as you want it. Do you know how many people would kill to be you? To be educated, safe, well fed, beautifully dressed, let alone married to a king?" The finger came closer and Ava mustered the fight to glare, daring it to come within range. She would bite it, she swore she would, the hardest chomp she could manage. "Most people wish for different lives. They wish for better health, or a larger income, or to be adored. You have all of those things and more, but you refuse to be happy."

Ava swallowed, shaking her head. Voice weak, she said, "You tried to trap me."

"Your father and I aren't stupid." Her mother angled her head. "You wanted time to sour the way the king viewed you, just like you did with Aron. We weren't going to allow that." The truth came out like dirty laundry and it stank between them. That Ava had always intended to defy her parents—that her parents had always intended to cut her off at the ankles. What a toxic game of family they played. "We heard about your display of animal cruelty this morning. The absurdity," her mother said with a derisive scoff. "Was your next plan to punch a horse? I don't even care. But you will set it right."

You will set it right.

After all these years, betrayal still choked her. She'd never truly thought her parents would rob her of love if it fell outside the bounds of duty. She'd known they would resent her, but what they'd done in order to set things right last time still butchered her heart.

She had hidden in numbness until she'd found defiance—a more sustainable defense against them, and she'd reassured herself that she would never be defeated again. That she would ultimately win back what they had stolen from her.

She'd been so close.

Her mother didn't know that Ava had intended to disappear in Monaco. She had no idea that if it hadn't been for the mass tragedy of Kiralian royalty, abruptly altering Ava's travel plans, the queen of Kelehar would never have seen her daughter again. Would she have cared? Would she have halted her schedule to mourn a lost daughter? Would she have cried, cursed herself, knowing she was to blame and wishing she'd done things differently?

Ava doubted it.

And that was what broke her. After months of anticipation and stress, after furtive conversations with Cyrus and hoping so hard she gave herself headaches—even after the loss of opportunity so close to the finish—Ava hadn't allowed herself to wallow in the emotional slurry surrounding her. She scarcely felt it, suspended by hope. *This is not my reality,* she'd repeated. *My reality is there, in the future, burgeoning with joy. I can see it. I will touch it.*

But there was something so wrong about believing her own mother wouldn't miss her that Ava's strength gave way, and she plunged into a present without hope.

"I can't do this anymore." The tears came with a surge of filthy feelings, pain and grief and blame that had spent years abrading her heart. She let the tears flow as she sagged down onto a divan, lowering her face. "I'm broken, Mama. You know you've broken me."

For a moment, her mother didn't answer. Then she said, "You broke yourself, Ava."

And she left.

Mark stood alone outside Ava's private chambers, cemented to the spot by the sound of anguish. Heaving sobs broke through the door. Not the tears of a mishap, but the cries of a damaged heart. He'd only heard pain like this once before, when a woman in Sage Haven had learned that her husband had died in the line of duty. He'd had tears on his cheeks listening, and he hadn't even known the man.

He didn't understand these tears. The princess's parents had departed for Kelehar less than an hour ago, and he'd assumed that despite the flush on the queen's cheeks when she'd followed her daughter from the meeting room earlier, Ava had won the following battle.

Mark had won his with Philip. He'd endured the man's outrage, owing him that much because Mark wasn't going to reconsider. He then informed his advisor that he'd be reviewing the existing palladium agreements. It could be worth more on an open market than an exclusive deal. They'd turn Kiraly's fortunes around without trading a princess like a broodmare in the process.

Despite their tension, he could have sworn Philip's nod held new respect.

He'd told the story back in Tommy's chambers to much grimacing and low whistles. Now he was on self-directed clean-up. He needed to meet with Ava to avoid ruining relations with Kelehar entirely. Even though she hadn't wanted the marriage, he'd still rejected her, and bruised pride could prompt nasty consequences.

Or a flood of soul-eroding tears.

The door to her guest chambers opened and Cyrus stepped out, his face troubled. The man jerked in surprise when he saw Mark and swiftly closed the door behind him.

"Your Majesty," the prince said.

There were several beats of awkward silence.

"Why are you here?" Cyrus's question was softened by genuine curiosity.

"I—wanted to check whether she was all right."

There was a pause, punctuated by a sob so deep it could have dredged iron from the earth's core. Cyrus glanced down the corridor, running a hand along his smooth chin. "She's not."

"I thought it was what she wanted." Confusion pinned Mark to the spot. Then he remembered this man was the heir of Kelehar. His equal into the future. And he'd just scorned his sister. "I didn't mean to disrespect her or your country—"

"Please," the man interrupted on a sigh. "I won't hold a grudge because you refused her hand. I'm more inclined to thank you."

But he didn't, and the sounds of Ava's weeping filled their silence.

"Should I get a doctor?" Mark paused. "Or chocolate? I've been told we make good chocolate."

"No. Thank you." The prince of Kelehar regarded him, and although it was a calm gaze, careful, Mark had the distinct impression he was being thoroughly scrutinized.

The door opened again, and Gul the bodyguard stepped out, his formidable figure sliding around Cyrus where he blocked half the doorway.

"She's still not respond—" Gul snapped his mouth closed as he caught sight of Mark. He tensed, his features unreadable as he scanned Mark's face. "Your Majesty," he said, and after staring in bafflement for a few seconds, bent at the hips. Then he straightened, standing stiff beside Cyrus. Both men watched Mark.

Ava's sobs strangled the silence.

"I should go." Mark turned, beyond uncomfortable. This wasn't something he had a right to overhear.

He was halfway down the corridor when his name traveled after him. "King Markus?"

When he glanced back, Gul had disappeared and Cyrus stood in an empty corridor with his arms hanging by his sides. His gaze was sad.

"Please try again later."

Ava didn't respond to the light tap on the door. She lay on the bed, her face buried in cashmere and cotton, her body crumpled amongst the blankets. She was exhausted. Cyrus had come and gone, sitting with a hand on her back while she cried herself hollow. Gul had replaced him, not touching, but sitting on the edge of the mattress and offering silent company. Now she was empty, alone with thoughts that would never bring her peace.

What if she couldn't execute her grand plans to escape? She'd fixated so completely on getting out that she'd never developed a strategy for if she had no choice but to stay. Gul was right. She needed better backup plans. She should assume nothing, not even a good mood after a win—Markus had refused the marriage, yet she was empty. A body outlined by skin with nothing inside. How could she celebrate when there was still so much that could go wrong?

"Princess," Gul called softly from the entrance.

She didn't have the energy to answer.

"Princess." He had moved closer to the bed. "King Markus is here to see you."

Shock shoved her onto her elbows. Light-headed, she pressed her eyes closed for a moment. "What?"

Gul was pulling a strange expression, partially apologetic, partially intrigued. "He asked to speak to you."

King Markus had come to her chambers asking to speak to her? "Regarding what?"

"I'm not in a position to ask that kind of question, Princess. Though, don't get me wrong, I desperately wanted to."

"I can't—" She sat up, panicked, her breath coming too fast. The king was visiting. Had he changed his mind? "What did he say?"

"All he said was that he hoped to speak with you."

Fear hammered down her spine. That could mean anything.

She ran a hand over her puffy face. Despite her recent behavior, he was still a king, and her dignity teetered on the brink. "He can't see me looking like this."

"I told him you'd been reading a sad book."

She sat up fully. "You what?"

"I thought it would help to explain your state." He looked sheepish.

"Oh, Gul." If the cover story was that she'd been reading, she couldn't very well turn the king away. Alarmed, she adjusted the covers, aligning quilts with pillows. She hoped he wouldn't ask the title, for she didn't know what book could possibly be this devastating.

Standing, she straightened the bodice of her dress and ran her hands beneath her eyes, wiping away makeup smudges. Then she patted her head and realized her silver circlet had fallen off on the bed. "My hair."

"It's mostly still in place." Gul ushered her from the bedroom and into her private sitting room.

She sat on the divan, her hands fluttering over her lap. Distress warbled her words. "What if he asks about the book?"

"It was so depressing you threw it out the window."

"That's too dramatic." Inhaling, she eyed the crackling fire. "Add another log. If he asks, I'll say I burned it."

"Not at all dramatic." But he did as she requested.

"Gul." Her heart was pounding, her hands shaking. There was no other reason for the king to be here. He'd changed his mind.

"Yes, Princess?"

"I wish you could marry and be happy enough for the both of us."

The log landed badly. Features masked with neutrality, Gul picked up the poker and righted it. Then he straightened slowly, not quite facing her. "And I wish you could use that ring without limitation."

She didn't answer. It seemed they both knew the art of a futile wish.

Gul emerged, his face impassive, and Mark waited for the verdict. Neither man had spoken about his earlier visit, but it was right there in the bodyguard's eyes—wariness and unmistakable curiosity.

After a long moment, Gul stood aside. "She'll see you now."

"Thank you." He took a step forward and stopped. "Gul," he said softly, glancing at him sideways. "Were those tears because of me?"

"Not even close, Your Majesty." He gave a soft smile. "Like I said, a sad book."

Nodding at the blatant lie, Mark entered her chambers. Airy and warm, the sitting room glowed amber around him and his stride faltered as he took it all in. The ceiling was a great sweep of gleaming gold, painted to look like the draping leaves of an enormous tree in the peak of fall color. Several branches dripped down the walls, matching the highlights of the room's furniture and blending warmly with the caramel carpet. The effect created a sense of light shimmering in every corner.

"What a room," he said, his attention falling to where Ava lounged on an elegant divan, her legs half-curled beneath her. She gazed out the window.

Casually, she flicked him a glance before returning her attention outside. "Your Majesty," she greeted, her voice neutral.

"Your Highness." Focusing, he studied her rounded shoulders, the weary sag to her eyelids. The tone of her skin was paler than usual, and she still wore the green dress, though the fabric looked creased. Her dark hair was slumped down her back, several pins sticking out of the slack tumble. "Did you enjoy the book?"

She inhaled, her breath ragged. "Not particularly."

He nodded, trying not to look at the pink stains on her cheeks, the swelling around her eyes. She must have hated that her heart was smeared on her face.

"I wanted to apologize for earlier." He moved to stand with his feet planted by the fireplace. He didn't want to loom too close, but he didn't want to hesitate by the door. The heat of the flame pattered against his back; it was an odd comfort to have in this warm season.

She kept her gaze averted. Her posture was tense. He suspected she was counting the seconds it took before he left.

"I hope my decision didn't offend you."

Her lips moved around his words. She dragged her gaze to him with a confused frown. "Pardon?"

"It was callous. The way I dismissed the idea of marrying you."

"Callous." Her voice was subdued, as if she had no spark left.

"Yes. And I want you to know that I didn't intend it as a personal slight. I'm sure you're—very nice."

"King Markus." She eyed him tiredly. "I've been nothing but awful to you. I worked very hard to earn that rejection. If I felt hurt, it would be my own doing."

"And do you?"

"No."

Gently, he asked, "Why didn't you tell me you had no choice?"

Her eyes were bleak. "You might have liked it."

He jerked back. "What?" Disgust pooled in his mouth. "Who would enjoy wielding that power over someone?"

Her inhale was rough. She didn't answer immediately. "You don't talk like a king."

"How should a king talk?" He inched away from the fire. It burned too hot. "Like your brother?"

He'd tripped her there—he could see it on her face. Evidently the prince wouldn't exploit a person's true wishes either.

"Your cousin Aron, at least," she murmured.

"So you can spit in my face?" He watched her wince. "You've spat at me many times since we've met."

She swallowed, curling an arm around her middle. Even then, looking small and miserable, he couldn't forget the wicked things she'd said.

"My brother is no fool," he said, coolly.

Regret poured across her features. "I know. I didn't mean that. I'm sorry."

"You were trying to make a poor impression. To great success."

Her body stiffened—she was shaking. "Are you really only here to apologize? Because if you've changed your mind and think it's funny to torment me about how you figured me out first, I wish you wouldn't."

He shook his head. "You think I'm a sadist, don't you?"

She regarded him, her face pulled back slightly, like a puppy being tugged on a leash toward someone it didn't trust. "I don't know what to think of you."

"I'm not here to torment you, and I won't change my mind."

"Promise."

"I swear it," he said firmly.

For a moment, she covered her face. Her fingers trembled across her cheek. Then she placed her palms over her knees. "Why did you say no?"

"Because I don't want to marry you."

The dullness of her eyes didn't change, but the corners of her mouth twitched. "It's all right, I don't need your sugared words. Just say it to me straight."

He tilted his head, offering a wry smile.

"I thought you were going to do it." She shifted, tucking her legs tighter beneath her. She looked cold, despite the stuffy room. "I was so sure. Will you sit?" Belatedly remembering her manners, or perhaps finally deciding that she was safe to use them, she gestured to the plump sofa opposite her.

He didn't want to stay, and he suspected she'd much prefer to be left alone, but it was an olive branch. He should take it. "Sure, thanks."

Before sitting, he lifted the lap blanket draped over the back of the cushions and passed it to her. "You look cold."

She met his eyes swiftly. "Oh." Seeming confused by the

basic courtesy, she took it and folded it carefully around herself as he sank onto the couch.

It took roughly six seconds for him to decide that he should have declined her offer to stay. An uncomfortable silence fell, in which she sat perfectly still, her gaze on the fine woolen weave of the blanket, and he replayed the memory of her cries, because the broken sounds refused to leave him.

"What's your garden like?" he asked, dragging them to a safe conversation.

She pinned him with a stare, sharper than he'd expected. The dull neutrality was fading now that she knew he wasn't here to pursue an engagement. "You overheard that much?"

He grimaced.

Shifting, her shoulders moving indignantly, she said, "It's a rainbow of colors and fragrances that delight and confuse me."

"Confuse you?"

"Oh." She arched a brow. "Are we pretending you didn't overhear the next part? I have no idea how to plant anything or keep it alive, and my garden is a constant reminder that I know nothing of any use."

His frown shifted as an idea hatched at her words, sudden and fully formed. "Your Highness," he said.

"Ava," she corrected tartly. "I'm more inclined to call you Cowboy than King, so I'll stick to your name if you call me by mine."

He paused long enough to raise a wry brow. "Ava," he said, and the informality of this woman's name was strangely sweet in his mouth. "Would you let me show you how to grow a garden?"

She blinked and the hand smoothing the blanket stilled.

"Everyone should know the land." He firmly believed that. "How to work with it and to respect how it works for us."

She shifted, frowning. "Why would you do that for me?"

"Well." He hoped this was a good idea. "I could teach you

something you want to know. And in return . . ." What *did* he want? "I'll come to you when I'm feeling out of my depth. You've lived this life from the day you were born. I haven't even been here a week." He couldn't turn to Philip. He needed to present a strong and confident front—not give his advisor a reason to doubt him. And he didn't want to worry his brothers. "You could be a voice of experience."

"I've never ruled," she said quietly. "Never been in charge."

"You've navigated expectation. That's what's overwhelming me." He tilted his head. "What was it you said? I need to preserve myself . . . use my title like an untrained soldier uses a shield in war?"

She blushed brilliantly and a hand rose to toy with her collarbones. "I've said the most horrible things."

"Kris might need an apology."

Mortification rounded her eyes. "You told him?"

"I tell my brothers everything." Mostly.

"Of course you do." Shame ghosted across her features. "I'll find him and apologize." She tilted her head, her frown cautious. "How do you propose we do this?"

Probably by both regretting it the moment he left her room. "It's a yes?"

"Yes." Then she inhaled a quick jagged breath that betrayed her earlier tears, and silence fell awkwardly as they both pretended not to notice.

"I guess I'll speak to the gardeners." With no clue how the two of them could work together, he stuck to the practicalities. "See if there's a space we can use."

"I can't prepare for helping you. Consider me on-call." She appeared to battle a smile and lose. It overcame her, lifting her cheeks, crinkling her eyes. "I think I like this idea."

So did he. Ava's advice could set his feet on solid ground. Unfamiliar ground, but solid nonetheless.

She twisted, looking out the window at the gardens as if she wanted to start immediately.

"It's meant to rain tonight," he said. "And I'm meeting with Philip most of tomorrow. How about we meet at four o'clock in the rose garden?"

Facing him again, she sat straighter, her features alive with interest. Her legs slipped off the divan, her feet landing on the carpet, crossed at the ankle. She was transformed from when he'd first walked in. "All right."

He stood, casting her a small smile. "You almost look chirpy."

"Oh, finally. I thought no one was ever going to call me that," she said, proving that even her sarcasm had returned.

His smile widened. "See you tomorrow, Your Highness."

She tilted her head, her lips twitching. "Don't be late, Cowboy."

8

Nothing could stop nightlife in this city. Not the death of the royal family, not the termination of public transport after sunset, and not a spring rain heavy enough to render Zara Nguyen's shoes unwearable.

It was dark and miserable by the time she left the women's shelter and struck home. Anyone sensible would be inside, but the average Kiralian wasn't sensible—they were indefatigable. After thirty-three years, Zara had learned to filter out the pound of bass and midnight explosions of outrageous laughter. Her people loved each other as much as this mountain they called home, and that clingy affection was a constant echo across the city.

She wove around patrons seated in front of restaurants and clustered outside bars. Her local pub had reached characteristic overflow as she shouldered past. People gathered around the open windows, chatting with friends on the inside as if there weren't the better part of a wall between them. Others had dragged out bar stools or sat on the pavement, passing around bowls of finger food, and others still were dancing to the beat of the guitar and kick drum that came from the stage inside.

"Zara, babe." A man caught her elbow lightly, letting go when she spun on him.

Gerard. A thread of guilt wove around her, loose and thin and irritatingly distracting. Trying to brush it off, she said, "When have I ever allowed you to think *babe* is an acceptable accompaniment to my name?"

"Since New Year's Eve." He waggled an inebriated brow.

So he'd been delusional for more than three months. Jamming her hands into her wet jacket pockets, she looked him in the eye. "Have I really?"

Slowly, the mischief slid off his face. "No. Can we hook up again?"

"No." Her impatience simmered at the irregular beat of the drums inside. It was clearly open mic night.

"Why not?"

"Because I don't really like you," she said, wiping rain off her face.

Gerard looked confused, like he wasn't sure whether he was hurt by that or not. "Why did you go home with me on New Year's then?"

Because she'd been lonely and empty, carved hollow by the news that a woman she'd tried to help had died at the hands of her husband.

When she didn't answer, Gerard urged her again. "C'mon, can't we be together?"

Jesus. "No."

He rocked his weight from one foot to the other and gave her puppy-dog eyes. Evidently, he'd decided he was hurt after all. "Why not?"

"Aside from me not really liking you?" She thought that reason was a winner.

"I'm a nice guy," he said in his defense.

"Yeah, you are." She wouldn't have gone home with him

otherwise. She chewed her bottom lip and then reached out to briefly clasp his bicep. "So stop asking nasty girls out."

She left him with that and pushed on through the rain.

Her apartment was an uphill journey from work. Handy for running late in the mornings, as it provided a swift and somewhat precarious bolt down to the women's shelter, but this geological spike from hell was less convenient for walking home after a day that had shredded her reserves like rags.

A day like today.

Three women had left the shelter. One into witness protection. One to make a new life for herself, free from the financial and social suckers of her abusive ex-boyfriend. And one back to her husband, her two kids in tow. *He'd never hurt the kids*, she'd told Zara, her backpack over her shoulder and kids' toys in hand. *Just me, when he hasn't paced his drinks, or I haven't kept up with the washing or something. He'll be better this time*, she'd said, nodding too much. *Now that he knows I'm strong enough to leave him.*

Maybe that was true.

Maybe it wasn't.

Zara banked left and started up a street so steep, it had steps in place of a sidewalk. True or not, she added the woman and her children to the cavern in her head. This was a coping strategy, designed to discard unsustainable stress. Years ago, she'd created an imaginary underground safe house, an expansive sanctuary, like Mother Earth had taken a particularly large breath to make space between her ribs for troubled women. There, Zara tucked away every shelter visitor she'd ever feared for—which was most of them. Although envisioning their safety didn't do jack shit in the real world, it was the only way she could allow herself to forget about them and retain her emotional and mental stability. Mostly.

As the rain reached her skin and her thighs started to burn

from the climb, she imagined handing the new family blankets and hot chocolate and inviting them to join the circle of music in the heart of the cavern.

"Zara."

She halted, snatched from her ritual. A man was coming the other way, slotted neatly beneath an umbrella, his glossy shoes clicking on each downward step. He tilted the umbrella back slightly and the streetlight caught on his blond hair and the tidy cut of his version of casual clothes. Silver glinted on his lapel—his silver pin, a capital A inside a circle. His first initial. He'd shared that story in a rare moment of conversation. It had been a gift from his great-grandfather on his sixth birthday. Zara's pulse flipped, instinctively reacting to this man's sentimental nature.

Talk about polar opposites.

"Hi Adam."

He slowed, passing on her left, and the rain stopped around her. He stood close, one step below her so they were eye level, and with a determinedly steady inhale, she said, "God-awful weather," and promptly wished the rain would drown her.

With a little smile, Adam raised an eyebrow and lifted his hand fractionally to offer the umbrella. "You're soaked through." His voice was a soft rumble; his eyes were light on her face.

She took the handle, clutching it like it was a part of him. "Thanks."

She knew better than to believe he was going to walk her back to their apartment—knew that if she entertained the fantasy, she'd be intensely disappointed. With his umbrella successfully transferred, Adam gave a nod and continued on down the street.

She stood, intensely disappointed.

Then she twisted, watching him go, her stomach tumbling down the steps after him. The rain swiftly blackened his gray shirt and then he turned the corner and was gone.

Groaning, she made the mistake of looking up to see how far she still had to go. The end was literally not in sight.

She lowered her head and soldiered on.

That night, Ava dreamed.

They strolled together, hand in hand, through the bustling alley market. Stalls surrounded them, gleaming with color, abundant with wares. They passed copper, paper, spices on one side, carpets, nuts, and jewelry on the other. People were everywhere, a torrent of frantic shoppers, but it was the most peaceful paradise with him by her side. His presence was like the glow of a thousand lanterns expanding right out of her chest.

"I don't have to marry him," she said delightedly. "I can come for you now."

The balls of her feet touched down lightly, springy steps that bordered on flying, and she could have pushed off into long glides—but she kept his hand and stayed by his side. She'd found him. He'd been here in the market all along.

The guards appeared suddenly. Wrenching their hands apart, dragging her back. Her insides tore but she couldn't scream. She couldn't fight. She saw his tears, heard his calls, and struggled to reach him, teeth, nails, lungs, but he was gone.

They were all gone.

She jerked awake in the dark, knowing her heart had been ripped out and her blood had gushed onto the bedcovers. But when she grasped the pain, her breast was intact beneath her hand, slick and sticky with sweat. Her pillow was wet with grief —her face, her throat—and it took the better part of twenty minutes before her breath came evenly.

She didn't sleep again.

"Let me get this straight," Zara said on the phone the next morning. "He's refused to marry you—congratulations, by the way—but you've opted in to one-on-one personal time with the guy. Are you insane?"

Ava sat by her bedroom window, phone on loudspeaker while Esther did her hair. Pain pulsed at her temples, the aftereffects of emotional exhaustion paired with yet another poor night's sleep. She balled her fists and hoped her expression didn't betray her. "Jury's still out."

"So, what, you have to keep up the act?"

"He promised he wouldn't change his mind about the engagement." She winced as Esther pinned her hair too tightly. "Esther, I thought we'd decided on simple. This doesn't feel simple."

"It's a ponytail for a princess, Your Highness."

"This princess has a headache. Could you please gouge with less vigor?"

She saw Esther bite back a smile in the reflection on the window glass. "Of course, Your Highness."

Ava returned to the phone call. "I can drop the act, Zara."

There was a pause. "You're sure it's an act?"

She frowned, wincing as another pin grazed into place. "I can be . . . pleasant."

"Gouge with less vigor?" Zara snorted. "But maybe it's not a bad idea for you to learn something normal like gardening. It'll help—you," she cut off suddenly, seeming to remember that it wasn't safe to discuss plans over the phone.

"That's the aim." Ava could learn things from Markus to help once she was away from here. She would ask him to show her other daily tasks after gardening, because she *was* getting out, and new skills might stop her sticking out as an inept princess quite so badly in her new life.

Her nightmare had reinforced her determination. She couldn't fall apart now. Her parents had returned home for two weeks. There was no threat of having to marry King Markus. Cyrus and Zara were working on a new plan. She had to believe it was all still possible—had to focus on staying positive.

"Yeah, but seriously, be careful okay?" Zara said. "Or you'll undo all your hard, bitchy work. The last thing we need is him realizing he was wrong to reject the alliance because you're not so bad after all."

"He won't," she said. And once Zara had hung up and Esther was still fussing, creating what had to be the most complicated style in the history of ponytails, she repeated to herself, "He won't."

"Let me get this straight," Tommy said over lunch. "You're voluntarily spending time with the woman you called rude and condescending, and who in turn called Kris a fool."

"She was pretending." Mark skewered a roasted potato. He'd already decided how to explain this to his brothers. "We're doing a knowledge exchange."

Tommy's mouth turned down at the edges. "Resourceful."

Kris glanced up, frowning as he chewed. "Do we trust her?"

"Well enough," Mark said.

His brothers both nodded. They returned to their lunch.

"Let me get this straight," Gul said, as he walked behind Ava along the western terrace. Exquisite carving laced the waist-high walls, a feature she could admire now that they didn't symbolize impending entrapment. "Your greatest fear is marrying King Markus, and you've stooped treacherously low in order to repel him, and yet, today you intend to willingly spend time with him in intimate proximity."

She led the way down a flight of mosaic-covered steps and into the rose garden where she trailed a hand over the soft new leaves of the hedges. The sky was a shiny blue and the air was sweet. "What intimate proximity are you referring to?"

Her guard made a faint sound of disbelief. "He's hardly about to teach you gardening with a hedge between you."

"He'll be my instructor. I'll treat him as one."

The following silence was bloated with Gul's unspoken observation on how intimately she'd treated a past instructor.

"It'll be nothing like that," she said coldly.

"Yes, Princess."

Minutes later, the path curved before straightening, and Markus came into view, standing by the marble bench amidst the roses, several guards positioned nearby. He was gazing up at the sky, his expression masked beneath the shadow of his hat, a thumb looped through his belt keeper. This man was not like any king she'd ever met—more comfortable in a checkered shirt and pair of cowboy boots than bespoke garments that distinguished his position. His jeans were intact today, no torn denim exposing the skin of his thighs, but Markus seemed determined not to wear anything that would set him apart from his upbringing.

The same upbringing that had filled him with decency. He was a good man. She still couldn't believe he'd visited her—*her,* with her insults and condescension and disrespect—and apologized for rejecting their engagement.

Markus turned and his gaze darted over her in obvious

surprise. Her belly knotted. Perhaps he'd thought her incapable of wearing jeans and a simple blouse.

"Ava," he greeted. "Gul."

Gul bowed. "Your Majesty."

"Markus." She looked around him and said, almost accusingly, "You're empty-handed."

With a wry smile, he gestured toward a small greenhouse visible above the roses. "It's all in there. Ready?"

At her nod, he led the way, several paces in front and clearly distracted.

Gul whispered, less discreetly than he was capable, "First-name basis, Princess?"

She glared a warning, and at the door, Gul positioned himself with his back against the outer glass. The slide of his eyes told her to be careful, so she ignored him and stalked inside. She didn't need his caution. Honestly. He was the one who'd tried to cajole her into thinking marrying Markus might not be *that bad*.

She jolted to find Markus directly inside, standing back with an arm braced along the door, holding it open for her.

A king—holding a door open.

"Thank you," she said, catching his eye. "Though if I'm to be your voice of experience, don't do that for anyone."

His lips twitched upward. "I'm not after advice on my manners."

"It's not what kings do."

"It's what I do, and I'm king," he said, and lifted his brows. "So I guess it is now."

Unsure how to respond, she kept walking.

"The royal gardener has set up for us." Markus's tone was preoccupied as he moved in behind her. Gul had been right about the proximity, curse him, for the greenhouse was full of raised garden beds and luscious hanging pots that left little ground space for separation. The air was thick, heavy with soil-scented moisture. A tall workbench was situated against a glass wall, and she stood with her ribs pressed into the ledge to put as much distance between them as possible. He sidled past, exceptionally close, spilling awareness down her spine like warm syrup. She breathed in, and alongside the humidity and soil was the intimate scent of a male body. She swallowed hard, her pulse slipping as he settled in beside her.

She hadn't been alone with a man, Cyrus and Gul excluded, for a very long time.

"You're not allowed to touch me," she said.

His blue eyes clashed with hers. "I—what?"

"During these lessons." She turned her attention away, her muscles taut with tension as she remembered the last time she'd been alone with a male instructor. The way it had ended. "You mustn't touch me."

There was a pause so awkward that even the silence seemed to cringe. Then he answered coolly, "That's not why I suggested this."

"I want you to remember who you're dealing with," she said, the memory making her far too defensive. "Since you so often forget who you're supposed to be."

She heard his inhale, his not-quite-steady exhale.

"Okay," he said, his voice pushing the silence apart like a pair of roughly calloused hands. "We don't have to do this at all, you know?"

"I know." She waited, rigid.

She desperately wanted to do this.

He cleared his throat. "Okay," he said again, and splayed a large hand on the benchtop. His skin was tanned and his nails cut short. "I'm not doing anything wrong. You'll stop treating me like I am."

She flashed a startled look at him.

He gazed back, steady now. "I didn't suggest these lessons to have you assume the worst about me or talk down to me. You did plenty of that before. If we're doing this, you'll at least pretend to treat me as an equal. But the next time you condescend or imply I'd touch you without you wanting it, well, I'm walking out of here and we'll be done."

"I . . ." Shame throbbed beneath her skin. "I'm sorry."

"We both want the same thing—we don't want to have to marry each other," he said. "I'd think that puts us on the same side."

Shame still strong, she answered quietly, "You're right."

After a moment, he said, "Good," and passed her a pair of gloves. "Put these on."

As she did, she observed the arrangement of items on the workbench. She leaned in, excitement overshadowing her tension at the sight of soil, ceramic pots, straw, pebbles, and an assortment of teacup-sized succulents in black plastic containers.

She settled back on her heels, frowning. "Why aren't we planting seeds?"

"Achievements are important," he said, not quite as obliquely as she'd have liked. "We can get to that another time."

Her pride bruised. She lifted her chin.

"Choose one you like."

She plucked a green star-shaped plant from the tray. She drew it close and examined it, strangely buoyed by the idea that this piece of life was about to rely on her for survival. She would take care of it, nurture it, and help it to grow. It had thick leaves splaying outwards in an attempt to catch the sunlight, cool and smooth to touch, and she imagined them stretching longer and stronger in her care.

When she looked up, Markus was watching her, brows creased.

"What?" Swiftly, she slid the plant away. "I've never looked at them close up before."

His face softened. "It's kind of sweet."

Confusion pinched her tongue. He thought she was sweet?

"Now choose a pot. Make sure its diameter is at least double that of the plant or it will outgrow it too quickly."

Wordless, she set a turquoise pot before her.

"Good. Since we're planting succulents, we're going to use a succulent-specific soil," he continued, casting a sidelong glance at her. She swallowed, her chest tightening with a nervous pulse of heat. Even an arm-span away, his presence pressed close. Those shoulders took up so much space. "But first, put a small layer of pebbles at the bottom of the pot so the soil doesn't trickle out the drainage hole."

She did as he instructed, feeling his eyes on her again. Her skin tingled.

"Now add the soil, about two-thirds of the way up the pot."

She added soil in small handfuls, bobbing down to gauge the level in between each addition. Finally, she scooped some out in the shovel of her gloved fingers, slid the pot back and forth to level it, and then eyed it again. "There," she announced, straightening.

She found him watching her again, his gaze warm.

"What now?" She refused to betray her discomfort by shifting. "Why do you keep looking at me?"

"Because I've never seen anyone concentrate so hard over such a simple task." Offensive words, but his tender delivery denied her the right to fire up.

Looking away, she adjusted her gardening gloves and asked, "Where are you from, anyway?"

"Sage Haven, Montana." He inclined his head as he spoke, an introduction with homespun manners. "My brothers and I run a—" He halted. "We *ran* a ranch. Quarter horses."

She rested her fingertips on the edge of the workbench. A trio of princes running a horse farm? She pictured the brothers riding through a sunny field, three abreast, cowboy hats on, and grins wide with boyish abandon. Ranch owners in name, but as princes they could have done whatever they wanted and operations would have bustled on around them.

"How did people treat you?" she asked.

He raised a shoulder. "It's a friendly town. Not so small that everyone knows everyone, but for the most part, it was a safe place to live."

She angled herself toward him. "I meant how did they treat you as royalty?"

Those blue eyes settled on the glass wall opposite as he wiped the back of his hand across his forehead. "They didn't know."

Disbelief loosened her jaw. "They didn't *know*?"

He reached for his succulent, his brow lowered. "Now we need to dampen the soil and form a well in the center."

Stunned, she used the watering can and mimicked Markus as he used his index finger to move soil to the edges. "How deep?"

"That looks right. Now get your plant and squeeze the pot around the edges to loosen the soil and roots."

She followed the instruction. "You didn't tell them you were royalty?"

"No," he said, after a pause.

"I honestly don't understand that decision."

"It wasn't our decision at first. Our parents concealed their identity when they first moved there. They didn't want to be treated differently, and they didn't want attention following them from Kiraly. They told us when we were old enough to understand. We, uh, we all went under the surname Jacobs, actually."

"And when you and your brothers were old enough to decide how you wanted to be treated?"

"It never felt relevant to us." He held the small black pot in his large hands. "We believed the crown would pass from our uncle to our cousin, and down the line from there. If anything unexpected happened, there was still our uncle Noel to ascend. The royalty in our blood felt like a recessive gene. We didn't want to be treated differently in our hometown because of a label that didn't fit us."

"You lied to them." She narrowed her eyes, hating the ugly pound of jealousy in her chest. He'd lived a normal life. He'd connected with people, formed relationships without having to wonder whether the behavior of his friends and lovers was influenced by his position. He had been truly free. "You lied to everyone you ever knew."

His throat moved as he swallowed. "Now splay your hand over the top, nestling the plant carefully between your forefingers. That's right. Then tip the pot upside down and ease it out, plant, soil, and all."

She turned the small plastic pot and couldn't keep from smiling when the weight transferred onto her palm. "I've got it."

"Good. Now discard the pot and use your spare hand to tickle the roots like this."

Slowly, she did as he did. The soil broke away, freeing the bottom roots, and she copied his action of flipping it carefully and placing it in the prepared pot.

"Keep it straight," he said, "and add more soil until it's level, making sure you pack it in so the plant isn't loose."

She coated the leaves in soil in the process and the result leaned decidedly to the left, but it was in and it was hers.

"You literally have no experience at being royalty," she said, following his lead and watering the newly potted plant.

He made a grim noise of agreement.

"I didn't realize the extent of it. I should have. I heard you greeted every last staff member of your household upon arrival."

He faced her, his gaze cool. "That was manners, not naivety. They deserve to be acknowledged. We're all working in this palace together."

"Oh, Markus." Curiosity brushed over her. "You can treat your staff with respect, but they're not your equals. Your position is not comparable to theirs. You're their king. Don't you understand that yet? There will always be a wall dividing commoner from royalty, constructed centuries ago, and you can't jump it as you please."

"My—" He faltered. "My manservant calls me by name. The sky hasn't fallen down."

Dismay made her gasp. "You asked him to?"

"Yes."

"Then he only does so because his king ordered it. Markus, please listen." She looked at him levelly. "Royalty transcends class. We experience incredible privilege and live under constant public scrutiny. People envy and despise us, swoon and obsesses over us. Tradition gives us form, for without it, what would separate us from a common politician or wealthy family? If you refuse to honor tradition, you deny the expectations of those who hold us together." She waved a hand in the general direction of the palace. "Your manservant doesn't think of you as an equal or a friend. He never will. You are his sovereign, and he's been raised to treat you accordingly—ask him to treat you as anything less than his king and he'll do it, but it disrespects his position."

Markus stared at the workbench, his gloved palms flat on the wood. His shoulders loomed broad and guarded over his tiny plant. "I don't know how to do this," he said quietly.

"Oh." She backed up, swiftly poking her head outside and murmuring to Gul, "I'm fine." Then she snapped the greenhouse door closed and returned to Markus's side. "Lesson number one: you can't say things like that with doors open. What if someone overheard? It's hardly going to inspire confidence in the hearts of your people."

He fisted a hand through his dark hair, gloves and all. Soil scattered down his chest and a few specks landed on his cheekbone. "At least they'd know the truth."

"Okay," she said, raising her palms and thinking fast. He'd faced down her parents without blinking—she *knew* he could do this. "Okay."

His glance was stricken. "I almost agreed to the engagement, Ava."

The confession hit her like a dagger.

"I almost said yes," he said, "because I thought that was what a good leader would do."

"Why did you say no?" She hated that her question was a whisper.

"It finally sunk in that making decisions for the benefit of my people shouldn't come at the expense of someone else's basic rights. You didn't want to marry me—and I almost made you, because I wanted to be a good king." He shook his head in what seemed to be self-disgust. "I don't know how to trust my own judgement in this place."

"This level of responsibility can slacken your grip on your humanity." She knew that only too well. "Go with your gut. It knows more than you think."

Frowning, he nodded. "I thought I could handle this. Trick myself into treating it like running a big ranch. But Philip told me this morning that my brothers and I have to attend a press conference on Friday. Aside from the fact that Tommy can't— and it's best if Kris doesn't—well, they could ask me anything. This country will realize I don't know what the hell I'm doing and—"

"Stop." She pointed a finger at him, changing tactics. "Your incompetency is embarrassing." She pulled a face of light disdain. "Clearly, life was nice and simple on the ranch and nothing ever really went wrong."

He eyed her, unimpressed.

She arched an eyebrow. "Did a windmill fall over or something?"

"You just potted your first plant—imagine keeping the soil of extensive pastureland in optimal balance for the horses' nutrition," he said. "Spending nights in the barn during foaling season when a storm knocks out the closed-circuit TV system. Spotting traps in contracts during a stallion acquisition. Making sure we don't miss when one of our bred quarter horses is up for sale at the end of its career, so we can buy it back and ensure it ages comfortably. Running a ranch is a road that never runs out of potholes."

"And I assume you didn't always know what to do then either."

He didn't hide his frustration. "I graduated college in business management and agriculture, but if I didn't know how to handle a situation personally, I damn sure knew someone who did."

"You mean someone like your head of public relations, who will be able to brief you on the kind of questions to expect from the press conference on Friday?"

There was a beat of surprised silence.

Then he exhaled long and hard, and said, "You did that on purpose."

She raised a hand, palm up, and then sighed. "You're capable of this, Markus. You just have to stay calm." She slid off the gardening gloves. "I'll help you to prepare."

"Thanks." His pride seemed unaffected by her unorthodox method of reassurance, though his fingers held the

141

edge of the workbench as he said, "Can you not share this conversation?"

"I've never been very good at sharing."

His lips curved, dry, and she gave a wary smile back. Then he moved behind her and said, "I'd better open the door before Gul breaks it down."

The base of her throat pulsed hard. Intently aware of him at her back, her sides prickled, and she half-expected his arms to circle around her.

"Markus?" she said quietly.

The prickles spread, thickening in the center of her back. He had paused directly behind her.

"Thank you for yesterday. I wasn't—wasn't feeling well, and you gave me something to focus on."

"You're welcome." The greenhouse filled with a careful silence. "The plant can live inside. You can put it on your windowsill." The tingle of awareness faded as he moved to the door. "And Ava?"

"Yes?"

His fingers were on the handle, his back turned, but he murmured in a soft voice that left pleasure flowering unbidden in her chest, "Jeans suit you."

9

The private dining room at the exclusive lakeside restaurant was more modest than Zara had expected. It had been arranged for afternoon tea for two, the honey-washed walls glowing in the sunlight that flooded in. The table was bare wood, engraved around the edges, and the chairs held cushions the color of pale pink magnolias, secured in place with little ties. Aside from the desserts and fruits filling the table, the room oozed understated luxury.

"Are you sure you wouldn't like more?"

She looked up into the dark, kind eyes of Prince Cyrus.

"Um, no," she said, tucking her hair behind her ears. It was like sitting opposite a mythical creature, his elegance beyond mortal measure. His black hair was thick around his ears, the natural half-curls forming a mostly tamed mess. He was lean, and calm, and graceful. He moved in a way that, if he were a glass of water, would never push the liquid up against the sides. Always level, always even. "I mean, yes?" She hardly knew what she was saying. "I'm sure I don't want more," she finished, flustered.

His small smile glinted in his eyes. "All right."

Cyrus had a beauty that wasn't pleasing only for people of certain tastes, or from a particular angle, or just when he smiled. He was beautiful everywhere, for everyone, all the time.

And in addition to him being a prince, and her friend's older brother—the most loyal brother on the planet—Zara didn't know how to handle the fact that she had an embarrassing celebrity-style crush on him.

Denial, mostly.

"Are you enjoying Kiraly?" she asked, leaning an elbow on the table. Then she realized what she was doing and hauled both hands into her lap.

"Very much. I've been exploring in between engagements."

"Quads aching yet?" A blush followed her question. Had she *really* just asked about his legs? His lean, sleek legs . . .

"Dramatically." He smiled. "Kiraly threatens to steal my grace."

She almost said, 'not possible', but seemed to experience divine intervention.

"Now, about Wednesday," he said, his gaze sliding to his right. The timber-framed glass doors had been folded back to expose an unobstructed view of the city's lake. The bright blue-green water shone like a gemstone in the spring sun, speckled with the yachts of wealthy tourists. Warm air wafted in, sweetened by the large pots of jasmine outside. "I've set everything up on my end. All it will take is a phone call to set it in motion."

This prince didn't meet her eyes as he spoke but had a habit of looking directly at her the moment he finished talking.

He stared at her now.

"Okay," she said with a nod. "We'll be good at the shelter. It's the perfect meeting point, because it's built for discretion. Her part could be the problem. A lot could go wrong."

"Yes." His brows dipped with concern. "But I don't see what else we can do."

"Your Highness—"

"Cyrus," he said, and his long lashes took her breath away.

She paused. "Cyrus." The sibilants teased her tongue. "I'm sick over this. I can't sleep, thinking of all the ways we could fail. It's hard to act confident around her."

"I feel the same." He set his glass down, somehow making no sound as it met the wooden surface. "Though I shudder to imagine where we would be without you, Zara. You've made a new life seem possible for her. You're her hope."

"Shit," she muttered. "There's some pressure."

"No." He briefly raised a hand. "Not pressure. Praise."

Praise was one of many things she didn't know how to accept. "Well, we have to get her out before your parents come back. The pressure stays for now."

His perfect features grew haunted, but he asked, "How is your cat?"

"I gave her away," she said in surprise. "I wasn't home often enough."

"Ah. Pity. She was more affectionate than Ava's cats ever were."

Zara had met Cyrus just once before. Six months ago, he had traveled to Kira City to discuss the details of Ava's initial escape plan, insisting on the privacy of a face-to-face discussion. He'd come to her apartment, wearing a black hoodie with a backpack over one shoulder, trying to avoid attention. She'd hardly been able to form sentences for the young prince on her couch, magnetic in common clothes and drinking bag-brewed tea without complaint.

Her crush had formed then, no doubt matching that of every so-inclined citizen of Kelehar. If Ava ever found out, she'd probably laugh. *Everyone is a little infatuated with Cyrus*, she'd say. *You'll get used to it.*

"Zara," he said, and his eyes rose to hers.

She hummed in question.

"Do I make you uncomfortable?"

"Do you—what? No. Why would you—God. Of course not."

His smile was strained.

"You don't," she said, pulling a face. "*I* make me uncomfortable."

"Well," he said carefully, his gaze lowering to the strawberry platter, "please stop. Your emails are different. Relaxed. Casual. You can be like that around me."

Could she? When she wrote emails to him, she focused so intently on helping Ava that she forgot she was contacting a prince. But in his presence, it was impossible to forget.

"Okay," she said, because she could at least pretend to be comfortable. "In which case, I am absolutely not finished eating. I need at least three more of those lemon tartlets, and do you really think I haven't noticed you kept those little cakes on your side of the table?"

He grinned as he offered her the plate.

She avoided his eye as she took one, unnerved that her blunt, cynical heart didn't find the fact that she was sitting across from a prince—like, an actual *prince*—too funny for words. Or funny at all. This foolish crush would fade when Ava escaped, and Cyrus had no need to see Zara ever again.

The day couldn't come soon enough.

Mark had been putting it off: the discussion that would reveal how little he and his brothers had moved on from their old lives.

Sure, they'd been doing all right. Adjusting to being royalty as best they could. But it was all surface deep and as much as it pained him, that had to change. *They* had to change. He'd chosen to honor his duty to Kiraly—and his brothers had joined him.

Those decisions had consequences.

He intended to bring it up at dinner. But Kris stalked in late, a reckless edge to his smile, and Mark knew better than to tear open a wound without first counting to three.

"I spoke to Mom and Dad today," Mark dropped into the conversation.

One.

"Yeah, I called them yesterday." Kris eyed him. "Dad was relieved to hear you weren't engaged. He said strategic marriage is a one-way ticket to a miserable life." He stabbed a potato with unnecessary violence. "And you met with Ava this afternoon. Wearing a ball gown, was she?"

"Not this time." Mark didn't know what he'd expected her to wear, but jeans hadn't been it. Burgundy and fitted, the everyday style had made him feel as if they had something in common. Made him feel more than that. Confined with her in that humid space, he'd been *attracted* to her. The prickly princess who had lashed him with insults since they'd met. He'd wanted to lean in closer, show her how to tip the plant by covering her hand with his and doing it with her.

"I taught her how to pot a plant," he said, trying to forget her unexpected appeal. "She told me to accept that I'm not the equal of anyone else in the country. Tomorrow, she'll help me to prepare for my first press conference."

Philip required all three brothers to attend. Mark hadn't figured out how to change that. But a room full of hungry journalists, desperate to learn the stories of their new royal family? That would induce another of Tommy's panic attacks.

As for Kris, well, he was unashamedly, almost antagonistically, only too happy to be himself. It would be safer if Mark handled it alone.

Tommy nodded, but Kris's narrowed gaze lingered as he chewed.

After dinner, Tommy said he wanted to show them something outside. He led them through the gardens, softly lit in the clear spring night, and into the alpine woods beyond. Figures merged into their wake, flashlights glowing white, and despite the security team's discretion, Mark couldn't help feeling like herded cattle.

The terrain spiked immediately, a steep ascent that made up for the levelling of the palace grounds within the mountain's slope. It was good to hike again. Kris certainly needed the exertion—he radiated tension, worked up over something as he powered along in silence.

Tommy held a flashlight, its beam lighting their route, and passed a second one to Mark. The trees were tall, sparse, and the undergrowth was springy under Mark's boots.

"When someone says, 'I want to show you something outside,' what do you assume?" Kris muttered beside Mark. "A full moon. Maybe a view from a nearby lookout. You don't think of a serious hike, because otherwise that person would have said, 'I want to show you something that involves trekking up a mountain. Perhaps you should bring a bottle of water.'"

Tommy reached into a backpack that Mark should have thought to query earlier, and extended a water bottle out behind him. Kris took it with a bark of laughter.

"This isn't a track," Mark eventually pointed out. The fresh tang of pine thickened the night air. "You know where you're going?"

"Yes," his brother answered, pausing with one foot in front of the other. It put an alarming bend in his knee.

"Want to tell us where?" Kris asked, breathing heavily.

"It's a surprise."

"Not really in the mood for surprises."

"Then change your mood."

"Much farther?" Mark asked before Kris could verbalize his scowl.

"Almost there." Tommy resumed the hike.

A muscle-working, lung-heaving period of time later, Tommy halted and shone the flashlight higher up the mountain. "There," he breathed, his other hand holding the thick trunk of a pine tree. "See it?"

The light beam passed over something that broke the pattern of the vertical woods around them.

A log cabin.

"What?" Kris said unevenly.

The darkness swallowed it completely. Mark could have walked six paces to the right and not realized the structure was there. As the light passed over a window, the glass flared with its reflection but the pitch black within skittered down his spine.

"Who lives here?" he asked, more out of breath than he liked.

"No one. I asked the security trailing my hike the other day if there was anything worth seeing up here. I was thinking more of a lookout over the valley, but they directed me here." Tommy moved the light around, revealing a small hunting cabin with a pitched tin roof and unlit windows either side of the door. The empty veranda gave no sign of life, not a chair, woodpile, or pair of boots. The ground around the cabin had been levelled and he aimed his flashlight high into the trees, showing branches that concealed it from above.

"Coming in?" Tommy said.

The front door was unlocked. As they stepped inside, Mark moved his light around. Structurally, it was a basic hut. There was a bench and cupboards forming a kitchen along one wall. In another corner, wooden slabs were mounted like bunk beds with foam slabs wrapped in plastic on top. A simple fireplace cut a hole in another wall, and firewood was stacked beside it halfway to the roof. There was a table with four chairs, a worn rug on the floor, and a small, walled-off section at the back that presumably housed a tiny washroom.

Mark dragged his thumb across the dusty tabletop. It hadn't been used in a long time. "Any idea why this is built on land directly above the Kiralian palace?"

"Royal bolt-hole." Tommy swung his pack off his shoulders. "I asked security. It's ours."

Kris snapped a sharp glance at him. "Bolt-hole?"

"A hunting cabin makes a good front. It's for emergency use only."

"Can't imagine bolting here in a hurry." Mark had only just caught his breath.

Tommy gave a cynical smile. "In the event of invasion, war, or a military coup, I suspect you'd surprise yourself."

Kris hadn't moved, his body stiff. "Is an uprising likely?"

"I meant historically. Chill out." Tommy knelt and unzipped his bag. "We've got ourselves a home away from home."

Mark turned in the open doorway. The forest was black outside. "You can come in if you want." He spoke into the dark.

"No. Thank you, Your Majesty," called a reply.

As Mark closed the door, relief worked through him. His muscles unwound and the tug along his shoulders seemed to ease. They had a retreat—a place to relax and escape scrutiny. He clasped Tommy on the shoulder. "Nice find."

In the following minutes, Kris scrounged around in the cupboards and came up with several cans of beans but no snack food, much to his verbalized disappointment. Mark found a rag in a bucket by the fireplace and wiped down the dust-thick table and chairs, and Tommy withdrew three longnecks from his pack and tossed a packet of crackers at Kris. Then they lounged around the table, smiled at each other, and raised their bottles.

"To King Markus," Kris said.

"My liege," Tommy added.

"Knock it off," Mark said, and they tapped the brews together.

They leaned back in their chairs, feet propped on the table. No surface in their old farmhouse had been too sacred for the heels of leather boots. For a few minutes, they did nothing but sit and soak up the solitude—the stillness outside, the smell of the untainted outdoors.

"Buck and Bull would love it here," Mark said casually. "We should bring them over."

Two.

Kris gave him a strange look as Tommy asked, "What do you guys like about Kiraly?"

Mark's gut hardened. He was too stressed to like anything about it. "I'm a fan of this cabin."

"The city." Kris balanced on the chair's back two legs, one hand holding his beer, the other resting over his stomach. "I went down again today. The people are great value. Welcoming, sassy in a good way." He swigged. "But the city—there's something for everyone and no one really gives a shit what others are into, as long as they can all eat and drink and dance together. They treat everyone the same." He grinned. "Even a prince. They played it cool, giving me space to go about my business—no excited squealing or pleas for selfies. Maybe they just don't want to scare us off now that the royal family is showing an interest in them. You guys should get down there and check it out. Especially you, Mark."

"Yeah." He just had to figure out when, in between

meetings with Philip, gardening with Ava, and freaking out with himself. Deflecting, he asked, "How're you coping, Tommy?"

"There are a lot of people," Tommy answered, picking at the label on his beer bottle.

Mark nodded. In every corridor, every parlor, at every turn.

"But I'm making myself scarce." He kept picking at the bottle label. "The guys that follow me around keep their distance, so it could be worse. How about you two?"

"Can't complain." Kris raised a shoulder, running his tongue along the inside of his cheek. Forced nonchalance to hide whatever had been bothering him when he'd arrived at dinner.

They looked at Mark and he drank to buy time. He should admit he wasn't coping, that every day made it more real and that being a king—*the* king—iced him cold. He'd always told them everything. Burdens divided three ways were lighter to bear and all that, and the only reason they'd uprooted their entire lives was to support him. He should let them do just that.

"Good," he found himself answering. His gut sank. "One day at a time."

Tommy nodded, stripping the label into smaller pieces.

"Thank God you were born first." This from Kris. "You've always been the honorable one."

Mark's answering smile was forced. Now. He had to do it now.

"Mom and Dad mentioned we've received an offer for the ranch," he made himself say. "A husband-and-wife couple. It's a good offer."

Three.

"We should sell," he added.

Kris and Tommy stared at him. Stunned, pained faces torn open by the blow.

"Sell it?" Kris hauled his heels off the tabletop. His chair snapped back to four legs as his feet landed loudly. Anger slid in his jaw. "Sell the ranch?"

The thought made Mark sick. "Yes."

Tommy released an unsteady breath. "We can't expect Mom and Dad to run it."

"What the hell?" Kris looked between them, practically snarling. "We can't *sell* it."

"But we're not going back," Tommy said quietly. "Are we?"

"No." Kris pushed out of his chair, throwing a hand against the nearest wall and leaning into it. He vibrated with outrage. "Not the ranch."

Stricken, Mark watched him. Loss pushed up into his throat. "Kris. Do you want to go back? You can run it. Tom, you too. You can both go back."

Kris rounded on him, a wild look in his eyes. "I can't leave you in this place!"

"I'm staying," Tommy murmured.

"Then . . ." Mark raised a helpless shoulder, hating that he couldn't make this right.

"Fucking shit." Kris ran a hand over his face, exhaling hard and ending on another curse. Then he collapsed back into his chair, folding his arms on the table edge and dropping his forehead on top. He spoke to the dusty floor. "Selling the ranch will be like ripping my heart out."

"I know." Mark's ribs ached already.

The sale would slam a final door on their old life. It echoed in their silence.

Then Tommy rapped his fingers on the table. Small movements often acted as his pressure relief valve. "Let's bring the dogs over."

Mark gave a small smile. "Yeah."

Kris looked up, his eyes sad, his chin on his forearms. Defeat had snuffed out his anger. "Yeah. Okay."

Better than having nothing at all, but it wouldn't change the hard truth.

Their lives would never go back to the way they used to be.

In bed, surrounded by darkness, Ava curled around an acute sense of loss. It had burrowed inside her years ago, wedging into a space she couldn't reach, nesting and expanding like a parasite. It weighed more than matter—more than her organs, or bones, or the bitter blood in her veins—and preyed on her at night when distractions dulled and her resilience waned.

She curled tighter, her hand sliding up and under the second pillow to drag her teddy bear to her chest. She felt no shame as she buried her face against its smooth cashmere fabric.

Loss reduced adults to children: weakened, ill-functioning, seeking comfort in tears and toys, foolishly trying to believe that it didn't mean the end.

It wasn't the end.

She would make sure of it.

"Gul tells me you're taking lessons from King Markus."

Ava eyed her brother across the breakfast table as he spread olive tapenade on his bread. He wore an exquisite tunic the color of apricots, embroidered with silk thread of the same shade. Cyrus had always been a master of refinement.

He was also an expert at expressing disapproval of her, because even Gul couldn't know that Cyrus was on her side.

"I potted a plant yesterday," she said, aware of her guard standing with his back to the nearest wall. "And we have another lesson planned for this afternoon."

"And will these lessons remain in the garden?"

She didn't answer as she narrowed her eyes.

Cyrus glanced up, his features neutral. "You know why I'm asking."

"I'm not sure," she said tartly. The same response she'd have given her mother.

"Ava." Cyrus placed his knife down. His tone was unimpressed. "Gul also tells me that you were speaking of *surviving on your own* the other day."

"Oh." She darted a betrayed glance at her guard. He stood with his feet apart, features impassive. He didn't meet her eyes. "It was offhand. I'd been telling him that I have everything done for me. I probably don't even know half the things people do to make my life this easy. I'm ashamed to be so ignorant."

"These lessons," Cyrus said, pushing. "Gul wonders if there's something more to them."

"I don't want to marry Markus." She tucked her head down. "I don't care what I've been ordered to do. I'm not winning him over."

"That's not what I meant. I know you hate this life and want nothing more than to run away." Her brother shook his head with a frown, as if he couldn't believe she was so silly. "But you're the princess of Kelehar. You can't disappear and expect no one to look for you. It's foolishness that would only embarrass us and you."

She stared down at her rosy tea, turning the glass cup gently in its saucer.

Cutlery clinked as he began eating.

"It's just something to do, Cyrus." She spoke to her cup. "I have an escape fantasy, yes, but it's just a fantasy. Do you think you would know about it if I were serious?" She waited until he pulled an expression of grudging agreement. "These lessons could help me feel more capable than I am. Our parents know

I'm useless—they know all they have to do is cut off my allowance to control me. I could argue until my tongue falls out, but I would have no choice but to show up for dinner if I wanted to be fed."

He looked insulted. "I'd feed you."

"Like a mouse in your wall?" She ran her fingers along the laced edge of the tablecloth. "There'd be no dignity in that. And it would just be another form of dependence." She hesitated. "These lessons with Markus are to make me a better princess. A better *person*. And I'll help him to be a more confident king. That's all. I'm not planning on escaping this life, and I'd hardly manage it by potting plants."

Cyrus added finely chopped herbs to his bread. Then he said quietly, "All right."

She glanced over at her guard. "Gul. Could you go get my cardigan? It's cool in here."

He nodded. Free to leave her alone in her brother's company, he strode from the parlor.

Cyrus flicked a glance at the empty doorway and ate his bread. Then, with their conversational performance over, he murmured, "I still don't know about him, sister."

She met his gaze. Gul confused them both. He was paid by the queen of Kelehar to watch over Ava. Keep her safe, keep her contained, and where possible, keep her compliant. Did his loyalty lie strictly with his employer? Or had his support shifted to Ava after guarding her so closely for the last three years? They had become friends. He knew of her past and empathized with her pain. She truly believed he wanted the best for her—but if that meant going against his duty someday, she couldn't predict which side Gul would choose.

"Neither do I," she said quietly. "He reports on me. But I know he cares."

"He's very observant."

"I'll be more careful."

She sipped her tea and waited for Cyrus to finish eating. She wasn't hungry.

After a while, Cyrus murmured, "Ava," in a careful tone.

She caught his eye, her stomach clenching.

"Wednesday afternoon, five-thirty."

Her heart latched onto his words like greedy fists, dragging them near. *Wednesday afternoon, five-thirty.* It was Monday. She had to wait two days. Those hours would feel longer than all the hundreds of thousands of hours she'd already lived combined.

"It'll have to happen fast."

She nodded quickly, urgently.

"It's Gul's day off." He lifted his glass teacup to his lips. "If you can give Erwin the slip, you won't be followed. Drive something understated, if you can resist the Vermilion."

"Yes," she breathed.

"And eat something," he said, frowning as his gaze passed over her face. "You look pale. You need strength. You don't want to fall sick between now and then, do you?"

At that, she ate until she could eat no more.

10

"This place is bogus."

Zara was perched awkwardly in Ava's sitting room, looking around like she was in a house of horrors. Ava should have found the bulge of her eyes entertaining, but instead it tied her pride in knots. They were vastly different people from vastly different worlds—her conversation with Markus the previous day had reminded her anew. They weren't equals, not really, and it was distinctly possible that Zara felt obliged to pretend they were friends simply because it was what the princess wanted. How could she have not considered it before? Every intimate word Zara spoke might be delivered in fear of offending royalty.

"Sorry." Zara cringed at her. In her loose-weave sweater and jeans, and hair in a messy topknot, she looked more like something the maid should discreetly brush off the sofa than someone who had legitimate cause to be sitting on it. "Must feel homey to you, huh?"

Ava stood by the window. Her turquoise pot shone brightly in the afternoon sunlight and was warm beneath her fingers. "Not particularly. I stayed in these rooms the last time I was in

Kiraly. Essentially, this mural is a reminder that surrounding oneself with gold offers no comfort in times of need."

"Oneself." Zara nodded, looking up at the painted ceiling with a downturned mouth. "Right."

Ava set her shoulders back. "Zara," she said, hating the small sound of her voice. "I'd like to ask you something, and have you answer honestly. I won't cut off your head if I don't like it, I promise."

"My kind of deal." Zara shifted, facing her fully. "Shoot."

"Are you only friends with me because I'm a princess?"

Zara pulled back, her features screwing up. "What?" Then she laughed. "God, sweetie, I feel blasphemous or some shit saying it in this place, but I'm friends with you despite that."

Ava blinked.

"You're royalty," she said, gesturing helplessly. "I can't find any significance in that. Crowns and ceremonies and castles—so much money sunk into perpetuating your own status. That money could be better spent elsewhere. Which"—Zara held up her hands, gesturing toward Ava like the contestant on a game show—"is exactly what you're doing with your women's shelter. I love that about you. You're generous and you've got grit, with a side serve of vicious conversational banter. Definitely not because of the royalty thing, cross my weird little heart."

The candid delivery gave no room for doubt. Pleasure buoyed from Ava's belly to her collarbones. "Oh. Good."

"And I'm soaking in every shred of your friendship right now," Zara said with a slouch, "so please don't start second guessing this and pushing me away."

Ava frowned, concerned. "Why? What's happened?"

"Just my housemate. He's still being really distant." Zara shook her head, looking down. "Unrequited appreciation. I'll get over it."

"He rejected your offer to go out for a drink?"

"I didn't ask." Her friend shifted. "Didn't bother."

"Will you regret having not asked if he moves out?"

Zara held her hands up, miming balancing scales. "Missed opportunity," she said, raising one hand above the other. Then her hands switched. "Certain rejection." She pulled a face. "Yeah, I think I'm good on this one."

"I'm sorry." Ava tried to figure out what her friend needed to hear. "His loss."

Zara sighed, and smiled a little sadly. "Thanks. Now come sit down and let's talk shop."

That morning, Ava had told Gul to expect Zara's visit. *"We've spent years emailing,"* she'd said to him. *"It'll be wonderful to finally collaborate on the women's shelter program in person."*

Now, just in case he stood with his ear pressed to the door, they verbally compared strategic plans and brainstormed ways to improve the delivery of services. The paper that passed between them, however, contained the new escape plan and how it would go down, step-by-step. Locations, directions, and who to expect—questions, fears, and shakily-written hope.

Several hours later, once Ava was sure she had her head around it, she exclaimed, "Oh, I've got this part all wrong," and tossed their notes into the fire.

"Let's take a break then." Zara leaned back to watch the paper burn. "How did things go with the king yesterday in your fancy ponytail?"

Ava smiled wryly. "The ponytail continued to exacerbate my headache, but I walked away with that little plant." She pointed to her succulent.

"Cute." Zara peered over. "It wasn't uncomfortable after the whole strategic marriage thing? Cos I can imagine that'd make hanging out majorly awkward."

"Um." It had only been awkward when she'd ordered him

not to touch her. After that, it had been . . . nice. More than nice. *Tingly.* Ava's cheeks warmed despite herself. "He said jeans suit me."

Her friend stared. "Get out."

Ava frowned, taken aback.

"He thinks you're hot. Holy mother, I told you this was a bad idea."

"He doesn't think I'm—" She halted when Gul knocked, entered, and announced, "King Markus to see you."

Zara whipped around to stare at Gul, then spun back to Ava with wide eyes. "Oh, my God, he thinks you're hot, and he's *here.*"

"We're not adolescents." Ava was struck by the terrifying notion that her friend lacked the required subtlety for the impending situation. Panic pushed her to her feet. "Can you act casual or do I need to jam you in a wardrobe?"

Zara actually paused to think about it. "Casual," she decided.

Ava stared her down, too alarmed to mitigate her glower of authority.

"Whoa, casual, casual," Zara said quickly, raising her hands. "I swear."

"Good." Ava's pulse tripped. Markus was here. "Now stand, don't sit down, and don't speak unless spoken to."

Zara leapt to her feet, lips pressed together, as the king strode into the room.

His arrival instantly put the dainty décor to shame. What good was gold and lace when her room could be filled with the rough-hewed masculinity of a born and bred cowboy? He wore a plaid shirt, red and black, the fabric invitingly soft and rolled to his elbows. Dark strands of his hair fell loose around his ears, scraggly and untamed, and Ava's inhale turned ragged at the shadow along his jaw. He looked tired, his eyelids heavier than usual, but still held himself tall, broad shoulders back and chin up.

Halting several steps into the room, his blue gaze traveled from Ava to Zara. Apology filled his first words. "I've interrupted. I'll come back later."

"Not at all," she said, and held out a hand toward Zara. "This is Zara Nguyen. Zara, this is His Royal Majesty King Markus of Kiraly."

Markus smiled, extending a hand. "Great to meet you."

Ava caught his eye with a frown. "You're a king meeting a citizen, not a friend of a friend."

He lowered his hand as Zara bowed, making no comment.

"And you're supposed to curtsey," Ava said under her breath.

"Shit." Zara gracelessly transitioned into a curtsey.

"You can't swear—" Ava raised a hand to her forehead with a sudden laugh. "I'm surrounded by ineptitude."

"A swan among starlings." Markus grinned, hooking a thumb into the waistband of his jeans. "Oh." He reached into his back pocket and withdrew a thin paperback, folded in half to fit, before holding it out to Ava. "This is for you."

The cover was creased, the corners curling with wear. A secondhand copy. She didn't reach out. "What is it?"

"A book to make you happy."

Oh. Pleasure warmed her. Such a simple thing, yet so much more. It confused her that this man had thought about her while they were apart, and so kindly. Unpracticed at expressing gratitude, she asked, "There's a book for that?"

His arm stiffened. "There are books that try."

Not knowing how to accept such thoughtfulness, but desperately wanting to, she took it and instantly feared she'd snatched. To cover her awkwardness, she flipped through the pages. Then she frowned up at him. "It's a picture book."

"It's a book of pictures that each tell their own story," he said, an edge of defense in his words. "Read into the illustrations what you will, but I like how they capture the innocence of human nature. A few minutes with that book restores my hope, which feels like a kind of happiness."

Thrown by his honesty, she placed it on the divan. "I'll return it when I'm finished."

Zara made a tiny noise in the back of her throat. When Ava eyed her friend's lowered head, Zara twisted her face toward her and mouthed *"thank you."*

"Thank you," Ava said, snapping her attention to Markus and blushing at her impropriety.

"You're welcome." Then he looked to Zara and his smile returned. "So, Zara, how do you know Ava?"

Zara straightened hesitantly. "We met last time she was in Kiraly, Your Majesty, and have stayed in touch since."

"That's great." He nodded easily, and with an odd sinking sensation, Ava realized that he was instinctively more relaxed around Zara than he was around her. "Are you a local here?"

"Yes, Your Majesty."

"Please don't call me that every time," he said, and then caught Ava's look of dismay. "That is, there can just be a mutual awareness of the fact that I'm the king, and that we are not, and never will be, equals."

His raised brow asked, *better?*

Her answering stare was flat, but her lips twitched.

"That's cool with me," Zara said, shrugging nervously. "But I have work to do, so I'll leave you guys to it."

"Zara." His brows lowered. "Before you leave, I wonder if you can help me. I haven't had a chance to visit Kira City yet. I want to get a feel for the people and lifestyle. Any recommendations on where I could go?"

Zara inhaled with what appeared to be an instant idea. Then she paused. "Somewhere fancy, you mean?"

"Somewhere normal."

"Oh, man," she said, slapping her hands together. "Let me narrow this down. Somewhere people will play it cool to have a king kicking around—that means locals only. Somewhere that won't represent the city at its messiest." She grimaced. "That really does narrow it down. Somewhere with good music, good food, and good company . . ." Her lips twisted as she thought. Then her eyes lit up. "Got it. The Bearded Bunting, just east of the western crest. It's super chill."

"Great. How do you feel about accompanying me in the next day or two?"

Zara's eyes popped and Ava's stomach jerked with irrational jealousy. "You want me to go with you?" Zara asked. "Because legit, I'm very mutually aware of the fact that we're not equals and never will be."

"Ignore that. I just want a night out."

Ava spoke before she could stop herself, her tone far too bitter. "Are you asking her on a date, Markus?"

The pair turned to her, their jaws loose.

Zara tilted her head, cheeks flaming, and mouthed, *"What?"* as Markus said, "No, but I hoped you might join us."

Oh.

"I don't go to normal places," Ava said, even as the invitation bloomed inside her. Some part of her *wanted* to spend time with him. The man she'd been desperate to avoid. Zara was right— she was insane.

"You'll love it." Zara sounded entirely unconvincing.

"I doubt it." Ava regretted the refusal as she spoke, but it was her default: avoid anything that might fool her into believing she could be happy the way she was. A practical fallback, for she couldn't lose the fight now. She refused to give up and settle. "You two go and enjoy yourselves."

Zara smiled at her tightly. "Could I talk to you for a little tick?"

Chin high, Ava followed her friend through the doorway into her bedroom.

"You're coming," Zara declared in a whisper.

"It's not the kind of thing I do."

"I don't care," she hissed. "I'm not going by myself!"

Ava battled her own urge to join them. "You know socializing is not my priority, Zara."

"Yeah." Zara's dark eyes were serious. "I do know. But your priority isn't coming until Wednesday afternoon. Treat this like reading a book at a bus stop—or private jet stop, or whatever. Catching the jet is your priority, but it doesn't mean you can't do stuff while you wait, okay? That's just wasting your life."

Ava clenched her teeth. Sometimes, her skin was too thin for her friend's hard truths.

"Besides"—Zara's voice lowered to a breath—"this will add to the rumor that you've run away with a commoner. Last seen together in a bar in Kira City . . ."

Floored by the opportunity, Ava stared at her. Then she smiled.

Grinning, Zara turned and dragged her back into the sitting room. "She'll come," she said to Markus.

Markus looked skeptically at Ava, clearly suspecting the decision had been made on her behalf. "You're here on vacation, aren't you?"

"Ostensibly," Ava said.

"Then invite your brother. And I'll invite mine." He nodded toward Zara. "Zara can bring anyone she'd like, and we can all take a break for the night."

Ava's hands were clenched by her sides. She forced them apart. "When did you say?"

Markus looked to Zara. "You good for tomorrow night?"

"Sure."

He raised a questioning brow at Ava and she scoffed to mask her panic. "Fine."

"Rad." Zara slung her satchel over her shoulder, wincing at Ava. "I really do have to get back to work." With a final bow-turn-curtsey at Markus, she departed.

Her absence echoed in the room. Ava was alone with Markus once again. Awareness of him moved down her chest, clustering in a flutter beneath her breastbone. He made her nervous, this man who had refused to trap her by his side, but it was a nice kind of discomfort, like being too warm by the fire in winter or singing along to a favorite song so loudly her throat hurt.

"Is after dinner tonight okay for your next lesson?" His question was a murmur.

Startled, she met his gaze. "Tonight?"

He nodded. "Philip needs me this afternoon, and I know I said I'd show you how to grow a garden, but I'm missing the smell of smoke on a cool night. How about learning how to build a campfire?"

A campfire. She instinctively raised a hand to the base of her throat at the thought of sitting on the cold ground before a makeshift fire with bugs in the air.

Then she said, "Yes," because it was important to reduce her aversion to unrefined activities.

He smiled with a raised brow. "Yeah?"

She gave a tiny nod.

"You'll need to dress warm and casual. And wear boots. It might be a long walk to find a good spot."

"I don't normally wear heels outside." She tucked her hair

behind her ear as embarrassment warmed her face. "You caught me on a vindictive day."

"I sure did," he said, and his smile faded. "Is tomorrow night really okay with you?"

"Is it okay with me to go out into the city with the man who refused to marry me, socializing in a public place with civilians and with no way to ensure that I receive service that honors my position?"

He looked like he was holding back a grin. "Yes."

She sucked on her bottom lip for a moment, relieved he couldn't sense the speed of her heart. Then she admitted, "I don't know what to wear."

With a small smile, his gaze passed over her figure. She wore a simple sundress of dusty red, modest around her neckline, fitted at the waist, and falling in soft folds above her knees. Tension locked her stomach tight, for his attention bordered on tactile, a visual caress that left her nerves twisting and her skin tingling. His smile faded and he swallowed, his gaze cutting to the window. "You want to avoid drawing attention to yourself?"

Self-conscious, she worked hard not to run her hands down her sides. "Ideally."

He looked back at her, his features tight. "I don't think that's possible."

And while she frowned at the implications of that, he murmured something about meeting her in the west atrium at eight before striding from the room.

.

11

Zara appreciated the personal escort from Ava's rooms. She would never have found her way out of the palace otherwise. Lost in the literal sense, she would also have been lost in time, staring at the ceiling frescoes and marveling at the magnitude of simple spaces like corridors and antechambers. She'd known the structure was gargantuan, for every day she eyed it from the city, awed and slightly nervous at how it cut into the multimillion-year-old mountain, but she hadn't anticipated the sheer beauty that resulted from the collaboration of artists over time. Each monarch had added their personal taste to the décor. Every wall and archway, ceiling and alcove had been used as an opportunity to sculpt and paint, erect and embellish.

It really was bogus—the wealth that lived inside these walls.

Her escort had observed her amazement and kindly offered a tour. They had just left a gallery displaying the portraits of the royal family throughout history and were on their way to the supposedly breathtaking concert hall, when two men emerged through a doorway on their right and set off in the opposite direction.

"You're actually serious? The king has invited you to drink tea with him?" one man was asking. "What an unprecedented prospect."

"It's unheard of—a manservant doesn't sit with his king," the second man answered in a voice so familiar that Zara spun around, too surprised to consider silence.

"Adam?"

He halted, turning back, his shoes as shiny as the marble floor and hair golden like the painted leaves in Ava's sitting room. In his black suit and blue tie, he looked more proper than King Markus himself. His eyes bulged when he saw her. "Zara?"

She forced herself to offer a small smile, hiding her sense of betrayal. She knew he worked in the palace, but he'd never told her he worked for the *king*.

"I'll be along in a minute," he said to his companion. The other man nodded with a curious glance at Zara and continued down the corridor. Zara's guide faded back into the gallery.

Adam faced her with a frown. He stood mere feet away, but it was as if he were farther away from her than ever. "What are you doing here?"

Nice to see you too. Her arms hung by her sides. "Visiting Princess Ava," she said. "And you?"

Shock burst across his face. "You're *what*?"

With quiet indignation, she said, "No. I asked you a question."

His features flickered with surprise, before his usual mask of composure settled. "I work here."

"For the king, I just heard." She hesitated, upset that this refined man put a stammer in her pulse. Why couldn't she fall for guys she actually had a chance with? "Look, would you mind moving out?" she asked, her words too loud. They echoed

169

through the elaborately carved arches—the harsh acoustics of a commoner. "Because I think you should."

Disbelief creased his face. "Pardon?"

"It's not your fault. But you might have noticed that I like you, and you haven't even told me you work for the king. Kind of big news. It seems I've overinvested in you, and you're uncomfortable around me, so you shouldn't stay."

He opened his mouth, inhaling, and then paused to scan her face. His scrutiny threatened to break her stare, but she held, refusing to be embarrassed by her own honesty. "You want me to move out?"

"I imagine you could live somewhere much nicer, serving the king directly."

He acknowledged that by inclining his head. "Yes, but—"

"I'm sorry. I know moving is a pain in the ass." She hitched the strap of her satchel higher up her shoulder. "But it's for the best."

Adam stood silently in front of her. If she didn't know better —and it was turning out she knew depressingly little about him —she'd have thought regret was darkening his eyes.

"Will you have a drink with me?" he asked, in that soft voice of his, and took a step toward her.

"No, I—" She halted, startled. *What?* "What?"

"I just . . ." His brow lowered, before he said carefully, "I've been distracted lately. As you can imagine, work has been overwhelming, and I struggle with being forthcoming. I'm sorry if you've interpreted that as me being disinterested in you."

She had. His disinterest had been unmistakable. Was this guilt talking? "Yeah, right," she said, and dug her fingers into her palms. To hell with it. One drink to find out for certain. "I guess you could come out with me tomorrow night," she said. "I'm meeting up with—friends."

"Okay." He nodded, his gaze fixed on her face. Her stomach flipped at the rare attention. "That'd be nice. Thank you."

She nodded, said, "Yeah, cool," and turned to leave.

His low voice pulled her back. "You said you were visiting Princess Ava."

She ignored the question hanging off the end of that sentence. "Yes."

He cleared his throat, but didn't ask.

"You want some palace gossip?" She rounded on him incredulously. He cringed a little, but didn't deny it. "Well, she's not a rumor to go around."

His frown was slow-forming. "That sounded protective."

Zara raised her chin. "Friends protect each other."

That seemed to strike his forehead, for his hand rose to cover the impact. "You're friends with her?"

"Why wouldn't I be?"

He didn't answer. Probably because there were so many answers to that question, he was overcome by choice. He stared, clearly astonished, and she suspected he was rapidly rearranging his impression of her.

She raised a shoulder and readjusted the strap of her satchel. "And King Markus dropped in while I was there. He's pretty nice. He asked me out, actually."

Adam's whole face seemed to blink in shock. "He *what?*"

"Anyway, I'd better go. Drinks are with Ava and the king tomorrow, just a heads up. I'm taking them to the Bearded Bunting. You know it?"

Mouth hanging open, he nodded.

"Meet you there then," she said, and left him standing in the middle of the corridor, a dashing picture of blond-haired bewilderment.

As she strode off to find her guide in the gallery, she shouldered impending loss. Sure, she'd get an evening of his company, but he'd only offered it out of guilt. Sitting there pretending it was anything more would be the worst kind of awkward.

And it wouldn't change anything.

She'd only asked him to move out to save her dignity. She'd seen through the crack of his bedroom door this morning—his bags still packed. Instigating his departure didn't change the rejection she'd felt at his neatly prepared luggage.

Adam was moving out.

Ava waited for Markus outside the west atrium. Her nervous energy meant she couldn't stand still, not with forty-eight hours until her life would change forever, so she left Erwin in the wide doorway and wandered the nearby paths, running her hand over the shoulder-height hedges. Tall panels blocked a section of the west wing, concealing the accident site, and a chill swept through her at the reminder that life didn't always go as planned.

At the sound of men talking, she turned to see Markus making his way down the sweep of outdoor steps, chatting to Erwin, two dogs trotting by his side. Her guard gestured in her direction, and with a smile, Markus broke off to meet her.

She faced him, pressing a hand to her middle, not sure whether she wanted to banish or protect the nerves that clustered at the sight of him. His figure was impressive; his leather-booted stride was sure.

"Hello," she said as he neared, linking her fingers together at her breastbone.

The dogs halted the moment he did, dropping to their bellies on the pebbled path. Not Bernese Mountain Dogs, but Border Collies.

"Hi." His smile enriched his voice. His top shirt buttons were undone, his sleeves rolled, and the hem hung loose over his jeans. His hair was damp around the edges and the light scent of lemon soap wafted over her, granting her a lungful of this man fresh out of the shower. The smell traveled through her, beguiling and warm, and she quickly inhaled again to capture it in her lungs. It tangled with her nerves in an innocent kind of pleasure–pain. This wasn't King Markus trying to do what was expected of him, nor was it Markus tackling each unexpected moment with kindness and common sense.

This was a man after-hours, unraveled and relaxed.

This was Mark.

"Hi," she said, and rolled her lips together to stop herself greeting him for a third time.

He laughed softly. "These guys arrived this evening. Hope you don't mind them joining us. They're restless, even though Tommy already took them out." He met her eyes, stiffening slightly, and gestured to the dogs. "Ava, meet Buck and Bull. Buck has the white stripe along his nose. They've traveled a long way to be here."

She didn't hesitate. She knelt at his feet and reached a hand out to each dog. They sniffed her palms, accepting her, and she scratched them both behind the ear. "Are they from your ranch?" She looked up at him as the collies wriggled closer.

"They are."

"They're soft."

"Yes."

He was motionless as she stood up, watching her. His eyes held a recent memory that smeared shame down her throat.

"I didn't want to hurt him," she murmured.

He hesitated. "I know."

"I just didn't . . ." She wrapped her arms around her middle and looked to the lowering sun.

"You just didn't want to have to marry me." His words were quiet.

She hadn't known what else to do. "It would have ruined everything."

A bird haunted the garden with its call, and a cool breeze moved over her.

"My parents' marriage was strategic." She shook her head. "They've never been in love."

He made a grim sound of apology.

"What about your parents?" She turned to him, realizing she knew nothing about his abdicator father or his wife. "Are they happy?"

"Yes." He slid a hand into the back pocket of his jeans. "Dad was third in line for the throne, so didn't have the pressure of marrying a future queen. My parents met at a community event and fell in love. They're still crazy about each other."

She wanted to say, *"that's beautiful,"* but couldn't manage it.

"Tommy ignores it, but Kris still makes kissing noises at them."

"And you?"

He answered softly, "If only I should be so lucky as to find someone who'd still make out with me when our adult children were in the room."

She let out a swift breath as the sentiment pierced her. Kissing a man she loved in the same place as their children, ageing and happy? Her throat tightened and she swallowed hard.

"It sounds corny," he said, raising a shoulder.

"Only a little." The breeze gusted up again and she shivered.

"You look cold." He swung a pack off his shoulder and stuck his hand inside. "The fire is a while off. Put this on." He held up a thick plaid jacket by the shoulders, many sizes too large.

"Oh." And then she realized he intended to help her into it. "Oh," she said again, turning and sliding her arms into the sleeves. It engulfed her, the hem reaching the backs of her thighs, and for several rapid heartbeats, she could have sworn she felt his hands graze her shoulders. "Thank you."

"Sure." He clicked his fingers and his dogs leaped to their feet. "Let's do this."

And they set off, with Erwin and a group of guards trailing behind them. Markus was silent, seeming focused on their route, and she said nothing, content to follow his lead as she angled her chin down and breathed in the heady, earthy scent of his jacket.

It was a good spot, not too far from the palace grounds. Mark set up a few flashlights in the fading light as he explained his choice to Ava—no tree branches overhead, a safe distance from surrounding growth—before passing her a pair of gardening gloves and asking her to help make a pit and fire ring.

"Will you wear gloves?" she asked, accepting them with a light frown.

He tried not to smirk. "No."

She tossed the gloves on the ground beside her. "Where do we start?"

He laughed as her appeal burned a little brighter. His jacket swallowed her torso and hips, and only the tips of her fingers poked out the ends of the sleeves. She'd worn fitted jeans with hiking boots, and something about all her class and elegance snuggling into his old buffalo plaid jacket—well, it did things to him.

"These pine needles have to go," he said. "Clear a pit down

to the soil. Do you want me to help, or can I go grab some rocks to form a ring?"

She'd started kneeling down before he'd finished speaking. "Go."

The mountain was untamed, providing an array of broken boulders and rocks for the task. Buck followed him back and forth, sniffing and exploring, while Bull stayed with Ava. Mark had built the ring by the time she'd finished clearing the pit, so he took her with him to gather tinder, kindling, and fuel wood.

"They'll go easy on you," she said, gathering sticks. "At the press conference."

He glanced over, pressing his boot on a fallen sapling and pulling up to snap the dry trunk into shorter lengths.

"It's your first media appearance," she continued, adjusting the stack under her arm. "You'll usually have staff to deal with the press for you, but your people want to know you first. They want to hear you speak. You three are still a novelty. Strapping, identical cowboys." She paused, angling her head as she eyed him. "Actually, they'll always love that. But all the media want are photos to splash around and sweeping statements about your good intentions."

Similar to what the head of public relations had told him that morning. Not that all three brothers would attend, because thankfully, Mark finally had a plan.

She straightened, facing him. "Don't make any promises you mightn't be able to keep. Don't let silence compel you to fill it. Stick to the time limit. Don't allow *one last question* more than once, or they'll know you're a soft target."

"Okay." He moved his foot and pulled the slender trunk upward again. It cracked, fibers tearing, and he twisted to separate it. "Will you be there?"

She grew still. "Friday, you said?"

"Yes."

"Do you want me to be there?" She looked down as she adjusted the pile of sticks under her arm again.

"Yes." He could draw off her calm to feed his own.

Her expression was odd when she looked up. "In what capacity?"

He wouldn't tell her, not yet, but he wasn't strictly lying when he said, "Emergency decoy."

"I . . . I'd like to attend."

He smiled. "Great."

She gave a tight smile in return.

Light fading fast, he led her back to the site, and she knelt beside him, rubbing her palms together in the cool evening air. The dogs settled nearby.

"Tinder first," he said, and nodded as she made a pile of the dry leaves and twigs in the center of the pit. "Okay, now some kindling. We want this to catch while the tinder burns. Make sure you leave space, don't just stack it on—yeah, that's better— because the fire needs oxygen."

Learning seemed to unlock her features. Her face softened, pretenses falling away as genuine concentration took control. As she carefully stacked the larger sticks, his attention moved between her work and the curve of her eyebrows, the little ridge in her nose, the serious pull of her lips.

"You're amused by my concentration face again, aren't you?" She nestled a final stick on the pile before sitting back and pinning him with a stare.

"Endeared," he corrected, before he could think better of it.

Her cheeks darkened. "Oh."

He pushed on. "Now lay the larger wood in a square around the outside. This style of setup is called a log cabin. Two parallel, then another two to form a square, resting on the outside edges of the first two. That's it. And build up from there."

The sun was almost gone. Her movements were steady in the growing darkness, but her breath came a little too fast. Being outdoors at twilight had always brought him peace, but it was possible she was unsettled by the surrounding forest and lengthening shadows.

"You okay?" he asked, resting the crook of his elbow on his upraised knee.

"Yes." She said it quickly, her gaze darting to his.

"We're safe here."

"I know," she said, but when she leaned back, she brought her body closer to his.

He passed her the matches and suggested she stand upwind to avoid the breeze blowing the match out. She carefully lit the tinder in several different places and added more kindling as the pile ignited. Within a few minutes, she was stepping around the flame and crouching down beside him again, her palms extended to catch the heat.

"Good work." He reached for his pack. "You've made a campfire."

Her smile shone in the firelight.

"And now for tradition." Grinning, he held up several packets.

"Marshmallows?" She sounded incredulous. "We're not children."

"Trust me." He'd brought marshmallows, chocolate, and the closest thing his staff could find to graham crackers. "You warm up, I'll handle dessert."

She tucked her knees up against her chest and zipped his jacket over her shins. A ball of warmth. If Kris were here, he wouldn't be able to resist nudging her over. With a small sound of pleasure, she held her palms out again. "Smells good."

"Yeah." The cool air, the tang of burning leaves, the smoke. The contrast of warmth and light amidst the press of a cold night. The solitude of nature, away from fancy halls and expectation.

"How did you know I'd get cold?" She wriggled her shoulders to indicate the jacket.

"It was more to protect you from flyaway sparks." He chose two sticks from the spare kindling pile, then held the ends in the flame, figuring she'd appreciate the sterilization. "They can put holes in clothes."

"Oh." She whipped her head around, one hand catching her balance as she stared into the trees behind them. "Did you hear that?"

He glanced over his shoulder. It had been a crunch and a snort, general sounds of life. Buck and Bull had looked up, alert, but hadn't bothered to stand. They were used to wild animals at night.

"It wasn't close," he said, and resumed threading marshmallows onto sticks. "Most animals stay away from fire. And"—because he'd be risking more than himself if he hadn't asked—"security assured me predators don't come this close to the city. Not that there are many in these mountains anyway."

"Predators," she repeated, and squirmed her knees out of the jacket to move closer to him.

He pretended not to notice just how *much* closer she'd come, but really, he was at the mercy of the soft attraction in his chest. It felt like an innocent part of her was clutching the hem of his heart and tugging him a little nearer. He'd scarcely have to sway for their shoulders to touch. "It's more likely to be a fox. And if anything does come too close, we've got the dogs here and half a dozen guards over that crest."

Not to mention me, he almost added.

"I'm sure you could handle it." She cast him a glance that sought confirmation.

"You're safe," he said with a smile. Then he held a marshmallow-topped stick in front of her.

She accepted it cautiously. "Are we roasting them?"

"Sure are." He put his into the flame, smiling again when she followed suit.

"Markus," she said, quietly, as they waited. "What's it like to be alone?"

His smile faded. What kind of question was that?

"I don't mean lonely." Her gaze swung to where he rolled his stick, and immediately, she started doing the same. "I know how that feels, even in a room full of people. I mean alone."

He frowned. "You were alone when I visited you the other day."

She breathed out a humorless laugh. "Gul was directly outside. He is always outside, if not right behind me. I like him. Love him, I think. But I don't know what it feels like to be alone —to be able to do whatever I want and not have someone watching or listening or simply knowing that I'm doing it."

He wondered, briefly, what things she had done with Gul standing directly outside while knowing exactly what she was doing. Had she taken lovers? Did her guard have to pat them down, run a security check, before they could be left alone with her? Mark's gut dropped. As king, would *he* face that kind of thing before he could be with a woman? Alarmed by the thought, he focused on her question.

"It's calming." He stared into the fire. "My mind slows down and only keeps pace with the things that matter. I used to go hiking or riding away from the ranch so I could forget the things I had to do."

"Does it feel . . . weird?" She twirled her stick. "Not to have another person nearby?"

"Not at all."

She nodded.

"Don't you have a royal bolt-hole?" he asked, thinking of the hunting cabin. "Somewhere secluded you could go for solitude?"

She blinked at him. "You have no idea where my home is, do you?"

He grimaced.

"It's in the center of Kelehar's capital city. The palace is like a crystal heart in a glass body, enclosed by skyscrapers of windows and hotels reflecting the blue of the gulf. The glittering pierces the eye and the heat is smothering. There's nowhere to go for peace and solitude. We have several royal safe houses, but I wouldn't be alone there either." She paused, her eyes widening. "My marshmallow appears to be on fire."

"Blow on it." He jammed his stick into the earth beside him, frowning. She made it sound like she lived in captivity. Always guarded, always surrounded. She didn't have the freedom of leaving her home to go walking alone or riding with the sturdy companionship of a horse. He held out two crackers, one holding a square of chocolate. "Lay it on here."

Yet he'd always had that freedom—right up until this past week. Suddenly, her existence held a mirror to his future. He would forever walk around the palace observed. Guards would follow him, inside and out, and Adam had mentioned security cameras. As king, his whereabouts would always be known. Even at the cabin, where he'd imagined finding peace and solitude.

He'd never be alone again.

"What's the matter?" Her attention flicked to him as she positioned the charred stick.

"Nothing." He forced a smile, squeezing her marshmallow with the crackers. "Pull the stick out." She did, slowly, and then he passed her the lot. "Eat up."

She made a sound of delighted horror when a sticky dollop landed on the ground. "It's so messy."

He grinned. "Have fun."

In response, she laughed—*laughed*—and leaned just far enough to nudge her shoulder against his. It was everything he could do to keep his shock from showing—to ignore the impulse to wrap an arm around her, pull her to his side, and eat the s'more from her hand. He wanted her outraged squeal. Her wriggling body against him. Her throaty laugh as he licked her fingers clean. Wanted, perhaps, the slow slide of what might happen next. Blood heating, he busied himself with his own crackers.

Campfires never failed to break down barriers.

This time, it might have broken down too many.

"Approved," she said, rubbing her empty hands together. "Now tell me why you looked panicked. I'll help if I can."

Hooking an arm over his knee, he held his s'more loose in his hand. "I guess," he said, and sighed. "I guess the more I talk to you, the more I realize how much my life has to change."

Looking down, she didn't answer.

"Not just never being alone," he said. "Or being no one's equal. But—" Regret made him hesitate. "I came so close to having my life partner chosen for me. That shouldn't happen to anyone."

She kept her face lowered.

"I'm sorry," he said, shifting, facing her properly. They were close, his knee almost touching hers. "For not refusing the whole thing sooner. For putting you through that."

"I've always known." The words were quiet. "I was forewarned so that I could take measures against falling in love with anyone else."

He quickly leashed his curiosity. He could *not* ask whether she'd succeeded.

"Ava," he said. "I'd like to think you're safe here, yet your bodyguards shadow you everywhere." Much more closely than his own guards. When not standing right beside her, Gul always waited directly outside the door. It was outrageously strict surveillance. At least his guards hung back, pretending they weren't there. He offered her his sweet-filled crackers as he said, "Is there a reason for it?"

She accepted his dessert carefully, her fingers not touching his. Then she looked to the stars and said, "Yes." Without elaborating, she started eating.

His curiosity bulged. He hadn't thought much about her— hadn't wanted to—but now they'd lowered their swords, he wondered about this prickly princess and her strange, guarded life. And the more he considered her, the more he questioned.

There was Gul, and the conversation Mark had overheard in the rose garden. Cyrus had given her something so that she could marry someone she wanted. Did she have a person in mind? Was that why she'd forbidden Mark to touch her? Troubled, he'd tugged on that line of questioning a few times. *You're not allowed to touch me.* She'd excused it on her rank, no one touched a princess, but her tension hinted that the reason lay buried under a heavier stone.

He slanted a sideways glance at her as a fresh memory surfaced, a dark shadowy thing with cries like a creature lost in the night. Cyrus had been there that day, and Gul, and neither man had been confused or alarmed. They clearly knew the reason for her grief. But concern left him wondering whether knowing was the same as helping.

He skewered another marshmallow and stuck it in the fire. Too many questions, and few he could ask. "What does Zara do?"

"Zara? She runs a women's shelter. For victims of domestic violence, though she says most of her residents are the children of victims." Ava's voice was neutral, detached. She pressed her fingertips together and apart, playing with the sticky residue. "It's her whole life. She pours every part of herself into it—does everything she can to help. Counselling, support groups, and skills workshops for women whose partners have prevented them from working. But she's also set up in-house education programs for the kids, and even gives male victims hotel vouchers to escape crisis, because she can't take them into a safe space for women."

He frowned. "Is there high demand for a women's shelter in Kiraly?"

Her lips pinched as she returned his look. "There's high demand worldwide, Markus."

His frown became a scowl. "What kind of scumbag mistreats women?" Then he paused as a memory rose in him like nausea. Silhouettes on a dark country road, six, maybe seven men, bodies jerking and shifting as they punched and kicked at two limp forms on the gravel—then scattering, worming away from justice as the headlights hit them, leaving their victims like an abandoned game of ball. Leaving Tommy lying there beside his bleeding best friend. Mark swallowed the image down. "Or mistreats anyone," he finished quietly.

She didn't answer him as she held her hands out toward the fire.

He refocused on the information she'd shared. "Zara doesn't have an easy line of work."

"No. She's the best person. Even though she's never received more than a dribble of funding, she keeps pushing on. She even mentored me in setting up a shelter in Kelehar, as if she has spare time for that."

"You started your own shelter?" Surprise pushed his brows up.

Cynicism lurked in the glance she gave him. "Can't believe I have a philanthropic streak?"

"I can," he said, too quickly.

Her arched brow betrayed that she didn't believe him.

"Okay, I can *now*," he said as the fire popped. "You met Zara last time you were here?" A natural extension of the conversation, but she suddenly went stiff and still and silent. "Must be good to catch up with her again. And tomorrow night should be fun."

"Oh. About that." She twisted her lips. "I'm not sure I'll attend."

Disappointment prompted him to lean closer to her. Voice lowered, he said, "Please come."

Her gaze snapped to his chest. There was a firmness in her expression as she looked back up. "Are these cowboy manners? Because I can't imagine you want me there."

"I want you there."

He hardly knew why, just that he *did*.

She swallowed. "You asked Zara first. I was an afterthought."

"You would have said no if Zara wasn't coming." Rueful, he smiled. "You said no anyway."

"Yes, but I didn't mean it," she said sharply.

His smile became an easy laugh, and he ran a hand through his hair.

"There's another reason." She tilted her chin up. "I don't know how to dance—not like I'm just a person at a bar in Kiraly." She picked up her roasting stick and distractedly snapped it in half. "I'm confident there will be dancing tomorrow night, and I don't want people to look at me. So I'll pass."

Gesturing to the open forest floor, he said, "I can show you how to dance like you're in a bar."

"No!"

Her cheeks colored, and he realized too late his voice had roughened with his suggestion. He lifted his palms. "Just a thought."

"We dance differently in Kelehar," she said. "I can't learn your straight-bodied shifting in a day. And what if someone films me trying tomorrow night and puts it online? I'd be the ungainly princess that goes viral."

His smile returned. "I'm sorry to break it to you, especially knowing how delighted you were to finally be called chirpy, but no one will ever, ever call you ungainly."

A blush darkened her cheeks again, and she gave a small smile. "Oh."

"You can't be every adjective, you know," he said.

With a lift of her shoulder, she said, "I feel like I'm not very many of the good ones."

"You're so many of the good ones, it's downright greedy." It should have bothered him how easily they sprung to mind. "Intelligent. Composed. Elegant. Observant. Bold."

"Five," she said after a moment. "Five adjectives. That really disproves my point."

"Sarcastic," he added.

"Not a good one." She rolled her eyes, turning away.

"You don't have to dance tomorrow night. I'll sit with you."

She jerked her head around, her eyes questioning.

"I've outgrown dance floors," he said, and wondered whether it was a bad sign that he didn't regret the offer.

"Oh." She hesitated for so long, he was sure she'd refuse. Then she offered a tiny smile. "All right. I've been nervous thinking about it." She paused. "I'll drive. Let's leave just after dinner."

Wait. Her bodyguards practically walked on her heels. "You'll drive?"

"Didn't you think a princess from Kelehar would know how to handle our largest export?" She was still smiling a little. "My parents left a few of our cars behind. You and Kris can meet us in the garage."

"Okay," he said, before noting she hadn't mentioned Tommy. She didn't assume he would attend, nor had she made a sideways attempt to glean information about him. Her sharp edges were softening without the threat of marriage, because granting Tommy that secrecy was almost . . . considerate.

Another, more surprising, adjective.

"I've had enough campfire for one night," she said. "The ground is hard and cold."

"Yeah, it is. You go." He stood with her—Buck and Bull leaping up beside him—and patted down the back of his jeans. He'd make sure the fire was well and truly out before he left. "I'll stay a while longer."

"Okay." She unzipped the jacket he'd lent her. "Thank you for this."

He raised his palms. "Keep it for the walk back."

Her hands stilled. "Are you sure?"

"I'm not saying keep it forever." He grinned. "It's my favorite jacket."

She winced. "I've wiped my sticky hands all over it."

"Then your next lesson had better be in the palace laundry."

Her answering grin nearly cracked his heart right open. It made her look so . . . *sweet.*

"Off you go." Distractedly, he ruffled Buck on the head. "See you tomorrow night."

"Okay." She snuggled back into his jacket. "Bye, Markus."

Her unusually commonplace farewell floated between them like a little bubble of vulnerability. No witty send-off or formal parting, but two words intended just for him, and for a heartbeat, the air contracted between them. A frown tugged between her brows as her gaze skirted over his lips and a shiver passed down his spine.

Then he turned to the fire, murmured, "Bye," and silently cursed irony for outdoing itself. The very woman he'd refused to marry, *promised* not to pursue—

And he was falling for her.

12

The next morning, Ava found Kristof in one of the palace libraries. He sat at a computer, typing faster than her eyes could follow. His profile was fierce, his body rigid. If she hadn't met him before, she might have decided not to interrupt.

Determined, she left Gul by the dictionaries and padded toward the prince in her soft flats, carrying caution and shame in equal measure.

When she wafted too close, Kris jerked around, minimizing the browser. His brows shot up and his mouth settled in a sneer.

"Hey there," he said.

It startled her all over again—how exactly he looked like Markus. From the cut of his features to the way muscle formed along his arms and torso. They'd grown the same—bulked up the same. Powerful, capable men, yet she could never mistake them. Markus had a grounding presence. Honest, calm. There was something immovable about him, like his kindness had roots deep enough to withstand any force. Last night, she'd known there was no safer place than by his side. Not just in the forest . . . anywhere.

But Kris—

He rippled with energy.

His broad, rancher build seemed to barely contain it. Restlessness. Frustration. Volatility, and a kind of dangerous sex appeal. It threw her off balance to face a man who looked like Markus but triggered a warning low in her chest. This brother was not safe.

"Just here to look, are you, sweetheart?" He'd leaned back in the chair, one palm loosely splayed on the desk. His head was angled in challenge.

The question curled her lip.

Markus would never mock her.

"I wanted to apologize for a comment of mine." Though he wasn't exactly evoking her remorse. "You're not a fool."

"That's a relief." His voice was hard. "I was on the verge of self-destruction."

"You don't like me," she said. "At all."

"Don't know why you'd think that."

She didn't bite. "You're more sarcastic than Markus."

"Everyone's more sarcastic than Mark. But Tommy's worse than me. You two would get on well."

"I'm not being sarcastic." She held his gaze, despite how it judged her. "I am sorry."

"Yeah, I know."

She frowned. They'd only met once before. "Then what makes you think I'm sarcastic enough to get on with Tommy?"

"You were going to marry my brother." He drummed his fingers on the desk, his gaze unwavering. "I asked around."

And he'd been told she was sarcastic? She really didn't have any good adjectives. "Who did you ask?"

His blue eyes glinted, but his silence refused to reveal his sources.

"What else did they say?" She crossed her arms, a nervous wring in her stomach. She had no idea what her staff thought of her, and that realization made her shamefully aware of how little attention she paid to them.

"One said you're so serious, you border on being brittle. Another admitted that you smile, sometimes, and appreciate those close to you." He eyed her oddly. "And another said that you were very sad."

Her pulse hitched and she said swiftly, "I can be a bit pathetic."

He gazed at her, silent, like he could sense her misdirection.

She clicked her tongue, uncomfortable. Her gaze moved to the computer. "You're working hard."

"When you want something done right . . ."

"You looked stressed." She kept the topic on him. "Stir-crazy. Do you hate it here?"

"I'm with my brothers," he said, not quite an answer. "Mark tells me we're going out tonight."

"Yes." She hesitated. "If you want to come."

"If *I* want to come?" He all but scoffed. "Inviting me to hang out with my own brother?"

"Perhaps you don't want to," she said coolly, and having done what she'd come to do, turned to leave.

"Hey," Kris said, and she looked back at his harsh tone. "Mark doesn't deserve to be curled around your finger."

Affronted, she said, "It wasn't my idea to go out."

"I'm suspicious of behavioral one-eighties," he said, ignoring her defense. "You were wicked to Mark. Now you're spending every spare second with him. If your plan is to change his mind about the marriage, then fair warning, you're not going to want me as a brother-in-law."

She tossed cold words onto the scald of that insult. "If that's what you think I'm doing, then you really are a fool, Kristof."

And she left him, discomfort leaning hard in her chest at the distrust she'd caught twisting his lips, as if he somehow knew that she'd slept in his brother's jacket the night before.

It was no surprise to Mark that Tommy refused to head into Kira City, nor was it unexpected that Kris was so keen for a night on the town that he pulled out his favorite shirt, vest, and neckerchief to wear with his jeans and boots. When they entered the royal garage after dinner, they found Ava and Cyrus waiting beside a lustrous cream car. The pair frowned as Mark and Kris approached.

"Good evening," Cyrus said pleasantly. He wore an olive-green, long-sleeved tunic over black pants, his outfit achieving a casual kind of refinement.

Ava had chosen a simpler style, possibly believing she was capable of passing as a regular citizen. The combination was right—burgundy jeans and a silk shift, her hair in a high ponytail —but somehow, the result was conspicuously beautiful. He recognized the jeans from their gardening day and swore the fabric had been tailored to grasp her body and hers alone.

He tried not to stare as she eyed Kris over and asked bluntly, "What are you wearing?"

Kris gave a sardonic smile. "Cowboy."

"Giveaway," she corrected with a frown. "I thought we were trying not to attract attention."

Kris snorted. "I never agreed to that."

"We're going into the city. It's implied."

"Not to me," he said. "Is this the part where you call me a fool again? Keep up the trend?"

She inhaled sharply.

"Let's go," Mark said, with a silencing frown at Kris. What was his problem? "Zara's waiting for us."

They piled in, brothers in the back, Cyrus in the front with Ava. The car was impressive, particularly compared to Mark's old farm truck. The upholstery was plush, not wearing thin; the gearstick seemed to move beneath Ava's palm like rushing liquid, not requiring any wrenching or cursing; and the steering wheel was the same flawless cream as the exterior paint, worlds away from his truck's simple vinyl.

In the city, she navigated down a narrow, cobbled alley and pulled into a single parking spot behind a cluster of multi-storied buildings in honey-colored stone. The Kiralian security team parked across the entrance to the laneway, and another pulled up at the opposite end, blocking it off. The guards hung back, granting the young royals a semblance of privacy, and even Erwin waited at a distance. A third team had come ahead, waiting for them inside the bar.

"Where do we go?" Cyrus smoothed the front of his tunic as he glanced around.

"Hey, Ava!" Zara's call came from one end of the laneway. "They won't let me through!"

"She's with us." Ava raised a hand at the guards.

In a blur of gray and bright yellow, Zara bolted across the distance and threw herself around Ava in a hug. "You guys really came!" When Zara sprang back, she scanned the men around her with a smile. "Anyway, how about we go and—oh, mother—" She clamped a hand over her mouth and dropped into a sharp curtsey. Her voice was stifled as she said, "Hey, Your Majesty. Your Highnesses."

Mark smiled, Kris grinned, and Cyrus looked at her lowered head with a fondness that suggested he'd met her before.

Ava looked at her friend, helpless.

"Good to see you again, Zara." Mark slid a hand into his back pocket. "Kris doesn't stand on ceremony either. Don't worry about it."

Zara straightened, looking apologetic. "Sorry, I can't believe how shit I am at propriety." Kris laughed as Zara's gaze slid to Cyrus. She tucked her hair behind her ear as she said, "I didn't think you'd come."

He frowned slightly. "Is it a problem?"

"Of course not," she said, her voice strained.

"Zara's invited her housemate tonight," Ava said, and looked at Mark. "Apparently, you'll know him."

How? Before he could ask, Zara gestured for everyone to follow her.

They moved along the alley toward an even narrower lane that ran between two buildings. It was as wide as Mark's shoulders and zigzagged in the middle, concealing the end from the start, but then they emerged into a sheltered courtyard so intense in its liveliness, he came to a halt.

The sound was loud, inviting, like a stranger throwing a welcoming arm around his shoulders and dragging him inside. People packed around tables, slapping surfaces in agreement, disagreement, and hysterics—shouting, laughing and gesturing, leaning against each other and embracing, and it all came together in a bellow of enthusiasm. Music underpinned the cacophony, an easy beat coming out the large open doors across the way. And as if the people didn't energize the space well enough, brightly colored bunting was strung in crisscrosses above them, stretching from balcony to balcony of the surrounding buildings, doubled-up with strings of fairy lights that sparkled in the darkening night.

"Welcome to the Bearded Bunting," Zara said, waving an arm before her. "I know the manager. Tonight, the bouncers have strict instructions to screen those entering and kick any indiscreet bastard out on the street—provided your guards don't beat them to it. You won't be bothered here."

"Thanks, Zara." Ava stood at the rear of their small group,

her back to the alleyway, her gaze shifting around the space. Her features were a mask of neutrality—just like that of the venue's security guard beside her, acting as if he hadn't admitted a group of the world's elite.

"Our table's over there." Zara set off, aiming for a vacant spot in the far corner.

Sensing Ava's unease in the crowd, Mark moved close beside her. Not close enough when a sudden holler made her jump, but then too close when her elbow brushed against his arm and fastened reaction around him like a clenched fist. She darted a glance at him, bottom lip disappearing between her teeth. He'd never seen her do that. She looked—startled by him.

His focus narrowed. She was softer than she let on. She'd betrayed herself last night, swallowed by his jacket, her features glowing in the firelight. She'd been willing to learn, to get her hands dirty. Unsure in the wild outdoors, God help him, and inching closer to his side. He'd imagined putting his arm around her countless times since, and now, he ached to draw her against him in this crowd.

She didn't look at him again, but when they reached the table, she sidled onto the wooden bench beside him, their backs to the wall, facing the boisterous bar. Cyrus sat on her other side, while Kris and Zara faced them.

"Cool kerchief thing," Zara said to Kris, reaching out to toy with the drinks menu.

Kris sent Ava a self-satisfied glance. "Thanks."

"I assume you left your six-shooters in the wagon?" Zara asked. "Also, just a heads up, this place has a strict no lassos policy."

Ava's smile was smug.

Kris adjusted the kerchief, running his tongue along the front of his teeth. "Montana's not laughing."

"Who wants a drink?" Zara asked next, glancing over her

slouched shoulder to scan the crowd. She turned back around, looking edgy. "My shout."

Ava slipped a note from her pocket and pressed it into Zara's hand. "The only shouting you'll be doing tonight is above this racket. Something with bubbles, please."

"I'll go with you," Cyrus murmured, sliding back out.

After a glance between Mark and Ava, Kris raised his brows and also headed into the bar.

For a while the two of them sat without speaking, observing the crammed courtyard. Mark tried to concentrate on nearby conversations, in case he overheard anything valuable about his city or people, but her presence rerouted his every thought right back to her. She was a constant tug beside him, the nearness of her body drawing at his skin. Her arm was close to his, warm and bare, and awareness coiled through him, heating, tightening.

"You okay here?" He pressed his back against the wall, trying to ground himself, but the hard render just increased the lure of her softness.

She nodded, her spine straight, her shoulders set perfectly. She didn't look at him. "It's fun."

He smiled wryly. Sure. He believed that.

"Did you get your jacket?" she asked.

"Yeah, Adam brought it in. Thanks."

She nodded again, her attention shifting up to the bunting and lights.

"Do you wish Gul were here?"

That earned him a surprised glance. "No. I told him to go out and enjoy himself."

"I meant to protect you."

"Oh," she said, her gaze dropping to his shoulder and back up. "No, Erwin's here."

He nodded, frowning. "You know, I've been racking my brains trying to come up with a way to get you alone."

Her stare was shocked as color rushed over her cheeks.

His gut dropped. That had come out wrong.

"Completely alone," he added swiftly.

"Pardon?" she said, her eyes still wide. Could she tell, just by looking, that her nearness made his pulse judder—that he was starting to gnaw at his promise not to touch her, feeling it drawing him back like a bit between his teeth? "You want me completely alone?"

"No, I—" Well, *yes,* it was starting to seem that way. He pushed a palm over his mouth. "I meant alone by yourself."

"Oh." She let out a breath. It was a while before she said, "You would help me?"

"I see no reason you shouldn't feel what it's like."

"You wouldn't."

"Do you?" he asked, because it was possible that even she guarded herself.

Sadness spilled over her face, and she hesitated before saying, "I ran away from my parents once." Her words were hushed. "The last time I was here in Kiraly. That's when I met Zara. I was alone, being entirely useless and unhelpful to myself. I'm lucky I found her." She glanced at a group at a nearby table as they erupted in laughter. "I'm no good to myself on my own."

Mark didn't answer as the others rounded the doorway to the courtyard, drinks in hand. The other patrons didn't outwardly acknowledge them, but the crowd parted at just the right moment to allow Kris to lead the way unobstructed.

"God, it's a jungle in there," Zara announced, slumping back down at the table and sliding a glass of bubbles to Ava. "I mistakenly hoped being accompanied by two charismatic princes might speed our wait, but clearly nothing comes between a drinker and their place in the bar queue."

Cyrus smiled, sitting next to Zara. "Their eye contact avoidance was masterful."

"Thanks for sticking with it." Mark accepted the glass Kris slid his way.

"Sure. So how was everyone's day?" Zara said next, before picking up her glass and tipping it back. After a few seconds, it became clear that she intended to drink to the finish.

Kris watched her, his brows creased, while Cyrus shifted his shoulders to face her, seeming alarmed. Ava raised a hand to her eyes.

As Mark wondered whether the night was going to get messy fast, his gaze caught on a familiar face in the crowd. Blond and round-faced, the man was scanning the courtyard looking distinctly uncomfortable. Frowning, he called out, "Adam?"

Adam glanced around, and Mark raised a hand to beckon him over. Zara slammed her glass down, her features rigid. She didn't turn to look.

"Hey, man." Mark smiled as Adam came to stand behind Zara, Cyrus, and Kris. Surprise filled the blond man's face as his attention moved from Mark to Ava beside him, possibly remembering their conversation about her temperament and wondering what had changed.

"Your Majesty." Adam bowed. He then flicked a look at each of the faces at the table and bowed again. "Your Highnesses."

"What are you—" Mark stopped as he realized. "You're Zara's housemate?"

"Yes." With the group watching on, Adam turned his attention on the only non-royal at the table. "Zara," he said quietly, his gaze lingering on the side of her face. "I'm here."

"Yeah, hey," she said, not turning around.

Cyrus turned to eye the newcomer with a level stare.

"You look nice tonight, Zara," Adam said.

She ducked her head a little, a faint blush on her cheeks, and Mark realized that despite her casual jacket and coarse attitude, she really did look nice. Her straight black hair had a loose curl woven through it, she seemed to be wearing makeup, and a delicate necklace hung on her chest.

Adam ran a hand down his opposite arm, casting a concerned glance around the table. "Can I talk to you?"

When Zara didn't move, except to slide a strange sideways glance at Cyrus, Ava said, "Zara," and delivered a blatant kick under the table. "Go talk with Adam."

Cursing nervously under her breath, Zara shoved herself away from the table and into the crowd. With a pained smile of thanks at Ava, Adam turned and trailed behind her.

Kris turned back with a wince. "Not exactly an auspicious start."

Ava glared. "Not one word against her."

Cyrus said nothing as he turned back around, his features neutral.

The music suddenly cranked louder. Applause broke out and everyone was up, pushing tables to the walls with the benches beneath, and swiftly stacking plates and glasses. Mark and the others watched on from behind a barrier of vacated tables, now piled with dumped handbags and jackets, as a buoyant, contagious energy rippled through the makeshift dance floor.

Kris was out of his seat within seconds, instantly lost in the mass. Cyrus lingered, eyes on his brandy, until his shoulders began to move, his head along with them, and then with a sheepish smile at his sister, he also slid off to dance.

When Ava sent Mark a quick glance, he smiled back, still relaxed against the wall behind them.

"You should go too," she said.

"I said I'd stay."

She sipped her bubbles and said with a wave of her hand, "I was being childish."

It was with thoughts far from childish that Mark murmured firmly, "I'm staying with you."

This time, with a cautious flick of her eyes and a smile on the blushing side of shy, she didn't argue.

"Zara, please wait."

Out the front of the bar, Zara finally turned to Adam. The loud beat of the music was muted out here, the night air cooler, thinner. Feeling more exposed without the shroud of heat and noise, she crossed her arms and stared at the shirt buttons on his chest as he stopped in front of her.

"I shouldn't have invited you," she said, a little dizzy from alcohol and the fact that two halves of her heart had just met inside. Cyrus might be a celebrity crush, but she'd fallen for Adam. A real and everyday kind of guy, even if his quiet self-reliance had seemed mysterious. "I like you—and you've packed your things," she said, and watched him stiffen. "Yeah, I noticed."

"Zara." His soft voice grew even quieter as he reached out and took hold of her hand. His fingers were warm, his grip stronger and more assertive than she'd expected.

He tugged her toward him, but she refused to budge, rolling her shoulder forward instead.

"Let me explain," he said. "I never meant to hurt you."

"Don't," she said, before his thumb brushed over the back of her hand and she was lost to a shower of shivers. Then she pulled out of his hold. "You're only saying this out of guilt because I've told you I like you. I don't need you to let me down gently. I'm already down. Please just leave."

"This isn't guilt," he said. "Look at me."

Hating her own weakness, she did as he asked—and weakened further, suspended in his steady gaze.

"Here's the truth," he said. "I was promoted to be manservant to King Markus the day after the royal family tragedy. The late king's manservant had resigned due to grief, and I'd worked hard to stand out. I came home to tell you that night." His blue eyes were wide with sincerity. "But you were distraught. It was the night—" His voice lowered. "You'd found out a woman who'd left your shelter had gone into intensive care. I came in, and you were crying on the kitchen tiles. I'd never seen you like that."

Anguish surged through her at the reminder. She hadn't realized he'd been there.

"Suddenly," Adam continued, "my work was weak, and my promotion was irrelevant. My position in the palace ensures the privileged remain that way—the very people who don't fund domestic violence support services. But your labor protects the vulnerable, Zara. You do it for the betterment of your community. You fight for women and enable their freedom and safety, working hard and selflessly as you do it." He paused and she looked up, stunned at his earnestness. "I didn't tell you about the promotion because I didn't want you to think less of me."

Disbelief left her staring.

"My job contributes nothing of value to society," he said, "while you give everything you have and more. You're brave and enduring—and I'm pompous and preened, and even if I were ten times the man I am, I wouldn't come close to the courageous woman you are."

"Oh, my God." Was he seriously telling the truth? "So . . . why are your bags packed?"

His expression flickered. "You're too good for me," he said. "I worked myself up into a mood one night, convinced you'd be better sharing your home with someone more like you."

"Stop it." She reached out, taking his hand in a tight grip. "I don't think less of you. I just want you to talk to me."

"I can do that," he said, his gaze on her as he brushed his thumb over her knuckles.

Nervous energy squirmed in her chest.

"All right," he said. "I guess that means I can stop avoiding you in an attempt to escape my own inadequacies."

"Yes, you can," she said, because she couldn't think of anything else to say. Then she shoved him lightly in the shoulder, smiling.

He caught her hand, now holding them both. "I don't want to move out. Not away from you."

She lowered her head, not daring to believe him.

"It's your call." His grip shifted, fingers threading through hers. "I'm genuinely sorry for upsetting you. You're just . . . intimidating in more ways than one."

Thrown, she snorted. "I'm sloppy and unsophisticated. I say stupid things because I can't keep my mouth shut, and swear like a sailor. What's intimidating about that?"

"For a man like me? Everything." But he smiled. "Will you dance with me, Zara?"

She grinned as delight made her head a different kind of dizzy. "Yes please."

He hadn't left her side.

Ava sat still as the courtyard pulsed with movement, arms pumping, bodies shifting, inhibitions checked at the door. Color was everywhere and she admired clothes of vivid turquoise, flame red, and mint green. She saw glimpses of laughing women, seemingly drawn to the untamed cowboy prince like beetles to a lantern, and before long, she spotted Zara dancing with Adam. Even Cyrus had disappeared into the crowd. The atmosphere enveloped her with its thriving energy, and she watched the dancing, the singing, the fits of laughter, all the while unable to tear her mind away from the man beside her.

Markus leaned back against the wall, his legs extended beneath the table. His hand rested on the tabletop, his fingers curled loosely around his beer. Relaxed and companionable, in no way did he give the impression that sitting with her was an obligation he'd rather be without.

His closeness pulled at her, a kind of pleasant static electricity that intensified every time he raised his bottle to his lips.

She eyed him as she shifted on the wooden bench. She wanted something to happen. She didn't know what, but her mind, her body, wanted *something* from him. A smile, a conversation to replay in her mind later, a stray touch of his hand . . .

But she'd forbidden his touch.

They hadn't spoken in four and a half songs. Nerves continued to discount any ideas she had for conversation. A question about his old life would make him wish to be on his ranch and away from her. A comment on the music might make him realize that he wanted to dance after all. A query about his absent brother might be misinterpreted as snooping. And so on, until she was convinced every possible topic would result in pushing him away.

So she sat, hands in her lap, tracking his every movement and wishing desperately that she were brave enough to break the silence.

"I've had one girlfriend in my life," he said, startling her by speaking and doubly with his topic of choice.

"Oh," she said.

"Her name was Sally." He leaned into her, leaving a wispy distance between their arms, a taut, tingly space, and continued over the noise. "We were together for almost eight years, starting when we were fourteen. By our early twenties, we'd become different people. I wanted to settle on the ranch; she wanted international adventures. It was an amicable enough ending." He nudged the bottle around on the tabletop. "Our relationship meant I had a comfortable youth, without the nerve-wracking misery of the high-school-dating scene. I'd done the hard part when I was too young to know how terrified I should have been."

Jealousy awoke in her. She had no idea why he was telling her this.

"Now," he said, "because of that, I have no idea how to flirt. Let alone tell a woman that I like her."

She inhaled sharply, dislodging the lump of hurt in her throat. "What are you getting at?" Perhaps she should have attempted conversation after all, and had the power of being the one to ruin the night. "You want me to teach you how to flirt as well as cope with being king? Because honestly, Markus, I can only handle one monumental task at a time."

"Ah." He shifted beside her, running a hand over his forehead. "No, I—" He sighed and caught her eyes. "That was me trying to tell you that I like you, Ava."

She blinked. *Oh.*

She stilled as the confession warmed her like the sun breaking through the clouds. No, not the sun. Warmed her like a rough, woolen blanket that smelled of this man, a blanket she wanted to bury into, draw closer around her until she felt the heat of her own breath as she admitted her own growing feelings.

I like you, Ava.

"Let's say I'm living in the moment tonight," she said, her heart pounding beneath her breasts. "And despite being out of practice, you decide to flirt with me anyway."

He fell still. Absolutely motionless. Yet she sensed something shifting within him, expanding, reaching for her. When he slid his attention to her, she could hardly think from the desire in his eyes.

"We could say that," he agreed, his voice coarse.

His fixed stare so close, so deliberate, released a flush deep inside her. Hot and lingering, it bloomed outward from her core. She found herself grasping the table edge. Was she really letting herself feel this after so long? *Should* she?

"First thing," he said, angling his shoulders toward her. She felt tiny beside him. "I'd follow up on our touch earlier."

Her elbow tingled. The brush of his forearm had been both insignificant and momentous.

"Okay." Her answer was breathless.

"Okay," he murmured, and his intent scrunched nerves low in her belly.

With the sun gone down, the bar was lit only by the strings of bulbs high overhead. The back corner, well away from the crowd, hid them both in shadow. No one could see him closing the distance between them, his arm pressing against hers, nor could they see the shiver that passed over her at the contact. Such a small change, to let their arms touch, but somehow it resonated within her as unspeakably intimate.

She heard his breathing grow shallow, felt the coiled tension in his arm as he pressed more firmly against her.

She actually jumped when his other hand rose to her face.

"No?" A careful question as he lowered his arm.

Swallowing, she said, "No, please, I—" and nudged his hand back up with her fingertips.

Her body strained. Every nerve, every muscle waited for contact. His body heat caressed her face a moment before his skin met hers, and she closed her eyes at his warmth. His palm was worn, well-used, but she leaned into the gentle abrasion. She wanted his touch—wanted it all over. His hand moved, his fingers traveling down her cheek, and his thumb brushed over her lips. *That* she felt right to her toes.

Opening her eyes, she met his waiting gaze. Dark blue and hazy. Nothing else existed. It was like being underwater—and only he was close enough for her to see.

Her chest hurt. He'd leaned in. His mouth was so close.

"This feels like more than flirting," she whispered.

His lips lifted at the corners. "I told you I'd forgotten how."

She started to smile back, but then he asked softly, "Have you been with anyone before?" and the moment shattered.

Yes.

How could she have forgotten? She was foolish for craving his attention, for aching for his touch. He had no place in her future—she would never see him again after tomorrow. This gorgeous man was nothing but a figure out the window on a long drive, a fleeting image of kindness and decency that she'd forget soon enough. And he'd do better to forget her.

With great effort, she masked her devastation with irritation.

"That's a strange question to ask the woman you refused to marry," she said, pulling back. "Or don't you remember that?"

He hesitated, then also drew back. Concern pulled between his brows. "You know I do, Ava."

"You remember that you promised, *promised,* not to change your mind?"

206

His voice was low. "I stand by that promise."

"Then why would you tell me that you like me?"

He shook his head, seeming at a loss. "There's a place in my chest. It's . . . disconnected from my mind. Disconnected from all the reasons it would be so much easier not to like you." He paused. "I was letting it speak."

Oh, God.

"I wonder if you've ever let that part of you speak," he said quietly.

Pain pinched in her chest.

It spoke to her all the time.

"I don't have such a thing." Her throat thickened. "I don't know what I've been thinking, spending time with you. But you're going to complicate everything, and I refuse to let that happen."

Suddenly, this gentle man at her side seemed more dangerous than the seething crowd before her.

Without another word, she went to find Cyrus.

13

"*It'd be better if we hate each other on sight.*"

Ava thrust herself through the pool, wishing the water would restore her stability because her encounter with Markus had left her teetering. She'd been wise talking to Zara when she'd first arrived last week—she'd known liking Markus would complicate everything. But after he'd refused their alliance, her caution had fallen away. Foolishly, she'd believed she'd reached safety.

Hours ago, Cyrus had driven her home from the bar and escorted her to her room. Erwin hadn't spoken as he'd followed behind, but she'd felt his curiosity. Evidently, that prompted him to send for Gul when her personal guard had returned from his own night out.

Gul had found her curled up on top of her blankets, staring at the wall.

"Oh, Princess." He'd knelt beside her bed.

Wrecked by confusion and chagrin, she'd murmured, "He likes me, Gul."

He'd paused and answered quietly, "But that's not a problem in itself, is it?"

"I like him too."

Instead of settling in for more, he'd suggested they visit the pool. She'd made a habit of swimming when her heart tried to cram itself into her head. The repetitive strokes sometimes shifted thought and feeling back into alignment, and she could swim suspended in the quiet space between.

It wasn't working. She kicked hard, tiny, fast movements, while rational thought continued to rage against raw feeling.

She'd backflipped this past week. She'd arrived knowing in her head that she might have to marry Markus and hating him in her heart. Now she knew she wouldn't wed him and liked him far too much.

It was unfair that being human allowed this mess of inconsistency. How was she even capable of appreciating a man when she knew nothing could come of it? Didn't her heart pay attention at all? And Markus—he knew she didn't want his affection. She'd once forbidden him to touch her and made him promise not to change his mind about marriage. How was it even possible for him to like her?

It was that place, she remembered, with a surge of dismay. In his chest that was disconnected from his mind.

Their hearts were both to blame.

He'd been honest, sharing everything, expecting nothing. He liked her, despite how sharp she kept her tongue—how nasty she became to protect herself. He liked her, even after she'd revealed that she was useless at real life. He hadn't laughed or thrown her incapability back in her face, as she'd surely have done to him. He'd offered to help her.

As she tumble-turned, a sunburst of joy subdued the turmoil. A blinding moment that rejoiced in the affection of such a kind man. Markus *liked* her. Then she balked, swallowed too much chlorine, and chagrin filled her once more.

He was the type of man she'd only meet once in her life, if at all.

And she had to leave him behind.

For a lap, that truth gouged her hollow. Tears merged with the water and she hauled in heaving gasps whenever she turned her head.

Then she pushed the loss down. She could do this. She swam on, longer strokes, faster kicks, and focused on her guilt. Markus deserved a woman as honest and considerate as himself. Not only was Ava selfish and unkind, but she concealed a truth so significant, every word she spoke that didn't confess it was a kind of lie.

It was better for him that she was leaving.

After pushing through another twenty laps, she pulled herself out of the water and pressed her face into a plush towel, drying her eyes, her face.

Then she saw him.

For a heart-stopping moment, she thought it was Markus. But his expression was wrong, too serious, too guarded, as were the rigid set of his shoulders and nervous energy coming out in the hand he raked across his scalp. It wasn't Kris either—his hair was too short, his tension too contained. It struck of anxiety, not volatility.

Prince Tomas.

She lowered the towel to her legs, eyeing him cautiously. This brother was uncharted territory. She'd only seen him once, at the funeral, when he'd been overcome by grief. He seemed to avoid being seen around the palace, and as far as she was aware, he hadn't set foot in the city. She'd wondered more than once what drove a man in his position to be such a recluse.

Regardless, he was here, his bare feet tapping restlessly against the gleaming white tiles from beneath faded jeans. She guessed that if she was looking at Prince Tomas, it was because he allowed it. He could have slipped away the moment he'd seen her swimming, but instead, he sat at the base of the polished concrete bleachers, shirtless, with a towel draped over one thigh. She took his presence as permission to approach.

Making her way along the pool edge toward the change rooms, she wrapped her towel around her torso and tucked the end under her arm. Tomas leaned back as she neared, not relaxed, but stiff-bodied, as if seeking to put more distance between them. His gaze was fixed on the water.

She stopped a few feet away and wrung out her hair. The water splattered lightly onto the tiles and he snapped his head toward her at the sound. On edge, this brother. His nerves threw her and before she could compose a kinder introduction, she said, "Have you just been sitting there waiting for me?"

Tomas shot her a swift glance. Sharp, piercing. Then he latched his attention back on the water. "You make it sound simple," he said, his words quiet.

She frowned. "You could have got in the water."

His lips tilted almost mockingly. "That's what I've been telling myself to do."

Half-joking, half-insulted, she said, "I don't secrete poison."

"For me, everyone does." His dry tone betrayed that he mocked himself.

She kept curiosity clear off her face, even as it reared up inside her. "I'm Ava."

"I know." He didn't introduce himself in return, nor did he look back at her.

"You know who I am?" She crossed her arms, an over-the-top gesture, because somehow, his understated reactions made her feel the need to compensate. "Well, now I'm nervous about what you've been told about me."

"Likewise."

"Nothing, actually," she admitted. "Your brothers refuse to talk about you. You're the enigmatic third prince."

"Second." And as he met her eyes again, she caught her breath. *There.* Through his anxiety, she sensed something greater staring back. Authority. Unease might muddy his surface, but beneath, Prince Tomas burned with command. Startled that out of the three brothers, it was this reclusive cowboy that ran deep with pure royal presence, she wondered whether he even knew it was there.

"Second," she repeated, still staring.

"If we're talking birth order," he added in a murmur, looking away.

She played up her reaction again, feeling like a clown even as she did so. "So technically, Kristof is the youngest." She shook her head with an exaggerated sigh. "Figures."

The edges of his mouth curved up.

Inordinately pleased to have amused him, she hid her own smile.

He said, "You take eight breaths per lap. It's a full-length pool."

She paused, her gut sinking. If he'd been counting, he'd been listening. Possibly, he'd heard the few minutes when her breaths had gulped for air, deep gasping intakes to match the struggle in her mind.

Uneasy about his perceptiveness, she arched a brow.

"As if you believe peace is at the end of the lane and you can't get there fast enough." Before she could respond, he added, "We swim the same."

"With observations like that, I'm grateful you make yourself scarce, Tomas."

He threw his gaze at her again. "I would have left when I

saw you, but I wanted to meet the woman who inspires trust in one brother and doubt in the other."

At his words, her guilt flared. "Kris is right to doubt me."

Tomas angled his face toward the tiles. If he'd been wearing a hat, she swore he'd be hiding beneath the rim. "But perhaps Mark's also right."

She shook her head.

"You returned without them tonight."

"They said they'd find their own way home."

"Home," he repeated softly, bitterly.

Her heart went out to him. If a hermit was torn from his shell, what did he have left?

"You should go." Tomas turned his head away, toward the entrance. "I'm making your man uncomfortable."

Surprised, she looked at Gul. His face was pink, his attention fixed on the concrete floor at his feet. His hair shined with product and the rims of his eyes were overly defined, dark, smoky smudges, remnants of his night out. In contrast to his imposing size, her guard was giving off the air of a shy youth.

"Oh." He got that way around beautiful men. And Tomas was a prince, and a half-naked one at that. Gul hadn't stood a chance.

Tomas ran a hand up his throat. The other hand ran along his jeans, his leg jittering beneath. "Apologize to him for me," he murmured, his gaze back on the water.

Frowning, she nodded.

The conversation was over.

She murmured a farewell and continued on her way, clinging to the distraction that meeting Tomas had offered. She changed into her clothes in the pool's powder room, thoughts on the reclusive triplet, and as she and Gul walked through the palace corridors, softly lit and silent, she identified the response that shifted through her with a strange sense of kinship.

She'd asked the wrong brother what it felt like to be alone.

"Right, spill your secrets to Auntie Zara."

Ava curled tighter beneath the covers, cradling the phone to her ear. Dawn light edged around the curtains, a new day beginning despite her sleepless night. She'd texted Zara a few minutes ago, asking to chat when her friend was awake. Her phone had rung instantly.

"You first," Ava said, her voice muffled by sheets. "I saw you dancing with Adam."

"Oh, that, yeah." Zara gave a breathless laugh. "Apparently he thinks the way I drag myself and others through life is admirable or something, and felt unworthy in comparison. We sorted it out. Then we danced. He's cute when he dances."

"And you . . . went home together," she prompted.

"Yes. Sharing an apartment kind of helped on that front. He drove me home and made me a cup of tea." Zara sounded like she was swooning and crashing at the same time. "Then he made me crazy by saying as much as he'd like to kiss me good night, he wanted to give me time to think about us, so asked if he could just hug me instead. And oh my God, all he did was hold me, but I was up for hours replaying it."

"I know the feeling." Ava's eyes stung with fatigue and her thoughts banked up in a dense clutter. "But that's wonderful, Zara. He seems like a nice man."

"He is, I think." Zara paused. "Now your turn. You left in a rush last night."

She closed her eyes. "Markus likes me."

Zara went silent, almost seeming to disappear from the line. Then Ava heard her slow exhale. "I'm sorry. I can tell you kind of like him too."

She pushed down regret. "I don't think I like reading at bus stops." What if she wasn't ready for the story to end?

"I'm sorry," her friend said again.

"I can't be here anymore."

"Yeah," Zara said, her voice subdued. "By later today, you won't be."

Tonight, at five-thirty: the revised escape plan. The other reason she hadn't slept.

"Yes," she whispered.

"Just think about that, okay? It'll get you through the day. I'll see you then. Don't be late."

Her friend's parting words were like an affectionate tweak on the nose, so with a small smile of terrified anticipation, Ava said, "I won't."

Mark slept poorly, because in some wishful corner of his subconscious, he kept thinking Ava was lying next to him. He couldn't shake the sensation of her arm pressed close, her soft breath on the side of his face, her warm body eliciting his thick-blooded desire. How many times he rolled into the empty sheet, desperate to drag her closer, he didn't want to know, but it took waking from a particularly roused reach and coming up empty for him to fully realize what was going on. He didn't just like her.

He *wanted* her.

God have mercy, as if his life wasn't complicated enough.

He'd awoken—definitively alone—to the curtains opening and had ended up on a couch in his sitting room, Adam awkwardly seated opposite.

"It was good to see you at the bar." Mark's eyes were gritty, his blood still too thick. He wanted to find Ava, talk to her, draw her near.

"Yes," Adam agreed, his expression pleasant. After a moment, he sipped his tea.

"Zara seems great."

"She is," he replied, nodding, and then eyed him a little too long. "Mark, I want to be a good fit as your first man. And that means more than providing you with room service and sharing our morning beverage. I hope in time, you'll grow to trust me and share the thoughts that weigh you down. I'm here to ease that burden."

Ava's warning caught him before he answered. He and Adam were not equals, and treating his first man like a friend disrespected the man's position. As much as Mark resented the idea of turning down a genuine offer of help, he had to start acting like a king.

"Thanks, Adam, but I'm not sure you'd understand," he said, not unkindly. *And nor should you.* This overwhelming pressure was for a king's shoulders, not those of his first man.

Adam inclined his head. "Then personal matters, perhaps."

Discomfort made Mark's shirt feel tight at the shoulders. Okay. So maybe they were going to discuss Ava, because he could use an opinion from someone who wasn't Kris. The repeated words, "*I don't trust her,*" hardly helped.

Sighing, he said, "I can't stop thinking about Ava. Last night, I was honest with her, and she bolted."

Adam was silent for a while. "Last night," he said eventually. "When I asked how Zara knew Princess Ava, she reminded me that she deals in brave people. And that Ava is exceptionally brave. Pardon my language, but her words were more along the lines of, *on the bullshit level of brave, like you can't even believe anyone in her position could keep walking.* Zara didn't provide specifics, but it made me wonder. Perhaps

Ava's not scared of your feelings, per se, but scared of the unexpectedness of them."

Mark's concern swelled, along with a growling protectiveness. "I don't want to push her."

The man pulled a face of apology. "As I've recently learned firsthand, avoidance isn't the best method of problem-solving when it comes to relationships."

"No. You're right."

Not that he was seeking a relationship, and Ava certainly wasn't, but he didn't want to end their strange, brief encounter by frightening her away. What he *wanted* was to kiss her, and he was sure from the hazy look he'd seen in her eyes last night that she wanted it too. He tapped his coffee cup. He'd give her space for the morning.

Then he'd find out where they stood.

Ava spent the morning and early afternoon in gut-wrenching anticipation. She drifted around the palace, forcing herself to admire the view from the high glass-walled corridors, angle her head to read the spines of books in the largest library, and deal with the simultaneous agony and ecstasy of waiting by pushing herself into a sweaty disaster in the gym. It was Gul's day off, so she couldn't even distract herself with tales of his night out.

Eventually, Erwin suggested she might like to pot another plant for her windowsill, so she ended up in the greenhouse, filling a burnt orange pot with soil. Apprehension had bunched in her stomach since Cyrus had first told her about the meeting tonight, but now it snarled and tangled, a constant ache right across her middle. Her hands trembled as she worked.

Trapped by turmoil, she was almost grateful when Kris found her. He materialized in a swoop, casting a sudden shadow on the workbench, and she spun around to see him grasping either side of the glasshouse doorframe. The tense set of his strong shoulders magnified his irritability.

Erwin stiffened and shifted, bringing himself in between the prince and his charge.

"I won't hurt her." Kris sounded insulted.

"He's my guard," Ava said, setting down her pot and turning to face him. "And you're very angry."

Kris took one breath, two, and then fixed his attention on her. "You're messing with my brother. You treat him disgracefully one minute, next you're exchanging lessons with him. Then you cozy up to him at the table last night—and flick him away like a fly on your shoulder. What the hell are you playing at?"

She didn't have the energy to answer that—not today. She discarded the verbal onslaught like sand tipped out of her shoe. "He confuses me."

"He's too trusting for his own good."

"You're right," she said, finding it hard to care. How much longer until she had to go? "And you overcompensate by not trusting me at all."

He didn't answer immediately. His gaze passed carefully around the greenhouse, before he glanced over his shoulder to the gardens. Then he stepped inside, closing the door behind him. Accusation chilled his blue stare when he looked back at her.

"I think you know why I don't trust you," he said, in a tone so hostile that Erwin cleared his throat and rolled his shoulders.

"Not at this moment." She rested her gloved fingertips lightly on the workbench beside her. Her mind slipped around the enraged prince, distracted, and she glanced at her watch. One hour. "But I assume you came here to tell me."

"I sure did," he said, stalking toward her.

Erwin refused to move aside when Kris drew near, forcing the prince to halt directly in front of him. For a few silent seconds, tension crackled between the two men. Erwin's stance was wide, hard—an elite royal guard in defense mode—while the prince radiated an intensity that dismissed Erwin altogether when he met Ava's gaze over the guard's shoulder.

Kris lifted a mocking brow at her. "Are you sure you want to hear it?"

Interest piqued, she angled her chin upward.

His features were stony; his lips curled in disdain. "I heard my cousin refused to marry you," he said, and her gut shrank. "That must have been infuriating. A dead-end for you and your parents. No hope of getting Kelehar's greedy fists on our mines."

She didn't move as his stare dug into her.

"That was three years ago. See, I've done my research. You haven't so much as dated anyone else in all that time. It seems strange to me that you'd be so affected by the rejection of a man you didn't even know. Unless you weren't thrown off your game at all—you were using the time to plan."

Premonition niggled at her.

"Now, you're back in Kiraly with a second chance at your marriage scheme. And all it took was for my family to die in a tragic . . . *accident*."

Dread crept down her spine. "What are you saying?"

Erwin stood as still and hard as granite in front of her.

They all knew what he was saying.

"Your parents," Kris said through his teeth. "And you."

Horror stopped her finding the breath to answer.

"It wasn't an accident." Those blue eyes burned. "It can't have been."

"Kris," she whispered, alarm breaking her silence. "Kris, be careful right now."

He leaned closer to Erwin and her guard slowly,

threateningly, turned his face toward the prince. Sensing it, Kris cut his attention to his right. Almost nose to nose, the men stared at each other with violence unspoken between them.

Then Kris's sharp gaze sliced back to her. "Because I'm right?"

"No." She shook her head and the world spun. Surely Markus didn't know about Kris's suspicions. He wouldn't allow Kris to shoot around like a wayward arrow trying to find a target. His theory wasn't just dangerous—it could be politically disastrous. "Because you're accusing Kelehar of regicide, and you don't seem to understand what that means."

Kris didn't break his stare. "It's the only thing that makes sense."

"Does it really?" His allegation squeezed her throat. "I don't even want to marry Markus. I don't *want* any of this. And my parents know that. I humiliated Prince Aron into rejecting me. They know I acted like someone Markus would loathe so he'd refuse to marry me. I'm too big of a risk factor for them to—to commit—" She couldn't repeat it. "Excluding the part where it's criminal and psychotic, why would they go to all that trouble when I'd sabotage the marriage anyway? That doesn't make any *sense,* Kris. Think about it."

Even if he didn't believe her now, when she disappeared from Kiraly in a few short hours, he'd realize his error.

Something in his eyes flickered—blame turned into agitation. He shook his head, emptying his lungs on a furious breath. "Damn it," he muttered. "I can't stop thinking about it. The timing. I'm stuck on the timing. Three years. You were last here three years ago. And that's when—" He swore again, looking away. "Can that really be a coincidence?"

She had no idea what he was talking about.

"Regardless," she said, not wanting to know, "you shouldn't

be talking to me about this. You have a head of personal security. Talk to them."

If he didn't, the hot-blooded Prince Kristof could be Kiraly's diplomatic demise.

"I've been trying," he said. "They're avoiding me."

"Contain your conspiracy theories." Her voice was spear-tipped like the ice in her chest. "And try harder."

His jaw slid. "It wasn't an accident."

"Perhaps that's true." The possibility leached dismay into her veins. Her parents couldn't be responsible, but the notion that *someone* had caused the balcony collapse made her fear their endgame. "And I'm sorry if it is. But talk to Markus about it. Maybe Tomas. Not me. And if you're going to keep pointing fingers, definitely don't talk to anyone else. This is how wars start, you know. You're a prince. You don't only speak on behalf of yourself anymore."

Silence fell. His tension prickled like a dog snarl.

"Kelehar didn't do it," she whispered, so softly the words scarcely touched the inside of her mouth. "I swear to you."

Erwin's hands were balled by his sides, his elbows bent a little. Poised. Pissed. On the knife-edge of being provoked.

The prince ignored him completely. Holding her stare, he suddenly looked like a man without a lead.

She turned her shoulder on him. "I'm busy. Will that be all?"

Kris didn't move. "Tell me what you want from Mark."

"I want nothing from him."

He watched her, too close, too intense, even with Erwin between them. "You must, or else you'd have left him alone when he refused to marry you."

Wrung brittle by nerves, she surrendered. "I want him to be kind to me. Everyone is polite to me, civil, respectful, following social order. But Markus is kind because of who he is, not because of who I am, and I've needed that like daylight."

Both men in the greenhouse seemed to stop breathing.

"You've insulted me enough for one day," she said coolly. "Leave me alone."

Kris didn't argue as his frown descended. Then he exhaled sharply and stepped back, running a hand through his wild hair. On a frustrated growl, he opened the door and was gone.

Shaken, she turned to Erwin. "Not a word to anyone."

His answering stare was furious.

"I know," she said, making her voice casual. "But he's confused. Thrashing around like an animal with its head in a bag. I don't believe he intended that as an official accusation, and we are not to treat it as one. That was simply a private conversation between the prince and myself, and I'm asking you not to divulge it. Can you do that for me?"

His answering nod came slowly. "Yes, Your Highness."

"Thank you."

And she went back to worrying about her own future.

The next hour passed unendurably, every second clinging onto the one before it. She potted plant after plant, a robotic process that kept her moving while standing in one place. She wanted to run without stopping, torching the energy banking up inside her, but she would need it.

Finally, between one surreptitious glance at her watch and the next, the air in her lungs turned to hot wire. A scalding, strangling mess in her chest.

It was time to go.

"Send someone to take these to my rooms," she said, stepping back and removing her gloves. "I'm finished for the day."

Erwin said, "Very good, Your Highness."

"I'll carry this one." She picked up the smallest succulent, strings of pale green beads.

She'd planned it. The women's bathroom on the ground floor had two access points, one at either end. Since she wasn't as close friends with Erwin as with Gul, he didn't know that she would never dream of using a bathroom that was occasionally made accessible to the public—or at least, he wouldn't feel confident speaking out about his suspicion of her using it. He positioned himself outside the door, his hands clasped and his feet apart, as she peeled off with an apologetic grimace. If he found it odd that she took the plant in with her, he kept that thought to himself.

Striding straight out the other side, she picked up pace, heading out of the palace toward the royal garage. The garden path that connected her route was bordered by a shoulder-high hedge, presumably designed to conceal the domestic bustle of staff from view of the palace. She clutched the potted plant in both hands. Adrenaline sped her breath and thumped hard against her ribs. *Breathe. Don't run.* It was four fifty-five. She would drive to the shelter, park around the back, and walk inside with ample time to calm down.

She heard a shout behind her. She sped up. It wasn't for her. She couldn't panic. It would be a gardener calling out for assistance or a called greeting between friends.

The garage came into sight, long and sleet gray, and the impossibility of the moment made her dizzy—until a second shout came from right behind her, loud and urgent.

"I've found her!"

She spun around, her insides sucking into a vacuum. A woman was staring at her, standing on tiptoes and reaching a hand high for all to see. Ava's face chilled, suddenly bloodless.

No.

She turned back, taking off at a jog, but the woman hollered again and trotted along behind her.

"Leave me alone," Ava ordered over her shoulder.

The woman fell back, but her footsteps continued to crunch the pebbles.

Dismay tightened her chest, and she made herself pause again. Had Erwin really noticed her disappearance so quickly? Surely not, but still, she couldn't let this woman follow her into the garage or it would all be over in a short city car-chase.

The woman bobbed into a deep curtsey when Ava faced her. "Your Highness." She addressed the ground. "I apologize for making a scene. King Markus requests your presence immediately."

Ava scarcely had air to speak, so she made the words thin and sharp. "King Markus has no right to request anything of me."

The woman flinched. "But he has the right to make requests of me, Your Highness. And I was to find you."

Then a man—a terrifyingly familiar man—rounded the bend in the path. Tall, lean, and ageing, he fixed his gaze on her with unmistakable resolve. She swallowed, tension pinching beneath her shoulder blades. It was Philip, red-faced and flustered.

The man who had tried to convince Markus to marry her.

With one look, he sent the woman scuttling off.

"Your Highness," he said, pausing a short distance away and sweeping into a bow, "we are in desperate need of your presence."

Panic fluttered at the base of her throat. "I'm previously engaged."

"Oh. Dear me. We would trouble Prince Cyrus instead, but unfortunately, he left the grounds not an hour ago."

She bit her tongue, hard, as her panic took on the edge of hysteria. Cyrus was waiting for her at the shelter.

"I'm afraid we've had a call from an influential online publication," Philip said. "They're threatening to post an article based on an anonymous tip that during his first week as sovereign, King Markus soured Kiraly's relationship with Kelehar by refusing your hand in marriage."

Dread cracked open over her skull. It dripped through her like acid. "That's silly."

"The magazine editor doesn't think it's silly that the new king has severed ties with a historically strong ally."

She started to shiver. "He hasn't severed ties."

Philip raised his palms helplessly. "But it could seem that way from the outside. Your parents have returned to Kelehar, after all," he answered. "The queen wasn't particularly subtle after the meeting, racing through the palace, careless of who saw her fury."

And Ava in the lead, distraught, as if she'd been scorned.

"If this gets out, it will ruin the king's reputation before his reign has begun. Please. Friday's conference has been brought forward—the media is already in the press hall. We are begging you to stand beside King Markus and put out the fire before it's properly lit." The man's gaze was riveted on her. "He needs you to do this. Just a few lines about the strong relationship between your nation and his—that's all we need for the truth to be told."

Despair rushed up her throat; prickled behind her eyes.

No.

"I can't," she whispered.

Don't make me.

"Please." Philip both startled and devastated her by going down on one knee. He clasped his hands. "Please, Your Highness, the young king has so much to give. He's a good man. This is difficult enough for him without enduring the disappointment of his people and the criticism of the world. Once started, the rumor mill will always spin doubt and distrust. And trust can be impossible to regain, even if it's taken away for false reasons."

Philip was right.

Her gasp was sharp, a snap, as if her lungs were made of fine bones that broke at the surge of air.

Oh, no, no.

Frightened, she looked around. Curious palace staff peered at them from around the garden, enough witnesses to substantiate the rumor if she chose to leave now. For what could possibly be more important than this press meeting, when she was known to be here on a vacation? Shopping, fine dining, a sunset cruise around the lake? Turning her back on Philip would seem like a deliberate slight of the king.

That slight would become condemnation when she never returned.

Philip was still on his knees, his palms pressed together, waiting.

She was cornered.

"Get up," she said, her voice flat. She cupped the plant to her solar plexus. "I have no time for this. The press gets two minutes. A statement, no questions, and then I'll leave. It's up to you to explain my haste."

"Thank you!" Then he was on his feet, hurrying across the grounds and into the palace. She strode behind him, every step like a lash on her back. It was four minutes past five. Five past, six, seven. Tears filled her eyes—why was the palace so big?—and she fought them down, telling herself that she would still make it. She would drive faster, park in the middle of the road, and tear into the shelter without a care for attracting attention.

She would make it.

She walked into the press room and the wall of sound

slammed her off-balance. So many people present to hear the king speak, and when they spotted her, cameras flashed and questions were called. She ignored them, striding directly to where Markus waited behind a tall petition to the side of the platform, his back to her. He'd dressed as himself in jeans, a plaid shirt, and boots, the wrong clothes for his first press conference, yet just right for him. His dark hair was uncovered, and he raked his fingers through it, an uneasy gesture—he was naked without his hat.

She was glad, suddenly, that she got to see him one last time.

She stopped behind him, her heart pounding, her knees loose, and her gaze fixed sightlessly on the nape of his neck. Last night, he'd confessed he liked her and she'd abandoned him. He had every right to be hurt, insulted—every right to dismiss her here where the press couldn't see.

Markus turned. His nervous frown quickly became concern. "Ava?" His voice was urgent as he leaned in close. "Hey, are you all right? Your lips are white. You should sit down."

She shook her head, her pulse jerking at his decency and at the time: twelve minutes past five. "Hurry this up."

She could make it.

"You look like you're going to pass out." His hand lifted, reaching for her shoulder. Then he seemed to think better of it. His hand lowered. "I'm sorry. This is my fault. I didn't realize you were unwell." Uneasy, he glanced around before shifting closer to her and lowering his voice. "I was the one who leaked the information of our failed strategic engagement."

A new kind of dizziness washed over her. "What?"

He looked stricken. "I couldn't put Tommy through something like this, and I don't want Kris speaking to the press until he's had more training. I needed to shift the focus. I'd hoped with your experience, you wouldn't mind. And you had said you'd like to be here."

She didn't have time to be upset. "It's fine." She forced herself to meet the innocence of his eyes. His gaze was serious, apologetic, and all about her. "I have plans to be somewhere else. Make this fast."

Reluctance shuttered his features. His stance grew, his shoulders rolling back. "You really don't look—"

"Please don't delay this." She swallowed, setting the plant down. "Please, Markus."

The crack in her voice seemed to disarm him. On a rough breath out, he relaxed, and his face tilted down toward her. "God, Ava. I worry about you." His concern was a low rumble, and she wished she could hide inside his gentle growl and let it drown out the rest of the world. "We're going to talk later. I'll come find you. Okay?"

She made herself nod.

"Okay." Then he turned and stepped onto the platform, and in a blur of faces and photographs, she joined him. Markus gave a short but warm greeting to the journalists, and then quickly moved on to reassure them that no tensions existed between Kiraly and Kelehar. In fact, he and Prince Cyrus had much in common and had even spent the previous night in Kira City together. When Markus glanced at her, she smiled and spoke about the positive conversations she and her family had shared with King Markus during their visit, concreting a strong alliance with the new monarch who would lead both countries into the future.

Observably, she was the perfect stateswoman. Her public persona was so ingrained that she stood at ease and looked journalists in the eye, and no one seemed to notice that her heart was disintegrating live on national television.

As Markus concluded, she spotted Erwin step into the back

of the room. Guilt inched up her spine at the betrayed look in his eyes—until Gul stepped in beside him, his features grim, and her stomach dropped. Erwin must have panicked at her disappearance and sought the boss.

God, she might not make it.

"Enjoy your evening," Markus said loudly, and then turned, hustling her off the platform. "Go," he murmured at her back.

On impulse, she reached behind her to find his hand. Instantly, his fingers gripped hers, warm and urgent, a touch so right that she wondered whether her fingerprints shifted to reflect the grain of his skin.

He resisted for a fraction of a second when she pulled away. Then, with her hand falling empty by her side, she picked up the plant and marched out of the room without looking back.

Tears blurred her eyes as she bolted through the corridors. Gul would know. He wasn't stupid. But she refused to hand herself over, and so she ran faster, outside now, pebbles flicking up under her feet, until the garage loomed in front of her.

He beat her to it.

She dashed through a side roller door, pivoted, and collided right into him. As she stumbled back, breathless, he saved the plant in one big palm and grasped her shoulder in the other.

"Princess," he said softly, using her title as both an apology and warning.

"Gul." Her voice was thick. She reached out and took the plant back but didn't move out of his hold. "I've never asked you to break the rules. I've always understood your position. But right now, I need you to help me. Not my mother, or my father, but *me*." He stared, his dark eyes wide with indecision. "No harm will come to me. Please let me go. Please." She was clinging to his sleeves, dragging him down into a bow as her knees sagged. "I need to see him. Just let me see him, Gul, please."

Gul's exhale was explosive. He ran a hand over his eyes and something like guilt settled over his features. Then, stunning the pain clear out of her mind, he said, "If you promise to convince your parents to accept my resignation."

Blindsided, she whispered, "What?"

"I want to stay in Kiraly." Sadness dulled his eyes. "I can have a full future here."

Oh. Her constant companion, the only friend who had weathered her every mood, and he wanted her help. She sank into his grasp, ending up against his chest, one arm tight around his middle. He deserved happiness, love, and he was asking her to grant it.

"I promise," she said, even as the words twisted fresh pain in her heart. She would never see this beautiful man again. But it wasn't an empty promise. She would ask Cyrus to help him.

Gul let her go.

Light-headed with urgency, she flung herself into the Cerulean and jammed the plant between her thighs. With no time for subtlety, she spun off down the palace driveway, out the gates, and into the city. It was five thirty-eight. *Eight minutes late.* Cars edged down the hill in peak traffic, and she screamed with the windows closed, frantic, before mounting the curb to access the closest side street. Back-road driving from there, she honked people out of her way, speeding and praying they valued safety over indignation, and then she was pulling up in front of the shelter, throwing herself out of the car, and hurtling through the unlatched gate and along the path that led to the concealed side entrance.

Her breath tore down her throat. Ten past six. He would still be here. They could still escape tonight. Cyrus would make sure of it. And Zara, Zara would help.

Halting at the glass door, scarcely thinking, she ran her hand over her cheeks and jammed her teeth together. She must look wild. She didn't want to terrify him.

She took a moment to press down the disrupted soil of her gift, wishing she'd thought of a ribbon, before pushing the door open and rushing into the musty welcome area to find them standing, just Cyrus and Zara, side by side, arms crossed and eyes red as they looked over at her, the sight splitting her hope into shards.

She couldn't escape.

Her son had gone.

14

Zara watched her go down. It was like Ava's body relinquished all control to her heart, and all her heart could do was shatter. She landed half-splayed out, a crumple that forced her face against the coarse carpet tiles. Her torso juddered with soundless tears and her fingers curled near the fallen plant, loose with defeat.

Ava had been in Zara's imaginary safe house for years—tucked away with her son, untouchable, always together—and experiencing the pair miss each other by fifteen minutes just about destroyed her coping strategy. Zara hung back, hugging herself, as Cyrus knelt beside his sister.

"We're going to try again," he murmured as his hand moved over her back. "Next week, while you and I are both still here, we'll try again. I promise you."

As he continued to murmur, Zara heard a faint scrape and turned, catching sight of several shelter residents in the hallway. They gathered in a close pod, silent and somber, their eyes hooded with empathy and attention rapt on the broken princess. Soon, Ava's grief found a voice and her sobs pushed the women away, a sound too private and painful for their abused souls to bear.

Careless of her own tears, Zara stayed.

She always stayed.

U

Cyrus explained how the plan had fallen apart. In her panic to leave the palace, Ava hadn't seen the journalists pouring out the front entrance, nor had she driven rationally, checking her side and rearview mirrors. If she had, she'd have noticed the cars on her tail, video cameras hanging out the passenger windows, determinedly tracking the princess who had fled from the conference and out of the grounds like plump bait for a juicy story.

Gul had watched it all.

He'd called Cyrus. "The princess is on her way," he'd said, "dragging an entire press conference in her wake. If what I think is happening goes ahead, we're going to have serious breach in confidentiality. You know our priority. This isn't going to work. I strongly suggest you shut it down."

So Cyrus had shut it down.

Keeping her son classified was critical. Having his photo splashed around the world in connection to her would cause a riot of speculation. It would put him on the media's radar and render a secret life with his mother impossible. Add to that, journalists following her to the shelter meant that escaping unobserved was also impossible. If she waited to slip away later that night, the media interest would be immense, with dozens of papers claiming photographic evidence of where she'd last been seen.

As Gul said, it wasn't going to work.

The security team who protected Ava's son had rushed the young prince and his guardian away just minutes before she'd arrived. Back home to his secret existence without her.

"Gul," she said once Cyrus finished explaining. She sat on the shelter floor, her mind an empty shell. "He stopped me. But then he let me go. He . . ." She didn't understand.

Her brother sat beside her. "I'm concerned that he called me. He's the head of your personal guard. Mine don't report to him. Why would he assume I'm a part of this?"

Her thoughts were blank.

"Could he have known where the shelter is?" he asked, turning to look up at Zara.

"Jesus." Zara raised a hand to her mouth. "I completely forgot. Last week, Ava picked me up a few blocks away, but she dropped me off out front. Gul was in the security car behind us."

Cyrus lowered his head. "He would have positioned a guard to monitor the building."

And when that guard had seen Cyrus arrive just hours ago, followed shortly by a boy and an unfamiliar team of royal guards from Kelehar, he must have contacted Gul—at the same time as Erwin would have told him of Ava's disappearance. An irrefutable correlation.

"What do we do?" she whispered. "Can't I follow him?"

"Gul will have people tailing him now. Darius has to go straight home."

Darius.

Her little king.

"We'll figure this out, Ava." Cyrus held her hand tightly. "I swear to you, I will fix this."

"What's going to happen?" Panic gripped her. "Gul knows."

"I don't think he suspects the full plan." Her brother rubbed his face. "If he mentions it, play that this was just a meeting, a stolen moment for you to see Darius. Don't talk about running away. If he'd realized you intended to disappear entirely, he wouldn't have let you out of his sight."

A stolen moment. Running away. Disappear entirely.

"Ava? Did you hear me?"

She nodded, her head heavy like stone. "He wants to resign," she murmured, the words avoiding her heart on their way out.

Cyrus frowned. "Resign?"

"He wants to stay in Kiraly."

He hummed. "What I wouldn't do for that man's portfolio," he said. "I'll press for it."

As heir, Cyrus was accumulating responsibility. Just months ago, their parents had given him the security portfolio concerning the royal bastard. Referred to as the Violin Project, it included Darius's whereabouts, weekly schedule, details on his guards and guardian, and a stack of profiles on anyone he'd interacted with in the local community. It was Cyrus's first closed-curtain obligation to ready him for one day taking the crown.

It had been his goal from the start. The reason he'd distanced himself from Ava in front of their parents and in public. He would never have been trusted with Darius if their parents had known he was on her side.

The instant he'd had the portfolio, he'd pounced. He made a single trip to the Italian village where Darius lived under the pretense of personally ensuring the portfolio matched reality. While there, he informed the guards that he was now solely in charge of this matter and any orders he issued regarding the boy were to be followed without question.

Such as taking Darius on a spontaneous day-trip to Kiraly to meet him in a women's shelter.

"I'll sort this out," Cyrus promised again, his voice low.

"And I'll deal with the press," Zara said.

Her approach to dealing with them involved delivering a fiery speech out front about the confidential nature of women's shelters, threatening that if any photographs of this location were made public there would be hell to pay, and that Ava running late for a meeting regarding such safe houses was *not damn well newsworthy, you pack of sickos,* but if they wanted a freaking quote for their trouble they could write that Princess Ava was progressively philanthropic and wasn't afraid to get her hands dirty in her quest for bettering women's shelters wherever she went, *now shove off.*

The street emptied in minutes.

Ava let Zara take her back to her apartment. She didn't remember the drive, or the walk up the apartment block stairs, or how she ended up in Zara's bed, but the blankets were soft and the smell was soothing. Her friend curled beside her, taking her hand and stroking the hair back from her face, and she closed her eyes and focused on Zara's warmth and the fingernails lightly raking her scalp.

"I took photos, honey," Zara murmured. "Tell me when you want to see them."

She wouldn't be able to see through her tears.

"Cyrus and I figured out a new plan once," her friend said. "We'll do it again."

"My parents come back next week. They'll take me home." Escaping from Kelehar was impossible.

Zara's hesitation was brief. "It'll be before that."

Ava's breathing eventually began to level out as Zara stroked her hair, and she slipped into an exhausted doze. She roused at one point, hearing the front door open and Adam call out quietly. She felt Zara lift her head, and there was whispering, hushed questions of concern, and then the click of the bedroom door closing.

"He said he'll make tea whenever you want," Zara murmured, settling her face near Ava's again. "Even if it's four in the morning."

She made herself nod. "Show me the photos," she whispered, and this time, when she cried, it was for the boy on the screen, sweet-faced and dark-eyed, and the three years of his life they'd spent apart.

After breakfast the next morning, Mark took thirty minutes to walk around the palace. He turned right when he'd previously turned left, and when a flight of stairs or narrow hallway caught his interest, he pursued it. Eventually, he would know this palace like the back of his hand.

As he strode through an archway into an unfamiliar courtyard—this one trickled and gurgled with ornamental pools and fountains—he saw Cyrus drawing his hand back and sending a stone skipping across a series of connected pools. The prince lowered his head, shoved a hand through his dark hair, and then dropped to one knee, picking up another stone from the path.

Agitation had replaced the man's usual composure. He probably wanted privacy, but Mark wanted answers. He'd visited Ava's chambers last night and found them deserted. No bodyguard, no princess, no one. It unnerved him. Paired with her distress at the press meeting yesterday, he was about ready to know what the hell was going on.

Cyrus swiveled at Mark's footsteps. Lines gathered beneath his eyes and there was a pasty tone to his olive skin. He stood and said, "Your Majesty."

"Morning." Mark leaned back against a nearby fountain ledge, crossing his arms loosely.

Cyrus gestured to where his stone had sunk. "I hope you don't mind—"

"Not at all."

Before Mark could ask about Ava, Cyrus sighed and sat abruptly on a marble bench opposite him. The prince stared at the ground between his feet, his hands bracketing his head. Then he looked up, his dark eyes imploring. "Am I older than you?"

Mark had no idea. "Twenty-five?"

"Twenty-nine." The prince nodded. "But I feel powerless. And you're in control."

He almost laughed. "That's a matter of perspective."

"Regardless, I envy your situation." Cyrus didn't lower his hands. His fingertips moved at his temples. "You didn't have to wait in the shadows of power. You just stepped right into it."

"Completely unprepared."

The prince grimaced in acknowledgement. Then he stood and moved to Mark's side, resting his forearms on the fountain edge and staring down at the clear water. "But you didn't spend years on the sidelines, waiting to be able to make a difference. It's killing me. It's not that I wish my parents bad fortune." Cyrus exhaled hard. "I just . . ."

The pause stretched on.

"Wish you could be doing things differently?" Mark suggested.

The prince turned inward, his expression fierce, locking his words between them. "I would never treat Ava the way they've treated her. They see us both as puzzle pieces. I am to be king someday—that is my duty and I accept it. But Ava doesn't fit into their big picture. They've been trying to jam her in for years, careless of how it breaks her. I wouldn't do that to someone." His voice was fractured by the same distress that widened his eyes. "I couldn't."

Unease blew a chill across Mark's skin. He was missing something here, something he desperately wanted—the truth about what Ava's parents had done to her. "Is she okay?"

On a long exhale, Cyrus leaned forward again and stared at the water. He shook his head.

"What was she late for yesterday?"

That wrenched the other man's attention. Cyrus looked alarmed. "Pardon?"

"At the press meeting, she told me she was running late. She was upset." Pupils blown and hands shaking, she'd seemed close to breaking point. "Is that what this is about?"

Bitterness glinted like shards in the prince's eyes. "Yes, but that's all I can tell you. It's a family secret," he said with uncharacteristic cynicism. It made this courteous man sound a lot like Ava.

"Can I help?"

"She likes you." Cyrus almost sounded confused. "That helps."

"I'm not so sure." He didn't hide the regret in his voice. "She bolted from me the other night, remember?"

"She's not used to it—she didn't know what to do." The prince looked back at the water. "You can help by liking her and letting her like you."

If only. "You know we've sworn not to marry each other?"

"Marriage is part of the problem. She hasn't been allowed to . . . socialize . . . without intent. It's never been about who she likes, but who is beneficial. Being able to relax and enjoy your company without our parents around, and knowing marriage isn't a possibility—she needs that kind of freedom."

It sounded a lot like Cyrus was encouraging a dead-end relationship with his own sister. The prince's hands were fists on the fountain ledge, his lips pressed thin.

"I think we can find a better outlet than skipping stones."

Mark straightened. "Why don't I introduce you to our stable master, so he can saddle up our fastest horse for you?"

Cyrus gave a humorless laugh as he pushed away from the fountain. "You have no idea how much I would appreciate that."

Ava borrowed a short gray skirt and black tank from Zara. Her heartsickness put a sluggish heat in her system, a kind of grief fever, and she couldn't care less if her short summer outfit raised eyebrows. After breakfast and the hundredth promise to try again as soon as they could work out a new plan, Zara walked her downstairs to where she'd parked Ava's car the night before. Gul was waiting beside it, his features grave.

"Chin up, sweetness," Zara murmured as Ava halted on the cobbled sidewalk, her eyes unfocused on the ground. "Your end goal isn't at your feet."

Gul escorted her back to the palace without a word.

She wanted to curl up in bed and lose herself to sleep, but she'd indulged enough overnight. Today, she had to function, walking and focusing and keeping her heart thumping. She shuffled along corridors and drifted around the gardens. Everything was colorless. The insignificance robbed the world of meaning and sound and substance.

Gul kept pace several steps behind.

Their silence was brittle; their accidental glances fraught. The events of the night before had cut through their friendship like blunt scissors. His loyalty to her parents lay on one side. Her scheme to evade him and Erwin in order to meet the son she'd legally given up lay on the other. She wanted to scream at him for wanting to leave her—scream for preventing her from a new life. She loved him. She hated him.

She said nothing to him.

She wandered through sitting rooms and great halls, onto balconies and through courtyards, and eventually came up against the barred archway to the west wing. "Under construction, Your Highness," explained the stationed guard. Blinking, she turned away and wafted up the stairs of the tallest tower, somehow finding her way to the closed door of the king's study.

Guards bracketed the entrance, but the men stared straight ahead, their faces impassive at her approach. She stepped in close and relief sputtered inside her like a tiny flame at the sound of a keyboard tapping inside.

She knocked.

After a short silence, the door opened and Markus filled the threshold. A cowboy king in denim and flannel, his hands built to calm horses and his heart determined to be worthy of his people's trust. Behind him, the desk was awash with papers and stacked high with reference volumes. His hat sat upside down on the far end.

"Ava," he said in surprise.

"You said you like me." Her voice was hollow. "How much?"

His forehead creased as he leaned against the doorframe. The movement brought his body closer, and she knew she'd subconsciously gravitated toward his sturdy strength like a falling stone. "How much do I like you?"

She nodded numbly.

"I don't know how to quantify it," he said, glancing distractedly at his guards. He emanated concern, his blue eyes tracking over her fatigued features. He lowered his voice. "But I want to help you. Tell me how I can."

Her mother had once told her that things would get better

when Ava learned to help herself. What the queen had meant was doing her duty, maintaining the reputation of the royal family, and putting herself to strategic benefit. At the time, Kelehar had barely recovered from economic instability and Ava had the power to prevent it happening again—but to give her country the benefits of her strategic alliance, she would have to give up her baby. The child would ruin her chances of marriage—her hope of a reputable life. She'd been unmarried and too young, and as her mother said, had she ever heard of a single-mother princess? Keeping the baby would disgrace the Veisi family in front of its citizens and the world.

Confused, shamed, and frightened, Ava had signed the documents that put her newborn baby into the guardianship of the crown. She'd done exactly as her mother had ordered.

And things had never grown better.

"Hug me," she whispered.

Markus stared, his chest rising and falling for several breaths. Then he said, "Thanks, I'd love your help," and stood back to invite her into his study. She stepped inside. He closed the door. And then he moved in, smelling like sunlight and safety, his strong workman's arms closing around her, his palms wide and warm, locking her against him. With her face turned to the side and her chin tucked down, her cheek pressed against his breast pocket, a soft fold of fabric that couldn't disguise the thumping of his heart. The embrace seemed so simple, so natural for him, that she pushed herself harder against his body, seeking the affection he gave so easily.

"Hey," he murmured, shifting so his shoulders curled in around her and his face pressed against the top of her hair. Pleasure spun across her scalp, thin webs of sensation, and she wondered how the crown of her head could be so receptive to comfort and kindness when it had only ever been subject to the weight of expectation.

He held her as the minutes passed, not once attempting to release her, or sighing, or shifting, or betraying that he had a million better things to be doing with his sovereignty. Instead of ruling a country, he gave himself to the insignificant task of mending a bereft princess. Then his palms began to move, slow strokes up and down her spine, and his touch drew out the numb grief that had set inside her, pouring warmth and comfort into its place. She breathed long and slow, eyes closed, and gave herself completely to his care.

"I like your hands," she whispered, and he laughed a breath across her hair, sending shivers down her neck.

"They're rough," he said, his voice more coarse than usual. "They've done dirty work and heavy lifting. I don't have dignified hands."

Dignified hands wouldn't take the time to rub life back into her like she was a newborn pup yet to take breath.

"I worry about you," he said next, echoing his sentiments from the day before.

"There's something I want," she murmured. He began to pull back, but she held on, unprepared to give up his embrace. "And I almost had it last night, but I was late. I missed my chance."

Markus groaned. "That's all my fault. I should have asked about the press—"

She shook her head against him. "You couldn't have known. But I want it so badly that I've spent years doing nothing but waiting. I've cut myself off from pleasure," she said, gazing at his rolled-up sleeve—and the corded muscle of his forearm. "I hardly understand why."

He was silent for a while, before he said, "As a boy, I had a horse called Mallie. She was big and slow and ageing, but she was affectionate, and took me where I wanted, and I loved her." His voice was low, and Ava found calmness in the rumble of his chest against her ear. "One day, she developed colic and Dad had to take her away for surgery. I refused to ride any other horse while she was gone. Not only because I missed her, but because it wouldn't seem right to enjoy riding without her."

She waited, listening to his heartbeat.

"But then my mom told me that a lack of living on my part wouldn't lessen my love for Mallie or my joy when she returned."

Ava closed her eyes. She'd done nothing but wait for three years, and all her plans had done were fall apart. There was no knowing how long the wait would be this time. What if it took months, years, of living a suspended life?

"You don't deserve to be my backup plan." She spoke into his shirt, as if the fabric might filter out her shame.

His voice was firm when he said, "Then I won't be a plan at all."

She hesitated. What did that mean? Uncertainty pulled her voice down to a murmur. "Are you asking me to leave?"

His hold tightened. *Really* tightened, squeezing heat up and out of the well deep within her. It flooded her. "No," he growled, his body hard, broad. "I mean we plan nothing, and whatever happens, happens."

She held her breath. Could she do that?

"I'm sorry I upset you the other night." His hands started moving slowly in small circles at her lower back, and her whole middle ached with wanting. "I should have started out by saying that I'm struggling with so much change and can't even think about a relationship right now. I wasn't telling you that I like you as part of a roundabout plot to marry you. That's way too many steps ahead of where I'm at right now. I like you, and I felt you deserved to know it. That's all."

Her face warmed and she buried a little deeper against him.

It was safe in his arms—safe to relax, safe to feel the strain of desire.

"People can like each other without anything coming of it," he finished, sensation rushing outward from where his palm brushed down her spine. Instinctively, she arched around his hand, pressing firmer against him. His breath caught and his body stiffened.

Her inhale was rough. "Can people touch each other without anything coming of it?"

He swore under his breath. "I want to say yes."

She wanted to touch him under his shirt. She shifted, angling her face up so her mouth hovered above the skin of his neck. He shuddered and her desire flared.

"I want to kiss you," he said, and she just about melted in his arms. "But I want you to be right there with me. Wanting it. Not using it as a distraction. And maybe whatever's going on with you means you'll never be right there with me. But the second you are—" Without warning he pulled back, disentangling himself from her. "I won't hesitate."

The world lurched. The endless view out the tower windows dizzied her.

She was alone again.

His sky-blue eyes were wary. "Am I wrong? About being a distraction?"

"No." She wrapped her arms around her middle. "I'm sorry."

"I have a question." His breath was still unsteady as he slid a hand into the back pocket of his jeans. "If I'm at risk of being a backup plan . . . what's your main plan?"

She sucked in a sharp breath.

Few people knew about Darius. Her parents and Cyrus. Gul. Zara. Several specialists and midwives who had been paid for their silence. Her son's guardian—Ava's own childhood governess—and of course, Darius's father. No one else.

She couldn't predict how Markus would react. He might run to Philip for advice and let the story loose. He might judge her, unbearable but possible, and shame her by telling the media about the scandal. Or he might be heartbreakingly decent and attempt to help, seeking guidance and sharing the story with someone less compassionate or discreet. He wouldn't be able to keep it secret. *I tell my brothers everything,* he'd told her, and she didn't trust them, not with this.

The truth could never be publicly known. Her mother had made a long-standing threat: the moment Ava revealed the existence of her son, the queen would ensure Darius was adopted. No longer legally in the custody of the crown, no longer protected as an illegitimate royal, he would become the legal child of a loving family. The family was all lined up, a tidy backup plan. The queen even claimed to have photo albums of Darius with them, taken intermittently, evidence of their years together. No court would tear a child from his family—not even for a princess. The threat effectively ensured Ava's silence.

The moment the world found out, Darius would be out of her reach.

"I can't tell you," she said.

Markus sighed and gave a single nod. Then he spoke quietly. "That book you'd been reading before I visited you, Gul said it was sad. I could see you'd been crying."

Stomach twisting, she looked up at him.

"If I knew the author, I'd make them wish they'd never written it."

The twist inside her yanked tighter. The intensity of his look betrayed he knew the book had been a lie. His threat was meant for someone else—whoever had made her cry.

Another reason she couldn't tell him. If he sided with her,

he would view the king and queen of Kelehar as his enemies. And even Ava knew that couldn't end well.

"I've interrupted your work," she said, stepping back. "I should leave."

"Actually . . ." He looked torn. "You came at a good time. I was about to send word to ask for your help."

"Oh. Of course." The palace was a void without him. She'd stay all day, if he'd let her. "What are you working on?"

"A speech for the Welcome Tea we're hosting on Saturday afternoon. And before you tell me I have a speechwriter for that, I know, but I want to do this one." He moved over to the desk, collecting a guest chair on his way and positioning it beside his own. No hierarchical seating arrangements with this king.

She followed him, affection glowing softly in her chest. "Who are you welcoming?"

"Our people."

She sat down more heavily than intended. "Pardon?"

He pushed his laptop between them as he answered, "I've put out an open invitation to the people of Kiraly." As he scrolled to the top of a text document, he reached out and dragged her chair closer to his side. He stilled when their knees touched, then turned toward her, his head tilted down, and the instant closeness had nervous curls of arousal spreading through her. Awareness darkened the blue of his eyes, and he directed his next words at her lips. "I don't want to build a sovereignty based on me and them." His voice was so low that she felt it in the base of her stomach. "To succeed as a nation, it has to be about us."

As he spoke, she focused on his half-full bottom lip. His mouth parted under her gaze, and the promise of the space between his lips just about undid her. *I want to kiss you.* She tugged at the hem of Zara's skirt and tried to focus. "You're inviting anyone and everyone into the palace for tea?"

"Yes."

The pull of his body made every second she didn't lean into him a battle. "All thirty-something thousand people?"

"Most won't come," he said, and she swore his mouth was closer than before. She was burning, her whole body alight. "We can't provide parking, and although we'll run a shuttle bus service, it can be hard to get up the mountain. But it's better than nothing."

"Why?"

He tilted his head. His forehead just about brushed hers. "When someone moves into a new town, they knock on the neighbors' doors and introduce themselves. Maybe with jam or biscuits. But I can't knock on everyone's door, so I'm inviting them to visit me instead."

And he would give his guests biscuits and tea. Once she would have scorned his naivety. Now, the gesture sparked her admiration. "You're going to be a wondrous king."

His smile was soft and he shifted, bringing his leg closer, imprinting not just his knee against hers, but the entire length of his thigh. A flare of sensation rushed outward from that pressure, upward, crowding between her legs, and she flushed at the unfamiliar yearning. She wanted him to touch her, his hands sliding over her body; she wanted him to draw her against him in a hug that involved mouths and tongues and skin on skin. Such genuine attraction was new to her, both tender and intense, and in that moment, it overwhelmed her. She wanted so much from him but didn't know how she could handle anything more than the press of his thigh.

She ducked her head a little and hid behind shyness. "Let's decide on a theme," she said, her words unsteady. She eyed his screen. "And develop the speech around it."

Markus didn't answer immediately. He seemed to be hauling himself back from an edge, somewhere that roughened

248

his breath and curled his fingers tightly around the base of his chair.

Despite everything, she longed for him to take her to that edge. Not as a distraction, and not as a backup plan.

"The theme," he said eventually, "is trust."

15

"You won't believe this."

Tommy led his brothers through the palace after dinner, avoiding eye contact with anyone they passed, but maintaining a strong pace out front. He was excited. Mark shared a glance with Kris, because the last thing Tommy had been excited about was an isolated cabin in the woods. It was about time that their brother was interested in something within these walls.

"At what point will I need hiking boots and a water bottle?" Kris asked as they started down yet another corridor with wide arches and painted ceilings. "How *big* is this place? I swear I haven't been down half of these halls."

"It's big," Tommy answered, ignoring the first question, and finally stopped in front of a grand set of closed doors. "This is the old map room." He pushed one door inward, holding it open, and with a shared look of curiosity, Mark and Kris walked in.

Mark hardly noticed the room itself. Small, with nothing but a table, map drawer, and single bookshelf in one corner. But the walls . . .

Old paper maps were pasted up everywhere. World maps from centuries past, and maps of specific countries, regions, and cities. Some were faded and flaking; others still held strong blues and greens and browns. On the plain wallpaper beside each map were old hand-painted illustrations, fanciful and detailed, that complemented the location. Mark slowly circled the room, passing elephants, pyramids, saffron-robed monks, and the paper sails of a traditional Chinese fishing boat. A fiery volcano, the ivory Taj Mahal, and various national flags. Bluebells bloomed next to the map of Kiraly.

"You've been hanging out in here?" Kris asked, also examining the old artwork.

Tommy closed the door, leaving the guards outside. "Not in here, no." His eyes gleamed as he picked up his backpack from where it rested against the wall just inside the door. Then he said, "Over here."

Kris's features mirrored Mark's bafflement as they followed Tommy to the bookcase in the corner.

Grinning, Tommy unzipped his backpack, pulled out a water bottle, and passed it to Kris.

"You're kidding me," Kris said, his tone straddling suspicion and disbelief. He took it slowly.

Tommy's grin widened as he handed Mark a flashlight. Incredulous, Mark accepted it and stared as his brother grabbed the side of the bookshelf, said, "Stand back," and pulled hard.

Cold, stale air wafted over them as the shelf slid sideways.

"What the . . . ?" Mark gaped at the revealed landing, dark and made of stone. He glanced uneasily at Tommy.

"No way." Kris snatched the flashlight out of Mark's hand, switched it on, and aimed it into the hole. The beam hit a wall several strides back. To the right, blackness spilled down in an unlit staircase. "You're kidding me," he said again, turning to stare at Tommy.

"Where does it lead?" Intrigue warred with Mark's discomfort that his brother had been walking around in the walls. Was it safe in there?

"These stairs go down four flights to take us to basement level. If you turn right, the tunnel goes all the way to the cabin." Tommy swung his pack over his shoulder, a second flashlight in his hand. "Told you it was a bolt-hole."

Kris was frowning intently into the darkness.

Mark eyed Tommy. "You said *if you turn right*."

"Yes." Tommy tossed his flashlight from one hand to the other. "There are passageways leading off every floor and several at the bottom."

Mark shifted his weight, unsettled. "All escape routes?"

"My guards aren't sure. Maybe old spy warrens, maybe secret servant passages, but most likely, our ancestors wanted the opportunity to snoop around their own palace. Apparently the largest entrance is hidden in plain sight in the throne room. Concealed by the blue velvet curtains behind the throne."

"Your guards talk a lot," Kris murmured. "Mine hardly open their mouths to say good morning. They showed you this?"

"Yes."

"Why?" Mark asked, because even Philip hadn't mentioned these passages to him.

Tommy raised a shoulder. "Because they thought I'd find it interesting. Not because they think we'll need it. Don't worry."

Mark was beginning to realize that the most pointless phrase anyone could say to him was *don't worry*. He was king in a palace lined with secret passageways and an escape route into the woods. The purpose-built potential of it made his skin prickle, even if it was centuries old.

"Are all of them dusty?" Kris turned on Tommy, his features hard.

"I didn't follow them, just shone the flashlight, but from what I could see, yeah. Why?"

Kris nodded, rolling his lips together. Something he did when he was pissed off but fighting it. His hands were bunched by his sides. "You didn't think to check?"

"I wasn't keen on getting lost. It's not like I had a map."

"No signs of use and no way to know where to go. What a great idea to keep going down to the basement."

"Yeah, I thought to myself, *Kris is going to hate this,* and took the stairs two at a time."

Kris's face was growing red. "Who else knows about this?"

"Everyone. I issued a press release." Tommy's tone was acerbic.

"This isn't a joke, Tom." Kris shifted, the seemingly unconscious movement effectively blocking his brother from the secret entrance.

Anger shadowed Tommy's features. "I'm not laughing."

"Right." Mark spoke firmly, and he and his brothers all shifted, facing inward.

Tommy glared at Kris. "What's your problem? Why are you getting weird?"

"Why are you so blasé?" he asked in return, his voice rising. "We don't know where all the passages lead. Shouldn't you find that out first? You're blinkered by that damn cabin. What if a tunnel connects this place to the city? What if people already know about it? They could get in without us knowing. They could be loose in the palace right now. These passages could be dangerous."

"What people?" Tommy pulled a face. "Loose in the palace? Where are you pulling this from?"

"We're new here," Kris answered. His knuckles were white around tight fists. "We don't know the situation."

"Security knows about these tunnels," Tommy said.

"They're fitted with infrared cameras. Nothing's going unmonitored. And my guards were in there with me, you boor."

Kris opened his mouth, but Mark cut him off. "Tommy's right; this isn't a big deal." Mark turned to Tommy and Kris grumbled. "But so is Kris. You need to be careful. Don't forget how we came to be here—not every part of this palace is structurally sound, and these passageways won't be any different, monitored or not."

"I understand that," Tommy said steadily. Then he turned to Kris and spoke more quietly. "My guards wouldn't let me go down there if it wasn't safe. I didn't put myself in danger, Kristof."

Kris hmphed, relaxing a little and as he ran his palms down his sides.

"I know you worry."

"Well, good," Kris answered, the tension falling out of his voice.

There were a few seconds of awkward silence and the argument seemed to be over.

"Do you guys want to try out the tunnel now?" Tommy looked between Mark and Kris.

"Sure." Kris nodded, aligning himself with Tommy as a way of apologizing.

Mark hesitated. They'd hike up to the cabin and the guards would wait in the tunnel, perhaps outside like last time. What if he asked them to retreat farther, granting complete privacy, just for a few minutes? Adam *had* said he had ultimate authority over security. . . He inhaled, torn over an idea.

"What's the matter?" Tommy asked, eyeing him.

"I'd like to invite Ava," he said simply, knowing that it wasn't simple at all. "Would you mind?"

His brothers exchanged a look.

Kris answered. "Would we mind revealing our concealed

passageways to the princess of a powerful country that you humiliated when you refused to marry her? A country we know next to nothing about?" He raised a brow. "Sure, that sounds really sensible and not at all in breach of palace confidentiality."

Mark forced himself not to bite back. Kris had a point, even if he'd sorely misjudged Ava.

"You're the king," Tommy said. "You decide who is in our circle of confidentiality."

Annoyance stiffened Mark's shoulders. "I don't decide anything exclusively. We're a family. We decide these things together. Kris, I was thinking of Ava also appreciating the break from constant surveillance—not that she might one day help lead an invasion into our walls."

Kris ran a hand over his mouth and looked away.

"You trust her." Tommy shifted the backpack strap on his shoulder.

Certainty had Mark nodding.

"Then it'd be okay with me." Tommy ran a hand over his throat, clearly apprehensive.

Kris had turned away, one hand curling around the wall opening as he leaned inside, peering down the stairs. His words were muffled as he said, "Not with me."

Disappointment lodged like a hook in Mark's gut. "Never mind then." It would be counterproductive if Tommy was anxious and Kris standoffish the whole night.

"Okay, let's go." Kris stepped onto the concealed landing, flashlight in hand. With a waggle of his brows, he started down the stairs.

Tommy didn't move. He was watching Mark. "Go get her," he murmured. "I'll cope."

Mark was tempted by the understanding in his brother's eyes.

"And I'll keep him in line." He jerked his head into the passageway.

"He said no."

"Because he's a jackass. Go."

Mark hesitated.

"He might struggle." His brother grinned. "But I've always been stronger than him."

"Thanks, man." Grinning, Mark strode across the map room.

God, he loved Tommy.

Ava turned the page slowly. She was sprawled stomach-down on her bed with the book Markus had given her, comfortable in a black camisole and pajama pants the color of red rose petals. Esther had braided her hair loosely and it hung over her shoulder, the ends catching in the pages. Ava dragged the book sideways, tipping over onto her back to hold it above her head.

The illustrations were simple yet intricate. Basic curves, no shadows, single lines for facial features—and yet those lines fell in just the right places to capture the essence of complex human emotion. Some showed a man alone in nature, or interacting with animals, or sharing life with a romantic partner, yet all depicted uncomplicated joy from simple moments of happiness.

As she turned the pages, she found herself smiling.

Then she reached a series of a man and child: the boy sitting on the man's shoulders in a windswept field, clutching the string of a magnificent kite; the man squatting down so he was eye-level as the boy proudly offered him an autumn leaf; picnicking on a grassy hill together, both with food around their mouths and smiles to their ears.

She lowered the book, her eyes hot with tears. *Darius.* Her shoulders ached to feel the weight of him perched there as they flew a kite, his little hand seeking stability on the top of her head. Her stomach ached for the fullness of their first shared meal. Her heart ached—

A knock came from her bedroom door. She blinked to clear her eyes. "Yes?"

Erwin opened the door a fraction and stood with his back against it, his eyes firmly fixed outward at her sitting room. "Your Highness, I apologize for disturbing you, but King Markus is outside."

She sat up so suddenly her head spun. "Now?"

"Yes, Your Highness."

Confusion brought her to her feet. "What does he want?"

"He says he'd like to show you something." His tone was admirably neutral.

Anxiety and excitement hit her at the same time. "At nine-thirty at night?"

"So it seems, Your Highness."

She hummed, feigning irritation as excitement overcame her. "I don't know about you, Erwin, but I'm too curious to send him away."

There was a pause. "I'm also curious."

"Well." She crossed the bedroom and past her guard. "Let's find out."

She opened the sitting room door herself to find Markus waiting in the corridor, fully clothed and booted. Their eyes met, and pleasure gusted through her. She smiled, unable to pretend to be anything but happy to see him.

"Ava," he greeted her, his gaze becoming strained. "I didn't mean to disturb you."

She raised a brow. "You seem to have made a habit of it."

"I . . . hadn't thought you'd be in bed." His discomfort was palpable, and she realized her nightclothes were responsible for the intensity of his expression. He hadn't looked away from her face. "I didn't mean to get you up."

"I wasn't asleep." She rested a hand against the doorway. "Erwin said you wanted to show me something. I want to see it."

Markus shifted his gaze to Erwin in the room behind her. When he met her eyes again, he said softly, "It'll take quite a while."

"Define quite a while."

"Hours," he said, and his hushed tone spread heat across her face and down her neck. Markus needed hours to show her something after dark? The flush seeped lower, deeper beneath her skin, and she remembered the smell of him, the pressure of his hands on her back, the strength in his working body.

"Hours," she breathed. "Where?"

His attention flicked to her guard once again, and his voice dropped further. "Somewhere private." Then Markus said, "You'll need shoes."

She blinked. "We'll be walking?"

His smile was tight. "The palace is big. It'll take a while to reach the map room. Your slippers might give you sore feet."

The map room? She tried to keep the disappointment off her face. "We'll be studying geography?"

"We'll be going to the map room," he said.

She frowned, and his brows rose pointedly. She was missing something. "I'll get my shoes."

"Boots," he added, quickly and quietly.

She arched an eyebrow. "And books? I love books," she said, loud enough for Erwin to hear. "Back in a moment."

Inside, she passed Erwin. "He wants to show me a book, apparently," she said, and went into the bedroom to find her boots. Too curious to waste time changing, she pulled them over her pajama pants, threw on a light coat, and returned to the corridor.

"I'm very curious," she said, and with a silent smile, Markus walked her through the palace with Erwin following behind.

It was almost ten minutes before Markus paused in front of a large set of closed doors. He turned to her guard. "It's a big book," he said. "An old atlas. With a long section on Kelehar. I think it's important for the princess to read it all tonight. We'll be hours."

Erwin frowned at her. Her escapades of the previous afternoon were fresh on his face.

She raised a shoulder. "I'll be out sooner if it's boring," she said, and followed Markus inside.

The room was dimly lit, shrouded in maps, and musty with the scent of old wallpaper. A pair of guards stood off to one side, waiting with their eyes lowered. Strange. Another pair had accompanied the king from her chambers and waited with Erwin outside. What was going on?

The thud of the door closing echoed off the bare stone floor, and as Markus moved in behind her, she looped the ties of her coat around her fingers, tugging nervously.

He rested a hand on the old table in the middle of the floor. "I hope you don't hate this idea."

"I'm still trying to figure out why I need boots."

"Are you claustrophobic?"

What? "No."

"Scared of the dark?"

"No, but considering this line of questioning, I'd like to point out that I'm not keen on being locked inside a box."

His features shifted wryly. "No boxes. Do you like walking long distances uphill?"

She smiled through her confusion. "I wouldn't say it's in my top ten, but I've always enjoyed walking. Uphill is fine."

"Would you hate spending an evening with my brothers?"

She tilted her head as she eyed him, still tugging on the coat cords. "Is this an unusual form of Twenty Questions? My turn. What's this all about?"

His gaze was wary. "I'm going to take you out of the palace in a secret tunnel to a cabin up the mountain, built originally as a bolt-hole, so you can know what it's like to be away from your guards. My brothers will be there, and our guards will be nearby, but we can go for a walk outside and leave you alone for a while—truly alone. You can move and no one will see. Speak and no one will listen. Close your eyes and know that nothing you hear is the result of another person."

Stunned, she stared at him.

"Or we can stay here and flip through an atlas," he said, running a hand along the back of his neck.

She whispered, "No to the atlas."

Markus latched eyes with her. "You're interested?"

"You'd have to lock me in a box to keep me away."

He smiled softly. "I said no boxes."

So he led her to a half-filled bookcase, slid it aside to reveal a hole in the wall, and shone a flashlight down a hidden staircase. The blackness pressed in around the beam and in both caution and exhilaration, she reached out to touch his arm. "Markus, should you really be showing me this?"

He placed a hand over her fingers, smiled, and gave her a gentle tug inside. "I trust you."

16

Markus hadn't been exaggerating about the long walk. Thankfully, the size of the tunnel wasn't suffocating—Ava suspected it had been originally scaled with men on horseback in mind—but the air was close, chilly, and the path was steep. They were unmistakably climbing the slope beyond the palace, and while such isolation could have been awkward and uncomfortable, even with his guards trailing a distance behind, Markus had started talking as they set off underground and simply hadn't stopped.

He told her about his dogs finding a friend in the stable master, and how he was desperate to go for a proper horse ride without being trailed by quad bikes, and how spring felt different on the other side of the world. He told her about the places in the city he wanted to visit if he found time, and how he hoped he hadn't put out the palace chefs by throwing the Welcome Tea, but that he had a surprise lined up for them as thanks. And Ava listened, lost in the sound of his voice and the comfort of his words, and marveled at how openly he talked when he was at ease.

She loved that he felt at ease around her.

"Your brothers," she said when he paused for more than two seconds. "Tell me about them."

He spoke about their childhood, and how Tomas—Tommy—had always been reserved around strangers and an avaricious reader, leaving books on fence posts and in the stables. "Once, he left a book in the grass to come inside for dinner, and we all had to hold hands after dark, the whole family, to sweep the field until we found it. Apparently he was up to a good bit."

Markus didn't mention Tommy's social avoidance, so she didn't ask as they continued to climb the mountain tunnel.

Then there was Kris. Impulsive, rough, yet somehow charismatic, he'd got in the most trouble during their younger years and had grown wilder during their adolescence. He'd gone straight for the girls and the parties, making a name for himself in Sage Haven as a one-night catch. Apparently, their peers had developed a simple method for telling the brothers apart: Markus was always with Sally, Tommy was always with his best friend, Jonah, and Kris was never with the same girl twice. But aside from messing around town, Kris had worked hard on the family farm and went away to study at college, as they all had, returning without a dent in his protective streak when it came to his brothers.

"They say people mellow with age, but he's become more protective of us, not less," Markus said.

Her brows rose. "You don't say."

His glance was questioning in the light of the flashlight.

"We've seen each other a few times since I called him a fool." That social breakfast seemed like weeks ago. "He doubts my motivation for spending time with you." She quickly decided to lie about his visit in the greenhouse. Better if Markus never had to worry about what his brother had said. "He seems to think I'm on my parents' side and intend to trap you in matrimony if it's the last thing I do."

Markus frowned. "Has he been difficult?"

"Nothing I can't handle," she said. "But he can be intense."

His jaw slid. "I'm sorry."

"You should be. I can't believe you let him live his own life like this."

He smiled. "But he's being difficult because of me, and I'm sorry about that. The one good thing about his temper is that it disappears completely when you win. No grudges, no lingering ill will."

"And if he wins?" she asked.

His smile became a grin. "Untested eventuality."

She laughed.

"What were you like as a girl?" he asked, and humor deserted her.

"Oh," she said, looking down at the stone floor as she climbed. "Spoilt, obviously, and not taught that other people had lives and feelings and dignity. I liked kittens, and so I always had new kittens to play with. I'm not sure what happened to them once they grew bigger, but I don't recall ever having a full-grown cat." She kept her gaze down as shame lined her words. "I yelled at staff and refused to eat breakfast if there weren't any flowers decorating the plate. I behaved in public, of course, and used to make my governess read newspaper articles if I was in the photo. Journalists used phrases like, *Kelehar's little angel* and *silent and endlessly sweet,* and I used to believe them."

Markus didn't comment, but his silence wasn't judgmental. He was just listening.

"I used to follow Cyrus around," she continued. "I love him more than almost anything—the only thing I like having in common with my parents." She paused, not sure what else she could tell him. "I went to boarding school in Switzerland. They were the best years of my life. I was finally around people of my own age and status. Most of them were down-to-earth and I learned not to embarrass myself by throwing tantrums when I didn't get my own way. Trust me, I was more imperious at twelve than I am now, and I know that's saying something."

He laughed before his features shifted into a light frown. "I hate to interrupt, but there's light ahead."

Her stomach jumped at the sharp series of steps and an open door. They had reached the cabin, along with Kris and Tommy.

Markus slowed to a halt and faced her. He wore a strange expression. "They won't harm you."

She almost scoffed. "I know that."

His brow creased. "I just thought since you're used to having Gul or Erwin around to protect you, you might be worried."

Oh. That would be a logical conclusion to draw from the outside. "I am a little," she said. "Thank you. Would you lead the way?" She didn't want to enter first.

With a nod, Markus moved ahead, ascending the steps and turning in the doorway to offer his hand. She took it and stepped in close beside him, her shoulder coming to rest against his chest as they both paused to look around at a steel-walled shelter. A bunker. The space was squat but long, furnished as a kind of sitting room. There was a closed door at the far end, hinting at other rooms, but Markus had turned to face the nearest wall with a surprised, "Huh."

He looked at a large and strange map of Kiraly. The palace featured heavily, with inset maps of each floor displayed on the right. Kira City spread out across the top with main roads labeled, the tourist precinct, and the lake. She frowned at the seemingly random bold lines in the palace floor plans—until she realized the whole thing was a map of the secret passageways within the structure and splaying across the city, one striking as far as the lakeside.

Opportunity burst open like double doors inside her, wide and flooded with light.

Reality slammed them closed.

She couldn't escape via these tunnels. Kiralian security would monitor them. Guards would catch up with her before she could so much as pass beneath the palace perimeter. Defeated, she turned away from the map.

"Well," Markus murmured. "It seems Philip gives me information on a need-to-know basis." He shook his head and turned toward the stairs on their immediate right. "Let's go up."

Cool, fresh air surrounded them in a tiny upstairs washroom, and she paused to take a few long breaths as Markus went ahead into the main space of a cabin, saying, "It's big down there."

She overheard Kris respond. "Did you see it all? There's a billiards room."

"Not yet." He turned back, his brow quirking as he waited for her. Suddenly uneasy, she made a fuss over adjusting her coat, wrapping each side as far as it would go over her chest and tying the cord in a double-knot. Apprehension twisted inside her. She was in their private space, outside their brotherly bond. She didn't belong here.

Her nervousness increased at the strain around his eyes, the slight stiffness in his shoulders. Markus knew it too.

Swiftly, she gestured for him to come back into the walled-off landing. He cast a glance at his brothers, and then stepped in close, his hands sliding smoothly into hers and lifting them to his chest. Hushed, he asked, "What's the matter?"

She swallowed. "I shouldn't be here."

"You don't want to be?"

She shivered as his thumb stroked her knuckles. "Do they know I'm here?"

His mouth lifted, and he tilted his head a little. "Yes."

265

"Kris hates me," she said.

Markus gave her a look that meant she was being childish. "He doesn't."

She tilted her own head at that, her eyes narrowing. Nervousness was getting the better of her, making her resist something she wanted. Because she did want to go out there and spend time with this man and his family, observing him around those he loved and the preciousness of their relationship. Three brothers bonding could surely be another illustration of simple joy.

Then Markus shifted closer, bringing his face inches from hers. The warmth of his breath reached her cheek as he murmured, "I don't need his approval to like you. Why do you?"

Her next breath was shaky. She raised a helpless shoulder.

"Okay." He stood back, sent her a grin that pierced right through her, and pulled her into the cabin. She staggered out in a few steps and half-crashed into his side. Standing firm, his hand dropped out of hers and slid around her middle, encouraging her to catch her balance against him. She fought a wave of attraction as she turned to face the others.

Kris and Tommy were watching her from where they sat at a timber table. One faced her; the other had twisted around to look. They both held a fan of cards, while the rest sat in a neat stack between them flanked by two piles of loose change. Several beer bottles stood down one end, with a lantern glowing bright.

For an instant, she had no idea who was who.

Then the closer one with longer hair rolled his eyes. "I don't *hate* you."

Markus sighed. "You've met Kris." He gestured to the far side of the table, his body twisting around her. She ached for him to wrap around her completely. "And this is Tommy."

Tommy's free hand clutched the table's edge. At her attention, his feet started jiggling beneath his chair.

"We've met," she said, inclining her head at him. "Hello again."

Tommy gave a little smile and didn't quite meet her eye.

There was a beat of silence as Markus and Kris frowned at each other.

"You've met?" Kris turned his back, facing Tommy. "What does she mean, you've met?"

"I wanted to meet her. So we met." Tommy considered his cards. "You folding or not?"

"Raise." His shoulders were stiff. "You've got nothing."

"Fold. Damn it," Tommy muttered, laying his hand on the table.

Kris laid his own cards down, not speaking, and Tommy slid several coins across to him. Tommy looked up when Kris asked, "Who else have you met?"

"You want a list or something?"

"Yeah, since you keep gallivanting around without telling us what you're up to. What if something happens?"

Tommy's features shuttered. He turned away, pushing out of his chair. "You don't tell me what you're doing," he muttered, moving over to the woodpile. The fireplace beside him was empty and unlit. "Why should I be different?"

"You know why," Kris said, voice harsh.

She regretted her comment to Tommy as Markus dropped his arm and moved away from her with a glance of apology. "Kris, stop it. Nothing's going to happen."

Tommy nudged a log with his foot. "He's just pissed because he hasn't heard from Frankie."

Friction wound the air so tight, so quickly, she didn't move in case it snapped. She really shouldn't have come. Self-consciousness had her cringing at her own intrusion, wishing she could disappear down another hole in the floor.

Then, as Markus murmured a scolding, "Tommy," she realized the beauty of this moment. She tried her best not to breathe, even as she soaked up every detail on the men's faces. She was watching these brothers *be brothers.* They spoke openly and aimed directly for pain points. Not out of malice, but seemingly because tiptoeing around issues would be futile. They knew each other too well. Their conversations took shortcuts, bypassing irrelevance and swiftly unearthing the roots of each other's thoughts.

It was tense, emotional, and glorious.

Then Kris startled her by slumping back in his chair. "She won't even answer my emails."

"Didn't you say she'd left on another job?" Tommy leaned a palm against the wall and looked at his brother sideways. "She's probably gone dark. She'll contact you when she gets back to the Haven, you know, wondering where the hell you are."

"She's going to hate me." Kris groaned and dropped his head to the table. "She already hates me."

"Her jobs can take weeks." Markus pulled out a chair and sat, frowning at Kris. "You have time to figure out how to explain all this."

"Yeah." The muffled answer sounded unconvinced.

"You could fly back," Tommy said, toeing another log. "Meet her. She might forgive you in person."

Kris just shook his head, grinding his face against the table.

"You didn't tell her you're a prince in an email, did you?" Markus asked.

"I'm stupid, but I don't have a death wish."

Tommy and Markus winced at each other over his lowered head. Evidently, Frankie had a temper.

"It'll be fine." Markus reached out and clasped Kris on the shoulder.

Kris didn't answer, but he did eventually straighten, shifting to sit side-on to Ava. He knew she was there, but clearly wasn't keen to invite her reaction. His cheeks were pink, his eyes fixed on the table leg beside him. His jaw was clenched hard.

When the silence stretched out, she decided that Kris didn't need another reason to resent her. So he felt exposed by his vulnerability. She could match that.

"I'm not sure what Frankie means to you," she said, and a darker flush rolled over his face as he muttered something about being just friends, "or whether she'll forgive you for keeping all of this a secret. But if it makes you feel better, my first and only lover was bribed by my parents to leave the country several months into our relationship. We'd kept it secret, but they—they found out. He accepted the bribe on the spot."

Fighting for the princess he'd accidentally knocked up had clearly seemed like too much trouble, so he'd accepted the responsibility-free card that had come with an annual payment for his continued silence. Last time Cyrus had checked, he was living it up without regret.

"He didn't say goodbye, and I haven't heard from him since."

All three men listened, motionless.

"He was common," she continued, a little ashamed of using that word in front of these men who didn't see differences in status. Her hands once again found the ties of her coat. "And even though that was exactly why my parents got rid of him, I felt that he was the one who'd rejected me. He could have resisted, or contacted me to apologize, or asked how I was doing." Her hands caught on each other, and she held them over her stomach. Her thoughts moved away from her first lover and fixed on her boy, wherever he was. "I also understand what it means to love someone from a distance, and the insatiable anguish of not even knowing how far away they really are."

Markus was the first to look at her. She saw sadness in his eyes and injustice tight on his lips. Tommy's face rose slower, but she swore respect lifted his chin a little higher than before. Solidarity in pain, or something twisted and human like that.

Kris cleared his throat and tapped the table a few times. "Well, that sucks."

She continued to hang back. "Yes."

"I'm sorry," he said next, and cut a glance at her. "Your parents sound like assholes."

And there it was again—bypassing convention and cutting straight to the core. She actually smiled. "They are."

Kris kicked out the fourth chair at the table opposite Markus. "Come on over." As she did, he added, "Just don't ever mention Frankie."

She sat down, her eyes catching on Markus. Sadness had morphed into concern that set his jaw and shaped his shoulders. She looked away, pretending to be interested in the cards on the table. "I won't," she said. "I'm too selfish to talk about other people."

Kris leaned back in his chair with the hint of a smile. "Beer?"

"No. Thank you."

"Should we deal you in?"

"What's the game?"

"Let's start something new." Tommy joined them. He collected the cards with a swiped palm and as he began to shuffle, he asked quietly, "Know any card games, Ava?"

"I could teach you tarneeb." She tried to sound offhand. "It's popular back home."

The brothers all pulled the same brows-up, mouths-down expression that she interpreted as impressed.

"You assumed I wouldn't know a single card game?" she asked, thankful that Gul had taught her tarneeb for dull evenings.

"Maybe," Kris said. "But I'm up for it."

Markus smiled across the table. "Let's go."

And so they played.

She taught them the simple rules of bidding and trick-taking, and as she won trick after trick, and Kris made increasingly mocking jokes at his own inabilities, and Tommy smiled widely enough to reveal a chip in his front tooth, and Markus looked at her with glowing eyes across the table, a strange sensation grew like a large bubble in her chest. Delight. The cards took the focus, so the brothers relaxed behind their hands, leaning back and laughing at their own misfortune. In sharing the game, they shared themselves.

When the second set was over, Tommy shuffled the cards again and said, "What's Kelehar like?"

"Oh." She hesitated. How could she describe an entire country in a few sentences? "In the city where I live, the glass buildings fill the skyline like sleek water pitchers and crescent moons. Sometimes I wonder how it doesn't all shatter in the heat. At ground level, there's color everywhere. Spice bowls and rugs, tiles and flowers. You'd be confused if you sought black thread at a market, because you'd walk away with gold and crimson and apple green instead. The food is superb, and the people will welcome anyone into their homes, no matter how little they have," she said. "Markus said you like reading. You would love the libraries at the palace."

"Plural," Tommy noted. "I love them already."

"Ava." Markus had been watching her intently. "Kris and Tommy and I might head outside for a while. Go for a walk. You can stay here. Okay?"

His brothers looked at him like he'd gone mad.

271

"She's never been alone," he said.

Kris and Tommy turned in unison to look at her, disbelieving.

"That's just not right." Kris placed a palm on the table and stood. "But I'll head back to the palace instead. The return trip will be enough walking for me."

Tommy also rose. "I'll come."

Dismayed that she'd prompted the end to the evening, she spoke more firmly than she intended. "Don't leave. It was just an idea Markus had."

But they kept moving, gathering the cards and empty bottles. "Sorry," Kris said, surveying the cabin and tossing the flashlight from hand to hand. "I have to leave. I hate you, remember?"

She tried to flatten her expression, but disappointment prevailed.

"Hey." He tilted his head at her, cocking up the corner of his mouth. "I've been . . . wrong. About everything. I don't hate you. But I'm still leaving."

Blinking, she looked to Tommy.

"Sorry, Ava, but it's getting late." He slung a backpack over his shoulder, not quite looking at her. "We'll do this again, okay?"

She caught the offer with a smile. "Okay."

He reached out toward Markus and received a kind of slap-shake goodbye.

"I say we race each other." Kris gave a small two-fingered salute of farewell before disappearing into the bunker.

Tommy followed. "Do you now?"

"Yeah. We'll see who can reach the palace the fastest while carrying the other. You go this time, I'll go next time. I'll set the stopwatch. Ready?"

Tommy's answer was faint. "Sure, come on over here."

A moment later, Kris gave a shout of indignation that faded into silence.

Markus was smiling when she looked at him across the table. "I was having fun," she said.

"I know. But you wanted to try this, right?" Only then did she notice weariness around his eyes.

Uncertain, she nodded.

He picked up the flashlight from his end of the table. "I'll head out for a while with the guards and you can see how it feels."

See how it feels to be by herself in the middle of the forest. She could switch off the lantern and feel night around her. Experience the improbable sensation of knowing she was truly alone. She could speak unheard and move unobserved. There would be no one within hearing or calling distance. No humans, anyway.

Her fingers curled at the thought. "Are there leopards in Kiraly?"

"Leopards?" Markus looked baffled. "I don't think so. Why?"

"It's just a—joke I have with Cy."

"You'll be safe." He was leaving, striding out the door, completely unconcerned that he'd be swallowed by the pine trees within seconds.

"Markus," she said, standing, her fingertips on the tabletop.

He stopped in the doorway and glanced back, brows raised.

"I don't want to."

He shifted, frowning, turning to face her side-on.

"I don't want to be alone with myself when I could be alone with you."

Her words seemed to melt across his face.

"Not as a distraction," she said. "Just right here, with you."

His mouth softened, and gentle lines spread around his

eyes. Closing the door, he slid the flashlight into his back pocket, the upward-facing beam backlighting his head and shoulders.

"Then be with me," he said, and extended a hand toward her.

Pulse tripping, she crossed the floor. Her hand met his outstretched palm and his fingers closed, drawing her near, while his other hand curved around the back of her head and cupped her toward him. His mouth, when it closed over hers, was hot and sure and sighing, and her heart kicked against her breastbone at the honest taste of him. This man might have forgotten how to tell a woman he liked her, but his body remembered how to show her. His lips shifted, waiting until she matched his movements before his tongue took over, pushing deeper to where taste collided with desire, unraveling like a spool of silk. His hands slid down her spine, tracing the waistband of her pajamas, splaying over her backside, gripping, pulling her closer. Her mind fogged as she palmed his chest, his shoulders, until a hazy memory lowered her explorations, and yes, there was the torn denim over the front of his thigh she'd seen the day they'd met. He kissed harder when her fingers found skin, pressing circles just shy of the lining of his front pocket, a tender space, and he groaned, his lips slipping on hers.

Desire squeezed harder, a knot constricted, when he found the cord to her coat. He untied it single-handedly and grasped her waist, his fingers curling, clenching when she rose to her toes and leaned her full weight against him. Time parted after that, as did the top few buttons of his shirt and her thighs around the bend of his knee.

This was how it felt to kiss someone in utter privacy. Not a thought spared for sharp ears, or fast mouths, or footsteps that might or might not be on a mission to intervene. Not a sensation lost or taste un-savored or touch received with distraction.

She would trade royalty for normality, forever, right now.

"Ava," he murmured eventually, pulling back for breath.

She moved with him, her torso fastened to his, her hands at his back. It was freedom, being stuck to this man.

"I—" He swiftly leaned down, pressing another kiss on her lips. He held still, eyes shut, his touch like a merging of puffed breaths in the cold of her soul. Longing replaced his mouth when he withdrew. "You make me feel adolescent."

She swallowed, shifting, placing her hand at the base of her throat. Her pulse flew in the hollows of her collarbones. "What does that mean?"

His answering smile held mischief, the wayward grin of a cowboy offering to share the saddle of his horse despite the rough ride.

"Actually," she said, her face heating, "I've just worked it out."

His smile faded. "I expect nothing from you."

And that was why she wanted to give him everything—wanted to accept the hand-up and sit pressed hard against his back. He gave her power over her own life. He was kind, and generous, and his gaze alone soothed her jagged insides. It wasn't just his body she wanted to share, but his journey forward. A traitorous thought flared before she could snuff it out.

Their match would make everyone happy.

Guilt struck swiftly. An instant clogging of her airways, her arteries. *No.* It would never make her happy. Nothing could, until her existence entwined with her son's. Without Darius, she was a torso torn open with the heart removed. She was an outline, a single dimension, a bolt of fabric yet to be colored. How could she think, even accidentally, of settling with Markus?

The quiet of the night seemed to expose her. Her heart suddenly feared her head.

Her inhale was sharp. "I can't be with you."

He frowned. Her skin felt cold, pale, under his stare. "People can like each other without anything coming of it, remember? No plans. That's what we're doing."

Overwhelmed, she withdrew. "I've been reading your book," she said, lapsing into her default. Deflecting her pain by causing it in another.

His inhale paused, a questioning hitch.

"I noticed it falls open to a particular page." A man standing on a mountaintop at dusk, his eyes closed, his head tilted back in contentment at the untouched landscape below. "And I wonder how a man who wants so little will be happy with so much?"

His gaze shuttered closed.

"Your life won't be spent alone with your brothers and horses."

"No," he said.

"You won't have days where you wake up with no plans and go hiking in the sunlight and return after dark."

His chest filled and emptied. His frown deepened.

"You'll never be able to forget what lies on your shoulders and feel unfettered joy."

"I'm not sure what your angle is," he said, his voice low, "but I know."

Her angle looped back to herself. "This evening, this moment, felt easy." She shook her head. "But you'll need to learn to take pleasure in abundance rather than absence, because you'll so often have more than less. This"—she gestured around the cabin—"isn't what royal life is like."

His brows knitted as he watched her.

"Nothing about your life will be simple."

"Ava," he murmured.

"You're deluding yourself, Markus. I need you to know that."

He tilted his head, his eyes sad. Somehow, she knew it was sadness for her, not himself.

"I'll worry about you," she said in a rush, cupping his face a moment before she stepped back from him entirely.

Her heart tore when he raised a hand to his cheek. "And I already worry about you."

His affection stung, like sweet tea far too hot.

"How long until you leave Kiraly?"

Panic jerked inside her. "Next week. Six days." She feared that were true—that she would return home with her parents, leaving behind any hope of being a mother to her boy. "If not sooner," she added in desperation.

"Right."

"I think—we should go back." She couldn't be here anymore. "Erwin will be out of his mind with bewilderment when Kris and Tommy come out of the map room."

Markus said nothing about the rareness of this privacy and how it wouldn't be so bad if they took an hour or two longer to explore the flame they'd lit in each other. He nodded once, his gaze sweeping over her, and gestured for her to lead the way.

He didn't fill the silence on the walk back.

17

Mark stalked the dark paths of the palace grounds an hour before sunrise. Buck and Bull trotted in front. He let them lead, hardly seeing the world around him.

He couldn't make sense of her. The facts were too random.

Ava seemed more frayed now than when she'd been under the threat of strategic marriage. She'd had somewhere to be during the press conference, something urgent, and hadn't made it in time. Cyrus had mentioned a family secret. Had that been what made her cry with such hopelessness?

The dogs banked right, heading for the rear courtyard. Mark shook his head. Gul and Erwin, who he'd assumed were her protectors, seemed to instead ensure she was always guarded. But why? What did they think she'd do?

There was something she'd been waiting years for. What? And what was her plan?

Frustration balled his hands. Whatever it was, he wanted to ease her pain. Wanted to spend more time with her, even once she returned to Kelehar. Wanted to hold her again, tight, right now, kiss her neck, the soft skin beneath her jaw, because damn it, he hadn't done it while she'd been in his arms. He wanted to bring her happiness and peace and freedom, and for her to trust him enough to share her burden.

Her life unsettled him. Something felt wrong, like seeing bruised skin as someone adjusted their clothing and knowing it hadn't been caused by accident. He'd seen too many of Ava's emotional bruises and burned to catch the hand that caused them.

He walked on, lost in thought, the cowboy in him determined to protect the woman he'd fallen for and the king in him opening his arms wide, swearing to use every resource at his disposal—pull every string, listen at every door—in order to stop those who harmed her.

Ava awoke to loud voices in her sitting room. Too exhausted to move, she opened her eyes and saw thick light edging her curtains. The air was warm, and her morning cup of tea had clouded over beside the bed. Had she been left to sleep late?

Gul spoke firmly on the other side of her bedroom door. "You can't go in there."

A woman with a low, throaty voice said, "I can and will. Remember being told that I'm the ultimate security in this place? Yeah. That's kicking in, so get back outside, buddy. I got it covered from here." And then the door to Ava's bedroom flew open and a woman strode in, throwing it closed behind her. By the time it slammed, she was halfway across the room.

Ava sat up, clutching the sheets around her nightclothes, and demanded, "Who are you?"

The woman had short red hair, shaved at the sides and spiky at the top. Her parakeet-green jacket was fitted with more zips than was strictly necessary, and the boots pulled over tight black jeans had far too many buckles. The shape of her face was pretty—wide, with a cute chin. Her expression, on the other hand, was no bullshit.

"Your Highness." The woman stopped by the bedside. Feet planted, she stared down at Ava with a hard gaze. Then she bowed fractionally, an obvious afterthought.

Confused, Ava lapsed into criticism. "You're supposed to curtsey."

"I don't prescribe to the enforcement of gender-based tradition."

Ava blinked. "I said, who are you?"

"I'm here to make a deal." The woman didn't look around Ava's room; she showed no sign of curiosity at all. Her green gaze held Ava's with unsettling steadiness. "You tell no one about this conversation—and you tell your guard to get his eavesdropping ass back into the corridor—and I'll help you."

"Help me?" Sheets slipping, she tugged up the neckline of her camisole and adjusted the strap. She didn't like the way this woman emanated authority. "With what? How to punk up my wardrobe? You can help by leaving."

But she didn't call out to Gul for help, and the woman didn't move.

"I'm head of personal security." The redhead's sharp gaze shifted over Ava's features. After a few moments, her lips twisted in dissatisfaction. "I know everything that happens here."

Ava's gut pitched. She prayed this was about her and Markus, because if it wasn't . . . "Gul, I'm fine," she called out. "Go back into the hall."

After a moment, the shadow of his feet disappeared from beneath the door. She heard the door to the sitting room snap closed.

The woman jerked her head. "Top choice. Like I said, you keep this meeting to yourself. The boys don't know I'm the one who lumped them all with guards, and you're not going to tell them."

The boys? The informality made her bristle. Who *was* this woman? Surely Markus and his brothers would assume they'd been assigned guards by the head of personal security. Why would it matter if they knew who that was? Unless—

"Do they know you personally?" she asked, her eyes narrowing.

The woman ignored the question. "In my position, I have access to security footage, guard reports, and palace gossip. I know more than anyone rightly should, and if you'll excuse me, Your Highness, your situation is fucked up."

Fear seized Ava's spine, but she forced herself to relax. This must be about being a pawn in her parents' game of strategy.

"It was," she said at last. "But King Markus refused the engagement."

The woman's expression didn't change. "I've had security follow you and your brother since you arrived. Your parents, too, while they were here." At Ava's infuriated glower, she continued, "If the alliance went ahead, not only did I want to be certain we could trust you, but that you would be safe in our city. Security in Kelehar would have done the same if positions were reversed. Besides, you were of special interest to me following your previous stunt with Prince Aron. And you've proven to be very fascinating."

Ava's insides went cold.

"Most notably, Wednesday afternoon, when paired with the reports of Prince Cyrus's activity."

Dread made her instantly sick.

"Explain yourself," Ava demanded, her voice thin but icy.

"I wouldn't usually do this." The woman paused. "But you've got Mark onside. He's asking every guard on my team about you. Cornering them one by one. It's not like him to use intimidation, but he's nailing it."

"What's he asking?" Ava's pulse sped. "What are they telling him?"

"Nothing. Because as individuals, they know nothing. It's only collectively . . ." She gestured to herself. "But he wants to help you. He's ordering them to find out what's wrong and report back."

Ava drew the sheets closer around her middle. "Will they?"

"If you do as I say, they'll have nothing to report." The redhead shoved a hand in the back pocket of her jeans, jutting a hip to the side. "I'm taking Mark's concern as his blessing as king for me to help you. Otherwise I could lose my job for this."

Ava's head was spinning. "What do you mean by *this*?"

"Getting you out of here so you can be with your kid."

This time, she almost was sick. Mouth clamped shut, she leaned forward to hold down a heave.

The woman knew.

Her rawest secret. The crown of Kelehar's greatest shame. Her deepest desire.

"Stop that." The woman sounded uncomfortable. "I'm not here to screw you over. I've done some digging, and it seems you've had enough people do that to you." She paused. "I saw a photo of the little Keleharian boy leaving the shelter. Another photo of you when you came out with skin like death." She paused and then said in a softer voice, "He looks like you."

Eyes closed, world ending, Ava said, "When will you report this to Markus?"

"This has got nothing to do with Kiraly. And it's not my secret to share."

Startled, Ava snapped her head up. She stared, disbelieving, until she finally said, "You . . ."

The woman stared back, waiting.

"You're really here to help?"

The redhead rolled her eyes. "Really."

The Kiralian head of personal security wanted to make the princess of Keleher's escape fantasy a reality. The woman could lose more than her job for meddling on this scale. "I'm not awake enough for this conversation."

"Then listen. I'm doing my best to run a tight ship and the palace security timetable doesn't change, except on the rare occasion of a large-scale event." She paused and arched a single brow.

"The Welcome Tea," Ava said, after a beat.

"We bring in contracted security to assist. They'll be covering the north and west grounds. Our guards will be overworked during the day, so we'll use a smaller team than usual for the night shift once the contracted team leave. At eight o'clock tomorrow night, I'll get them to change posts—clear of the west wing. It's still under construction, but it's been assessed. It's structurally sound." She tapped her fingers against her side. "Go in through the blocked entrance on the ground floor—off the atrium to the western gardens—and you'll find an opening to the underground tunnels. I've been told Markus has already shown you one of them. Take the stairs to the basement and turn left. That tunnel goes beneath the city and emerges in a laneway behind the lakeside cafés."

Shock held Ava still, her mouth open.

"I'd originally thought your son could meet you at the lake, but if that Gul guy is keeping tabs on him, then he'll be followed, and you need a clean exit. Instead, your kid and his guards will come to the palace during the Welcome Tea tomorrow afternoon. All guests will be ID-checked at the gates. Your son and his guards will be allowed in—anyone else from Kelehar, who may or may not be security shadowing them, will not."

Ava couldn't speak. This strange, hard-edged woman had spent time planning this—for *her*.

"I'm about to go talk to your brother, and then to your friend at the shelter. Prince Cyrus will instruct your kid's team to lay low. A room will be arranged for them to wait in without disruption until the change of guard tomorrow night. You can't wait with them because I can't guarantee that you won't be observed. They'll meet you in the west wing just after eight. Cyrus will meet you here, in your rooms, and will dismiss Gul. Then he'll go down to the west wing with you and I'll erase all the surrounding security footage." She blew out a breath. "You'll head into the tunnels. An unmanned car will be waiting in the parking lot near the lakeside toilet block. You'll leave Kiraly for your desired destination."

"Luxembourg." A tiny town in the country's north, scarcely on the map. Cyrus had organized a house on its outskirts. It had a garden, window boxes, and a fireplace in the kitchen.

"I'll spread the cover story that you've run away with a commoner. Anyone who cares will be looking for you paired with a man. Not with a child. You'll spend today being seen around Kira City to give credence to the idea that you met your commoner lover here for a rendezvous. You'll cut your hair?"

"I—" She hadn't thought of that. "Yes."

"You speak German?"

Ava nodded. "And some French. I've been seeing an accent coach at home." Language wouldn't betray her.

"You know how to plant something useless in a tiny pot?"

She opened her mouth to answer, before halting with narrowed eyes.

The woman tilted her head, the first hint of humor slanting her lips. "I see you've armed yourself with all the important things."

"I can light a fire now," she said defensively.

"Then your usefulness is no longer in question. Good luck." Then she gave a single nod and strode toward the door.

"Wait." Ava leaned to watch her around the bedpost. "Kristof wants to talk to you about a security matter."

The woman glanced over her shoulder, her fingers on the door handle. Her expression was as impenetrable as a locked iron door as she muttered, "Does he now."

"He—" Ava hesitated. "He has a theory. It would be prudent if he didn't talk about it with anyone else."

The redhead clicked her tongue, looking pissed.

It was the familiarity of the movement that finally caught Ava's attention. The almost intimate eye roll that implied she didn't think Kris would be trouble. She *knew*.

"You didn't tell me your name," Ava said.

Something in the woman's gaze flickered. "Frankie," she said, and her voice sharpened as she continued. "Don't tell Kris. I'll handle him when I'm ready."

Ava stared as the door slammed shut, startled by the realization that the friend Kris had left behind in Sage Haven was actually the head of personal security in Kiraly. It seemed she'd already known he was a prince; that he wasn't the only one who'd kept monumental secrets.

Then Ava's stomach writhed and shimmered with nerves.

Escape plan—take three.

As instructed, she spent the day in Kira City.

She endeavored to be seen by as many types of people as possible, making herself hard to miss by pairing her electric-blue dress with a sunflower-yellow scarf. The more eyewitnesses to confirm that Princess Ava had been in the city—and to speculate that she definitely could have met up with a man while there—the better.

She had morning tea in an average café known for giving customers the "Kiralian experience," which she could only assume meant loud clientele, laughing counter staff, brightly colored chairs and walls, and food that tasted roughly five hundred times better than it looked. She chatted with the waiters and asked the locals for directions.

She shopped in the elite precinct that curved around the lake and ate lunch in a restaurant reserved for the global cultural cream.

She visited tourist attractions. Walked the length of the pier, stared at the central train station's intricate architecture, and forced herself up a wide set of steps known locally as The Scepter, beautifully cobbled and wickedly steep, stretching many blocks from the center of the city directly toward the palace. She stopped to talk to people as she climbed, fixing herself in their memories, and gazed above to where the palace sat on the horizon. Due to the angle of the hill, the crest concealed the remaining stretch of civilization that lay between the city and royal family, creating an illusion of being on the monarch's doorstep.

The illusion could also make a susceptible mind wonder whether the king was gazing down from his study, his attention caught by the speck of a princess on the slopes of his city.

She thought about Markus every moment of the day. She imagined meeting him on the street, a man with country manners and an easy smile, and being drawn to those steady hands as he pointed out directions. She imagined him recommending the cardamom pastry twist with black tea at his favorite cafe, and her shy invitation for him to join her. In her mind, he sat beside her, and she didn't hear a word he said because she was too busy watching the way his mouth moved, the swell of his bottom lip and the lift at the corners, always on the brink of smiling. She could fall hard for a man like him. She imagined him strolling by her side along the lake edge, showing her the sights, and by midafternoon, she would let him hold her hand. Under the watchful gaze of the palace, he would kiss her atop The Scepter—a sweet, cautious embrace that would leave her heart in his breast pocket at the day's end.

If she were a restless royal, Ava could have been tempted to run away with a man like Markus.

Gul was her actual companion. He shadowed her without speaking, and she refused to turn around. It had been two days since they'd shared an intentional glance, let alone a conversation, and silence weighted his presence behind her until it felt like her bulky guard was literally hanging off her back.

By the time they returned to the palace in the late afternoon sunlight, the weight had become so unbearable it had crept around to tug at the base of her throat.

It choked her to think of leaving him like this.

"Gul," she said abruptly, throwing open the door from her guest chambers. He straightened from where he stood with his back to the corridor wall, surprise clearing the gloom from his face.

"Yes, Your Highness?"

Her heart tore at his use of her proper honorary title. "Come inside."

She stepped back and he moved in, cautious, shutting the door behind him. Then he stood, silent, his gaze on the golden rug beneath his feet. She didn't back away but stayed opposite him until her throat thickened and tears warmed her eyes. She wanted to be close to him. She didn't want to lose him, this man she couldn't trust who just so happened to be one of her best friends. She swallowed and said unsteadily, "You stopped me."

His head snapped up, his features hurt. "I had no choice."

"You know everything." Betrayal hushed her words. "How could you stop me when you know everything?"

"How could you put me in that situation, knowing that I know everything, and knowing who I work for?"

She glared through hot eyes. Answerable only to the queen, Gul would be held personally responsible if Ava vanished. She wrapped her arms around her middle, hating that in her single-mindedness, she hadn't wanted to consider that making her life richer could destroy his.

"And I let you go," he said, a firm thread in his soft voice. "I didn't stop you. I delayed you. I let you go, Princess."

"You delayed me," she said. "And then you called Cyrus and—" Her lips trembled. "I missed him."

"It wasn't going to work." His hands balled by his sides. "You created a scene, driving off like that. It would have exposed everything. Too many people saw you."

She hardly heard him. Words hollow, she repeated, "I missed him."

She might miss him again.

"Don't blame me for this," he said, voice wavering.

"Who should I blame?" Tears fell and she almost believed it when she said, "Myself?"

"You know I don't—"

"It's always been my fault. I was stupid and foolish for falling for a common—"

"It's *never* been your fault!" Gul's shout startled her, and she stepped back suddenly. He exhaled, pressing his palm to his forehead, and bowed deeply. "Forgive me."

She blinked, her lashes wet. He had never raised his voice at her.

"I'm scared for you," he said next, his face lowered. "I get angry that I can't help."

She wanted to lift a hand to the lushness of his black hair. Her beautiful friend. Softly, she said, "You want me to help you to resign."

He lifted his face to her, broad and broken. "If you will."

She nodded, stricken, and waited for his explanation.

His eyes shone with regret. "I can't do this anymore. I care too much about you. I can't live with myself for keeping you from him. But if I don't do my duty, your parents could stop me from ever finding work again, perhaps more than that." He exhaled roughly. "This situation is highly sensitive, so I fear I have a lot to lose if I fail."

Her arms locked tighter around her middle. "Cyrus would defend you."

"Don't." He shook his head. "Please don't make me choose between you and them."

Her stomach roiled. He was asking her to wait until he successfully resigned before she attempted another meeting with Darius.

And she intended to deceive him tomorrow night.

"I don't want to lose you." Her voice wavered.

He nodded, his features pained. "Me neither."

She swallowed bitterness. "I've learned something recently."

He waited.

"It's possible to miss someone when they're right beside you."

His mouth puckered. Then his chin lifted. "I know what you mean," he said, his words unsteady. "I hope you'll keep in touch."

She wished she could promise him that.

Instead, after the silence stretched out, she said, "Oh, I bought these today," and moved to her boutique shopping collection. Her hands trembled as she picked up a cream fabric bag with silk handles that held several boxes. One box held a wind-soft silk shirt, another a blazer of deep burgundy velvet, both items much too large, and a third box contained dark eye makeup.

"I was shopping for something to do. I don't actually want any of it." She held the bag out, her stomach twisting. "Could you take them away?"

The silk handles slipped onto his fingers with a gentle hiss.

"Make sure they end up with someone who'll love wearing them." She had chosen the shirt to match the silk scarf she had given him the other day.

Gul didn't quite meet her eyes as he lowered the bag to his side. "I will."

She covered the impending silence. "Would you like to stay for a while? We can chat." He loved chatting. She hadn't ever chatted with him enough. She tried to smile and her cheeks strained.

"Yes. Thank you."

They talked into the evening, a disjointed, stilted conversation as they went out of their way to avoid the truth lying between them.

He planned to leave her.

She planned to leave him.

All too soon, they would never see each other again.

The light tap on Mark's door came just before midnight. Five quick knocks—just like when Ava had found him in his study a few days before. He tossed his laptop onto the couch beside him, almost finished with the final details for tomorrow's event, and strode to open the door.

She wore red pajama pants and fluffy slippers. Her hair was braided and her eyes looked puffy with sleep debt.

"Hello," she said.

Silently, he stood back to let her in.

He'd grilled his security team about her. Had they seen anything suspicious or untoward about her and her family? No, nothing to report. Had they observed anything odd about her staff or the bodyguards who shadowed her? No. Nothing. Could they provide him with details of her previous stay and everything that had transpired? Nothing had been recorded, for Prince Aron had wanted her visit wiped clean. Mark suspected he was simply aiming too low on the security chain, but he hadn't yet managed to coordinate a meeting with the head of personal security.

Ava's sweet fragrance knocked his thoughts away as she entered the room. He'd been kissing her this time last night and had missed the feel of her all day. She closed the door, turned to face him, and leaned her shoulder blades back against the ornate wood.

"I'm like a pendulum," she whispered, gentle on his senses like the quiet lighting of his single corner lamp. "Swinging toward you, swinging away. You must be getting sick of me."

He shook his head, as if it didn't matter. "Are you all right?"

"I, um." She paused. "I feel like I haven't slept properly in years."

He almost said he knew how that felt. But he suspected, compared to her, he wouldn't know the first thing.

"I must be almost delirious," she said, and laughed under her breath. "Or hysterical or delusional or unbearable to be around."

"I can bear it," he said.

She tilted her head, smiling, but the humor didn't reach her eyes. Her gaze traveled down his shirt and up again. "I'm going to miss you."

His heart stretched and he shifted closer. "You don't have to miss me."

"But I will," she said, and moved into his arms. Her kiss was demanding, voracious, and he moved fast, laying her back against the door, one palm on the wood, the other in her hair. She had come here for this. Not an exploration of taste and texture, but the release of sensory hunger. Her lips were rough on his, and her body moved with small, hard slides, as if she sought to squeeze through a crack that refused to let her pass. His hands moved up her sides and the warmth of her smooth skin cracked a whip on his lust. His shoulders rounded, confining her against the door, and he pushed his hands away from naked skin, down over the fabric on her hips. His body strained to strip her bare, but he fought desire, knowing that decision was hers.

"I would run away with you," she breathed, her words thick, as his lips moved down her chin. "I'd wear your shirts at breakfast and picnic with you in overgrown fields."

The romantic imagery bloomed in his mind. Then thorns dug into his throat.

They could have lived like that in Sage Haven.

His kisses reached the underside of her jaw. Her skin smelled like addiction.

"I would learn the names of all your horses and wait on the porch for you to come home."

He pulled back, his blood hot and his mind trying to focus. "The palace wouldn't stop you from learning the names of my horses." In a fluid movement, he shucked his shirt and handed it to her. For breakfast in a future she thought they couldn't have. "You're regretting things you don't need to."

His naked chest momentarily stole her attention. Then she

292

met his eyes, raising the shirt to her nose, clenching the flannel in her fist. She didn't answer.

"I want to help you," he said, moving in close again. Her knuckles pressed against his bare chest. "Please let me."

"I don't need your help," was her whispered response, her breath heating the hollow of his throat. "It's all going to work out. I just need to touch you."

All too easily swayed by her palms, he let her take what she needed. Open-mouthed kisses, her hands on his stomach, the crush of his arms around her. And when she finally slipped out the door, his shirt in her hand, her hair no longer braided and her lips swollen with attention, he was left with enough fire and urgency to ward off sleep for the entirety of his reign.

18

Mark and his brothers stood on the balcony adjoining his study, looking down at the front courtyard as guests arrived for the Welcome Tea. They hadn't spoken. They'd hardly moved, but for the occasional adjustment of the traditional suits that Philip had insisted they wear. Blazers and slacks the color of budding bluebells, piped and fringed with gold. Kris had scorned the glossy shoes provided and wore his old boots, while Tommy continued to tug at his cuffs and collar.

Mark shifted, one hand gripping the railing. His instructions were being carried out well.

Guests entered through the gatehouse, and palace staff directed them either through the front entrance or around to the eastern grounds, depending on the guest's preference for shelter or sunshine.

Live music would be playing in the gardens and grand ballroom. Various areas had been set up to accommodate their guests—the banquet hall, the recital hall for people who preferred to sit, and the grand ballroom. Security blocked all other doorways and staircases, along with any garden paths leading from the designated outdoor areas.

Food was to be served throughout the event. The menu featured dessert recipes from Montana—treats the brothers had so often received as thanks for helping a neighbor with heavy chores, or wolfed down on the walk home from a bake stall in town. Cinnamon rolls, huckleberry pies, sandwiches, and giant bowls of cherries.

"Look." Tommy pointed at a group of women making their way up the great steps.

Kris gave a laugh and Mark grinned. They each carried a plate piled high with what could only be home-baked goods. A symbolic gesture, presumably in response to the royal family's leading example of a sharing community.

Tommy whacked Mark on the back. "This was a good idea."

He glanced at his brothers. "We ready?"

"Sure." Kris nodded.

Tommy's tone was sardonic. "Always."

The plan was for Mark and Kris to mingle, circulating separately so guests wouldn't cotton on to the fact that only two princes were among them.

"I'll come down for the last part," Tommy said, stepping back from the ledge. Guests from higher positions in society had been invited to stay for an extra hour in the ballroom, along with the press: politicians, executives, and people of influence across all sectors, from mining and engineering, to education and social services. The brothers wanted to meet Kiraly's decision-makers.

Mark wouldn't hold Tommy to it, but said, "See you then."

Kris was rumpling his hair and adjusting his blazer so only the middle button remained closed. He flicked a hand into his back pocket, exposing a wedge of his belt. Apparently finished preening, Kris met Mark's exasperated gaze with a self-satisfied grin.

"Let's go meet the neighbors," he drawled.

Ava sat to the side of the string quartet in the grand ballroom and waited for her body to give out around her. It couldn't maintain such levels of anxiety—too much of her was affected. The emotion wasn't confined to her mind or chest but seethed and flexed all over. It clenched her gut, pressed her lungs, and channeled restless energy into her legs. She couldn't stop swallowing. She was sensitive to touch, hyperalert to the shifting details around her, yet simultaneously disengaged. Her heightened physical state made it difficult to retreat entirely into her head, but she came close in her obsession with a single thought.

I'll be with Darius tonight.

The Welcome Tea unfolded around her. She'd positioned herself on the side edge of the stage before guests started arriving, safely outside the clutches of interaction. Gul stood several feet in front of her. Let the guests think that only a seat this close to the musicians was good enough for the Princess of Kelehar.

The day's hours had blurred, meaningless, around the pinpoint in time that would change everything.

Just after eight.

Hands clenched, ridden with anxiety, she waited.

Guests gradually filled the room, some standing awkwardly near the walls, others chatting in excited groups. Attire, as usual, was as bright as a rainbow, and ranged from tidy jeans and blouses to beautiful spring dresses. Some men wore suits, while others stood in the overalls that they'd likely worn to work that morning. All spoke in hushed voices, allowing the music to dominate, aware that the social rules of being a guest were exaggerated in this context.

It was almost bewildering that everyone was oblivious to the nerves thrashing inside her.

She waited. More people came.

A line of tables to the side of the room served tea and sweets. Guests lined up, perfectly orderly, and ate using the very tips of their fingers. Did they think the underutilization of the body was a sign of sophistication? Perhaps they weren't mistaken. They stood in small groups. Older couples, teenage groups of friends, families.

Children.

She waited, closer to the edge of her chair, her quads burning.

Kris entered at one point and slowly prowled the room. He clasped hands and made small talk, leaving a sea of beguiled glances in his wake. He reserved a lopsided grin for a handful of guests, tilting his head just so, striking a hand through his hair and receiving every shade of reciprocation in return. A shy tinge; an ardent blush. He worked the room with as much effort as a lover grazing a finger over skin, yet still the guests reacted like he'd promised them a lifetime.

Then he left.

Time must have passed.

Gul caught her attention when he pulled his phone from his pocket and answered a call. It was brief. He faced the room, stiff back to her for a long while after he hung up. When he finally turned to look at her over his shoulder, he bore her betrayal like a gash across his handsome face.

Guilt was no match for her deranged joy. Darius must have made it into the palace—and Gul's guards must have been refused at the gate.

She swallowed. She waited.

Markus was announced and her mind lunged into focus. He was a figure of clarity in a haze of faces. His eyes found hers

297

with his first step into the room and her nervousness burgeoned. She would burst soon, skin tearing and folding open, puckering apart like eggplant smoked too long. Markus watched her for longer than he should, careless of the attention of his guests, of how they turned to follow his gaze to the princess sitting alone at the front edge of the stage.

He raised a hand with a small smile, tilting an invisible hat in her direction.

She inclined her head in a whisper of a movement.

He circulated, shaking hands and asking questions. People began to leave. The crowd thinned. Then it built again with a finer type of person, well dressed, more confident, and without children in tow. The press entered next, dispersing like an insidious spray.

Zara appeared by her side in a sudden swoop. "Oh my God," she said in a rush, kneeling beside the chair and grasping Ava's hands. "This is epic."

Ava tried to focus on her. "Epic," she repeated.

"You look like shit, sitting up here." Zara squeezed her hands, and she shot a look at Gul's back. He was too many paces away, the general chatter too loud for him to overhear. "People will have noticed. In hindsight, it'll be easy for them to believe you've been pining for your gorgeous common lover."

Ava's gaze drifted over Markus. A canker weighted heavily, low in her belly.

"It's good. It means the story will hold." Her friend leaned in closer. "He's here. Safe. You remember what to do?"

She could recite every word. She nodded.

"Good, good. Hey, that Frankie's something, isn't she?" Zara patted the back of Ava's hand, and then twisted her head to read Ava's slim gold watch. "God, I'm so nervous. I keep having to pee. Only a couple more hours. How are you?"

"So nervous," she breathed, the words scarcely hinting at the mess inside her.

"Yeah, wow. I'll be there later." She darted another glance at Gul, before leaning in for a parting hug. "I'm going to find Adam. Try to enjoy yourself," she whispered. "Store up on royal life. You might miss it sometime."

Then she disappeared into the crowd.

Gul turned to eye Ava. His features were blank.

Pain shredded her pride, yet it was only a shadow of her mounting fear. What if this plan failed too? She looked away and saw that Kris had returned. Markus moved to greet him by the entrance, gaining enthusiastic attention from the press. Cameras flashed and they posed agreeably, grinning, arms around each other's shoulders. Then the flashes intensified, excited by something new, and as the light faded, she saw that two brothers had become three.

Tommy was here? It was interesting enough to haul Ava out of her stupor. She didn't know the root of his troubles, but crowds clearly hurt him. His skin was pasty, his features tight. His fingers didn't stop thrumming against his thighs and his eyes seemed weighted to the floor. He hauled his gaze up, over and over again, as the flashes continued.

Markus and Kris bracketed him, arms around his shoulders, both relaxed and easy, body language claiming that everything was all good.

Within minutes, she overheard people saying that Prince Tomas wasn't feeling well. "Must be coming down with a bug," someone said to their partner near the stage. "So much change in such little time. But don't they look grand in the royal blue?"

Then the room hushed, and Markus delivered the speech she'd helped him prepare. Trust, integrity, and intention. Despite having read the final version, she couldn't follow what he was saying and vaguely worried that it made no sense at all. But people applauded and cameras flashed and she assumed everyone else had understood the disjointed string of sounds.

The brothers did their best to interact with every person in attendance. Markus peeled off first, a king in high demand, and she watched how Kris continued to talk in Tommy's ear, strolling with him around the room, signaling that these two brothers were having fun together and wouldn't be separated.

Then a group of his admirers gusted around Kris and he was dragged away.

She shifted, her hands curling around the base of the chair. Tommy was close to the front of the ballroom now. His expression was neutral, but she could see the strain around his neck and the rigid set of his shoulders. Kris laughed amid conversation, taking the chance to do a subtle eye-sweep for his brother. With too many people between them, he found Ava's gaze instead.

She understood his silent plea.

Tommy's path had scooped in front of the stage. He hadn't noticed her. He turned his back, seeming intent on the exit.

"Your Royal Highness," a journalist said nearby. "Prince Tomas."

He stilled. His hands became fists. He turned, raising a brow, his features almost pleasant.

"You've kept yourself private since you arrived," the man said and raised a small recording device, "leaving your brothers to do the social heavy lifting. Why is that?"

Tommy scratched behind his ear. He looked politely puzzled, but his soft voice was unsteady as he answered, "Is that an appropriate question to ask a prince?"

"What compelled you to leave solitude behind this evening?" the man instantly rephrased.

Tommy's skin was too pale. "The occasion."

"You've hardly been seen since you arrived. What's kept you so busy?"

"Google *royal obligations*," he said.

The journalist laughed. "You're set on avoiding my questions. Are you struggling with being thrown into royal life? Perhaps, as a man of the land, you think monarchy is antiquated?"

Ava stood so suddenly, the room blurred around her.

There was no safe answer to such a question.

"I'm weary," she declared loudly. The front third of the ballroom looked her way, Tommy's predators included. His eyes clashed with hers. "And exceptionally bored." She pushed a pin back into her hair. "I've hardly had a moment of suitable company all day." She set her attention on the reclusive prince. "Prince Tomas," she called, moving past Gul and down the few steps off the stage. "You're an angel come to take me away. You, at least, can talk about something more interesting than how *amazing* the ceiling is or how *special* it is to be invited to stand around all day. The mundanity of this crowd . . ."

His eyes were wild, but he jerked his head in a nod. When she reached him, she had to hold her hand up, eyes darting pointedly to his elbow, before he extended his arm.

"Your Highness, Princess Ava—" the journalist began.

"The *mundanity*," she repeated, her voice harsh as she looked directly at him.

She and Tommy made for the exit.

As they neared the large double doors, propped wide open, she noticed Markus positioned to farewell those departing. Entirely inappropriate for a king, yet she melted at his decency. He was a good man. How ironic that she was going to escape the world he'd just entered when his existence would have finally made that world bearable.

He caught her eye as she departed with her hand on

Tommy's arm. It was the kind of look where features didn't change, expression betrayed nothing, but both parties instinctively knew the meaning behind it. He thanked her for looking out for his brother. She acknowledged that she'd simply done what needed doing. And then she was leading Tommy down a bunting-bright corridor, wondering whether their final instant of eye contact had meant what she'd thought it meant.

Markus would come for her later.

Tommy let her lead. She took him upstairs, right to the top floor, and along the corridor with glass walls so they could look at the night sky above the city. The sense of openness, endlessness, was more endurable than closed walls.

It was later than she'd realized. Her watch was nearing seven.

"Thank you," he said.

"Stay with me." Gul wouldn't question her about Darius while she was with a prince of Kiraly. Her guard remained partway down the corridor, out of hearing range, his eyes trained on her. She didn't deserve full privacy. "As a return favor."

So Tommy remained and in an odd way, she found relief in his anxious companionship.

"Are you okay?" he asked, his soft voice sliding through the silence.

She stared at a flickering star. "No."

It was a solid half-minute before he said, "Neither am I."

She eyed him with dulled concern. She cared. But her heart was overfull with her own fear. "I'm sorry."

"Nah," he said, smiling bitterly at the sky. "You didn't cause it. And you got me out of there." A single chime came from Tommy's pocket. Frowning, he pulled out his phone. Then he glanced at her. "Mark says he's left the Welcome Tea, but Philip has cornered him for a debrief. He's asked if I'm still with you."

A different kind of nerves tumbled inside her. "You appear to be."

Tommy's thumb flew across the screen. Then, "I've been turned into a messenger."

She arched a brow.

"He wants to know if you'll meet with him. He wants to talk to you."

She had less than an hour. It would keep Gul at bay. "Tell him to come to my rooms."

Mouth lifting wryly, Tommy typed back.

"Where is Kris?" she asked.

"Um." His thumb kept moving. He paused for a moment, before saying, "In the kitchen."

"Would he mind coming up here?" She couldn't keep Tommy strapped to her side until Markus was free. She would take advantage of his other brother. "I want to talk to him, just for a moment."

After a pause, he said, "He's on his way."

Somehow, the man by her side seemed to understand that she didn't want to be alone. He waited as more and more stars glinted into view, until finally Kris appeared at the far end of the glass corridor. He approached with a swagger, a one-sided smile, and a sandwich.

"Did you know we have a planetarium?" He shook his head as he neared. "I accidentally found it instead of this corridor."

"I knew." Tommy looked at her, his features neutral.

"Thanks Tomas," she said. "Have a good—night."

She wouldn't see him again.

His brow flickered. "You too."

Kris slapped his brother on the upper arm, a parting gesture. "You should get a sandwich."

"Yeah." Tommy gave a nod. "I'll head down to a kitchen packed with chefs and assistants, stressed out of their minds after today's event. That'll help me wind down. Help them relax too. Great plan."

Kris bit into his sandwich and gave his brother the thumbs up. He grinned as he chewed.

Shaking his head with a smile, Tommy left them. As he passed Gul, her guard stepped back out of the way, lowering his head, just as Tommy stepped in that direction to cut behind him. They almost collided and both sprung back as if scalded. Tommy raised his hands apologetically, while Gul's chin pressed against his chest, his cheeks flaming.

Tommy actually jogged to get away.

"Awkward," Kris said.

She glanced at him. If only he knew the awkwardness of his own situation—the woman he coveted was watching his every move. "Yes," she said.

He took another bite. "You wanted to talk?"

"You were right about me."

His jaw froze mid-chew. Disbelief flashed in his eyes.

"I didn't know you were right at the time." She swallowed and realized that her inability to stop swallowing had eased at some point. The nervous habit kicked back into gear. "I've messed with him. I've made him think I like him, because I do, but I'm going to leave him anyway."

His chest expanded and he lowered the sandwich. "I don't think you get what it means that Mark really likes you."

"It means I have something I don't deserve."

"Yes," he answered, his voice hard.

That added density to the canker in her gut. An ache for Markus formed in anticipation of leaving him behind. It already hurt, but like a shiver of fear preceding an event assured to be terrifying, she knew she'd felt nothing yet.

"No," Kris said next, looking down and shaking his head. "It means you have something you don't think you deserve. It means . . . it doesn't matter why you don't think you deserve him, because that's never going to matter to Mark. When us brothers came into existence, he got all the decency. Tom and I do all right, but we're not decent. Men don't come better than Mark. He makes everything okay. Okay?"

She could have agreed, or at least nodded. Instead, she said in an empty voice, "Will you walk me back to my rooms?"

He sighed, running a hand over his mouth. "Sure."

They walked without talking. The next time she traveled along the palace halls would be on her way to the west wing. She halted several times, overcome by fright of the unknown, and Kris's frown got deeper each time.

"You haven't looked well all afternoon," he said as they rounded the corridor that led to her guest suite. Her heart lurched at the sight of Markus approaching from the opposite direction and Kris halted immediately. "Anyway," he murmured, raised a hand at his brother, and set off the way they'd come.

Panicked, she glanced after him and inadvertently met Gul's eyes from half a dozen paces away. Her guard's expression went blank.

Markus had stopped outside her door. He didn't speak; he didn't need to.

She swallowed and let him inside.

With the door closed, locked, she crossed the sitting room and started opening the windows. She couldn't breathe. Her pores were blocked; her lungs weren't taking in enough oxygen. Almost dizzy, she darted into the bedroom and opened the double doors leading to her balcony. Cool night air enveloped her, a hushed touch, and she gasped it down, closing her eyes. Then the air shifted, tightened.

She turned to Markus.

He leaned against the doorframe, his arms crossed loosely. Concern lined his brow. "You're not yourself," he said.

She was herself, heightened.

"You don't know me." Not an accusation, but a pained confession.

His forehead creased further. "Ava."

"I'm leaving earlier than expected." And she wasn't coping.

"When?" A frown deepened the question.

"Tonight."

He pulled back, his open heart seeming to retreat with his body. Confusion flashed across his face, then hid behind impatience. "What?"

She touched a shaking hand to her face. She swallowed again.

"Why do you need to leave tonight?"

"Because," she said, granting herself one confession. "My future depends on it."

He stared at her, backlit by the golden glow of a single lamp inside. In a low voice, he said, "That's hard to hear, because it feels as if my future depends on you staying."

"Markus—"

"I don't know what's going on with you." He stepped back, shaking his head, and disappeared into the bedroom.

Distressed, she ran her hands along her bare arms, stepping forward, stepping back, then pushing herself forward again into the bedroom. He stood with a strong hand gripping the wooden poster at the foot of the bed, his back to her. The royal blue of his blazer and trousers looked black in the dim light. He'd worn the color with the assurance of a king—a man at home in the bold, striking tone that set him apart in the crowded room.

"I've done this wrong." She stood just inside, the open curtain brushing her elbow. "I should have stayed away from you."

"Too late for that." His back stayed turned.

"I have a plan." A single focus. "You don't fit into it."

"There's no accounting for the people we meet," he said, and faced her. His broad shoulders looked bigger in the faint light, a dark stretch of body that she ached to curl beneath. "I had a plan too. I was going to run a ranch with my brothers. I was going to wake up every morning to a big open sky. I'd care for the horses and take the truck into town. Maybe I'd meet a woman; maybe she'd settle into our lives and I'd end up with everything I could ever want." He paused, eyes on her face. "And you know," he said, "it didn't happen."

She swallowed, her throat tight.

"Now I'm a king. I live above a city. I arrived here believing I'd have nothing I'd ever wanted. But then I met you. And I've realized that you're my open sky—the home for my cowboy heart."

Despite everything, her own heart tumbled with sodden joy at his words. A pathetic, mangled emotion that made her ache to feel happiness that wasn't drenched in sorrow.

"Sometimes, Ava, plans can change, and it still works out okay."

She shook her head, a fraction of a movement. "You don't understand," she whispered.

He didn't ask her to explain. "When can I see you again?"

His question gouged a new wound inside her. She didn't answer.

Never.

His brow bunched at her silence. "This isn't okay," he said next, shaking his head with a sudden exhale. "You won't tell me what the hell's going on. You've spent days looking like a ghost has walked through you." He paused. "You cry like someone's got a knife in your soul."

She blanched. When had—

"I heard you." He shoved his fingers through his hair. "After the meeting that day, I came to make sure I hadn't ruined relations with Keleher. And I heard you."

She turned away, that truth lodging in her chest like her breastbone had cracked and slipped sideways. She pressed a palm against it. Those tears had been for Darius. "That was private."

"Yet I can't unhear it." His voice softened. "And it rips me up knowing that pain is still there—knowing that you won't let me help get rid of it."

"It's my pain." She rounded on him, stung by his desire to heal her and her desire to let him. "You can't take it away from me."

At his stricken stare, her thoughts collapsed into a possible future where this third attempt to escape failed and she returned to Kelehar with no chance of disappearing. Guarded, shadowed, observed every second of every day. What then, but to allow herself a different kind of happiness with Markus? He would soothe her heart with love and kindness, and maybe, after a time, the pain of missing Darius would lessen to an ache of a life unattained.

She held her breath. *No.*

The queen of Kelehar had chosen her husband over her daughter. When Ava's father had delegated the problem of Ava's pregnancy to her, the queen had chosen to let her daughter suffer in order to please her husband.

Ava refused to prioritize a man over her son.

No matter how much she'd fallen in love with him.

"Please leave." She pushed herself to the bedroom door and gripped the open edge. It was the only thing that kept her upright. "Now."

He crossed to her, his jaw tight, his body tense. He stopped so close her stomach jolted, remembering her careless visit to his room the night before. She'd intended to say goodbye, but instead been derailed by the intensity of his touch, the excitement, the hook and ache between her legs. She'd hardly been able to stop shaking afterward. Gossip would be rampant among his staff—she had talked her way into the most private wing of the palace in her nightgown.

Once again, Markus was so near their shoes touched.

"You see me as a king, not a man," he said roughly. "Dominating, taking without asking." In a few swift jerks, he'd removed the blazer, balled it, and thrown it across the room. Discarding the clear symbol of his status. "Treating you how you expect to be treated."

She didn't move.

"Is that it?" His voice dropped to a murmur. His breath fluttered over her face. "You expect me to replace that pain with something that hurts just as much?"

She shook her head, but she wasn't sure of anything anymore.

"Ava," he said. "I want to help."

"I see you as a king, because it's what you are," she whispered, her hands slipping off the door. "Every second of your life will be scrutinized. Even if I trusted you with everything, we could never be together. I need to be unseen to be happy. And you will always be seen."

His eyes bored into hers; his chest ballooned with breath. Her words seemed to travel through him, a ball bearing rolling along a tunnel, dropping through a hole, before passing along another dark tunnel. Working out, perhaps, that not every problem had a tidy solution.

Then he said, in a voice quite unlike his own, "No one can see me now."

She stared, her heart pummeling her ribcage.

He stared back.

The passing seconds seemed to discard everything between them—doubt, fear, breath—until Markus slowly lifted a hand and placed it on the door. With a small shift of his shoulder, he pushed it closed behind her.

The bedroom was silent. A cool breeze moved in from the balcony. He didn't pull his arm away. Her shoulder was a hair's breadth beneath it and her skin strained for contact. She closed her eyes, but it only heightened the pain of having him so near without touching. She had just under an hour before she'd walk out of his life.

She had to make that time count.

"Yes," she said, and looked up at him.

His elbow bent as he closed in on her, his mouth taking hers, his body bearing down until the doorknob dug into her side. The magnitude of her nerves—about this, about everything—converged at the taste of him. It lit her up from within, a ball of raging feeling seeking release.

With a shaky reach, she unzipped her dress. It puckered around her breasts, fabric falling forward. Markus drew back, slipping the straps off her shoulders with warm palms.

Trembling, she ran a hand over what was left of his traditional attire. "I don't want to see this." Duty and responsibility had no place here.

He obliged, his pupils wide, dark. His shirt went first and then his belt. Swiftly, his hands worked the top of his trousers, and after dipping into his back pocket, he discarded them. When he made to move in, she raised a hand and he halted near-naked in front of her.

He was faultless. Resilient muscle reinforced by hard work. Rigid torso, strong thighs, and skin made rough with dark hair. She scarcely breathed as she circled him, one hand gathering her dress at her waist, the fingers of her other hand trailing along his shoulder blades, his bicep, the taut rise of his nipple—a princess contemplating every angle of this man deemed worthy of her.

She stopped in front of him, watched his shoulders rise and fall. With a tilt of her head, she beckoned him.

Done waiting, he dragged the dress down over her hips, kneeling with the fabric as it gathered on the floor, and eased her feet from her shoes. Then he straightened, locking her against him. His skin was hot, his body stone-strong. A flush of longing heated deep inside her.

He had her on the mattress in several steps.

Her heart expanded, blood flooding in at the strange feeling of him on her bed, then constricted as he nudged her down onto her back. The covers were cool, lush with silk. He pressed himself over her, awakening her breasts with open-mouthed kisses, and when he shifted, moving down her body, the golden canopy of the four-poster rippled above her.

The times she'd spent with her violin tutor had been fresh, thrilling. She'd been young and he'd been hypnotic, an impassioned musician who knew how to use his skilled hands to get what he wanted. And in those long, secluded lessons, her rebellion had allowed him to take it.

Markus didn't do fresh. The slide of his hands on her body was like gravity settling, an ancient, time-honored force. The calloused pads on his palms swept her thighs apart, exposing her, before his thumb stroked and her pleasure rose like a furious, feverish blush.

She twisted, sighing, as his fingers entered her. Crazed and edgy, need built inside her, low and swelling fast. His elbow whispered against the inside of her leg, glorious contact, and his glides grew slick with her heat. Her breath was shallow, her head tipped back. She struggled with his shoulder, gripping and slackening as her pleasure mounted.

She lay open to him—trusted him.

He straightened, startled, when she sat up. His dark hair was loose around his face, jaw flexed, lips parted. Then his brow creased. "Are you—?"

Her kiss cut him off, a rough shove of her whole body that drove him back onto his spine. Her dismay presented as fury, appalled at the unfairness of finding a man she trusted right when she had to leave. Life seemed to drag her in circles, waiting until she saw only darkness before teasing her with a shining light. This time, she'd crawled toward the glow of her son only to be blindsided by the love of her life.

Her kiss took that out on him. She bit his lips and tugged his hair and marked his skin with her nails. He let her do it, gently grasping her hips and pulling her around to straddle his waist. He let her do it until she broke away, clutching his biceps with a noise of infuriated defeat.

"Ava," he murmured, easing her hands off him.

"I hate you," she said, sitting up with a hand on his chest. Her lips stung. His probably stung worse. "You accept everything."

His face was shadowed, his blue eyes seeming almost black. Grasping her hips once again, he slid her down his body so the juncture of her thighs pressed over his erection, and she clenched above him, warm and needy and desperate. His eyes closed for a moment. "I don't accept that you hate me."

"After the way I've treated you?" All she'd ever done was hurt him. The dismay faded, replaced with a spluttering emptiness. Her fingers slipped, her nails raking down his stomach to the waistband of his briefs. "You're too trusting."

"I trust you." His hand closed around hers and guided it over the cut of his abs, the hard swells of his chest. Her body ached to gather him close and she dropped her head, her hair spilling over her shoulders as he said, "You can't convince me not to."

And he pushed up onto his elbows, covering her mouth with his.

She didn't try to convince him.

He flipped her onto her back again, tracing the tender bend behind her knee, the hollow between her breasts. It was bliss; it was torture. He reached for her grandfather's ring where it rested over her solar plexus on a rose-gold chain. A reminder that she would choose her own future—that she had already chosen, and Markus had no place in it.

He lifted it up, as if to unloop the chain from around her neck.

She grabbed his wrist. "Leave it."

She wanted to feel the band trapped between them, heated with the imprint of his skin, the intricate pattern of his pores. It was the closest he would come to wearing it.

He watched her, serious, before inclining his head in that sweet cowboy acquiescence. It broke something inside her. His willingness to concede was not a weakness, but a sign of picking his battles. Not a stubborn man, but she suspected that when he dug his heels in, nothing on earth would move him.

"Ava," he murmured. "Maybe we shouldn't do this now."

"Please." Her breath shook in her chest. "I want to."

He frowned down at her. "You're not happy."

"I am." Somewhere in the mess inside her, she was radiant. "I just—wish things could be different. I'm guilty over you. Torn up. I can't stay. But I want this, with you, more than anything."

"Are you sure?" The question came out as a rumble.

"Yes." She found his shoulders and tugged. He resisted, busy with a small packet, and then in a single movement, he covered her. Broad, heavy, and safe, just as she'd imagined, and she shifted, tucking herself more completely beneath him.

He pressed his mouth to her forehead as he brought his hips down, a warm weight that thickened the arousal between her thighs. She rose to meet him, her body melting as he entered on a soft groan.

"Don't leave tonight," he murmured, combing a hand into her hair and pressing his face against her neck. Slow at first, he moved into an aching rhythm, each stroke just shy of meeting the pressure building inside her. She clamped around him, a tight clench that smoldered on each slide. "I'll take you riding tomorrow."

She closed her eyes. As her pleasure gathered, sorrow matched it, ache for ache, at the base of her throat. She couldn't stay—couldn't be with him tomorrow. Her breaths hitched through the growing lump, hard with loss.

"This feels sad," he murmured, his lips against her neck as he moved inside her. The curve of his palm spread down her side, a stroke of reassurance. "Don't be sad."

She turned her face into his hair, her mouth against the curl of his ear. The confession of her heart budded on her tongue but it would be wrong to mention love, not on the brink of leaving. "Don't ask me to stay," she managed, her voice strangled by too many forces.

His movements slowed and he propped himself up to look at her. Frowning at what she failed to keep from her face, he found her hand and brushed his thumb along the insides of her fingers, a delicate scrape that shivered right to her soul. When he raised it to his mouth, her palm became the source of all feeling.

Then he smiled, a small, loving thing, and she wondered what it cost him to make it look so easy. "Okay."

His lips returned to her neck, kissing gently as his thrusts grew harder. She angled her hips to take him in, her body bright-edged with heat, and tension reached out, urging him further. Once more and again, until he was there, right where she needed him, a bursting energy inside her that shattered her stress and dreams apart, every thread, thought, and vapor.

He ground out her name on a final shudder.

Empty, her body unwound. The covers caught her. She couldn't move—and with him full of life above her, she didn't want to.

The mother in her regained balance first. She ordered the lover to pull herself together, reform her heart without Markus in it, because this next part was not going to be easy.

She did as she was told.

19

Mark's breath came fast. His heart sped faster, tripping over the distance Ava had already put between them. Making love hadn't been like this before. Exquisite like summer rain; excruciating like a whip down his spine. He hadn't known the jagged edges of intimacy: the pain of a too-full heart, the hollowness of a moan, the tragedy of a woman's body moving beneath his for the first and last time.

Nor had he truly known the luster of another's release. Rich and gleaming, he'd chased Ava's satisfaction with the desperation of his own.

The bed shifted as she slid off the mattress and passed him several tissues from a box on her nightstand. After cleaning himself up, he watched as the lamplight cast shadows across her naked body and ached to drag her back into complete darkness beneath him all over again.

Instead of pulling on her pajamas or returning to the formal dress she'd worn that day, she moved to a tall wardrobe, opened it, and withdrew a neat pile of clothing. She dressed methodically. Thick, dark leggings. A simple tank, layered with a thin long-sleeved top, covered by a dark button-up jacket that looked plum purple in this light. She sat on a quaint dressing chair to tug on socks and the shoes she'd worn on the long walk to the cabin, and something in his chest constricted like mud suctioning around a heavy work boot.

These were her going away clothes.

She hadn't looked at him. She stood and gathered her hair, twisting it into a loose bun at the nape of her neck. It was a style he hadn't seen on her before, and as she secured it, he frowned at how ordinary it made her look. It softened her cheeks, lessened the austerity of her usually exposed neck. He made himself smile, waiting for her to meet his eyes. After the sadness that had welled between them in bed, he wanted to give her warmth.

"That was goodbye," she said, her voice neutral. "You can leave now." She disappeared onto the balcony without glancing at him.

He sat up, stiff with protest. As he pushed off the covers, his hand slid beneath a pillow and met unexpected resistance. Frowning, he pulled, and was startled when he ended up holding a teddy bear.

"What's this?" he asked quietly.

It was a classic teddy with moveable arms and legs, the smooth fabric white and checkered with forest green. The same green lined the pads of its hands and feet, and formed a bow around its neck. Clearly handcrafted, this teddy was worthy of royalty—but it was still a stuffed toy in a grown woman's bed.

She didn't answer. In a swift glance he saw that she was frozen on the balcony, staring in at him. Her skin looked bloodless.

This, he sensed with unease, *is important.*

Off the bed, he dragged on his trousers and moved outside with the toy in his hand. She'd turned her back on him, her fingers closed around the balcony railing. Her features were tight, her lips pinched white as she stared out at the palace grounds.

"It's cute," he said, and raised the bear, maneuvering stuffed limbs so it seemed to sit on the railing. It didn't have the aged look of a toy that had survived childhood and lived on in adulthood. He pressed a finger upward along the teddy's neck and made the head move around. "Does it have a name?"

She didn't move, except to swallow. Her throat pushed downward like a stiff pump. "Darius," she whispered.

"Hello, Darius," he said, and then made a disastrous miscalculation. In an effort to keep the mood easy, hoping to lure a conversation out of this moment, he lifted the teddy and tossed it lightly into the air. It was a playful gesture, like a father tossing a child only to catch them again beneath the armpits a split-second later, safe and sound.

Except the toy tipped midair and he fumbled to catch it properly. The teddy hit the railing, flipped, and dropped off the balcony.

He'd never forget her small noise of horror. A chill struck his gut.

"No," she said, and the simple negative carried so much torment that he stepped back, blaming himself for something he didn't understand.

"I didn't—" he started to say, but she'd spun around and run inside. He circled a palm over his chest, troubled, as he followed on her tail. "It's okay. We'll find it. It landed in the magnolias."

She sniffled as she shot out of the bedroom. What was going on here? He paused only to find his shirt and jam his arms through the sleeves, knowing a half-naked chase through the palace wouldn't help anyone.

She ran fast. By the time he hit the corridor, Gul was disappearing around the far end. Mark bolted after them, confused and alarmed, buttoning his shirt as he ran. She seemed to know the shortest route, taking a narrow flight of stairs reserved for staff, racing along another corridor, and then down the sweeping staircase that would take them to the west entrance hall.

It wasn't until they were halfway down that he noticed she had a bag on her back. She was leaving now? In common clothes, racing away from her bodyguard with a backpack that looked stuffed full to bursting? Panic lurched in his middle.

There was something very wrong about this.

"Princess," Gul called, his voice low, taking the stairs on a swift angle. "Whatever this is, don't do it."

She ignored him.

She reached the marble floor and sped across the expansive atrium toward the exit, an indoor fountain on her right, the barred entrance to the west wing on her left. Two short poles held up a silk rope that blocked the double doors and a sign on the slightly ajar door read: *Area under construction. Strictly no admittance.*

It happened in the blink of an eye.

As Ava passed the sign, a small child slipped out from the crack between the doors. So out of place, Mark's first thought was that the boy had become lost during the afternoon's event. Dark hair, high cheekbones, he had a face that looked so much like the princess it was uncanny.

Gul made a strangled sound and his stride slackened as he fumbled for the banister. Did the man recognize—

Mark stopped dead as shock slammed him.

Too much like her.

"Hello," the boy said to Ava's back as understanding rushed through Mark like a hurricane. "Are you Ava?"

319

Ava turned so suddenly she overbalanced. Her knee hit the floor hard, followed by the slap of her palm. Her eyes didn't leave the boy. He was so small, yet so big, with a thatch of black hair. His skin was several tones darker than hers, his eyes alive with innocence. A smear of sugar swept up his cheek—he was chewing, food still in his mouth. Casual, inquisitive, spectacular.

Her heart raged like a trapped animal. Something momentous swelled inside her, a thick surge of emotion, but she swallowed it down and held still.

"Darius," she said, without voice.

He frowned and turned as a tall woman with graying hair slipped out beside him, swiftly reaching for his hand with a soft reprimand. Yasmin, Ava's old governess turned guardian of her son. The woman snapped her face toward Ava, a startled glance that softened with kindness.

"Dear girl," the woman murmured.

"Not now, Yazzy." Darius twisted his hand from hers and stepped forward. His attention returned to Ava.

She wanted to stand.

Doubt winded her, keeping her down.

She'd imagined this moment in a million ways. She'd wriggled and cried over it for years. But now that Darius stood in front of her, the lifetime of things she had to say felt like naïve fantasies. She couldn't say she loved him. She couldn't say she'd missed him or that she'd never leave him again.

Just because he was her walking heart didn't mean she was his mother.

He looked calm, unaffected, and she realized the black twist of role reversal. This must be how people felt around her. The obsessively fascinated public who followed her existence like a religion. She embodied a fairy-tale: a princess who seemed to lead the perfect life. People copied her various styles in an attempt to capture the glamor they admired; they bought overpriced magazines because her face was on the cover. They screamed in the streets when she drove past and waited for hours in blistering weather to watch her arrive at an event. They brimmed with desperation, arms outstretched and ribs bruising on barriers, seeking to touch her and attain emotional fulfillment.

Look at me. Say something to me. Touch me. Validate me.

And she'd scarcely noticed them.

She wanted to reach for Darius, scream for his recognition of her as his mother. She wanted it so intently, she feared herself.

And then the big feelings consumed her.

The sobs started at full force. Convulsions that doubled her body over and pushed her eyes shut. She struggled to breathe through sorrow and joy and hurt. The grief of giving him up overwhelmed her all over again, as did relief that the years of separation were over. She sobbed for every second she'd missed of his transformation from infant to small boy. For the old agony of breasts engorged with milk but no baby to feed. For the fleeting sound of his newborn cries she'd forgotten too quickly. All that and more, feelings so big, they were impossible to process.

"Are you okay?" he asked, his voice thick with young age, almost cloggy. She could listen to it forever. "Yazzy, is she okay?"

Ava lifted her head but couldn't see him through her tears. She sobbed harder because she was crying so hard she couldn't speak to him.

She nodded.

"Yazzy talks about you." He sounded cautious, confused. "She says you're nice."

Darius took another step toward her.

Her body activated.

She inhaled through her tears, suddenly frantic to smell him, to catch scent of her boy, because the last time she'd breathed in his delicate musky odor, the need to keep him had pushed her into hysterics. Her skin stung with the ache to fold him into her arms. Her very heart changed shape, bulging and lengthening, until her whole chest pulsed with the need to cradle him.

But she couldn't hug him, because he might hate it. He didn't know her. He might cry or thrash or form a vivid childhood memory, a moment he'd recall years from now with shadowed feelings of discomfort, distress, or fear.

She covered her sobbing mouth with both hands. She had to stop. She would scare him.

She couldn't stop.

"Who are they?" His question was quiet, and with a wave of nausea, she remembered they weren't alone.

Protectiveness rose in her like a shot of adrenaline, a dozen shots, roaring in her ears and quaking in her heart. She coughed, choking on her tears, and staggered to her feet. Spinning around, she raised her arms by her sides to block her son from the man hired to keep them apart.

Darius was hers. Her parents wouldn't take him away this time. She'd resist; she'd fight. She'd smash them in a tailspin of truth. A scandal that would disgust and titillate a world sustained on the horrors of others.

Gul stood close, his feet apart and his gaze on her son. Devastation warped his features.

"No," she said, guttural with grief. Tears still streaked from her eyes. She seemed incapable of stemming them.

Gul's mouth bowed downward. His chin puckered.

She raised her arms higher. "I won't let you."

Tears glistened in his eyes. "Why now?"

New movement behind Gul snagged her attention. Her

blurry gaze caught on Markus, toward the bottom of the staircase. He was holding his shirt with both hands over his collarbones, as if the appearance of the child had interrupted him mid-button. His stricken gaze was moving from her to Darius. She met and held his next glance.

Her skin stiffened and flushed, swollen with expression and endless tears. Not apology or shame, but gentle defiance, knowing this revelation would change his opinion of her, because there was no way it couldn't.

This is what I couldn't tell you, she hoped he saw in her eyes. *You understand why I can't be with a king. I'm not heartless. My heart is too full.*

The obvious truth stole the rest of the blood from his already pale face. He reached for the bannister.

"Ava." Gul pulled her attention back to him. "Please."

She inhaled raggedly and exhaled on a sob.

"I can't . . . can't let you leave." Pain splintered his voice. "Is that what you're planning? Leaving? You can't. You know that."

"Gul." She didn't speak his name like a plea, but the offering of a last chance. "I've tried to give you what you need to feel whole—to feel like you're finally yourself." An emerald-green scarf. A velvet blazer. Liner to showcase his beautiful dark eyes. "Can't you give me what I need?"

Mortification crumpled his features.

"You can't stop me," she said.

He shifted his weight and her entire body curled inward; her mind hunched like a wolf coiling into a crouch. The dropped toy had triggered a poorly timed escape, executed before Cyrus arrived and Gul had been dismissed. But seeing the bear—a present for Darius—slip through Markus's fingers had struck her cold, and she'd bolted before she'd seen reason. Bolted from the memory of their lovemaking, the traitorous urge to stay with him; bolted to find the toy before the escape was set in motion. This altercation wasn't part of the plan—but Darius was breathing through his nose behind her, one nostril whistling, and she knew she would resist Gul like a street-fighting mongrel, because that was her boy and she was too close to go soft over three years of friendship and the plea in his eyes.

They stared at each other. Silent, distressed. She had to keep blinking to clear the tears. He didn't make a move, and she didn't turn her back.

Gul's expression flickered a moment before she heard the noise. Footsteps, running hard and fast down the passageway on the far side of the fountain.

Seconds later, a red-haired woman tore into the atrium wearing an expression of fury and a jacket the color of tangerines. A piece of pizza flopped in her hand.

Gul spun around fully as Frankie shot at him, fast as a bullet. He took a quick step back, startled, and said, "You."

"Me." She pulled up short, hardly out of breath. "Get in the west wing," she ordered, and bit into the pizza. She spoke around the mouthful. "Now."

Gul said, "I'm not—"

"Argue behind that door." Frankie grasped his shoulder, her arm on a steep upward angle, and gave a push. "Because if you lock horns out here, all you need is one staff member with long ears to walk past and half the palace is going to know every detail. So even if you win, her secret's out and your job will still be forfeit."

Gul didn't move for several seconds. Then he turned silently, expressionless, his gaze set over Ava's head. He cut around the silk rope that barred their entry and disappeared into the west wing.

Frankie's attention moved around Ava—and down. She put a hand on her hip. "I told you to stay in there." Discomfort softened the hard set of her jaw as she seemed to struggle with scolding a three-year-old. "What happened?"

"Nothing," Darius answered, sheepish. At Yasmin's gesture, they followed after Gul.

Frankie seemed at a loss as she turned to Ava.

Ava stared back, trying to stem her sobs with great sniffs and gulps.

"What a scene." The hard lines in the woman's face returned like a protective barrier against pain. She moved toward Ava, gesturing to the doors. "What the hell were you thinking?"

"I wasn't thinking," Ava answered, turning and gasping her next inhale. "I was feeling."

"Always a stupid move," Frankie muttered, right behind her until—

"Frankie."

Markus spoke quietly from across the atrium.

Ava's heart imploded as she looked to the man observing everything and understanding nothing.

The shock on his face was purely that—no judgement, no horror, no panic—and his unaligned presence ran softly through her. Of course he still stood apart from them. He'd asked no questions, made no move to intervene. He hadn't presumed to include himself despite having authority over everyone and everything in this palace.

She covered her mouth as a feeling, clean and precise, cut through the overwhelming torrent of emotion. It wasn't complex, what she felt for him. It was blindingly, beautifully simple.

She loved him.

"Frankie," he said again.

The woman's chin rose as she turned. She didn't move as

she held his confounded stare, but the thumb she jerked by her side was half-hearted. "Get inside, Mark."

"How are you even—"

"Not now. After. Get inside."

He didn't move. Her betrayal was a bruise in his blue eyes. "Does Kris know?"

For several seconds, Frankie didn't move. Then she turned and cut past Ava, her shoulder banging against hers. Through the tears that persisted, Ava caught the ferocious look on the woman's face, the hurt. At the last moment, Frankie gripped Ava's hand and dragged her into the only unmonitored wing in the palace.

She was inside before she could look back.

The main corridor of the west wing was dark, lit by dim uplighting lining the walls. A small group of people clustered in an antechamber on the right: Zara, Yasmin, and half a dozen guards whose sole responsibility was the safety of the illegitimate royal. They stood at odd angles to each other with an air of anticipation.

Darius was by Yasmin's side, his small hand reaching up to hold hers. His face was pressed against the older woman's thigh, seeming shy now that he'd been in trouble, refusing to look at anyone.

Within less than a minute, Cyrus arrived, sliding into the hall, looking harried.

Markus remained by the doors, silent, pale.

"Right." Ava jolted at Frankie's abrupt tone. "Let's get this going." She gestured at Ava like a stage manager giving the cue for her entrance. Or in this case, her exit. "Ready?"

Ava squeezed the straps of her backpack. How could one

word encompass so much? Was she ready to leave her entire life behind; ready to trigger a cascade of events involving the royal family of Kelehar? Was she ready to position Cyrus under their parents' guillotine, for his involvement in her escape would be unmistakable; ready to live with her son after three years of grief as her constant companion?

Always had been, never would be.

"Yes," she said.

"No." Gul moved forward like his body was shackled to the atrium behind him. He stopped in between Ava and Darius. "I can't let you go."

Frankie made a noise of impatience. She flapped her half-eaten pizza slice at Cyrus.

The Prince of Kelehar moved forward, taking the directive in his stride. "I contacted my father last night," he said, stopping in front of Gul and holding the man's gaze. "I requested to take over your portfolio. It makes sense, since your position as Ava's guard directly relates to the security of the Violin Project. He agreed."

Gul stared, a giant in distress. "My prince," he started.

"Your resignation has been accepted," Cyrus said.

Gul blinked. His stare turned blank in disbelief.

"Effective immediately." Cyrus's tone was gentle. "You have no obligations here. No authority. I expect you could be gone from the palace by morning."

Relief collapsed over Gul's face. His body sagged, his knees bending, and he covered his cheeks with his palms. His exhale was jagged.

"Isn't that sweet?" Frankie patted Gul twice on the shoulder blade. "All sorted. Now move, you lot. I have to get tampering with the security footage out there."

There was a swell of activity from the guards as they

gathered around Darius and Yasmin. As a group, they started moving down the corridor.

"Is she coming?" Darius asked Yasmin, looking back at Ava.

Ava's old governess looked back, meeting her gaze with an awed smile. "Yes."

Ava was trembling. She gripped the straps of her pack so tightly her fingertips were losing sensation.

Gul turned to her. "He looks so much like you," he murmured, his eyes glistening.

Loss tugged at her throat. She nodded.

"I'll miss you." He tilted his head to the side with a sniffle. "I love you."

"Me too," she said.

"I can't watch you leave." He bowed, his torso falling below his hips, and straightened to meet her gaze one last time.

And then he left.

Before Ava could process that she would never see her friend again, she was suddenly in Zara's fierce embrace. The woman who had ushered her toward this moment since they'd first met. She hugged back, breaking apart with gratitude.

"Yeah, I can't watch either," Zara said, covering Ava's hand and squeezing infinitely harder than Ava had herself. "I'll be in touch."

Then she too was gone.

"Ava." Cyrus came forward, his features disbelieving. "I'll find a way to see you once things have settled."

Beautiful, bighearted Cyrus—she'd hug him to death if it didn't mean she'd end up without him. She buried her face in his shoulder. "Thank you."

"It'll all work out. I'll handle our parents. I'll make sure Gul is okay. And you won't want for money. If anything happens, no matter how small, you tell me and I'll sort it out. But you'll love the house. And the quarters next door for the guards, I made sure it had—"

"Cy," she murmured, a tear slipping down her face.

"I know." He stepped back and nodded, face down. "Be well, sister." He retreated to the nearest wall.

Breathing fast, Ava looked at Frankie.

Frankie arched a brow. "You ready? Or do you wanna . . ." She jerked her head to indicate behind her.

The blood in Ava's ears quieted. Her trembling stopped.

Was she ready to leave Markus?

She turned, her breath held, her body wooden.

He stood just shy of the double doors leading in from the atrium. Shock still darkened his eyes and bewilderment parted his lips. His arms hung by his sides. His hair was disarranged, a fleeting keepsake of their lovemaking. The hem of his shirt didn't line up, buttoned in the wrong holes, and his feet were bare beneath the perfect cut of his traditional trousers.

He could have said a thousand things. *Why didn't you tell me? How can you possibly have a child? Where are you going? Do your parents know about this? Would you have told me you had a child if we'd become strategically engaged? What will it mean for Kiraly that you're disappearing under my roof? You lied to me. I can't trust anything you've said. I'm king here. Why should I let you leave?*

Instead, he said in a voice that sought to hold her up, "You'll be better now."

"Yes," she managed to say.

"You won't have to cry like that ever again."

She blinked wet eyelashes. "No."

His expression didn't change. The skin sagged around his mouth and beneath his eyes. Probably what it looked like to slam into an emotional wall he couldn't have seen coming.

Lungs burning with regret, she said, "I didn't mean—"

"I know." He ran a hand over his mouth. The corners still sagged when he pulled it away.

"It's just that I haven't—"

"It's okay." His voice was soft.

She nodded. Don't try to give him a raindrop when they didn't have time for the whole storm.

They didn't have time for anything.

"Go," he said, his frown taking on a despairing edge. "Your future depends on it." And then he gave that small loving smile that wrapped itself around her, but it didn't look as easy as it had before.

Fraught, she looked to Frankie.

The woman's features softened. "Good luck."

Knowing she could hesitate forever, Ava turned after her own flesh and blood.

"In here, Your Highness," a guard said, and stood with an arm extended, directing her into the third room on the left.

She glanced back over her shoulder.

The corridor was empty.

With blood hot in her ears and overwhelming change battering her heart, she stepped into the room that concealed another secret entrance to the tunnels, finally on her way to a new life.

It was done.

20

Sighing, Mark closed his laptop on the detailed correspondence from his health minister. It was a report regarding the new mental health program that would be rolled out next month. One of Tommy's first matters of priority, and Mark had seen it done, along with a sweep of social funding that included support services for victims of family violence.

Standing, he stretched his neck and tried to loosen the tension gripping between his shoulder blades. Fractionally more relaxed, he moved onto the tower study's balcony. Kira City was magnificent below him. The sun was setting on another early summer day, and the sky that had been intensely blue was dulling to a fuzzy peach, leaving the honey-stoned buildings glowing like radiant embers.

Even after three months, he still felt like a tourist looking at the city's beauty. The haphazardly populated mountainside boasted the state buildings, elevating them high on crests, while houses of citizens crushed together in the geographical dips and divots. The people might live in tucked away places, but he saw them all.

He breathed out, grasping the carved railing and dropping

his head. His attention caught on the cluster of potted plants in the balcony corner. Some were raised on stands, leaves spilling down onto the tiles, while others grew in ceramic pitchers and wide basins. The tiniest was a succulent in a turquoise pot.

It was growing. It would need repotting soon. He'd nursed it since discovering it on the golden guest suite windowsill, just days after she'd left.

He shifted, leaning his elbows on the railing.

Those had been impossible days.

Frankie had explained what she knew on that first night, blatantly ignoring the elephant of her own presence in the room. She'd rushed him from the west wing to the security suite and talked of Ava while finishing her dinner and running through surveillance footage. "It's not my place," she'd said, her fingers tapping, "but she's not likely to get the chance to tell you herself, and Cyrus and Zara have filled me in on most of it."

Ava had fallen pregnant to the violin tutor she'd once told Mark about: the same man who'd been bribed by her parents to leave the country, and who had accepted without hesitation. Apparently Ava had suspected the baby early on, but had been too afraid to confide in anyone. A nineteen-year-old unwed princess couldn't fall accidentally pregnant to a commoner. Not in Kelehar, not anywhere.

She'd finally told Cyrus, and he'd told their parents on her behalf. Without even speaking to Ava, her mother had issued a press release of the princess's "planned" trip to study abroad. The university destination was undisclosed to the press because she wanted to focus on her education. Ava was then relocated to a private, royally owned property where she studied political science by correspondence and carried the baby to full term.

"Her mother is foul," Frankie had said, her eyes glued to the screen. The queen had offered no options or alternatives that would allow Ava to keep and raise her baby. She'd offered shame in abundance, though, and lashings of vitriol. "Ava could have been the most well-resourced single mother in history. But no, screw that."

Vulnerable and terrified for herself and her son, Ava had been coerced into signing his welfare over to the crown. Darius became a ward of the state and on the day of his birth, he'd been taken away with a nursemaid and Ava's own governess. She had never been told where.

By the time her panic settled, it had been too late. The queen had refused to give ground and disgrace the royal family by bringing the child back. She'd threatened to adopt Darius out the instant Ava went public. She would cover her tracks, as only a queen could, and ensure that the adoptive family could claim to have raised him themselves from a newborn. Just because Ava was a princess didn't mean she could change the rules of adoption. How selfish to assume the public would support her bending the law to indulge her own privileged regret. No one would stand for it. She had signed him away. She was no longer entitled to him.

As for Ava's claims that she had been coerced, did she really want to take on the crown in court? Because it would never even reach court—surely she knew that.

"She should have told me." Markus had paced, wound tight with outrage. "I could have . . ."

"Could have what?" Frankie's expression had been skeptical. "You're a good guy, Mark, but this was seriously delicate."

"Ava isn't." She was brave, tenacious like a bulldog, her jaws locked on her dream of reuniting with her son. Nothing had shaken her bite.

Not even him.

"No," Frankie had agreed. "Those prissy dresses threw me off at first. But your woman's got grit."

Fresh pain had throbbed at that. "She's not mine."

"Don't have to be together to belong to each other. Now get going. I have thirty-six minutes to finish this before change of shift."

He'd bristled. He wasn't going anywhere. "Thanks for helping her," he'd said, getting it out of the way. There'd be no gratitude in the next part of this conversation. "You must have a soft heart under there somewhere."

She'd paused her frantic editing to face him, cocking up one corner of her mouth. "How dare you."

He'd held her stare. "How dare *you.*"

Instantly, her features had sobered.

"As far as you ever told us," he'd said, "you were a born-and-bred American. Different accent now, I've noticed. Going to explain yourself?"

She'd stood, gaze wary. "I'd prefer not to, if it's all the same to you."

"It's not all the same to me."

"It's complicated and personal, and we both have other things to do tonight."

"You lied to us—to Kris."

She'd stared at him, her features haunted.

"All this time." He'd shaken his head. "You came looking for us. Embedded yourself in our lives. Why, to monitor us?" The sting of her betrayal filled his words. Then he'd realized. When Philip said they'd been watched in Sage Haven, he'd meant by Frankie. *Frankie.* Kris's friend—the woman he was secretly mad about. "Your friendship with Kris was by design."

Stricken, she'd said, "At first, but—"

"You've used him." Repulsed, Mark had said, "I have to tell him."

"Don't." She'd stepped forward and gripped his wrist. Her

usual fierceness had flashed across her face. "Please, Mark. Don't tell him."

"He's my brother," he'd said, his voice low. His gut had heaved as he'd remembered Ava's instructions. "And I am your king."

Frankie had looked startled. She'd snatched her hand away and dipped her head. "Your Majesty."

"Mark," he'd told her, relenting, but no less furious. "But I'm not the same Mark you knew in Montana. Don't treat me like it. You've hidden yourself since we got here. Now I want to know who works for me, and how they came to be here, and that includes you."

"Understood," she'd said, her face still lowered. "Can I edit now?"

Edit the security footage of Ava's escape. He'd run a hand over his mouth. Frankie had only exposed herself to him in order to help Ava—for that, he owed her his silence. "I won't tell Kris. But you had better."

"I—will."

She'd then deleted every frame of footage recorded in the atrium that evening, and he'd felt each deletion like a cut inside him, a methodical removal of the princess he'd known so briefly.

Hollow, he'd followed Frankie's final instructions to return to Ava's rooms and close the door. "Then walk out in the exact clothes you were wearing when you first arrived. Look casual and return to your own rooms. I'll move that footage back so when someone investigates the disappearance, you'll be clear. I'll show her running out later, with Gul following, and no one else."

But in the end, Frankie's precautions had all been unnecessary.

The following morning, Cyrus had contacted his parents to

inform them that Ava had gone missing. He suspected she was with a commoner she'd met in Kira City.

The queen had arrived six hours later, believing Ava was still in Kiraly and intending to find her before a story broke out. Not once did she seem to consider that Ava was long gone. For three days, she scoured the city for news of her daughter, and only then did Cyrus mention that there was an issue with the subject of the Violin Project—it had also gone missing.

The subtext had been a thousand miles deep.

The queen had immediately requested a meeting with Mark.

Still slammed flat by shock, he had sat opposite her in his study and listened in nauseated fascination.

"This is most embarrassing," she'd said, her tight expression giving nothing away. "I hope you'll enable us to be discreet. She always did find herself attracted to the lower classes, and we saw no other way to support her attraction to this man than to encourage her to slip away in the night. We can't be seen to support it outright, you understand, but at least she'll be happy this way. I am sorry she chose to run off while in Kiraly. She must have distressed your staff by disappearing like this." She'd tapped her fingers on the arms of her chair. "I'd like to issue a statement while here. Do you mind if I use your press room?"

The queen of Kelehar had then force-fed journalists a story with saccharine insincerity.

Princess Ava has chosen to relinquish her royal obligations to the crown of Kelehar. While we cannot pretend that we aren't shocked and saddened by the suddenness of these events, we willingly support her in this decision. Although it pains us to let her go, we wish her peace and privacy in the life of her choice. Princess Ava remains our beloved daughter and a jewel in the crown of the royal family of Kelehar.

Mark had stood in the wings, aghast.

He didn't understand this game. But he'd decided to play a round anyway.

He'd requested the queen return to his study. She'd entered, looking irritated by the inconvenience, and Mark stood from behind his desk. He didn't smile, nor did he offer her a seat.

"You won't look for her," he said. "You won't even think about looking for her."

Her torso had inflated with indignation. "I beg your—"

"Darius is with his mother now," he said, and watched dread ice her features. "And Kiraly might provide Kelehar with palladium and discretion in this matter if you don't look for her. For either of them."

"Might?" The question was faint.

He angled his head and waited.

"We will wipe clean your debt to us," she said quickly, her eyes wild. "You owe nothing."

"Thanks." He took that without offering confirmation of his discretion.

"I—King Markus, I—"

"Will leave now. And you'll never be received in Kiraly again."

Afterward, Zara had come to see him at his urgent invitation.

"Power play!" She'd held up a fist and he'd bumped it without enthusiasm.

"What happens next?" He'd sat opposite her, aching with tension. He had to know what could happen if the queen took his words as a challenge. "Is she safe?"

Zara had raised a shoulder. "She's out, and that was the trick. If they find her and try to separate her from Darius now, she'll reveal the whole thing. They can't knee-jerk him into adoption. Not when he's with her. She's finally got access to her

337

parents' underbelly while protecting her own. They can't touch her."

He'd sat heavily, his face in his hands.

She'd then told him much the same story as Frankie, though she'd added an extra insight. "She's run away before, you know," she'd said, perched awkwardly on the lushly cushioned chair. "That's when I first met her. She'd just convinced Prince Aron not to marry her and slipped out of the palace. She searched out my shelter. She said she was trapped in a psychologically and emotionally abusive family dynamic, and that she needed to find the son they'd coerced her into giving up. Unfortunately, giving a princess the tools to start a new life doesn't follow the same checklist as other women."

Zara had encouraged her to return to the palace. "The timing was wrong for an escape. She didn't know where Darius was, and even if she had, her parents would have assumed that was where she'd go. They could have adopted him out on the spot. No. It would only work if he was a moving cog in the escape plan and met her halfway."

Which he had.

And now she was gone—had been gone almost three months.

Mark stepped back into his study and retrieved his water glass from the desk. He hadn't drunk enough today, could feel a headache forming, but back outside he knelt and poured the rest onto the star-shaped succulent. He needed it to keep growing.

He knew he was growing as a king. Ava's escape had blinded him to it for a while. Every day, he buried himself in paperwork and policies, meetings and official appearances. He had crammed his head with obligations, for otherwise he would think of Ava and nothing else. Occasionally, even the rigors of royal life couldn't fight the urgency to let her into his mind. As she'd once said, it was insatiable anguish to love someone from a distance and not even know how far away they really were. Was she still in Europe or returned to the Middle East, or had she crossed oceans in order to find safety?

Once, Tommy found Mark on a bench in the rose garden, staring sightlessly at the ground. Kris had come across him in the stables, leaning on the handle of a shovel, stall only half-mucked. Even Adam had entered Mark's rooms in the early morning to discover the king sitting on the couch in the previous day's clothes, unslept and baffled by the sudden dawn. But mostly, Mark worked.

The ache of her absence—of the unknown life she must now be living—had consumed him so completely he hadn't noticed at first that his plummet into sovereignty had slowed. His feet were far from on solid ground, but he was no longer free-falling. He woke each day without panic or doubt. Confidence drove his steps through his palace and purpose fueled his interactions.

He drew on his brothers' strength. He sought Philip's counsel. He worried about making the wrong choices for the wrong reasons, but tried to make good choices for good reasons. He rode his new horse every morning to remind himself of simpler days and treated people with respect and knowledge that they were not, and never would be, his equal.

His cowboy brothers were princes, his lost love a princess.

And Markus Jaroka was king.

Ava passed as a commoner.

She breathed in, the sweetness of warm grass catching in her nose. The summer day had been hot, and Darius had begged her and Yasmin to eat dinner outside in the shade of the house. The clutter of dirty plates and cups had since been shoved aside to make room for their full-bellied sprawls on their backs so they could watch the stars come out.

The wonder and terror of this masquerade still had the power to seize her in the quaint Luxembourg village streets. Three months into her unfathomable new life, and all it took was for someone to look at her sideways or take a fraction too long to respond to something she'd said, and her pulse would shudder and her blood would run cold. She'd barely refrain from pushing Darius behind her, utterly convinced they'd figured her out. She might be safe from her parents, but she'd always fear the threat of her son being hauled into the spotlight.

Yasmin said that Ava's imagination far outdistanced that of anyone in town. "It's not a simple mental leap to conceive of a runaway princess hiding in their midst. And that's assuming anyone here cares about the family affairs of international royalty."

If they did care, they'd be looking for the glamorous Princess Ava with a mysterious lover by her side. Not the single mother of a toddler no one knew about, living with an older woman who appeared to be her own mother.

Whatever the reason, she passed as one of them.

Ava hadn't lain outside to watch the darkening sky before. Not for as long as she wanted, and without observation. Discomfort was stiff inside her at such unregulated living, an edge she hadn't been able to soften, but she no longer feared letting her guard down. In that, at least, she had changed.

So much had happened.

Her hair had gone that first night, parked off to the side of the mountain road, great ribbons of it falling away beneath Yasmin's brutal chopping. The pixie cut had opened up her face, exposing the layers of sleep deprivation beneath her eyes and the fatigue puckering her skin.

Just hours after arriving in the village, she had benefited

from the new style. It had kept clear of her face as she'd emptied her stomach in the toilet.

"Exhaustion," Yasmin had said, gently laying the back of her hand over Ava's brow. "You've got nothing left. Off to bed."

Another upheaval had stemmed Ava's protests.

The sickness had taken several days to pass. Darius had mostly steered clear, but tagged along when Yasmin brought her soup and tea. He'd been cautious around her, nervous even, in those early days. She supposed she would be wary too, if a strange, sick woman was suddenly living with them in their new home.

Then she'd shaken off bed rest and journeyed through culture shock. First had been an exhilarating honeymoon phase. The smallest things delighted her. Walking from her bedroom to the kitchen in the early morning and realizing that no one had monitored her passage. Choosing her own clothes based on weather and mood, not her impending schedule. Washing them and hanging them out on the sagging clothesline beside an old pear tree, savoring the size of Darius's clothes as she pegged, cooing over his little socks.

She'd soaked up the tiniest details of their house, determined to remember every quirk and chore, from the creaky floorboard in the passageway and the wrist-flick required to halt the blinds in place, to how to recycle the household packaging and clean the grout between the shower tiles.

After a time, frustration had extinguished her enchantment.

What did it matter if she could open the blinds and put cardboard in a bin? She still didn't really know how to do anything useful. Yasmin still had to manage the house, regardless of how determinedly Ava followed instructions. She didn't think to do a stock-take on items like detergent or pepper before they went shopping. She didn't know when to change the bath towels or start cooking a meal so that it would be ready by the time Darius suddenly realized he was ravenous. She didn't know how to cook at all. Her lessons with Mark had been too brief, too shallow to equip her for anything more than lighting tinder and watering growing plants.

"So get in the garden." Yasmin had ordered when Ava had shared her ineptitude. "The dandelions are out of control."

She'd dirtied her hands, pulling weeds like they'd insulted her. What she hadn't mentioned to her old governess was that no amount of pretending to be common would make Darius warm to her. He kept himself at a distance, week after week.

But Yasmin wasn't blind.

"He doesn't know what a mother does," she'd told Ava. "He's waiting for you to show him."

Despair had bubbled over inside her. She'd thought of her own mother and wondered what it had been like for the queen to have two children. Had she ever wished she could love easier? Ever wished she'd made different choices to support them?

Did her mother miss her, despite everything?

"I don't know what a mother does either," Ava had quietly said.

"No one knows." The woman had smiled wryly. "But I've raised him to know that I'm not his mother—that you'd be coming one day, when you could. He's been waiting for you."

It was dangerous to wait for something for too long. The idea of having a son had grown so big in her mind, so loaded with pain and love and expectation, that she was too scared to approach him now that they were together. And it seemed Darius felt the same about her.

Small things made their separation excruciatingly clear. She would help him choose his clothes in the morning, but he'd become increasingly distressed by her suggestions, until she stepped away and he'd settle on an outfit that made no sense with the season. "It's the colors," Yasmin had explained eventually. "He doesn't care about the heat."

Ava would try cutting up his food, but he'd stare at his plate like she'd just smeared it all across the floor. "Not too small," Yasmin had confided. "It makes him feel like a baby. It's perfect if he can skewer it with the fork and bite one end, bite the other, and then eat the last piece."

Ava would read him a bedtime story, but instead of nodding off to sleep, he'd become more and more awake, aggravated because she was getting the voices wrong. "We'll get new books for you to read him," had been Yasmin's suggestion. "He's too used to the way I read those stories."

But no matter how she'd tried, asking what color he wanted to wear, cutting three-bite-sized pieces, and reading new stories with different voices for each character, there was always something else she didn't know, something she got wrong, and her ignorance continued to upset him.

And her, like an arrow to the heart.

His mother should know him better than anyone.

Then a gift had arrived.

A package addressed in Zara's handwriting. Darius had gone crazy with excitement. Their first delivery in the new house! A cardboard box full of possibility! He'd bounced on Ava's heels all the way into the kitchen, and she'd ached to do a lap of the property first, just to keep him there, his hand brushing the back of her knee. Instead, she'd knelt on the rug beside the dining table while Yasmin peered over from the couch.

Love had bulged inside her as Darius settled on his haunches and met her eyes in bright anticipation.

"Goodness," Ava had said, praying it wasn't something boring inside. "You open it."

He'd struggled with the tape, so she'd helped peel it off, her knuckles bumping against his impatient hands. Then he pulled open the folds on top and dove into the packing peanuts. Glee lit his face a moment before he squealed and pulled out a forest-green-checked teddy bear.

"Who's it from?" he'd demanded, scrunching it to his chest so the bear's arms and legs splayed backwards.

She'd inhaled raggedly. She'd answered through a tight throat. "It's from me."

His face had widened. "You?"

"He's your age," she'd said, her voice unsteady. "I hope you like him."

Darius hadn't stopped hugging it. "He's *green*."

"He's different." She'd nodded, noticing a folded piece of paper poking out of the packing peanuts. She'd fished it out. "Just like you. You can call him whatever you like."

"I'll call him Cyrus." And if her heart hadn't melted completely at that, he then tumbled over the box to wrap his arms around her neck. His feet and knees had formed an exquisite jumble in her lap. "Thank you." That beautiful cloggy voice had spoken in her ear. The soft warmth of his cheek had pressed against hers, and with trembling hands, she'd carefully closed her arms around him. The first hug he'd instigated in six weeks. Emotion had pressed at the top of her ribcage, a pressure that billowed when he let the embrace tighten.

Then he'd pulled back, stumbling out of her lap, attention set on the cashmere toy. "I love him."

"Me too," she'd whispered.

Collecting herself, she'd opened Zara's letter. But it wasn't from Zara.

"I found him in our tallest magnolia. I thought he'd like to finally find home, and Zara offered to get him there."

There was a line break and Ava had noticed tiny dots of ink, as if the pen had been lowered and lifted several times, hesitation ultimately getting the better of him. Greed had flared in her, wishing he'd written more, pages and pages, but instead, he'd finished on the third sentence.

"There's a kiss for you on his left ear."

Wordless, she'd handed Yasmin the note and smiled at Darius. "May I see the teddy?"

She'd held it to her face, her lips brushing the soft left ear, and just the thought of Markus pressing his mouth to the fabric, intending the kiss for her, had torn her insides apart with longing.

After that, Darius had started to relax around her. He called her "Ava" and still ran to Yasmin when he was confused or upset. He needed Yasmin to tuck him into bed each night and worried whenever she left the house without him. But he would also curl up with Ava on the couch, and hold her hand on a walk, or help her in the garden. It was an adjustment period for them all. Ava had learned to ask for a hug at the end of the day. Yasmin had learned to redirect some of his queries, slowly teaching him that it was okay to seek Ava out first.

He had asked Ava if they could eat dinner outside tonight.

The grass tickled the back of her neck. She turned her head, scratching lightly, and saw that Darius had drifted off to sleep using the teddy as a pillow.

She reached out, stroking the bear's ear, and loss opened up inside her.

"You all right, my love?" Yasmin murmured, perceptive as ever. She'd probably noticed Ava's lips brush the toy every time she got half a chance.

"I should be happy." Ava's hand dropped to her son's ankle, rubbing lightly. "I am."

For years, she'd believed that this was the only way she could ever be content. But she'd never conceived of a man like

Markus—never dreamed that she'd be so greedy as to want more than this, after everything.

The prompt came gently. "But you're incomplete?"

Incomplete. "Yes."

No matter the endlessness of her love for Darius, no matter how full and radiant he made her heart, the happiness he brought refused to overflow into the hollow Markus had left behind. She was like an outline that Darius was slowly but surely coloring in, but his vibrant scribbles continued to miss a section, regardless how long he spent circling the pencil. *"You missed a bit,"* she imagined saying. And he might say, her wise little child, *"It's not my bit to color in."*

She slept in Markus's flannel shirt. She read his book of illustrations every night, knowing she should send it back, but unable to part with it. His letter lay on her bedside table and the dots of ink drove her crazy.

"I miss him so much." She rolled to face her governess with her hands tucked under her cheek. "But these are early days. I'll move past it."

Yasmin raised a dark brow. "Do you have to?"

"Oh, come on, Yaz." She'd chased these thoughts around her head night after night. There was no way to banish the truth. "Darius is safe like this. That's all I've ever wanted for him. I can't drag him from a home to a palace. I can't make him share daily life with hundreds of other people. I can't—can't be the reason he'd be hounded by the media everywhere he went or accosted by random people who seem to think they're entitled to an opinion on his life." She curled her legs to her stomach. "I couldn't bear him growing up to think he'd have been better off without me."

"Oh, Ava."

"No, it's fine." But it wasn't. "If I'd fallen for an everyday kind of man, this would be different. He could join us here.

But I can't even entertain the idea of taking Darius back there."

"From what I've heard, you did fall for an everyday kind of man," Yasmin said.

Ava stared in disbelief.

"He just happens to be a king," the woman finished.

"Don't." Ava's hands settled over her solar plexus, tangling together. "Please don't."

"Darius has been nervous around you, but he's quite the performer. I've often wondered if he wouldn't mind the spotlight."

"Not as a child." Ava couldn't bear it. "Even if he doesn't know any better, I do."

"Well, all right. I just wonder, after what you've been through, why you'd stop short of having everything you deserve." Yasmin pushed herself upright with a soft groan. "Still, I don't see why you can't at least visit Markus. It's been long enough. This isn't exile."

The words swirled color in that empty space inside her and Ava sat up quickly, her heart beating hard. What kind of thing was *that* to say? She stared at her old governess. "How?"

"Let's say you put him to bed while I clean up." Yasmin collected the stack of plates. "And then we get in touch with some friends of yours and see what we can do."

Zara lay on the couch with her head in Adam's lap. The apartment windows were propped open in a desperate attempt to cool the stuffy space, but the summer night air refused to budge. A fan oscillated in the corner, rattling as it turned, and the drunken shouts of party people several floors below carried up at infuriatingly irregular intervals.

"Ah, the ambiance," Adam murmured, turning the page of his tedious book. Their reading tastes did not overlap, she had learned, because she liked escapism and he preferred political nonfiction. He wanted to be a reliable confidant for Markus, able to provide well-researched advice as well as a confidential ear. Zara liked to forget politics existed.

"It's nice that they're trying to include us," Zara said with a roll of her eyes, putting down her book as her phone buzzed. It was from Ava's new number, which Zara had memorized but not saved. Swiping the text, she read Ava's request for a phone call in the morning *because it was about time they organized a visit*. "Huh."

"Everything okay?" he asked in that distracted tone that always made her want to kiss him until she was the only thought in his head.

Until he was the only thought in hers . . . because sometimes, just sometimes, he wasn't.

She hadn't seen Cyrus since Ava had left. He'd come to her apartment the day after the escape, breathtaking in a teal tunic embroidered with silver. No undercover common clothes—the Prince of Kelehar had come to her door. He'd asked how she was feeling—if there was anything he could do. She'd struggled to answer, because he'd shifted closer to lean against the doorframe and his warm, steady gaze had all but sought permission to see her soul.

All in her head.

He was a graceful, glorious prince. He'd find nothing of interest in a soul like hers.

Then Adam had walked out of the bathroom, towel around his waist, and Cyrus had swiftly departed.

It was mortifying to be so captivated by a famous figure. Celebrities, sports stars, royalty—she wasn't alone in this kind of crush. It was normal. And it didn't rule out real relationships.

She was happy with her gorgeous, refined live-in boyfriend. She really was.

"Yes," she answered Adam's question. "It's just—Ava."

The fan rattled on. Adam ran his fingers down her arm and slowly lowered his book. "Zara."

She sensed it. He was finally going to ask.

Ava's disappearance had blown gossip across the city, an infectious topic that still had people talking, and Adam hadn't asked Zara what she knew. It had affected Mark to the point that Adam continued to come home from work discouraged that he couldn't help, and he hadn't asked. It had pushed Zara into a low mental state for weeks, a weird reaction for the biggest success story of her career, and he still hadn't asked.

It was intensely private. As confidential as matters came. And Adam had known that just because he was first man to the king and lover to the princess's close friend, didn't mean he should know what had happened that night.

"Zara," he said again, and she twisted to sit up, crossing her legs so she could look at him properly. His gaze was strangely intense, and she resisted the urge to squirm into his lap. "I never want you to feel like you have to tell me anything you don't want to. Your line of work requires discretion, and I respect that. But you carry a lot on your shoulders." He reached out, tucking her hair behind her ear. "I'm here for you. I want to support you. Ease your load, if you ever feel like sharing, because . . ." He hadn't looked away. "I love you."

Oh. *Oh.*

Her mouth went dry. Something pounded hard in her head and she was pretty sure she'd stopped breathing. *This* was how it felt to be told she was loved?

"Wow." He loved her. Loved her? Was three months soon to say that kind of thing? It felt soon. Did she love him? Her heart hammered as he watched her. He was a thoughtful man.

Patient. Stoic, in a polished way. The kind of man that women at her shelter prayed to meet—that Zara was beyond lucky to have in her life. "Well. Adam. I, uh—"

"Don't have to say it back." He smiled gently and reached out for her hand. "I just wanted you to know."

Letting out a hard breath, she returned the smile with a cringe as relief eased the pound in her head. He understood her —genuinely didn't expect more than she was willing to give. She might not be sure whether she loved him, but she wanted to give him something. A sign of trust.

She texted Ava and asked permission to share the story with Adam.

Ava responded with, "*If Markus trusts him, I trust him.*"

"Okay," Zara said, flopping back onto his lap and meeting his curious gaze. She settled in for the long version. "Here's the thing."

21

M ark needed this.

He folded his cards and propped his booted heels on the cabin table. Poker and beer had become their Tuesday-night ritual: a slice of sacred family time that often carried late into the night. Tommy brought the beer, Kris sweet-talked a supply of snacks from the kitchen, and Mark wrangled himself out of any social engagements Philip had booked on his behalf. Buck and Bull always joined them and were currently sprawled under the table.

"I have a bad feeling about this." Tommy was studying his cards. Then he eyed Kris and sighed. "Fold."

"Ha." Kris set down an abysmal hand.

Tommy swore under his breath and swigged from his beer.

"Nailed it," Mark said to Tommy. "He'll never figure out that we let him win."

"Ha," Kris said again, collecting the cards. "Do I smell sour grapes?"

Tommy rolled his eyes. "If you did, you'd probably eat them."

As if reminded of his stomach, Kris grabbed a handful of pistachios from the bowl next to him. "Another round?"

"Nah." Tommy scooted his chair back a bit and extended his legs, crossing them at the ankle.

"Your loss," Kris said with a grin that implied *literally*.

Mark reached out, easing the glow of the lantern.

"Met anyone interesting while kinging?" Tommy spoke the words in Mark's direction. It was a vague enquiry with a very specific subtext.

"No," he said, turning his head away.

The silence was too quiet. His brothers were exchanging a look.

"It hasn't been that long," he said, looking back in exasperation.

"You hadn't known *her* that long." Kris placed several pistachio shells on the table. "The break after Sally made sense, but excuse us for not wanting you to fall into another lull that takes you into your thirties."

"I miss her."

"We know." Tommy moved his bottle back and forth in front of him. His brothers had gone camping with him a few times, slept under the stars, while Mark had tried and failed to turn over a new leaf. The emptiness traveled with him.

"And it's kind of hard to move on when I don't even know where she is." He hated not knowing which direction to look when he thought of her. "I can't stop thinking about all the things I don't know."

"Join the club," Kris muttered, clasping his hands behind his head.

Mark grimaced as guilt ground his pride. He'd honored his word to Frankie and hadn't told Kris that she was in Kiraly. He hadn't told Tommy either, but keeping it from Kris was far worse. It was obvious that going so long without contact from his closest friend was slowly gutting him.

Mark had tried to talk Frankie around several times, but she was a force of nature, and when she dug her heels in, he might as well have been trying to persuade a tidal wave to change course. She couldn't hide from Kris forever, but she was clearly prepared to give it her best shot.

Then something clicked. "Hold on," he said, eyeing them both. "Did Philip put you up to this?"

Kris raised his brows, splaying a hand on his chest in melodramatic offense.

Tommy said, "Yes."

"Come on, man." Kris kicked him under the table.

Mark shook his head. "I can't believe it." Philip's preparations for social engagements had begun to include the phrase: *I believe you'll find her very interesting*. Which Mark had worked out was the verbal equivalent to an unskilled cupid drawing back his bow.

"I know it sucks." Tommy eyed Mark. "But it's something Philip has to think about. As it stands, we're the last of the Jaroka family line."

"So it's up to me to get heiring?" Mark's dinner turned bitter in his stomach. He shoved his beer aside, exhaling hard.

"I don't know." Tommy raised an apologetic shoulder. "I just—I don't know."

"I'm not interested," he said flatly. "Philip knows that. I refused marriage with Ava because I didn't love her." His words scraped painfully in his heart. Too little, too late. "I'm not about to marry someone just because she's *interesting* so we can start having royal children."

"That's not what he means." Tommy reached for the nuts. "He just . . . worries that you're hung up over the one who got away."

"I let her get away." Mark stared at the table, haunted by this truth. "I told her to go."

"It was the right thing to do," Tommy said. "But now you're comparing everyone to her and no one will ever compete."

Mark smiled without humor. Who could possibly compete with Ava?

"He's not trying to set you up with another princess." Kris spoke reluctantly, as if perhaps Philip had made him promise to clarify this part. "The public loves rags-to-riches stories. He'd support your union with anyone." He paused, rolling his eyes. "Provided they have the potential for elegance, public speaking, and a background that checks out."

"No scandals?" Mark's attempt at derision came out stale.

"No scandals," Tommy agreed quietly.

His advisor didn't have to worry. The only scandal Mark would give him was a king who never married.

It was only a small noise that caught his attention.

An insignificant little bang, like two tree branches knocking together, or the cabin shifting in the wind, or an owl landing suddenly on the roof. Really, it shouldn't have even been worth noticing.

Except it came from downstairs.

Mark frowned and eyed his brothers. Guards always accompanied them on these nights, positioning themselves in the forest outside and at the entrance to the tunnel. But they were always silent, taking care not to remind the royal family that they weren't alone. Kris brought his chair forward onto all four legs and Tommy's head tilted, his eyes narrowed. Mark shifted so he sat sideways, his back no longer to the underground entrance.

After several seconds of silence, he said, "It is a windy—"

A new sound cut him off. The tread of footsteps coming up from the bunker.

"One of the guards," Tommy said. "Maybe something's happened back at the palace."

"Maybe," Mark said, still waiting, watching. The footsteps paused at the top, hesitating in the tiny room that housed off the bunker entrance.

Tommy started drumming his fingers on the tabletop.

"Oh, for God's sake," Kris muttered, before calling out, "What's going on?"

"Come on in," Mark said, smoothing over his brother's intimidating tone.

They all heard a hard exhale, followed by a quiet, fierce muttering that sounded . . . feminine. Mark exchanged a frown with his brothers. There were only two female guards in their combined host, and both were positioned outside tonight. The footfalls moved toward the door.

Ava stepped out.

All three brothers shot to their feet, their chairs skidding out behind them.

For months, Mark had lied to himself. He'd pretended he was proud he'd encouraged her to leave—pretended that in their final moments, he hadn't considered asking her to stay. But deep down, he'd housed selfish desires, and when she'd looked at him that last time, tear-stricken and brittle, his ego had screamed for her to stay. It had pounded on the back of his tongue, pleading, knowing that circumstances like that didn't come with a second chance.

But he'd told her to go, and so she had.

"Hello," she said.

Disbelief choked him. His blood roared in his ears.

She looked different. Her hair was short, incredibly short, and instead of designer clothes, she wore regular jeans, a blue T-shirt, and walking shoes. The same backpack from the night she'd run away was slung over her shoulder, and she seemed softer somehow, like she was the kind of person who would accept a hug from a friend of a friend, or laugh if someone forgot her name in public. Yet she still stood with faultless grace. Her chin rested on an invisible ledge that tilted her face fractionally toward the ceiling and her unwavering stare came from a lifetime of never being the first to look away.

She was staring at him.

Mark's world was pitching and he didn't know where to reach for balance. "Ava—"

"Let me speak," she said, and even her voice sounded softer than before. "I've been rehearsing the entire walk up from the lake, and I need those hours to have been good for something."

Kris took a step sideways. "We should go—"

"No," Ava answered, though her eyes didn't leave Mark. "Stay."

Kris stilled. Tommy hadn't moved.

Every part of Mark was reeling.

"I've been thinking." She inhaled a sudden drag of air that shuddered in her throat. "Thinking of you, Markus. A lot."

She shifted the bag on her shoulder, a nervous movement.

"I lie awake at night," she said. "I lie there and think of you."

Hope and hurt formed a bittersweet knot in his chest. Why was she here? What could possibly come of this?

"But then I think of how I treated you." Shame lined her features. "I have to get out of bed, because I can't bear to stay still when I remember the things I've said and done. I tainted my memories by treating you poorly more often than I treated you well."

He frowned.

"It's true," she said, her brows rising in earnest. "Trust me, I've run through every moment in my head. Even after you refused to marry me, I was awful. I was scared of falling for you, because I knew I had to leave. Nothing was allowed to change my mind and you threatened that. You were honest about how you felt, and I scolded you and ran away. You trusted me, and I kept secrets. You made love to me—"

Kris muttered, "I really think we should—"

"And I ran away from you." Pain cut the sophisticated sheen from her voice, leaving it rough and raw. "I was supposed to be happy in my new life. But you niggle at me, Markus, and I can't concentrate on being content, because I'm not *ready* to be, and that's your fault."

There she paused, that dark gaze steady on his, finally granting him the chance to speak.

"You've cut your hair," he said.

She stared back for a long time. Then she gave a tiny smile. "Yes."

"You walked here all the way from the lake."

"It was a long walk," she admitted.

"You've come alone."

"Yasmin and Darius are staying with Zara," she said, and set the bag down at her feet, "while I visit you."

"Visit." The word bit him. He looked away, running a hand over his mouth.

"That's why I need your brothers to stay here." She remained across the cabin and that distance felt as long as the horizon. "I don't want them to leave me alone with you or I might never leave at all."

Her words struck that dark space inside him, the space that thought only of himself and festered with his unvoiced protest to her escape. She was going to leave him again. She expected him to be decent and let her go, because of course she needed to be with her son, and only an asshole would demand she fulfill his desires.

But he couldn't live with that regret twice over. It wasn't fair on her—but coming all this way just to visit wasn't fair on him.

"Do you have to leave?" he asked, his voice quiet.

Her inhale seemed to get stuck halfway down her throat. Sadness creased her face a moment before she swooped to pick up her bag. "I shouldn't have come—"

"No." Mark moved fast, blocking the door to the bunker but stopping short of touching her. The distance between them writhed against his skin. "Don't go."

"This was stupid." Her voice trembled slightly.

"It wasn't." He'd let her go once. He wasn't doing that again. "Please stay."

"I—can't." She slipped her arm through the second bag strap and settled the pack properly on her back. "I just had to see you again. Tell you how I feel. Maybe . . . get closure."

"How do you feel?" Greed rose in him. Months. He'd endured months without her, and now this closed-up, contained, *perfect* woman was offering him her feelings. "Tell me."

The question seemed to spook her. She clearly hadn't thought this through—hadn't thought he would close in. But he wasn't the easygoing cowboy she'd first met. He'd become a king. And she was his equal, not only in status, but in his heart.

"I love you," he said, denying her the closure she sought. "That's how I feel."

Her bottom lip curled as sorrow drove her face down.

Pain arced in him. Why did their most precious interactions always cause her sadness?

"When someone climbs a mountain to see me, I'm not in a hurry to let her go." He wanted to reach out, pull her into him. "We're going to make this work."

"There's no way around it, Markus." She looked up and her eyes were huge, wider now without her hair closing in around her face. "You're king. You'll never escape attention. Everyone has an interest in your public and personal affairs, and by extension, that of your partner. And if that partner happens to be a princess who vanished earlier this year and has resurfaced with a child who's unmistakably her own, well, I can't imagine I'll have much hope of being left alone. And neither will Darius."

Mark was shaking his head.

"It's finally over," she said. "I can breathe again. I got so tired of acting. Tired of suffering under the scrutiny of strangers. Tired of people obsessing over my life as if it was their own. I don't have the reserves to drag Darius into this life and constantly defend him, and me, and probably you, for being with me." Her eyes were glistening. "I want to be happy, like the people in your book, and that's not possible standing beside a king."

"There must be . . ." But he trailed off. Not a single solution came to mind. Not even something wild and foolish. Regret weighed in his stomach.

He still couldn't let her leave.

"I'm sorry for coming," she managed to say, and a tear spilled down her cheek. "It was selfish. I wanted to see you again. Perhaps to say goodbye properly, because it wasn't right, the way I left you. Another awful thing I can't forget."

"You're not awful." He took her hand and attraction flared between their fingers, a heated burst that fed off their months apart. He yearned to follow the trail of goosebumps that had risen at his touch, up her arm, beneath her T-shirt, and beyond. He swallowed, his throat thick. "It's not one of your adjectives."

Her eyes flickered down, brushing over his mouth. "It is."

"No." He shook his head. "It's not. You have a very strong grasp on your priorities." And in this moment, so did he. "I need you to stay with me. We'll figure this out."

"I'll stay a while," she whispered. "But not forever."

359

Forever with Ava flashed in his mind—an overexposed dream. It faded, leaving him blind.

"Actually." Kris spoke from behind them. "I have an idea."

Mark had almost forgotten his brothers were in the cabin. Startled, he turned with Ava and Tommy to look at him.

Kris stood on the far side of the table, his palms pressed flat against the wooden surface. A shadow hung over his features, but his eyes burned fierce.

"A prince can avoid the spotlight easily enough," Kris said.

Tommy pulled a face. "What's that got to do with—" Then he halted with a sharp inhale. The blood drained from his face. Wordless with horror, he turned to stare at Mark.

"No." Sick with understanding, Mark rejected everything about the idea. "Nice thought, but no." He turned away.

"Don't dismiss me."

Shocked, Mark looked back at his brother.

Kris was glaring at him, all but bearing his teeth.

"I'm dismissing the idea," Mark said.

"You said you'd find a way to make it work. This is the way."

The selfish darkness in him thrummed, greedy for what his brother offered. But again, he made himself say, "No. Besides, it would be Tommy—"

"Skip Tommy," Kris said, so harshly Tommy flinched. "Skip him and go straight to me. I'll do it."

"Sorry, but what is the idea?" Ava's bafflement had Mark catching her eye. Hope burned there, because she'd heard the promise of a solution without understanding its impossibility. "I don't speak triplet."

Anguish drenched his answer. "Kris." He halted. "Kris is suggesting that I abdicate."

"Oh." Her eyes pressed closed, and she looked pained. She took several breaths, slowly, unsteadily, through her nose. Then she set her attention across the room. "Kristof," she said, "renouncing the throne is not something a king does on a whim to get the girl."

"I understand that." He spoke in a growl. "But I don't think Mark sees you as a whim."

Mark tightened his grip on her. "You won't cope, Kris." He forced himself to be harsh, to remind his brother of the truth. "It's not as fun as your public appearances."

"Fuck fun. This is your *life*, man. I'm doing it."

Ava squeezed Mark's hand. He met the plea in her dark eyes as she murmured, "He could try."

"What?" Disbelief staggered him. "You just agreed that abdication wasn't the way."

"I said it wasn't to be done on a whim."

"He's torn," Kris said roughly, "because he always tries to do what's best for others. And accepting this would be doing what's best for him."

Mark shook his head as a war raged in him. He couldn't let Kris do this. His brother had given up the ranch, his beloved life in Sage Haven, to support him. Mark couldn't repay him like this. And yet—the darkness in him fought back. Enraged at being suppressed for so long, his selfishness overpowered his need to protect his brother.

He'd do anything to be with the woman he loved.

Kris continued, "You were born twelve minutes before Tommy—forty minutes before me. You're the oldest because you got your head in the way first, okay? This doesn't have to be on your shoulders."

"It's not—" He fought because he'd hate himself if he gave up so easily. He spun his gaze to the right. "Tommy?"

But Tommy stood unmoving, his features masked. He gave a small shake of his head.

Kris swore suddenly, bringing his fist down with a bang.

"Enough, Mark." His tone was unyielding. "You're not a sacrificial lamb. There are three of us. I'm doing this."

Stunned, tongue dry, he shook his head.

"Markus." Ava tugged lightly on his hand. "It doesn't have to be absolute, not immediately. It's not as if anyone will even know it's Kris."

There was a pause as they all turned to frown at her.

Then Kris picked up that idea and ran with it. "Exactly. We're identical. We don't need to tell anyone except Philip, maybe the guards. Nothing official yet, but I'll stand in for you, Mark, and see how it goes. You could spend time with Ava and no one would know. We could test the idea. If—*when* it works, you can formally abdicate and live with Ava and Darius, all happy and unseen."

"I couldn't move away." Not after his brothers had both moved to Kiraly for him.

"Then stay," his brother snapped. "I told you already, our people treat everyone the same. They play it cool, give their royalty space. It could work."

"Kris." Dullness washed over Mark with the realization. "My coronation is in three months."

Doubt flashed across his brother's face. "I'd better learn fast."

"It's not long enough—"

"Just say thank you, for God's sake," his brother said loudly. "Then Tommy and I can leave you two alone."

Mark swallowed, light-headed. His pulse pummeled his ribs. Was he really going to do this?

Ava turned, silent, and buried her face in his shoulder.

"Thank you," he said.

"Okay." Kris was breathing fast. He eyed Tommy, seeking final confirmation. "Okay?"

Tommy raised a shoulder but didn't answer. His face was pale, his hands balled in fists.

"Let's move." Kris strode around the table, collecting Tommy by the arm and hauling him toward the bunker. Numb, Mark stepped aside and watched them disappear down the stairs. Neither of them looked back. The dull sound of their footsteps faded as they descended into the tunnel and were gone.

Sucker-punched, he turned to Ava. "What just happened?"

She smiled up at him and wonder shone like an open sky in her eyes. "Kris is giving us a chance."

They were alone.

Markus pressed her against the cabin wall, his fingers laced through hers, pinning them up by her shoulders while he drew in great breaths of restraint. His need for her was like the sun, and she basked in the burn, skin and soul, beneath him.

He didn't kiss her, not yet. The grip of pleasure-pain held her taut and trembling, savoring the wait, not daring to move first and end the agony so soon. They were together, yet not quite together, and she held still, struggling to believe that months apart hadn't inflated her memory of him. He was as all-encompassing as the cowboy king in her dreams.

His features were twisted, his eyes closed, brow knotted. His toes touched hers and his chest grazed her breasts. She wanted all of him—wanted this torturous promise of fulfilment.

"Do you hate what Kris proposed?" she whispered, her eyes on his mouth.

He shook his head, the tip of his nose brushing hers. He kept his eyes closed. "I hate that I want him to do it."

She spoke as softly as she could. "You could say no."

His answer was a growl. "I'd give up the ranch for you, if I had no kingdom."

She held her breath and released it. "I have a son, you know."

His eyes snapped open, clear blue and serious. "Darius."

"Darius." She turned her palms, moving them gently in his grasp, seeking the stimulation of skin moving against skin. "If Kris goes through with this, all the way through, then I need to know that you won't walk away from the throne only to baulk from the reality of a woman with a child."

"I won't." He shifted, leaning forward so his forehead touched the wall above her shoulder. "I've thought about you, about him, this whole time. I don't know the first thing about kids, but I'll learn. For him, for you. For us. If he'll allow me in his life—I want it all. Everything you are, I want it, Ava."

Of course he did.

"Markus," she whispered, and he shifted, drawing back to look down at her with darkened eyes. "Markus, I have something to ask you."

This fraction of time splintered in between Kris's vow to take Markus's place and whatever ended up happening—it couldn't be wasted. If their lives were destined to part, then this had to be done now.

"I'll need my hands," she requested, and almost rose to her toes and kissed him at the unwillingness in his eyes. "I'll give them back."

Reluctant, he released her and spread his empty palms on the wall by her shoulders. He kept his body close.

She reached beneath the neckline of her T-shirt, and fumbling, she drew out a long, rose gold chain. Her grandfather's ring hung heavily in the center.

Markus grew very still, but his breath quickened.

"I don't know what's going to happen with us," she said,

unclasping the chain and sliding the ring free. Her hand shook and her pulse shuddered. "But I know that you're the only man who'll ever deserve this."

"Ava," he murmured, and when she looked up, his features were burdened by heartbreak. "How can you keep making happiness feel sad?"

"It's not," she said firmly, believing it this time as she took his left hand in hers. "This time it isn't sad. I've made many plans that have failed, and still haven't mastered the art of a solid backup, but perhaps it's time to have no plan at all. Let's start walking and see where we end up." And then she held the band over the tip of his ring finger and rose onto her toes. He didn't pull back, but held steady for her to bring her mouth against his and murmur, "Will you be mine, Markus?"

"Only yours," he said. And he closed his mouth over hers in a kiss that promised to walk with her, through dark memories and bright futures, for the rest of their lives.

22

I t had been an eventful ten days.

Ava's world had been upturned once again, spinning, tumbling around her like flakes in a glass globe. She'd spoken to Darius that first night. She knew they'd only recently moved to a new house, but what did he think of living in Kiraly instead? With Yazzy, of course, and a nice man named Markus. There was more to do here than in the village. A lake for swimming and boating. Mountain trails for horse rides. Cafés, and shops, and everything else the city had to offer.

"And a palace," he'd said excitedly, because Zara's windows pointed straight at it.

Yes. And a palace that no longer filled her with fear and bitterness.

The second step had been to brief Philip on the eccentric plan. They'd gathered in the king's study, overlooking the lush lands of Kiraly, and explained to the bewildered advisor that Markus would be stepping down from the throne—and Kris would train to take his place.

They'd expected indignation, red-faced anger, and the man's absolute refusal to support such an outrageous arrangement. Instead, he'd absorbed the plan in silence. Not moving, not interjecting. Paling, as was only human, when they revealed the truth behind Ava's disappearance, and her hope to settle safely in Kiraly. Sadness shadowed his eyes as he'd looked to Markus. "You would do this, Markus, for the one you love?"

Markus had squeezed Ava's hand. "I would."

"Sacrifice your crown?"

"Yes."

"Once it's official," Philip had warned them, "it can't be undone."

Unhesitating, he'd said, "I understand."

And still he was willing to sacrifice it for her.

Ava had turned into him, right there in front of the others, and pulled his mouth to hers.

"Then I ask just one thing of you, Markus," Philip said next, his attention sliding across the grand tower room to settle on the roguish cowboy lounging against the desk. "Help your brother to realize he can't do anything he pleases just because he is king."

Kris had pulsed his brows with a wicked, tameless grin.

No doubt about it, the plan was shaky. Markus would stay in Kiraly with Ava and Darius, not in the palace, but in a private royal property that Philip suggested out of the city. Markus would act as a second advisor for Kris, and Ava would lend her knowledge where she could. Philip agreed that a trial period was wise before they announced the unorthodox crown swap. He would give Kris one month. If Kris couldn't handle it, then they would all need to meet again and have a very serious discussion.

"I'll handle it," Kris had said, almost savagely. "Don't worry."

She believed him. She'd experienced his protective streak firsthand. When that spread to incorporate all of Kiraly, the

367

nation would have a fierce king doing everything in his power to keep them safe, prosperous, and happy.

With change beating in her heart, Ava had then returned to Luxembourg with Darius, Yasmin, and their guards. They'd spent time packing and saying their goodbyes to neighbors and new friends. Despite the pull in her chest, the endless yearning to feel Markus's touch, she refused to rush Darius. They would do this at his pace.

On the ninth day—yesterday—he'd declared he was ready.

She'd spent the drive back to Kiraly with her heart unfolding; opening into a brighter beat.

"And these are the gardens," Markus was saying, bringing her thoughts back to her tour. "You'll love them."

Ava took his hand as he stood back, holding the door open to a cobbled patio. She took in pots of overflowing petunias, vines of sweet-scented jasmine on the honey-stoned walls, and a fountain that sounded like peace. This property lay beyond the outskirts of Kira City, hidden from the road by a stretch of pines and protected behind a walled perimeter. It was a mansion, with suites for all. Darius. Yasmin. Quarters for the house staff and guards. Darius was already in his room, having eagerly convinced Yasmin to help him unpack. Ava thought of the light-flooded bedroom she would share with Markus, the bed where they would talk and learn and flare in each other's arms. Tears warmed her eyes.

This would be their home. *Theirs.*

"Hey," he said, smiling gently and drawing her against him. "I thought you were done with tears."

"I'm just so happy," she said and smiled when he pressed his mouth to her forehead. "We're going to live here. Together."

"If you're really sure." His words were warm on her brow.

A conversation they'd had many times already. He knew living in Kiraly wasn't something she'd ever wanted. Yes, they would live in relative isolation, in this sprawling secluded home on the mountainside, but they would have to brave the city eventually. The people might play it cool, like Kris claimed, but there were the tourists. She'd be recognized eventually, and the rumors would fly about Darius.

"I'm sure," she said, closing her eyes.

She intended to take control of the rumor-fueled wildfire with a press conference. She would tell her own story, a heavily modified version of the truth, something about a scared nineteen-year-old who had grown to learn to keep those she loved by her side. Then, she would never talk to the press again.

"You've given up your crown to be with me," she said. "I can sacrifice anonymity to be with you."

He pulled back just enough to look at her, his arm still strong around her back. "And Darius?"

Ten days had given her time to think—to understand that one royal upbringing wasn't the same as them all. She wouldn't expect him to be any one thing, wouldn't control his life.

"Darius will learn that in Kiraly," she said, "to be royal means to be yourself."

He smiled, eyes softening.

"Besides," she said, winding her arms around his neck. "Someone once told me that plans can change, and things still work out okay."

"More than okay." His mouth found hers, and he kissed her until she heard the hum of an approaching car.

Drawing back, she frowned as the black luxury vehicle stopped at the top of the driveway. Strange. That car was an Obsidian: sleek, magnificent, and originating from Kelehar. But Cyrus couldn't visit for another few weeks, so who was the man stepping out—

"*Gul!*"

Joy flooded her as she raced to him. His grin became a laugh as she flew right into his arms, burying her face into his chest. "Gul," she said again, out of words from happiness.

"Princess." His greeting rumbled in his chest. "You miss me?"

She stepped back, her cheeks aching from her smile. "Every day."

Color stained his cheeks as he said, "That must be why you've moved to my city."

She laughed, glancing at Markus as he came to stand beside her. "I hear you work in the palace now."

Her old guard nodded, eyes shining. "That's right."

"Gul," Markus said, smiling and shaking the man's hand. "Glad you could come."

"Wouldn't miss it."

"Miss . . . ?" She looked questioningly between the two men. Her eyes narrowed when neither answered, their features suspiciously neutral. "Miss what?"

"I might walk these gardens," Gul said, and moved away with a wink.

"Tell me, Markus." She put a hand on her hip, angling her chin high.

He let out a soft laugh as he turned into her. "The first time I met you, I never would've thought you'd end up putting a ring on my finger."

She clicked her tongue, softening a little. "Are you trying to distract me?" She took his hand, running her thumb over the gold band.

Propose to someone you want to marry, Cyrus had said. *By this token, the crown of Kelehar supports your choice.*

"You know," she said, turning the band around his finger. "It's ironic that despite my determination to choose my own future, I ended up proposing to the one man my parents had approved for me all along."

"Occasionally," he said, "irony isn't a complete bastard."

She laughed. "I never would've imagined this," she said, scanning his face. His eyes, an innocent shade of blue. His dark brows, kind mouth, and bold jaw. "You were so . . . different."

About to say more, she was distracted by another car coming up the driveaway. No. Another *three* cars. Through open windows, she could see Kris and Tommy in one, Zara and Adam in another . . . and was that Philip in the third? She lanced Markus with a suspicious glare. "What is going on?"

"I couldn't wait, Ava." Emotion darkened his gaze, and he shifted away from her. "I know you only arrived a few hours ago, but I couldn't wait another day."

"For what?"

"Our engagement party," he said, and lowered to one knee.

Delight flung a hand over her mouth.

He grinned and pulled a delicate gold ring from the pocket of his checkered shirt. Holding it out so it glinted and sparkled in the sunlight, he said, "Ava, I haven't always known the true you. But even protecting yourself, you were smart and brave and fearless. Later, I learned that you were strong and sensitive and resilient, and everything I could imagine cherishing for the rest of my life."

Her smile was so big she choked on it. Or was that from her tears?

"I loved you before I knew everything about you," he continued, his blue gaze like a midday sky. "And once I knew everything, I knew I'd never love anyone else."

She laughed again, tears running down her face.

"You proposed first." His smile grew crooked. "Because this should always have been your choice. But I can't stop thinking about how I once said that you and I would not be married—that it was my final decision. I spent months wrung-out and empty without you, those words eating away at me. They eat away at me still, and I want to end them. End them with vows and rings and a celebration to shake the skies. You asked me to wear your ring," he said. "And now I'm asking if you'll marry me, Ava Veisi, as soon as we possibly can."

A wedding that would bind their futures with royal extravagance and small-town values, private and intimate, yet larger than life.

"Yes," she breathed.

As his own eyes glistened and he slid the ring on her finger, Ava looked at the man she loved, and at the home they would share, and at Darius as he ran squealing out of the house toward them, and she knew from this day on, her life would brim with fulfillment and happiness and freedom.

And she would never yearn to be alone again.

HER COWBOY PRINCE

**Meet the cowboy royal who will never be tamed—
and the best friend sworn to protect him.**

Kris Jaroka didn't sign up for this. He and his triplet brothers
were uprooted from their ranch to inherit the throne of Kiraly.
His duties keep escalating, and no amount of shirking his guards
can stop the gut-ache of leaving his best friend, Frankie, behind.

But his biggest challenge lies ahead.

For years, Frankie Cowan has secretly monitored the safety of
Kris and his brothers. When Kris's recklessness forces her to
reveal herself as the head of palace security, her duty to protect
him and his refusal to be tamed meet head on.

Bound together, their lies and hurt soon surrender to their
chemistry, and Kris burns to offer her his future. But Frankie's
past isn't fit for a cowboy, let alone a prince—proving that the
person she most needs to protect him from is herself.

ACKNOWLEDGMENTS

This book is my first full-length story, and as the first in a trilogy, it required waaay more planning than I've previously attempted. Character brainstorming was my primary function for a long time, so my first thank you is to my endlessly supportive partner, Dom, for always launching yourself down fictional rabbit holes with me. Also for the gorgeous cover design.

To my family, for story discussion and reading and proofreading. Clio, for literally climbing a mountain for phone reception while traveling around outback Australia in order to discuss it with me. Zara wouldn't exist without you. Grace, for always reading and giving feedback whenever I ask, and Mum, for your enthusiastic (but always pertinent!) use of correction pens.

To my friends and writing partners, Louise, Janis and Sandy, for your critiques, advice, and support. You connect me to my genre, my muse, and I adore your friendship. Also to Alissa Callen for your years of support and guidance during the ups and downs of this wild publishing journey. You've always been there for me, and I can't thank you enough.

Very special thanks to Shelagh Merlin for beta reading. Your encouragement keeps me going.

Delighted thanks to Lauren Clarke and Anna Bishop from Creating Ink. Lauren, your structural edits were *perfect*. The core of the story is stronger because of you!

To the Madeline Ash Sweeties, my incredible advance review team. Thank you for investing your time in my writing by reading and reviewing. I am SO grateful for your generous support.

As this is my first self-published novel, thanks also to the Indie Royalty facebook group for openly sharing your experiences and knowledge.

For Coby, for years of being my writing companion. Sometimes it feels like you're still curled up snoring at my feet.

I would also like to respectfully acknowledge the Boon Wurrung people of the Kulin Nation, who have traditional connections to the land where I live and wrote this book.

And to my readers, old and new, for giving a cowboy king a chance when publishers and agents alike told me he wouldn't sell. THANK YOU for proving them wrong.

ALSO BY MADELINE ASH

Rags to Riches series

The Playboy (#1)

Alexia needs to become sexually confident for an upcoming acting role and playboy Parker agrees to teach her. Now all they have to do is let each other go.

Her Secret Prince (#2)

2016 RITA Award finalist

As a teenager, Dee had her heart broken by Jed. Years later, he's back in her life—but will a surprising royal discovery ruin their second chance together?

You For Christmas (#3)

2016 RUBY Award finalist

Black sheep Regan arrives on Felix's doorstep to take up the debt he owes her. Will they act on their feelings this Christmas or are their pasts too painful to bear?

Breaking Good (#4)

2017 RITA Award finalist

2017 RUBY Award winner

Years after spending a night with bad boy Ethan, Stevie runs into him again. She's shocked to discover that he's alive—and she has to tell him he has a son...

Morgan Sisters series

The Wedding Obsession (#1)

2019 RUBY Award finalist

After life-changing surgery, Emmie is overwhelmed by the urge to marry. Despite his love for her, her best friend Brandon struggles to believe her proposals—until a shocking revelation changes everything.

His Billionaire Bride (#2)

Business investor Carrie is guarded for good reason, while artist Edwin—rejected by his family—will only settle for commitment. Their intense chemistry builds them so high she's blinded to the fall. And the only way out is to break both their hearts.

ABOUT MADELINE ASH

Madeline Ash is an Australian contemporary romance author and two-time RITA Award finalist. She has won Australia's Romantic Book of the Year award (RUBY). She delves deep into the hearts and minds of her characters, creating flawed and compassionate leads—who are always rewarded with a happy ending.

madelineash.net

BB bookbub.com/profile/madeline-ash
f facebook.com/MadelineAshAuthor
🐦 twitter.com/Madeline_Ash
📷 instagram.com/madelineashauthor

Made in United States
Orlando, FL
08 September 2022

22132008R10231